BATTER DIPE

The wedding party seemed to be lining up for pictures, and the guests were starting to corral near the tent. When I got inside, my crew was nowhere to be seen. I could see Paul through the window on the opposite side of the tent. I went in search of my staff and nodded approvingly when I walked around the first few tables with beautifully lit candles positioned around the pink Stargazer centerpiece. From here the wedding cake appeared to be holding up nicely. I moved closer.

My smile faltered and I squeaked in surprise.

My hand went to my parted lips.

On the floor in front of the wedding cake table lay Lucy, covered in what could only be funnel cake batter . . .

Books by Kate Young

SOUTHERN SASS AND KILLER CRAVINGS

SOUTHERN SASS AND A CRISPY CORPSE

SOUTHERN SASS AND A BATTERED BRIDE

Published by Kensington Publishing Corp.

Southern Sass and a Battered Bride

KATE YOUNG

KENSINGTON
PUBLISHING CORP.

www.kensingtonbooks.com

KENSINGTON BOOKS are published by

Kensington Publishing Corp.
119 West 40th Street
New York, NY 10018

First Kensington Books Mass Market Paperback Printing: May 2021

ISBN-13: 978-1-4967-2149-5
ISBN-10: 1-4967-2149-7

ISBN-13: 978-1-4967-2150-1 (ebook)
ISBN-10: 1-4967-2150-0 (ebook)

10 9 8 7 6 5 4 3 2 1

Printed in the United States of America

For Nita and Rita, who love to laugh as much as I do

CHAPTER 1

The temperature hovered around a near-perfect eighty degrees as the sun began to set over the ocean, and I watched the bride walk down the aisle. My childhood sweetheart, Deputy Alex Myers, stood at the front under a beautiful arch of flowing white fabric, and from my vantage point in the reception tent, he looked dashing. He wore linen pants rolled up at the ankles and a white button-down shirt rolled up at the sleeves. Soft music and murmurs of the wedding rehearsal mingled with the light breeze. The wide expanse of the Atlantic Ocean lapping the shore was their backdrop. It viewed like a scene out of a Hallmark movie.

It appears perceivably untamable Alex Myers can be tamed.

The groom lifted his bride in the air and spun her

around, their laughter traveled, and my chest constricted. With a deep breath of salty air in my lungs, I turned away.

"You okay?" My best friend and coworker, Betsy, continued to smooth out and adjust the tablecloths.

"Yep. Perfectly fine." I glanced around the large tent, with lovely cream silk drapings from the tent peaks, lit with elegant string lights and strategically placed chandeliers over the twenty-five round tables covered with champagne-colored tablecloths. Faux bamboo chairs painted gold reflected in the light. The tables being set up around the whitewash dance floor must have cost them a fortune. Lucy must have a trust fund or a nest egg she's been saving for her big day, because Alex surely didn't have that kind of money. Oh well, not my business. I was paid to do a job, and I'd do it and do it well.

"You're not perfectly fine and you know it." Betsy tightened the tie over her fire-red mane. "And how could you be? Y'all have history."

With a sigh, I moved one of the centerpieces adorned with dripping candles closer to the center of the table. Betsy was right, we had significant history. Her cousin, Alex, had been my first love and on-again, off-again boyfriend since high school, except for the two-year period when I'd been married to the jerk of the century. Alex and I sort of picked up where we left off shortly after I moved back home. Enter *Lucy*.

"I want Alex to be happy, I really do. I just hate he chose *her*." That woman and I started out on the wrong foot from day one. She being the reason he and I were no longer together. Or at least they shared a pivotal moment in our relationship's downward spiral. I'll never forget the onslaught of emotions I felt when my brother told me he'd spied Alex at the Beach Bum Bar getting cozy with a tourist. And though Alex vehemently denied Sam's account and any wrongdoing, he later went on to secure said tourist a receptionist job with Peach Cove Sheriff's Department, and I'd later found out that the two had been spending a lot of time together. Innocent or not, he'd lied to me, and we'd never recovered after that. And though I made attempts to remain civil when they became a couple, Lucy belittled me at every turn. The woman was a total nightmare. Honestly, for catering her wedding, I deserved a peace prize.

"I hear ya. My cousin is an idiot. And his bridezilla is even worse." She let out a long, noisy breath full of frustration, and gazed out of the tent, where the rehearsal was in full swing. The small group appeared to be going through the ceremony all over again. "I just always thought the two of you would get married and we'd be family for real." Betsy gave me a sad smile, and I returned it before reaching out and taking her hand.

I gave her fingers a squeeze. "We are a *real* family. And, Bets, he's your relative. Don't let our friendship and your hatred for the bridezilla cause more problems. I'm good. See?" I beamed. Or tried to. I really was okay. Still, it was hard to see Alex moving on in the fashion he had before I did. Not that I was ready to say *I do* to anyone. It simply stirred up all sorts of emotions.

"Uh-huh. You look like you're good." Betsy put her hands on her hips. "And I know you aren't inferring I'm the one causing the rift in the Myers family."

I pursed my lips.

"What are you sayin'? It's my fault?"

I gave my head a shake. "I'm saying that what happened at the bridal shower can't happen again. He's marrying her now." Seeing her on the verge of a hissy fit brought back the encounter and caused my shoulders to knot up. I took my part of the blame. It had been a mistake for me to attend the shower. Lucy thought I'd shown up to monopolize the family, which wasn't the case. She'd invited me, a gesture that had shocked me to my core, and initially, I'd planned to politely decline. Then Betsy pleaded for me to go and stupidly, I had. Attempting to be the bigger person had backfired. After a plethora of hateful scowls, Betsy and I left early. Lucy had followed us outside the church and the onslaught of snarky insults ensued. It was almost as if she were looking to spar, and I made the perfect punching bag. When Betsy rushed to my defense, Lucy turned on her. It went south from there. Alex had been livid.

"Don't tell me you feel guilty?"

"We could've walked away and should've."

"Whatever. I don't feel the least bit guilty. She totally started it!" Betsy huffed and puffed for a few seconds, glancing out the tent as cheers echoed from the beach. "You know what?" She pointed in the direction of the rehearsal. "When it comes down to it, Alex is the root of the problem. No one likes Lucy. You think I'm the stumbling block in this whole family drama, ha! You should hear Aunt Vi rave on. She prattled on to Aunt Regina about her son ruining the only chance at happiness when he lost you. And she called him a fool for not seeing the rattlesnake he'd snuggled up to." Knowing Betsy's aunt Vi my entire life, and living with her for a short period of time, I could only imagine.

"Let's calm down and finish up here." I attempted to get us back on track.

"I'm calm." Betsy bared her teeth in a failed attempt to

grin. Her red perspiring face made me worry she'd give herself an aneurism with her blood pressure spike.

"Marygene."

Betsy and I turned to see Paul Fowler making his way through the tent with another man I didn't recognize. Paul and I had been dating for a couple of months. He'd waltzed—or more like splashed—into my life at a time I needed it most. In fact, it had been during the same weekend Alex announced his engagement to Lucy. I'd skipped our usual Sunday lunch and decided to drown my sorrows in natural vitamin D and salty water. I was soaking up some rays on a float in the calm surf, trying to float my troubles away, when a man on a paddleboard wiped out and took us both under. I'd broken the surface, sputtering, and so did he. Red-faced and mortified, he introduced himself. Paul and I spent the rest of that day together and then several days following. I'd needed a distraction and like magic, he'd appeared. The man was game for anything I wanted to do, and we discovered we had the exact same taste in movies. He was everything Alex wasn't: gentle, well-read, and had opinions about politics. It was refreshing.

I smiled at Paul as he spoke. "This is Christopher Davis, the new manager of our office."

I moved through the space and extended my hand. "Nice to meet you. I worked with your predecessor, Adam, on several events, and they were each a great success."

The older round man smiled and released my hand to wipe the perspiration from his brow. "I'm pleased to hear it. I'm from Sunshine's Savannah branch. I wanted to make the introduction personally with all our partners.

We look forward to many years of successful events together."

"As do my sister and I." I nodded with a smile. The Sunshine Murder Mystery Company had brought in more business for the Peach Diner's catering operation than we could have hoped for, and now had us on the list of partners. Jena Lynn and I were extremely pleased at the expansion of our little family business. My enterprising Nanny had used the talents and money she managed to scrimp and save to open the Peach Diner when her husband lost his fortune in moonshine and gambling. The women of the Brown family were foodies to our core.

"Glad to hear it." Christopher's phone rang and he excused himself to answer it.

Once his boss was out of sight, Paul leaned down and gave me a kiss on the cheek. His cologne smelled stronger than usual, and his hair looked slightly damp, making me wonder if he'd recently showered. Odd for this time of day.

I pushed the thought from my mind. "What happened to Adam?"

Paul ran his long fingers through his thinning sandy-blond hair. "He decided he needed a change, I guess. He was MIA for a couple of days and then Mr. Davis showed up. No one at Sunshine knows anything other than that."

"Well, that's weird." Betsy took up residence beside me.

"Oh, hello, Betsy. I didn't mean to be rude. It's been a topsy-turvy day." Paul and Betsy hadn't quite become friends yet, but they both were trying, and I appreciated it.

There wasn't a future for us if Paul couldn't get along with my nearest and dearest. If I'd learned anything from my past, it was I would never allow a man to control my life or have a say in who I kept company with ever again.

Not that Paul and I were anywhere near contemplating a future at this point, but I wanted no confusion on the subject. Early stages of a relationship were a fragile thing. Some days, I could see myself making a life with him, and others I sensed a bit of unrest within him, or maybe it was me I sensed it in, but it gave me pause. I wasn't certain. However, I cared about him and would just take things one day at a time.

Betsy's smile appeared more as a grimace. She'd had a little thing for Adam, and they'd planned to go out. "He just left without a word? That's doesn't make a lick of sense."

Paul shrugged his thin shoulders. Apparently he wasn't concerned with where Adam's sudden departure left the company. "Well, I'll leave you ladies to finish up. I've got two more stops to make with Mr. Davis before we end for the day. See you later tonight, Marygene?"

Tonight I needed to be alone, to ponder choices and deal with closure.

I gave my head a shake and Paul's mouth thinned into a flat line. My past had left me with issues I couldn't ignore. Healing and self-care would always need to be a priority and I'd adjusted to that fact. I'd also learned I didn't need to apologize for it or feel guilty. It was okay to say no. "After the reception tomorrow, we can go out for a bite to eat." I patted his arm. "Okay?"

He nodded but didn't look happy about it. "See you tomorrow then. Call me if you get a chance or change your mind." The way he looked at me with some sense of urgency gave me the impression he had something on his mind he was eager to discuss.

Weddings had that effect on some people. For me, I was content with the way things were and didn't feel ready to move to the next stage of the relationship. Maybe my intuition would be wrong. I sighed as he turned to leave.

Betsy waited until he left the tent to start her rant. "That just makes no sense. Adam and I had a real connection. We had a date for next Saturday. He wouldn't leave without telling me!"

"Maybe he had a family emergency. He might call you." I turned my attention back to the tables.

"Yeah, I guess. Sunshine won't be the same now. We'll have to see a lot more of the scarecrow."

"Scarecrow?"

She threw her arm in the direction Paul had left. "He's the spitting image of the scarecrow from *The Wizard of Oz*."

"No, he isn't." I shook my head at her silliness.

"He is! Just picture him standing out in a field. Here, I'll help." She threw her arms out and made a painful-looking face. " 'If I only had a brain . . .' "

"Bets"—I covered a snicker with a cough—"you said you'd try."

Betsy scrunched up her face. "I lied."

"Betsy!"

"Oh, for the love of Pete"—Betsy rolled her eyes—"you can't actually be into that guy. He's not your type." She didn't wait for me to respond. "He's too tall and skinny. Plus, he's a Yankee. Topsy-turvy? Who do you know that says topsy-turvy?"

I pursed my lips for a second and scowled at her. "Don't give me that Yankee nonsense. Javier is a Yankee and you had the hots for him."

"Javier is different. Sadly, he and I weren't meant to be. I need a man with a sense of humor." I laughed, thinking back to Betsy and Javier's date, where she'd attempted to charm him with her fluent pig Latin.

She chortled when I reminded her.

"Yes, I'll freely admit Paul is a different type than I normally date, but I think that's what makes him appealing. Besides, it isn't serious. We're just getting to know each other and seeing where it goes." I'd made my mind up to go slow and be sure of what I was getting into before leaping. The issues I had that resulted from the abuse I'd incurred in my horrendous marriage a couple of years ago taught me to be cautious when it came to committing my life to another. It took me a long time to gain the strength to walk away from Peter Hutchinson. And even longer to open up to anyone about it. Today, I'm stronger thanks to a great therapy group, my amazing friends, and family. I still had bad days when ugly issues surfaced, but I'd learned in therapy I could box them all up and put them away—via my coping mechanisms—and I could repeat the procedure as needed. One day at a time. It's how I lived. And I was proud of my progress.

"Fine. Whatever. I'll get this to the work area." Betsy went to take the deep fryer to the small tent adjacent to the large reception tent. The small workspace afforded us enough square footage to position two refrigerators, three worktables arranged in an L-shape, and storage cabinets. Now, thanks to Alex's insistence we serve funnel cakes, his favorite fair food, we also had two deep fryers. Jena Lynn and I did our best to try and talk him out of it. It certainly didn't go with the menu Lucy decided on and even she protested, but in the end, he'd won. I guess he needed to win something, since she monopolized everything else. Thankfully, my brother and diner grill-cook, Sam, would be manning the fryer.

Betsy rejoined me as I finished arranging the final food station. The stations consisted of multiple buffets positioned throughout the wedding reception tent. It allowed wedding guests to mingle with others and sample a variety of menu items.

"Hey, since you're not exclusive with Paul, you should go out with Javier. He's uber sexy, even if he doesn't have a sense of humor. And the two of you have that sexual tension thing going on. That's plain to anyone with eyes. You know he's into you. He's made that clear, and you totally have the hots for him."

I opened my mouth as my eyes went wide.

Betsy waved her finger in my face, scolding, "Don't even try to deny it. Plus, he knows about your little affliction."

I could argue, but her expression told me she wouldn't be letting the subject of my love life go. Deputy Javier Reyes and I did have a magnetic attraction between us, but there were several problems right off the bat. The most important being he worked for my dad, the sheriff of Peach Cove, and with Alex, plus he was another alpha-male type. I wanted a partner, not a boss. And with the passing of my thirtieth birthday, I needed to make wiser decisions.

"Maybe you should tell Paul about your *affliction* and see if he runs for the hills." Betsy smirked as if to say, *Gotcha*.

As to my *affliction*, a term Betsy had dubbed it, I was dealing with that better now. As ridiculous as it sounded, my mama, Clara Brown, had been tied to the island since the day she passed. She wasn't what you'd call a pure heart in life, and now the powers-that-be forced her to remain in limbo on Peach Cove until she made amends. I wasn't sure what qualified as amends, or what it would take to satisfy the requirement. For all I knew, she could be here my entire life span or be gone tomorrow. What I did understand was if a soul was forced to remain as an island spirit, it created an energy around the person they were communicating with. An aura, if you will. The deceased were drawn to said person, i.e., me. The possibility that I might be insane had lurked in the back of my mind often. Either way, I had to deal with Mama on a regular basis.

"That is not going to happen."

"I know, I'm kidding. Just don't settle. You can do way better."

I smiled at my friend. She meant well. "You have my word. No settling." I glanced around one last time. Everything appeared as in order as it should at this point. "I guess we're through here."

"Yeah. I promised Meemaw I'd go to the rehearsal dinner at the Beach Bum." Betsy squinched up her face when the last word left her lips. She must have realized her faux pas by bringing up the restaurant where Alex was caught flirting with a tourist who turned out to be Lucy and making the off-again part of mine and Alex's history permanent. "I'm sorry. I'm an idiot."

"Don't be, and you're *not* an idiot." I waved her apology away. "It's ancient history. I've moved on."

Alex and I had to make a point to stay out of each other's way. We'd made a go of it and it hadn't worked out. Before he'd proposed to Lucy, there were times he attempted to rekindle what we'd had. When we weren't focused on real-life problems, neither one of us could see why we weren't still together. Then the sensible side of me emerged and I reminded him of our history.

CHAPTER 2

I strolled down the beach near the water's edge, a lone sandpiper running ahead of me. The foaming water lapped at my toes as the wind whipped my blond hair around my face. Soul-soothing Heaven. The spans of beach space utilized for beach weddings and receptions was a short drive from my house on the east side of the island on Laguna Beach, but today, I'd decided to walk. I glanced toward Aunt Vi's Pelican Cottage, where she usually enjoyed a glass of wine. This evening the patio remained empty. She'd be attending the rehearsal dinner with Betsy and the rest of the wedding party. I was glad I didn't have to attend. I could imagine the uncomfortable tension and awkward small talk.

Next door to her cottage stood the newly renovated Sand Dollar, where Javier resided. It also appeared to be empty. He must be on patrol tonight.

I let out a sigh and continued down the beach toward the first real home that belonged to me and only me, Beach Daze Cottage. It'd been love at first sight with the property's exposed high beams and ample square footage. My friend Yvonne, our popular island designer, had come in and worked her magic, adding wall-to-wall windows with pocket doors that faced the ocean. I had my dream kitchen and just enough money left over to furnish the entire cottage with pieces from estate sales and discount furniture outlets.

When I'd arrived back home a couple of years ago after my horrible marriage ended, I'd moved into my childhood home Mama had left me. Now my sister and her family of three filled the newly rebuilt home with love and laughter. It was as it should be. Jena Lynn had a wonderful husband and a beautiful baby I adored. She'd told me after they'd moved in that her life was everything she'd dreamt it to be. She lived in the perfect home with her little family, the Peach Diner's business boomed, and we were all together on the island again. The joy I felt for my sister was immeasurable.

When I thought of my own life, there were days I had to focus not to allow loneliness to seep into my bones. My life hadn't exactly gone to plan. Though I'd grown a lot, I had a great deal more to work to do. I'd been blessed with a wonderful group of friends and, even though my family didn't fit into the perfect mold, we loved each other and would move mountains for our tribe. Having Mama around complicated a lot of things. Whenever anything out of the ordinary transpired, I was on edge until it turned out not to involve me. On the other hand, the predicament had afforded us time to work through our troubles and have a healthier relationship. If having a relationship with a dead person could be healthy.

Determined to shake this impending blue mood, I decided to open a bottle of wine and assemble the antipasto platter that awaited me in the refrigerator. I'd enjoy it on my lovely back deck and watch the sky go dark. I'd read somewhere that smiling for fifteen seconds, whether you were faking or not, immediately lifted your mood. I gave it a try as I started up the path through the dunes toward my cottage. The bright green herbs growing up from my planters on my deck came into sight. *One, two, three . . .* The space was lovely and just what I'd always wanted. I fumbled with my little cross-body bag in search of my house key as I climbed the steps. *Ten, eleven, twelve . . .*

"Marygene."

I froze and my smile faltered. *What is he doing here?*

Slowly I turned around and met Alex's deep chocolate gaze as he took the steps two at a time.

"You ruined my smile count."

"What?" He shook his head in a bemused fashion. "Never mind. I forgot who I was talking to." He winked, his attempt at charming me. He'd failed.

"Aren't you supposed to be at your rehearsal dinner?"

His shoulders rose and fell. "I had to talk to you. May I?" He motioned toward the back door.

"I don't think that's a good idea. We can sit out here." There was no way we were going inside. The last time he and I were alone, we'd had a heated discussion that ended in a passionate encounter. Not that I'd go down that road now that he was engaged, but still. In my current state, I didn't want to take any chances. Wiser decisions, check.

I opened the door and flipped on the outside lights, bathing us in a soft yellow glow.

Alex moved toward the bench; the chives blooming behind him swayed in the breeze as he frowned. "Marygene, this turmoil between us is shredding me. I—"

"Alex—"

He sat and slapped the tops of his thighs in frustration. "Please, just hear me out."

I waved a hand for him to continue.

"My family is in an uproar because they feel Lucy is the reason you and I didn't end up together."

I fought an eye roll. The entire island believed she was the reason.

Alex blew out a breath. "I was never unfaithful to you."

I narrowed my eyes.

"Yeah, I know you think my flirting was out of hand, but it never went farther than that." His eyes pleaded with me. "I'm an honorable man, and if life hadn't fast forwarded with Lucy the way it did"—he glanced off—"well, none of that matters now."

I studied his face, reading definite conflict in every muscle twitch. With the tiniest bit of encouragement, he'd divulge everything. After fifteen seconds of debate, I decided not to encourage. He'd be married tomorrow, and his confidences should only be shared with his wife. And I *wasn't* nor would *ever be* accused of being the other woman. "I don't want to be the reason you're at odds with anyone, especially your family. I told Betsy something similar earlier today."

He shoved his hands through his thick, wavy black hair. "That girl has always been a handful, but lately she's gone too far."

"She just worries about you. Betsy has a heart of gold.

She's loyal and will always have your back. You just have to be honest with her and hash this out."

He glanced upward before scowling. "We're talking about Betsy here. She's nuts!"

I ignored his reference to Betsy's sanity. "What do you want from me? I can't force your family to accept Lucy."

"I know that," he groused, sounding petulant. "But she's a little scared of you and she's terrified of Betsy."

I chuckled a little and the corners of his mouth turned up slightly. Maybe he was beginning to see his over-reaction. The woman clearly had nothing to fear from me and from Betsy—well, a little fear could be healthy. "Alex, this isn't like you. You've never cared what people thought and you used to laugh at rumors. It'll take time for every-one to adjust to you marrying Lucy. You know how folks are. Why are you really here?"

He sat back against the backrest, but his shoulders were still rounded forward. "You're right, of course. I was just venting to my friend. Because we promised to remain friends, and I don't know how to exist if we aren't. This wedding is driving me insane. Lucy is beside herself with worry that something will go wrong or that you and Betsy will sabotage the whole thing."

"Why would I sabotage an event my business is cater-ing? It would be career suicide." I sat on the built-in bench next to him.

He moved a little closer and when I didn't move away, he let out a little sigh of what I read to be relief. His tone softened. "When you say it aloud it does seem nuts."

The wind blew and a thick curl danced around his forehead.

"You just don't know how she is. For the last week she's been nonstop going on about the way my family loves you. She thinks they care more about you than me and I should do something about it."

I patted his shoulder. "You know that isn't true."

"At least Mom likes her."

Well, that isn't a surprise. His mama was the queen of mean. If you ever got on her bad side, watch out. But, his mama's meanness notwithstanding, we'd promised each other we'd remain friends. And I certainly hadn't kept up my end of the deal lately. "Listen. I care about you and I always will. Our lives and memories are linked since childhood. I want you to be happy, and if Lucy does that, then I'll try to get past our history." I clasped my hands in my lap. "But let's face facts. I'm not ever going to be her number-one fan and honestly, she doesn't want me to be. I mean really, Alex, it's absurd."

He had the decency to blush and glance away.

"And while we're on absurdities, for the life of me, I can't fathom why she'd want us to cater her wedding, but I've been nothing but civil and accommodating. I won't lie, she did her best to make our lives hell with the preparations. Jena Lynn is a saint, and even her patience was tested."

Alex's face hardened. "It's *her* wedding day."

I raised my hands in a defensive posture. "I get it. But changing the wedding cake design six times is excessive, and then four days before the wedding she insists I make her original choice. I wouldn't have taken that from anyone else. Because of you, I did it."

Alex blew out a breath and ran both hands through his hair before letting them drop. "Yeah, that was pretty rotten. She can be difficult at times. She's nothing like you." His hot gaze bored deep into mine and he reached out and took my hand.

Alarm bells sounded inside my head.

"She'll never be you."

"Alex." I pulled my hand away and scrambled to my feet.

"It isn't like a switch I can turn off." He tapped his chest. "You're ingrained inside me. I'm not saying I don't care for Lucy. I . . . do. We're just . . . different." His eyes darted around as if searching for the correct words. "I don't know how to put it. You get what I'm saying, right?"

Yeah, I did. "I suppose you'll always have a place in my heart, too. In time, it'll grow into something else. A fond memory. We were combustible, for sure."

He gave me a lopsided smile and sadness crept into his eyes.

I thought back to when he was spinning Lucy around and the warmth in his face as he gazed up at his bride. They shared a connection for sure, and as their lives grew together, it'd deepen. I sat back down and stroked his arm. "Hey. Life turns out the way it's supposed to. We learned a lot from each other, and you helped me through the most difficult time of my life. I will never forget that or cease to be grateful. Go into this next chapter of your life knowing you have my support and I'm genuinely happy for you. Lucy is pretty terrific, right? She must be if you decided to settle down after insisting for years it wasn't for you."

He stiffened slightly. "Lucy can be mighty convincing."

Our gazes locked. "When we love someone, they have that power over us."

"Do you love Paul?"

Surprise caused me to hesitate a second. "Too soon to

tell. What does my relationship with Paul have to do with anything?"

He hesitated. "Nothing, everything."

My heart rate sped.

"There's something I need to tell you—" His phone chirped, and he let out another long, ragged breath after he checked it. "I've got to go. I was expected at the Beach Bum twenty minutes ago." He looked at the cell phone. "She wanted to host the rehearsal dinner there. It's where we first met and all."

And there it was. A comment that meant nothing and everything all at the same time. I let out a small chuckle and stood. "Go. Your future wife is waiting." I went inside, closed the door, and counted to ten.

Mama stood there with her hands on her hips. Her face was drawn with concern.

"What?" I gasped. Putting my hand over my heart.

"Something is wrong. Dreadfully wrong. I'm feeling very uneasy about this catering job."

When Mama warned me of something, I'd learned to listen. I began to get a little light-headed. "Everything is ready to go. Can you be more specific? No one is going to die from food poisoning, or anything, are they? I could rid the menu of the item in question." My stomach knotted.

She shook her head and her brown curls bounced. "I can't get a clear picture. I just know something dark and grim hovers over this union."

"You're saying it has to do with Alex and Lucy? The tragedy?"

Her brows furrowed. "Maybe. The puzzling part is the darkness surrounds you too." She began to fade. "Be careful."

CHAPTER 3

The reception tent buzzed with Sunshine workmen and the Peach employees.

Jena Lynn rushed around the tent, her brown bob moving about her face while she doled out instructions to our staff. "You need any help?" She paused briefly at the cake table.

Hannah, Jena Lynn's sister-in-law, had become my right hand in the catering side of the business. She proved a proficient baker. Unfortunately, she'd gone out of town unexpectedly this week with a sudden death on her husband's side of the family. We were all a little stressed to be shorthanded but were managing. The warning Mama had given me weighed heavily on my mind. I'd keep my eyes and ears open. I was hoping the darkness had to do with the controversy that surrounded this union. It could be.

"I'm good. Don't worry. It's going to be fine. Trust

me." With steady hands, I carefully positioned the top tier of the wedding cake and gently pressed the rods into the tier below.

Betsy signaled the tier was centered perfectly, and Jena Lynn moved on. I let out the breath I'd been holding. It was always precarious work assembling a cake on-site, especially when the outdoor elements had to be considered. I descended the stepladder and grabbed my piping bag from my kit and began piping little pearls around the layers we joined with clear dowel rods. It was a gorgeous cake, prosecco sponge with a delicate strawberry filling that I'd perfected over the summer. The kirsch liqueur made the flavors come alive and burst into a symphony on the taste buds. I couldn't wait to see how it was received.

"Oh, Marygene. It's stunning." Aunt Vi came up beside me and gave my arm a squeeze. The plus-sized woman in her fifties had the same fire-red hair as her niece—the shade now came from a bottle—and emerald-green eyes. She wore a white spandex dress with flamingoes on it and matching pink flamingo earrings. The dress matched her personality. She'd stand out in this crowd for sure. Not that she gave a flip what anyone thought, a trait that had her topping my most-favorite-people list.

"Thank you. I must admit the flavors are to die for, and are even more impressive than the decorations." I took in my confection creation and smiled. The four-tiered cake with brilliant Italian meringue buttercream frosting offset with champagne-dusted icing pearls and freshly cut Stargazer lilies from the florist would be the centerpiece of centerpieces.

"I'm sorry we have to enjoy it at this clown show." Aunt Vi flung her arms around.

"Now, now, Aunt Vi, you promised not to make a scene." Betsy smoothed out her floral green chiffon dress.

"Me, make a scene? Girl, I have no idea what put that idea in your head. I'm a peaceable person. The bridezilla is who we have to worry about."

Betsy and I exchanged a smirk as Aunt Vi asked, "Speaking of the bridezilla, has she reared her head yet today? Change the menu—or wait, I know, pull a runaway bride?"

"No to the first two, and not that I've heard on the runaway bride scenario."

Aunt Vi laughed. "Wouldn't that be wonderful. We could enjoy the party without her. I had enough of her last night at the rehearsal dinner."

My ears perked at the mention of last night. I wouldn't say anything about Alex's visit beforehand, and I held out hope the couple smoothed out their issues and would live happily ever after. I'd decided before bed I'd keep well wishes in mind and forget about everything he'd said. Everyone got cold feet before their big day, didn't they? And he certainly wouldn't want to be reminded of it.

"Alex showed up late and she made a big show. She flew across the room the second she laid eyes on him and planted a big wet one on him for all to see," Betsy said. "It was so fake. I don't know how he can go through with this."

Aunt Vi nodded in agreement. "The boy is whipped for sure. But we were good. Neither one of us made a nasty comment or slapped the mess out of her when she went to bragging about all her wedding gifts. Did you know that none of her family are attending the wedding? Not a single person."

I shook my head in surprise.

"Apparently, they fell out a while back and she hardly speaks to them."

That could certainly contribute to the darkness factor. As Mama grew in her sensitivity, she'd told me she could now see more than looming danger. She could also see heartache and grudges that tore people apart from the inside out. It'd been obvious to me at the time how difficult this new development was to handle.

"Huh, that's sad."

Betsy and Aunt Vi shrugged. They both had the same look that I took to mean they believed the fault probably lay with Lucy.

I didn't want to dive down that rabbit hole. "Well, I haven't seen her today. I'm going to keep happy thoughts that she's pleased with the way everything has turned out."

Paul came in with his iPad, jotting down notes as fast as his workmen doled them out.

Aunt Vi rubbed her hands together when she spotted him. "I'm excited to see who gets whacked in this murder mystery. Hey you, young man!"

Paul turned toward Aunt Vi. His eyes went wide when he noticed her ensemble. He cleared his throat. "Can I help you, ma'am?"

"Can I whack whoever has it coming?"

Paul half laughed. "If we decide to go the enactment route, I'll give you a shout. Could be entertaining."

We all laughed then. Maybe this wouldn't be as brutal as I imagined.

Aunt Vi gave him a thumbs-up and whispered some-thing to Betsy, and the pair fell into a fit of giggles before leaving the tent to go and take their seats. I gave Paul a full appraisal as he turned to speak to a fellow employee, wondering what it was about him they were so put off by. He had a nice face and smile. Since his move to the island several months ago, he'd immediately taken a job at Sun-shine Mystery Murder Company. It was steady work he enjoyed, and he gave it his all. His ambition was evident with his desire to work his way up and perhaps own a franchise one day. I couldn't figure it out. Sure, he wasn't Prince Charming or smoking hot, and our chemistry didn't produce fireworks, but life wasn't a fairy tale. And some-times safe and boring could be appealing.

Disturbed by my own admissions, I focused on my tasks. In the prep tent, I checked to ensure the refrigerator was still working. We had a horrific experience last year on what was the hottest day of the summer when a refrig-erator quit working, chock-full of mousse tarts.

My brother was hauling an air-conditioning unit in-side. "I can't stay in here running fryers without some air. Alex will have to eat the cost, since he wanted these fun-nel cakes."

"We shouldn't have to operate deep fryers at all. Fun-nel cakes at a wedding." I shook my head. "I have the most amazing wedding cake to serve, who's going to want a funnel cake over that?"

"I'd want both. It's kind of awesome, if you ask me, to have fair food at a wedding." Sam secured his white ban-dana. Blond hair the exact shade of mine peeked out from underneath.

I shook my head.

My half brother was the spitting image of his father,

Sheriff Edward "Eddie" Carter. Technically, Eddie was our father. Not knowing that fact for the first sixteen years of my life, I'd never gotten around to calling him anything other than his given name. Until that night when it all hit the fan and I found out about the affair that resulted in the conception of yours truly, I'd believed my sister, Jena Lynn, and I shared the same father. Even though she was the spitting image of Mama and I bore no resemblance to either her or Jena Lynn's dad. When he passed, Eddie and Mama had picked up where they left off. Needless to say, it had been a traumatic period in my life.

I'd inherited the gray-blue eyes, blond hair, and easily tanned bronze skin, but Sam got the height, towering over my five-foot-five frame.

"We okay?" Jena Lynn sidled up next to me.

"Fear not." I shut the door to the refrigerator. "Cool as a cucumber." I smiled at my sister, whose amber eyes had dark circles under them. "Little Olivia still not sleeping?"

Jena Lynn's shoulders slumped. "I don't think that child is ever going to sleep through the night. The pediatrician says it'll happen but, sweet fancy Moses, I'm dying here. Last night after I put her down, I literally army-crawled out of her room so she wouldn't see me from her crib."

That got a laugh from both Sam and me, which made Jena Lynn smile.

"I feel bad that I've had to lean on you so much over the last few months. You've run everything single-handed and haven't complained a bit." Jena Lynn blinked back tears.

I gave my sister a quick hug before the waterworks commenced. She was still dealing with hormone surges, and the dam could break at any given moment. "I haven't minded. And after the two years you ran the diner by yourself, it was high time I pulled my weight. Plus, Livie is definitely worth it."

She grinned. "She is. I can't believe she's almost five months old."

Wet spots were developing on my sister's short-sleeved chef's coat. The embroidered peach on her left breast was leaking. She glanced down. "Oh no!"

I snatched a hand towel off the table and handed it to her. Sam pretended to not notice and focused on his batter, giving Jena Lynn a minute to make her escape. And I went to ensure the staff was setting up properly.

The guests were beginning to arrive and filling the chairs to await the ceremony. Betsy and Aunt Vi were seated on the first row of the groom's side, with Meemaw and Alex's mom. Zach was seated on the back row with chubby Olivia on his knee. That child melted my heart. Eddie was seated next to Zach, with Eddie's girlfriend, the lovely Doc Tatum, on his left, his graying hair shining in the sunlight. He glanced back in my direction, and I lifted a hand. Doctor Lindy Tatum and Eddie had been seeing each other for over a year now. Seeing them happy made me overjoyed.

Aunt Vi's revelation about Lucy's family made me take in the bride's sparse side. If I were in her shoes, I'd have the guests spread out on both sides, instead of leaving one side empty. She'd made a few friends on the island since moving here. Her maid of honor was a coworker. It did surprise me that not a single member of her family came to the most important day of her life. I'd heard from Betsy and Alex that she didn't have a lot of relatives, but neither one of them said anything about the type of relationship she had with them. Not that it was any of my business. I felt bad for her. It must be difficult gazing out over an empty row of chairs.

I checked my watch. If the wedding started on time, the event would go off without a hitch. I moved around the exterior perimeter of the tent to inspect it was enclosed properly. The last thing we needed was a gust of wind to blow sand all over the buffet tables and wedding cake. It'd happened before and had been a nightmare to manage. Though, manage we had.

As I made my way around to the back of the tent, I spied Alex coming down the walkway with Javier at his side. They both looked dashing in their silver-gray linen suits. The shade offset Javier's olive complexion, making his hazel eyes pop in the sunlight. They both noticed me, and Alex paused for a second and our gazes met. He froze.

I had a horrible sinking feeling in my stomach and my eyes slid away briefly. When I glanced back, Javy patted Alex on the shoulder as Alex seemed to gather himself, saying something low to his best man, and the two continued down the pathway.

Javier took a detour, his intense hazel gaze trained on me. "You all right?"

With squared shoulders, I faced him. "Why does everyone keep asking me that?" I knew the answer, but my pride made me go deep into denial with my responses. Still, I couldn't stop myself. "Alex and I have been apart for more than a year now." Without thinking, I brushed a bit of lint off his lapel.

All the relational stumbling blocks I seemed to have with Paul didn't hold with the man in front of me. He wasn't much taller than me but had to outweigh me by a hundred-plus pounds, and there wasn't an ounce of fat on him. Where I liked to indulge in pastries and sweets, he ate clean and exercised a lot. He had a torrid past full of danger and a disastrous marriage that had altered him. An experience he and I shared. He was harder than other men. In the year I'd known him, I'd grown to respect his character and integrity.

When I glanced up, he intently searched my eyes. "Alex had a few drinks too many after the rehearsal dinner. He mentioned your name a dozen or more times. Luckily, Lucy had gone home before he hit the regretful phase."

The more I heard about the bride and groom from other people, the more my opinion on the matter solidified within me. Mama had to be sensing the turbulence within their relationship.

The more I attempted to forget the conversation I'd had with Alex, compiled with Javier's scrutinous gaze, made me edgy. Then I understood why. "Ah, he told you about coming to my cottage. Last minute jitters is all." I shrugged and made up my mind to believe my statement. "Alex wouldn't go through with a wedding if he didn't love Lucy." I smiled for emphasis. *I'm okay, Alex is okay, we're all okay.*

"He's a fool." He stepped into my personal space. "People on this island stay stuck in the past. I plan to help you move into the future. One day you'll stop wasting your time on the wrong men and see the right one standing in front of you." His tone was thick and gruff.

I gasped when he thrust his fingers into my hair and crushed his lips to mine. I was breathless and staggered when he released me, and the earth beneath me must have been scorched. He rocked back on his heels and a small satisfied smile spread across his face as he steadied me with his hands on my rib cage.

Lost in the moment, I almost grabbed his head and pulled his mouth back down to mine and, what's worse, I think he could tell. Seconds stretched out like hours as I wrestled with the decision. Suddenly, his expression altered as he glanced over my head, and the spell was broken. I dropped my arms.

Before I could turn around, he slowly and methodically leaned down and kissed my cheek, as he allowed his hands to drop. "That'll give you something to think about." He left.

Seconds later, Paul stood a few feet from me. By the expression on his face, he'd seen everything.

"Don't say a word. You can be angry at me later if you want. Not that I encouraged any of that." I waved to where Javy had been. "We have an event to work and it will be a success if it kills me."

"Fine. But I think we need to talk sooner rather than later. You didn't seem to be resisting." He was right, I hadn't.

I was sure his mind went in all sorts of directions. Funny, though, I didn't really care all that much, even though I now believed Javy had an ulterior motive.

"The reason I sought you out, Marygene, is I need to know if you're ready for me to set up the props and clues. I didn't want to have my guys in your way."

I nodded. "Yes. We're ready."

CHAPTER 4

Everything was in its proper place, and we were as ready as we would ever be to host the most complicated wedding reception, complete with a murder mystery, by the time the music began and the bride descended the wooden steps and started down the aisle sprinkled with white rose petals.

"Wow, it looks like half of Peach Cove came out for the wedding." Sam stood next to me in the entryway. "A hundred bucks says they all came out for the murder mystery. Sunshine sure is making a killin'."

They'd been excellent for business, for sure. The juxtaposition of a wedding and murder mystery had become a profitable one.

"I'd have to agree. The excitement from the guests at every mystery event I've attended is palpable. Which is probably the reason Lucy moved her wedding date. With-out Sunshine, the crowd would be sparse."

"Honestly, the woman is so self-absorbed, I don't be-lieve she'd even notice everyone here is either a friend of the Myers family or wants free booze with a little enter-tainment."

We settled in silence as those in attendance stood. My brother flung his arm across my shoulders as Lucy joined Alex at the front. He didn't ask if I was okay or offer any consoling comments. Something I appreciated. When I wrapped an arm around his waist, he gave me a squeeze. This was big stuff for Sam. He wasn't a sensitive type of man. Unlike most of our friends and family, he never saw me with Alex in the long run, though he'd never said I told you so.

The loud rumbling of a motorcycle carried down from above the dunes. Even the bride turned.

"Who owns that sweet Harley?" Sam whistled as he lowered his sunglasses to get a better look.

The man in a biker jacket, wraparound sunglasses, and a bandana stared down over the ridge.

"Must belong to a tourist checking things out."

He revved the engine and the popping sounds echoed before he sped away.

"Rude." Sam was grinning.

I shook my head at Sam's enjoyment of loud, dangerous vehicles and my eyes drifted to the dark and delicious best man. Javier smiled in my direction. Or at least I thought he was smiling. It was hard to tell from this distance.

The crowd cheered, and I'd completely missed the groom kissing the bride. Javier's calculated kiss and the obnoxious biker bystander proved major distractions.

"Well, that's done." Sam dropped his arm and we got busy.

I made my rounds, and Sam went back to the tent to fire up the fryers. With everything in hand, I went outside to have a quick cuddle with my niece. Jena Lynn was standing next to Zach, holding the little doll with a peaches-and-cream complexion, in her arms. Olivia had her chubby fist stuffed into her mouth, with drool sliding down her chin.

I reached for her, and Jena Lynn passed her over. I wasn't sure if I would ever be mother material; but an aunt, I had that down to a science.

"I think she's teething. Hence the drool." My sister wiped her baby's chin with a burp cloth with Daddy's Girl written on it in pink.

I kissed her squishy cheeks. "Aunt Marygene doesn't mind a little drool, no she doesn't." I baby talked, and Olivia cooed. She let out a little squeal of delight as she peered over my shoulder. I didn't need to turn around. I was fully aware Mama stood behind me, making faces at her granddaughter. Unbeknownst to Jena Lynn, her daughter had met her grandmother and was quite fond of her. Babies had that ability. It shouldn't alarm me, but I wouldn't lie and deny the fact that it worried me a little. Never in a million years would I want this beautiful little doll to endure an island spirit. I pushed the thought from my mind and laughed as the baby giggled.

"I think she favors me," Mama said from behind me.

Jena Lynn and I thought so too. She'd be a beauty for sure, just like her mother and grandmother.

"She always gets so happy when you hold her." Jena Lynn beamed as she wrapped an arm around Zach, who kissed the top of her head, and she wiped her eyes. "Don't mind me. I'm a weepy ole mess."

Zach enveloped her with his arms and Jena Lynn nearly disappeared. "You're wonderful."

I gave the baby one last kiss before handing her back to her parents. "I hate to give her up, but Aunt Marygene has to go work." I smiled at my niece before I glanced back at the crowd. "The natives are getting restless. Olivia is lucky to have a mama and daddy like y'all."

"I'll see you in a few minutes," Jena Lynn said, and I nodded.

The wedding party seemed to be lining up for pictures, and the guests were starting to corral near the tent. When I got inside, my crew was nowhere to be seen. I could see Paul through the window on the opposite side of the tent. I went in search of my staff and nodded approvingly when I walked around the first few tables with beautifully lit candles positioned around the pink Stargazer center-piece. From here the wedding cake appeared to be hold-ing up nicely. I moved closer.

My smile faltered and I squeaked in surprise. My hand went to my parted lips. On the floor in front of the wed-ding cake table lay Lucy, covered in what could only be funnel cake batter. Mama's words rang in my mind and my knees felt weak.

"Sweet Lord! If I hadn't seen this with my own eyes, I wouldn't have believed Paul." Betsy snickered and looped her arm through mine. "She volunteered to be the victim in her own murder mystery reception!"

Oh, thank God! *Get a grip, Marygene.*

"Paul said the batter's a clue as to who killed her. What's wrong with you. Your face is pale."

I tried to laugh, and it came out nervous and shaky sounding. "I just can't believe she'd do this. Her dress! Her hair!" Impressed and stunned by Lucy's lack of vanity nearly left me speechless. I supposed I could have underestimated her. Surveying the area, I made sure the walkway was clear. I didn't want to have anyone slipping on the batter. This really wasn't a good place to set this up. Thankfully, none of the batter spilled around Lucy. I would have a word with Paul about it. Never again. I didn't care if the batter was being used as a clue. This could be a lawsuit waiting to happen.

"Did she say if she liked the cake before going into character?" I hoped Lucy would hear me and pop up for a second to speak to me. She didn't. Oh well, I'd done my best.

"Maybe she told Paul before she got whacked. She has to play dead really well, too." Betsy leaned down. "The guests are coming, Lucy. Don't make a peep or the whole reception will be ruined. I'll just fix your legs so it looks more realistic." My friend maneuvered Lucy's legs in the most unladylike fashion. Betsy admired her handiwork and began all-out guffawing. To my utter surprise, Lucy didn't break character.

"You're evil, Bets. Lucy, if you slap her for this one, I'll not come to her aid." Amused, my head shook involuntarily.

My best friend, what a joker. I supposed Lucy would grow accustomed to her antics now that she'd officially become part of the family. Another thought struck me. Could this be Lucy's attempt at fitting in? My opinion of the bride rose at the notion.

Rebecca came rushing in through the back of the tent with a chest full of ice. Wisps of her long dark hair escaped her ponytail and her face was flushed. "Marygene, I've been looking for you. The ice machine has some error code on it. It's stopped making ice."

"Did you tell Sam? He usually knows how to reset it."

"Yeah, I did. He's on it." Rebecca wiped the sweat from her forehead.

Lord help us if we couldn't keep the shrimp on ice. I rushed toward the prep tent. I'd told Jena Lynn last month we needed to order a new ice maker. The machine had malfunctioned on more than one occasion. Sam, being the tinkerer he was, had managed to breathe new life into the machine each time. I prayed his luck would hold out.

"Sam! Talk to me."

Bent over the machine with his tool kit, Sam grumbled something unintelligible but, a second later, the low hum of the ice maker began, and then it roared back to life.

"Sam, you're a miracle worker." I held my hand over my heart.

"That's what all the ladies say."

"Yuck." I laughed and threw a towel at him before I went back out to the reception tent. The guests were milling around and already forming lines around the food stations. Everything was going to plan, and a swell of pride filled me at pulling off the most complicated wedding reception of my career.

"Oh my God!" Alex seemed to be really getting into character.

"It's starting." Betsy sidled up next to me with a plate of food. She was stuffing her mouth with roasted shrimp cocktail and laughing at the same time.

I feared she'd choke herself.

"You shouldn't have positioned her that way. You're so bad." But I snickered along with her.

If I'd been Lucy, I wouldn't have stood for it. She was going all out with this thing.

"Somebody call nine-one-one!" Alex shouted.

Guests were getting excited and ready to join in. Betsy and I moved closer as Alex shouted again.

"It's the groom! He's the killer," an older woman shouted from the table closest to where Lucy lay.

"No! It's the caterer! Only she would have access to the batter."

I turned to gape at the table behind me. Several older residents already seemed to be tippling the champagne from the fountain at a rapid rate. *Terrific.* There were always messes when people started knocking them back too early.

"Ohhh! You're going to the clink!" Betsy died laughing and pointed at me.

Alex lifted his bride from the floor and clutched her to his chest. When he turned, that's when it clicked something was amiss. I knew Alex. He wasn't acting.

My heart pounded and I rushed next to him. "This isn't part of the game, is it?"

"No! Marygene, I can't get a pulse!" Alex's face wore the expression of a madman, with wild eyes shifting as they searched mine. "Sh . . . she's pregnant," he croaked.

All the blood drained from my face. "I'll get help." I ran.

CHAPTER 5

Chaos ensued. I ran right into Javy and nearly bounced off until he steadied me by the arms. I'd shouted something a little incoherent about Lucy and Alex and needing help. He'd jumped right into deputy mode and instructed me to get Doc Tatum before he whipped out his phone and called for an ambulance. When I found Eddie and explained what was going on, he'd informed me Doc Tatum had a medical emergency at the hospital and had left ten minutes ago. The person with the most medical experience on site was Theodore "Teddy" Gaskin, our funeral director/coroner. At Eddie's behest, he rushed inside the tent to offer what help he could provide, and I followed. Javier began ordering people to file out the side. Some of the guests believed the ordeal to still be part of the game. Others were in a state of panic. My staff stood confused.

I sidled next to Javier and didn't protest when he took my hand and wrapped his fingers around mine. Eddie was on the ground next to Alex, encouraging him to release his bride and let Teddy work. I held my breath as Teddy attempted to get a pulse.

Many thoughts flew through my mind at a rapid-fire pace. Mama had warned me and I'd disregarded it. I could have called for help earlier. Like the second I'd found her. When someone was ill or injured, every second counted. Then I wondered, had Lucy been ill? Had there been some complication with the pregnancy? Then the fact that the large mass in attendance greatly outnumbered the small Peach Cove Sheriff's Department concerned me. With so much going on, how could they possibly gain control of a crowd near pandemonium?

Teddy's dark brows were knitted together, and his mocha-colored skin lacked its usual glow as he began CPR. His treatment appeared rough as he pressed on her chest. Her lifeless form moved with each press.

Alex's eyes bulged and his body began to shake. "Get off her, you idiot! You don't know what you're doing. You're a freakin' funeral director!" He shoved Teddy away and poor Teddy hit the ground with a thud. Through the blurred vision of tears, I watched the distraught man as he cradled Lucy in his arms and began rocking. Begging her to wake up.

Without a thought, I went to my knees next to him and wrapped my arms around him as he wailed. I had no words. Still, I attempted to form some and managed, "I . . . I'm so sorry. So very sorry."

His eyes were wild, his face contorted in both rage and agony, his nostrils flared, and a little spittle hit my face as he shouted, "Get away from me! You aren't sorry. You hated her!"

I scrambled backward as Javier and Eddie fought to pull him off Lucy.

"Come on. Son," Eddie said softly. "An ambulance is on the way. Let Teddy see if he can help the girl until they arrive."

I longed for the sirens of the ambulance, and I pleaded to God, praying Lucy could be helped and, by the downcast eyes and solemn expression on Teddy's face as he worked, I feared they couldn't. Guilt consumed me. If only I'd listened to Mama and hadn't looked for another solution.

"I don't want her in here," Alex said, and I met Eddie's gaze.

He nodded toward the exit. Javier aided me to my feet, and I backed out of the tent.

My heel sunk in the sand as I stepped out of the way of the line of attendees that trailed behind Javier, who exited right after me, back to where the wedding had taken place only moments ago. The sun's rays were blistering, making us all wish for a gust off the Atlantic to cool our sweaty brows. I wiped my face clean, my stomach still in knots.

Betsy and Aunt Vi flanked me a few yards from the tent. The rest of my staff, including Sam, stood behind us. The Sunshine Murder Mystery Company's staff mingled with mine as I scanned the faces in the crowd for Jena Lynn, Zach, and Olivia. There were too many people.

Mama walked out of the tent toward us. Her yellow dress with white daisies blew in the wind. She held her dainty hand up to block the sun. "Something isn't right here."

You could say that again.

"If the girl passed on, I'd feel it, and I don't." It was a rarity to see Mama's face twisted in such deep confusion.

I overturned my palms as inconspicuously as possible, giving her the "what gives" sign.

"I wish I could tell you. Something is wrong, either on my side or that girl still lives." She faded from sight. Sirens were louder now, and I knew the ambulance had arrived. With Mama's declaration, I held out the tiniest shred of hope Lucy would either receive medical attention for whatever was wrong or we'd find out this all had been an elaborate ruse. Lucy was known for her theatrics. This would certainly be burned in the memory of all who attended. My instinct immediately refuted the second notion. Alex's reaction had been real. There wasn't any denying that. Would Lucy enact something so horrific and not inform her husband of the plan?

Alex came out of the tent, assisted by Teddy. The thin man had a difficult time holding Alex's weight.

"Oh no . . ." Betsy mumbled.

"Poor baby," Aunt Vi said.

"This is awful," I whispered.

Alex stumbled a couple of times before falling to his knees. Eddie hurried over and helped. My heart rent into pieces at the sight of Alex's ashen face, his eyes devoid of their normal playful warmth. He didn't lift his head as the two men hauled him toward the chair Javy had dragged over.

"Let me go to him!" Alex's mama shoved against Javier and rushed to her son.

He leaned into her as she consoled him. His shoulders shook, and I fought the tidal wave of emotion welling up within me. I willed my inner strength to rise. I had to be strong.

It helped that Betsy was close. She kept glancing over at her cousin, her eyes red rimmed. She loved Alex more than he knew. It was his mama that kept her and Aunt Vi at bay.

Aunt Vi shook her head toward where Alex sat. "This is just awful. Where are those dang medics?"

"They're up on the ridge." Sam came up behind us.

"Oh, thank the Lord." Vi rubbed her forehead. "I'm going to have to find another place for Mama to sit."

I glanced over toward the ceremony site, where Betsy's meemaw sat under her small umbrella. I turned around and whispered to Sam to help Aunt Vi.

"I don't think the medics are going to be able to do anything. Her lips weren't the right color." Betsy looped her arm through mine.

I hoped she wasn't correct.

"Sam, use the extra tent and the portable air conditioner. It's way too hot for her to be sitting outside."

"On it," Sam said.

"Thank you, dear." Aunt Vi patted his arm.

Everything happened so fast from there. I found it hard to follow the flurry of movement and the squawking guests as the EMTs rushed into the tent with their little bags. Alex followed them inside with his mama plastered to him. The next thing we knew, Alex was yelling, and his mama started calling for Eddie. Seconds later, the EMTs left the tent *without* Lucy. Betsy and I huddled together.

"Oh my God. She's dead." Betsy gripped my arm tighter.

"Why'd they leave her body inside?" I sniffed.

Eddie and Javier were scurrying around with hardened expressions.

"This isn't right." I chewed on my bottom lip. "Something is terribly wrong, Bets."

"You're just now figuring that out?" Betsy shook her head, not understanding my meaning.

Before I could elaborate, Javy called me over, and I followed him a distance away from the others. "Have you been in the same spot the entire time?"

"Yes."

"The entire time? You didn't go anywhere, not even for a minute, or was your attention divided?"

I searched his face. "I . . . I might have glanced away for a second, but I didn't leave. I sent Sam to set up a spot for Meemaw." I pointed to where Sam had improvised by putting up our small pop-up tent we kept around for extra storage and set Meemaw inside with an air conditioner. She'd been joined by a few of her contemporaries. It was too hot for them to sit out here exposed.

Javy nodded. "Did you see anyone coming or going?"

I understood he meant the reception tent.

I gave my head a shake. "What's happened? She wasn't murd . . ." My tone trailed off.

Javy leaned his head close to mine. "She's gone, as in physically gone. We can't find her. And, in her condition, it's highly unlikely she got up and walked off without being noticed. The coroner couldn't get a pulse or thinks he couldn't." Javy shook his head. "Alex pulled Teddy off before he finished CPR. Now Alex's in there grilling him, and Teddy is so shaken up he actually claimed he can't say for a hundred percent."

My fingers went to my parted lips. "My God."

"Someone had to remove the body, and if that's the case—"

"Foul play."

Javier's brows furrowed, and his mouth thinned out into a flat line as he nodded. "And if we're being completely candid here, the body should have never been left unattended in the first place." Javy didn't blame Eddie, but by the way he was staring over in his direction alluded to his disapproval.

I started to defend my father, stating that this case hit close to home. Eddie viewed Alex as more of a son than simply his deputy. But the argument died in my throat when Eddie used his megaphone to address the attendees, and I jumped.

I swallowed hard and turned around to where Eddie stood. Most of the guests had moved closer to the tent during the commotion.

"Everyone must remain at the ceremony site until further notice. I understand you're all upset and want to know what's going on. But I'm going to have to ask for your patience."

The megaphone dropped by Eddie's side, and he waved Javier and me over. "Where is Paul Fowler?"

"I . . . I haven't seen him." I searched the faces in the crowd.

"Paul!" Eddie blared over the megaphone. "Paul Fowler."

"Here!" Paul moved through the group standing behind Betsy. He must have slid in when I wasn't paying attention. I wondered why he hadn't joined me at the front. Though he hadn't any ties to Alex or Lucy, still, this would affect the company he worked for. Front and center was where he needed to be.

Eddie's serious expression had Paul taking a step backward. "Young man, I need you to be up-front with me about what's going on here. Is this some ruse? Part of your company's event?"

I gaped at Javier. This wasn't an angle he'd mentioned that the sheriff's department was exploring. His attention stayed with Paul and Eddie.

"No, sir." Paul's face paled. "Miss Carmichael stressed her desire to be the focus of the murder mystery. She was perfectly fine when she positioned herself for the event. This"—he waved his hand toward the tent—"I assure you was not part of the plan. Why? Is she?"

"Please wait back over there with the staff." Eddie pointed his index finger at Paul. "But stay put. I want to be able to locate you the second I need to."

Paul did as instructed, casting a worried glance toward me before standing in the exact spot he'd been moments ago.

Surely he didn't think I had something to do with him being singled out. It was procedure, whether Paul had any clue what had happened to Lucy or not, and the fact that it obviously wasn't a stunt. Even I knew that. Alex would have never fallen to pieces the way he had. And Lucy certainly wouldn't enact some elaborate performance without the knowledge of her husband. The notion seemed absurd.

Eddie pointed to the tent. "Deputy Reyes, we need to cordon off the entire perimeter and try and get a handle on things before it gets even worse. Theodore claims he couldn't get a pulse. Almost positive he couldn't. But clearly, the girl is gone. Fowler appears credible, and, until we know otherwise, we'll have to consider this a crime scene."

Javier glanced over to where all the guests were. "We'll need to clear it first. We can't run an investigation with all these people around. The scene's probably been contaminated already with all the foot traffic and people touching everything."

"It's a nightmare, for sure." Eddie rubbed his forehead. "We're going to need to check all the vehicles before we can allow anyone to leave. Make sure there aren't any traces of the victim and keep on alert for anything suspicious. I'll start with the business vans, make sure they're all accounted for, and then help you with cars, taking the folks in groups. That way we can check each one thoroughly before they drive away. I'll get Sam to help since Alex will need to sit this one out. I also need to ask him what vehicle the bride arrived in."

"What can I do?"

Eddie glanced at me as if seeing me for the first time. "If you could get your keys to Javier and try to calm your and Sunshine's staff, that would be helpful. We'll need the keys to their vehicles as well." He rubbed the back of his neck.

My head bobbed in a grim nod. "They'll need to go back inside the tent. Most of them stashed their purses inside the little locker in the back tent."

Eddie shook his head just as Javier spoke. "Having them trample back through the crime scene isn't ideal."

"Does Sam know where the locker is?" Javier asked.

I gave a single head nod, feeling numb.

"I'll go with him to retrieve it and bring it out to the staff. Sheriff, with it being just the two of us, we'll need to use the coroner as a deterrent for nosy guests. Station him outside the tent and make sure no one else enters."

Eddie agreed and moved through the small crowd and paused to speak with Teddy.

I glanced at Javier as he scanned the area like a hawk. "I'll go have a word with your brother while you give the staff your update." He held my gaze for a couple of seconds. "Keep your eyes and ears open."

His jaw tensed, and his brow furrowed. He wanted to convey something to me. I believe I understood. Where Eddie wrestled with the notion that something sinister occurred here, Javy did not. Eddie grew up in a different world than Javier. He'd once told me the types of crimes he'd worked before relocating to Peach Cove after his divorce. Drug lords and hardened criminals were a part of his daily life. Eddie hadn't had to deal with such crimes. We trusted one another and expected good to prevail.

"I understand. I'll be careful." The wind kicked up as we moved with a purpose toward where the staff had gathered. I focused on my surroundings and those within it.

Whispers were audible but kept low. Confusion and fear were palpable. The seagulls' calls overhead sounded louder than normal. The salty air stung my exposed skin as it mingled with sweat.

"Where is she?" Alex bellowed and seemed to appear out of nowhere. Ms. Myers kept attempting to take hold of his arm, but he wouldn't allow it. He stepped in front of me, inadvertently knocking me off balance, and shot a furious glare where the staff stood.

I regained my composure as the scene unfolded.

At first, I thought he was pointing at Betsy and then he hurled, "What did you do to her, Fowler?" Alex's entire body appeared rigid. He was on the balls of his feet with his fists clenched. Without waiting for a response, he rushed toward Paul.

Sam moved between Alex and Paul and attempted to defuse the situation. "Hey, man, let's calm down here, buddy, before you hurt someone."

"You stay out of this, Sam." Alex's lips peeled back, exposing clenched teeth. He shoved Sam, who fell into the crowd and to the ground, taking a couple of Sunshine employees with him. The remaining staff parted like the Red Sea, allowing Alex to grab Paul and snarl, "I'm giving you one chance to tell me where she is." He fisted Paul's shirt in both hands and shook him violently.

"I . . . I assure you I have no idea what you're talking about," Paul said with trepidation, his gaze darting around nervously, but he held his ground as he grasped Alex's wrists and tried to pry his hands away.

"This was your event. *Yours!* It was your idea she be the victim and now she's missing. What have you done with her?"

I feared for Paul's life. The crowd around us grew as they heard that the bride they thought was dead was now missing.

Folks were shouting, and a couple of Alex's old football buddies egged him on. "Kick his ass, Alex!"

"It wasn't my idea. I suggested one of the bridesmaids." The wobble in Paul's tone alluded to his faltering nerve.

By the time I reached them, Sam was assisting Javier hauling Alex off Paul as Eddie walked around the tent. Eddie told Paul to go and wait with the other guests at the ceremony site. It would give Alex a chance to cool down and Paul a moment to compose himself. Eddie gripped Alex's shoulder and placed his head closer to his deputy's, a fatherly gesture. My heart ached.

His voice was low and gentle when he spoke. "You've

got to get it together. I know you're upset. You have my word I'll do everything within my power to find her."

Alex held on to Eddie.

"Okay, bud? You have to trust me."

Relief flooded me when Alex began to nod.

"Now, I need you to take me to the car she arrived in and point me to whoever has the guest list, your mom perhaps," Eddie said.

I wrapped my arms around myself.

Alex's chest heaved and he put his hands on the sides of his head, gripping his hair. "You're right. I'll get you the guest list Lu—" He cleared his throat. "Lucy has her binder with all the wedding plans in the truck. Since we hadn't hired a wedding planner, she wanted to keep her notebook close. She rode over here with her maid of honor, Trixie."

When Eddie called everyone on the list in for questioning, he'd have to bring them in groups too. There was no way he'd get all those people into his little department at one time.

As Alex and Eddie walked off, Javy threaded his way through the crowd, preparing them for the process ahead. Groans and complaints flew from the attendees' lips along with the women assaulting Javy with concerns and questions. I wasn't sure he'd ever gain control. When he finally did, he spoke with Sam and the two went to retrieve the locker.

When my shoulders slumped, I let out a deep breath and started back over to where Betsy and the others stood. Alex's mama intercepted me. She was a hardy woman, with black curly hair, and brown eyes lacking the usual warmth of her son's. She pointed her sausage-like finger right at my nose. "Don't you think for one second you're going to get away with any of this. You couldn't stand it my boy was happy without you."

My mouth dropped open.

"That girl had it all, beauty and brains. You hated her! It wouldn't surprise me for one second if you killed her and had your lover over there get rid of the evidence." She'd nodded toward Javier and Sam as they walked off. Since she couldn't be referring to my brother, that left Javier.

Betsy rushed to my defense. "Aunt Regina, you know Marygene. She couldn't hurt a fly. You're just upset."

"Ha! And you!" Pure venom spewed from her lips as she narrowed her eyes to slits. "You've never been right in the head, just like Viola. I heard about the threat you made. And now that I think about it, you were probably in on it too! Maybe even the ringleader."

The guests were edging closer.

Betsy folded her arms across her chest, her face full of outrage. "You're insane! I've been on my best behavior. Aunt Vi and I even contributed to the rehearsal dinner when you were struggling to pay for it."

Regina Myers's head whipped backward as if Betsy'd slapped her. She took in the growing crowd and her face colored to an unhealthy shade of puce.

I shot Betsy a *What in God's name are you saying?* gape and forced my mouth closed before attempting to defuse the situation. "Let's just calm down and—"

"You shut your yap!" Ms. Myers poked me in the shoulder.

Betsy knocked her finger off and whirled on her aunt. "Don't you talk to my best friend that way. The family has always been there for you, even after Uncle David died. And you have the nerve to accuse me of this? He's my cousin. My own flesh and blood! It's shameful. Meemaw will hear about this."

"See! Y'all heard. You're all my witnesses! She's threatening me just like she did my poor sweet daughter-in-law." Regina played to her audience, crowing in theatric fashion. This was getting way out of hand.

"Betsy, let this go. It is not the time," I whispered to my friend.

"I've got this." She waved my concern away and went toe to toe with her aunt. "I ain't got nothing to do with any of this, and I dare you to prove otherwise. I've been the best niece I know how to be. But you make it impossible. You're a first rate bi—"

"Betsy!" I grabbed her arm. Why would she antagonize this woman?

She ignored me.

Regina continued, incensed. "You watch yourself, you little heifer."

"What did you call me?" Betsy jerked her arm away as her eyes flashed with white-hot fury.

"You heard me! And I can prove it! You told her she didn't want to mess with you or Marygene because y'all knew how to get rid of a body!"

Betsy's face paled.

Regina poked her in the chest. "That's right, missy. I've got your number. You. Are. Busted."

Intakes of breath traveled over the wind. Murmurs and accusations floated around. Betsy appeared a tad shell-shocked. Now, I didn't believe she'd realized what she was doing when she decided to poke the mama bear in front of us. We were beginning to receive dirty looks, and if Eddie didn't get back over here soon, Betsy and I were going to have to make a run for it. And running made everyone appear guilty.

"Regina! For the love of God." Aunt Vi waddled over, her cheeks flushed and her hands flying. "I understand you're grieving for your boy, and Lord knows we love him too and hate to see him hurting. None of us know what's going on here. For all we know, that girl could've just got up and walked away on her own. I'll tolerate a lot, and have over the years, but you start in on Betsy and we're going to have problems. And when I say we, I mean *you* are going to have problems." The stern warning Aunt Vi gave Regina had her sputtering for words and fighting for composure.

Betsy and I both gaped as Regina backed away sheepishly and stuttered, "A . . . Alex needs me," and hurried off.

CHAPTER 6

Three hours later we were told we could leave. Betsy had sent Aunt Vi to take Meemaw home and she would be riding in the company van with me. I finally found Jena Lynn. Eddie had allowed her to sit in her car, with the air, to keep her baby out of the sun and away from all the commotion. She and Zach were on their way home now with my promise I'd handle everything from here.

Since we were forced to leave all our equipment inside the tent, there wouldn't be anything in the van except extra equipment we brought for backup purposes. Standing off to the side of the tent opening, I was numb. Normally, I would have been perturbed at the sight of my masterpiece now a disaster. The flowers had wilted, the icing ran down the sides of the cake, and the bride-and-groom topper had fallen off the top tier and somehow wedged itself in the side of the cake. Now it didn't seem important. Still, I needed to be practical. There wasn't anything I could do for Alex or Lucy. "Eddie, I don't want to sound insensitive, but that wedding cake stand cost me a fortune. Are you sure I can't take that with me?"

"I'm afraid not. Everything will need to stay put until it can be processed."

He was right. I knew that. And the more I mulled this whole situation over, the more I wanted to scream and let out some frustration, followed by interrogating every single guest myself. "This is lunacy. It doesn't make sense. I mean, if Lucy were dead, she couldn't get up and walk away. And no one took her. You checked all the vehicles."

Eddie scratched his head. "No one took her that we're aware of. I'll admit this is a puzzler. Someone knows where she is. All I have to do is find out who." He made it sound so simple. Neither one of us believed it would be. He opened his mouth and closed it a few times. Since our pow-wow a year ago regarding Mama and my uncanny ability to discover victims, he'd avoided the subject. Now he appeared to be struggling with how to phrase his question. He wrapped an arm around my shoulders and pulled me close. His back was damp. "Do you have, um, any feelings or whatever it is you get?"

"I don't know for definite if the girl is dead or alive. If I could help, believe me, I would. Alex is crushed and confused. His mama is completely out of control." I still couldn't understand the woman's logic. I rubbed my brow. "She knows us. Has known us all our lives."

He gave me a quick squeeze. "She's upset. I wouldn't worry about her rants. We'll figure it out. I've got to stay here until forensics finishes. You and Betsy go on. Tomorrow is going to be a long day."

My mind spun as Betsy and I walked toward my work vehicle. Alex's face when he found Lucy, the bomb he'd dropped about her being pregnant, and his mama's accusations. The mere idea that she could even suspect us in any of this broke my heart. Then there was Lucy. What happened to her? Could this all be some elaborate stunt? Could Mama be wrong and Lucy had died? Teddy believed he'd been unable to get a pulse. And as Betsy pointed out, her lips were a blueish color. Was there something more sinister going on, as Javier suspected? I rubbed my aching forehead.

"Can you believe this?" Betsy ranted beside me. "Someone is trying to set me up! Aunt Regina is falling for it too. Any idiot that knows me understands that if I'd killed her, no one would have found her body. I'd have her chopped up into tiny pieces—"

"Betsy, hush!" I glanced around to make sure we were alone. "No one is trying to set you up. Your aunt isn't thinking clearly."

"I just hate this." Betsy stamped her feet. "Hate it, hate it, hate it."

The sound of loud footfalls came against the asphalt behind us. Betsy groaned and I cast a glance over my shoulder.

Paul ran up behind us, surprising me since I thought he'd already left. "My God. This is going to be bad for business. Christopher is flipping his lid."

Betsy folded her arms. "Business? How can you possibly think about your job at a time like this? Some of us have real concerns."

I scowled in her direction. The last thing we needed was to instigate another confrontation.

Paul raised his thin brows. "I'm sorry. My words were tactless. Forgive me. I just assumed you'd both be concerned about the financial consequences. It might be bad for the Peach too."

"That was tactless. Where we come from, family is everything and he's my cousin, for heaven's sake!" Betsy leaned forward and enunciated slowly. "My cousin." She snorted. "Leave the thinking to those of us who have a bra—"

"Betsy!" I understood how upset she was, but that gave her no cause to be so hateful.

"No, Marygene, it's okay. I understand and apologize." Paul looked abashed.

It certainly wasn't okay. I pursed my lips at Betsy before attempting to smooth things over. "We're just shaken up. Betsy didn't mean anything by that. She's trying to sort things out while dealing with hurt feelings." We stood next to the van in the nearly empty parking lot.

Paul concentrated on his shoelaces. "I get it. All that was pretty unnerving."

"That's putting it mildly, but I understand your meaning." I rested my back against the van. "I don't know what to think."

"Yeah, me either." Paul lifted his gaze to meet mine.

Betsy threw unapproving glances our way. "I know what to think. Lucy crossed the line, and someone punched her ticket. They were just too stupid to do it right. And now they're trying to frame his family." Betsy took a step forward and stared suspiciously at Paul. "It's always the quiet ones. They keep all the frustration deep inside, then one day, they explode. Bam!" Betsy threw her arms in time with her bam.

Paul jumped.

"Give us a minute, won't you?" I gritted my teeth at my friend, who always pushed a little too far.

"Yeah, I'll give y'all a minute." She pointed her two fingers at her eyes and then at Paul before jerking open the door and hopping inside.

The van door slammed shut with a clunk.

"Sheesh. She's a piece of work." He kept his voice even, but his eyes flickered with more anger than I'd ever seen before.

For a second, I didn't recognize the guy before me.

He must have seen my reaction and took a step back. "Sorry. This just has me rattled. She needs to be careful throwing around accusations."

"I'll speak to her." I kept my tone low, and it didn't escape either of our notice how guarded I sounded.

Sweat broke out on Paul's upper lip as he shifted on his feet. "At least the police were here when it happened. Never in my life have I experienced such a shock. And the poor groom. His ghosted face will haunt me."

Betsy tapped on the window, then opened the door. "It's hot as Hades in here. Hurry."

"Sorry." I dug through my bag and handed her the keys before turning back to Paul. "Didn't you find it unusual for the bride to choose to be the victim? I mean, Lucy was all about her appearance and this was the biggest day of her life. Didn't you find that a little odd?"

He glanced upward, as if thinking it over. "Not really. The batter wasn't part of the original plan. We added it this morning. She thought it would be clever to lead the guests down the wrong path. Her appearance shouldn't have been altered. She instructed my staff to make sure the train of her dress draped so people would see the intricate sequin work. She had pictures of models she brought with her during the consultation. They were called 'death spreads.' She thought it would be hauntingly beautiful and completely original."

Death spreads? "You mean images of people posing as dead? Not real dead people?"

He nodded. "Models posed as the deceased. She thought it would leave her guests beautifully awestruck. Her words."

There wasn't anything beautiful about that idea to me.

"Well, I guess we better get going."

I nodded absently, still thinking.

"Do you need a hug?"

I glanced up. Paul's expression conveyed exactly who needed the hug. I leaned in and held on to him for a few seconds. Betsy blew the horn three times in succession.

"I'll be right behind you." Paul gave me a small reassuring smile before jogging to his vehicle, and I went around to the driver's seat of mine.

"Nice, Bets. Really nice." I backed out of the space.

"Somethin's off about that dude. I'm telling ya." Betsy sat staring out the window. "He's got those beady little killers' eyes."

"Dude?"

"Yeah, dude. I'm bringing it back."

"Let's not and I think you're misjudging Paul. He's just different." And considering the way he freaked out, I couldn't see him killing anyone. He wouldn't have the stomach for it. "You were awfully hard on him."

Betsy and I rode up the winding road toward the entrance ramp. In twenty minutes, we'd be back in the town's center. When I glanced over in her direction, I

could clearly see her struggling to keep it together. She
kept picking at her cuticles while she bounced her foot,
her gaze never leaving the passing palm trees.

"It's going to be okay." I gave her a quick pat on the
arm before focusing back on the road. "Talk, it'll make
you feel better."

"I don't need to talk. You know me, I'm a rock. Stuff
bounces off me or breaks on impact. That's the way I get
by in life. I'm tough as nails. I'm concerned for you is all.
I should probably talk about that." Betsy, like the rest of
us, tried to believe she could withstand anything.

"Sure. Go ahead."

"I bet you feel just awful the body disappeared."

I stopped behind a car and waited to merge onto the
highway. "I think we all do."

"Yeah, but you especially because truthfully, you're
glad Lucy is gone."

That caught me by surprise, and I turned in my seat.
"Glad?"

Betsy wouldn't meet my gaze. "Without a body nobody can test for DNA. You're glad because your best
friend's DNA could be all over her. All it takes is a single
hair, and you know how my hair sheds. Mine sheds almost as bad as Killer's does." Her elusive cat, Killer, did
shed a lot. In fact, since he made himself so scarce when
I was around, it was the only evidence of his existence.

"Lucy was lying on the floor where there was a lot of
foot traffic. There could be DNA from loads of people.
You've nothing to worry about." I moved up a couple of
car lengths, rolling to a stop. "Javier is already concerned
about the contaminated crime scene. It would be difficult
to convict anyone on DNA alone."

"That's what everybody says. 'Don't worry, it'll all

work out in the end.' You ever seen that show on Netflix where those guys were railroaded? Well, those poor folks were targeted by the police. And nobody could do a darn thing about it. They're still stuck in jail."

I scoffed. "How confident are you they're innocent? Besides, Eddie and the Peach Cove Sheriff's Department aren't trying to railroad you. Alex is your cousin, for heaven's sake. We should be focusing on him."

Betsy undid the clip in her hair. Waves of frizzy curls fell around her shoulders as she rubbed her temples. "I am worried about Alex. I'm not callous."

"I never said you were. You love him."

She chewed on her fingernail. "I do, and I just hated that girl, and everyone knows it. I have a hard time keeping my opinions to myself."

"A lot of people didn't care for Lucy. Let's take a deep breath and hope they find the body, or her alive."

"She ain't alive."

"It's hard for me to believe she's alive too. Still, Mama claims she would know. She sounded certain when she told me she has no knowledge of Lucy's passing. I'm holding on to hope. It might only be a sliver, but I'm holding it nevertheless. You should too." We merged onto the highway and had just gotten up to speed when a car changed lanes in front of us without signaling. I hit my brakes.

The pedal went all the way to the floor. "Oh my God!" Unable to stop, I steered around the car. The van gained speed as we went downhill and around the bend.

"What are you doing?" Betsy leaned forward and braced her hand on the dashboard. I was forced to weave in and out around other cars. The drivers were blowing their horns at us.

"The brakes won't work!" I swerved around another car, nearly sideswiping a sedan.

"Do something!"

"Like what?" A minivan with a baby on board sign hit their brakes in front of us. "Hang on!" I swerved off the road and onto the shoulder. I steadily pumped the brakes, but the van wouldn't slow.

We went down into the ditch and into the tree line. Betsy screamed as I navigated off the road and ran right through Mama before the world went dark.

My ribs hurt and my legs were bumping against something hard. With great effort, I forced my lids open and the world around me spun. I became aware someone was dragging me across the grass and I was powerless to do anything. Something warm and wet ran down my face and into my eyes, stinging and blurring my vision as I was laid down. I made several attempts to focus before I eventually made out a figure dragging Betsy toward me. My heart raced as her head lolled to the side, and I thought I might be sick. Her frizzy red curls dragged on the ground. Fear unlike any other gripped my heart like a vise. A loud explosion caused my ears to ring. Flames were blazing from behind the figure and Betsy. She was laid next to me and the figure dashed away. Flashing lights for the second time today were visible and, since I was unable to hear sirens, I feared my eardrums had burst.

My head rolled to face my friend. I rasped out her name and attempted to sit up, but my body wouldn't co-operate. She lay next to me, unmoving. Over and over I attempted to shout her name.

Someone loomed over me. I tried to shove them away toward Betsy. *She needs help!*

Finally, I managed to get my vocal cords to cooperate above a whisper and managed to scoot my arm across the ground. I wrapped my fingers around hers and squeezed with what little strength I had within me. "Betsy."

Her eyes fluttered open and her head rolled to the side to face me as a blurry figure checked her vitals.

"Thank God." Relief flooded me. Tears streamed down my cheeks.

Her cracked, bloody lips were moving. I strained to hear, and I think I made out, "Oh good, we're in hell together," before I passed out.

CHAPTER 7

The throb in my skull made it feel like it'd split apart when I woke and the bend of my arm itched. My fingers fumbled on something hard. As I cleared the cobwebs, I saw the IV taped to me. Small red lines covered my arms. The blood pressure cuff squeezed the other arm, making a low humming noise. I took in the sterile room that smelled of bleach, with a large window. I blinked a few times when I saw Javier slumped over with his suit jacket tucked between his head and the back of the high-back chair. His white shirt was untucked and rumpled. He stirred and suddenly his eyes went wide.

He sat upright, the jacket falling to his lap as he ran a hand over his military cut. "Hey. How are you feeling?"

"Water," I croaked.

He grabbed the little pink cup on the table tray and

filled it with water from the matching pink pitcher. A straw was put to my parched lips and I sucked greedily.

"What happened?" I croaked again through a raw throat once I'd satisfied my thirst. *Oh, the accident.* Before Javy could answer, I sat up and blurted, "Is Betsy okay?"

The room spun.

"Whoa. Take it easy." His hands went to my shoulders and he eased me back on the pillow. "Yes, other than a minor case of whiplash, your friend is just fine. They ran an MRI to make sure she doesn't have a serious head injury. Scan came back clear. In case you're wondering, you have a concussion and some bruising, with minor cuts on your face and arms. You might have to be here a few days. You both were lucky."

My fingers went to my stinging cheeks. Tears filled my eyes. "Is it bad?"

The corners of his mouth turned upward, and his hazel eyes softened. "No. There won't be any scarring. Like I said, you were lucky." He gave my hand a squeeze and something inside me warmed.

I was beyond grateful to not be alone.

As I recalled the crash, or what I could recall of it, I took in a ragged breath. *We were lucky.* And it was a relief to hear my friend hadn't sustained any serious injuries. I couldn't live with myself if she'd been seriously hurt—or worse, I lost her.

"I should go see her." When I tried to sit up, the room spun wildly and the pounding commenced like a jackhammer. I gave up. "Maybe not just yet." I'd have to settle for sitting up a little. "Lift the bed, will ya."

Javy pushed the button on the side of the bed and my

head raised like magic. "The sheriff just left. He's been here all night. He didn't want you to wake up alone and he had to leave."

"Thanks for staying." I attempted a smile. "Ouch." I gingerly felt the tiny cuts on my cheeks and forehead. I must look a fright.

Javier didn't seem to be freaked out, so I wouldn't focus on vanity just yet.

"Your sister and brother were here last night as well. Jena Lynn wanted me to tell you she would stop by your place and make sure your cat has food and water."

My sweet sister always thought of everything. And Mr. Wrigley would be grateful.

"We've already taken Betsy's account of things. I don't want to rush you, but, as you know, the first recollections of events are important. Can you tell me what happened in your own words?"

He was absolutely correct. "Yes." With my hand to my forehead, I told him about the brakes malfunctioning and avoiding other vehicles by swerving and driving down in the ditch, then Betsy and I were dragged from the van by a Good Samaritan seconds before it exploded into flames. I recalled the heat I'd felt as the fire billowed from the van. I shivered when I remembered how Betsy's head lolled to the side. Thank God she was okay. The guilt overwhelmed me. "We take great care to ensure our vans are in good working order. I . . . I don't know how this could have happened. We just had the routine oil change and maintenance check." I let out a giant ragged sigh and remembered the shadowy figure who saved our lives. "Who was our Good Samaritan?" My gratitude to that person knew no bounds.

"Paul." He swallowed and his face held an expression I couldn't discern. "It was Paul who pulled you and Betsy from the wreckage. He was behind you and called nine-one-one when you began driving erratically. Dispatch wasted no time when his panicked call came in."

Javier handed me a tissue when, too overcome with emotion, I struggled to speak. I took in a deep breath. "Thank God for Paul. Is he here?" I wanted to waste no time in thanking him.

Javier gave his head a shake. "He was here. I'm not sure where he is now."

"Did Eddie find out what happened? Brake fluid leak?"

"You know him well. When it came over the radio you'd been in an accident, I'd never in my life seen a man go so pale in a matter of seconds. He pestered everyone and wouldn't leave your side until he knew you were okay. He made sure the top neurologists read your MRI results. He wanted nothing missed."

That was my father. Relentless. I smiled without think-ing and instantly regretted it.

"He wouldn't be able to relax until he went over the vehicle himself." There was something else on Javy's face. Something dark. "More water?"

I massaged my temples and gave a small nod.

He brought the cup back to my lips and I drank from the straw.

The door swung open. "Marygene!" Betsy shouted as Aunt Vi wheeled her into the room. Her face was scratched up and her neck was in a brace. "Someone tried to off us! Can you believe that junk?"

"Betsy, should you be out of your room?" Javier asked.

"We ain't stayin'." Aunt Vi nabbed this wheelchair from the hallway. "We're gettin' out of here before they steal my organs."

Aunt Vi nodded. "That's right. If you're an organ donor, I'd advise you clear out as well. I saw a show on some crooked surgeon who sold folks' vital organs on the black market for megabucks. I'm not lettin' that happen to my girls. You want me to get you one of these babies, Marygene?" She patted the handles of the wheelchair. "We can waltz right out the front door before anyone notices. I'm sure the big hunk of burning Latin love will push your chair."

"Hold on a second. We'll discuss this asinine escape plan in a minute. What are you talking about? No one tried to kill us." *Had they? Surely not.*

Aunt Vi wheeled Betsy to my bedside. "The van exploded, Marygene. Use your noggin. Ask him." Before I could utter a single word, Betsy exploded with, "Aunt Vi heard Javier say something about a bomb when he was talking to Eddie over the phone a bit ago."

My mouth fell open. "What?" I turned toward Javy and held my aching head. "Is that true? Did someone tamper with the van?"

"I was just about to discuss this with you. Ladies, I'd advise you to keep that information to yourself." Javier's hazel gaze darkened when he turned back to me. The hard lines of his face told me he blamed himself for not being more careful with his word choices while on the phone with his sheriff. It wasn't like him to make that sort of mistake. "A pipe bomb was found on the underneath side of the vehicle and we're surmising the brake line had been punctured, causing the brake fluid to leak. That's why it took a bit for the brakes to fail."

"See!" Betsy waved her arm toward Javy. "Thank God Paul followed us, or we'd have been crispy critters."

My stomach lurched.

"I might have been wrong about Paul. He ain't so bad. You could do worse." She licked her top lip, which began bleeding. She'd reopened a few wounds. "I'm parched. Can I have a sip of this?" She leaned forward aggressively and reached toward my bed tray for the cup. Her hand faltered and fell to my lap. "So dizzy."

"You have to be careful." I knew that dizzy feeling, and it was awful.

Her face turned an odd shade of green. "Uh-oh." She slapped both hands over her mouth as her cheeks bulged in time with her eyes.

"Bathroom!" I pointed to the open door across from my bed. Aunt Vi rushed her inside and the door slammed behind them. Poor Bets.

We learned something new about my best friend. She liked to let everyone in earshot know she was puking. Never in my life had I heard anyone shout so loud with each hurl. Javier covered his mouth with his hand and covered a laugh with a cough.

Aunt Vi came running out seconds into the ordeal with her fingers pinching her nose. Her watery eyes spoke volumes. "Guess we might better heed the medical advice and let her stay after all. I'm sure they won't go after her organs with a police presence. I'll be sure to let them know we're on to them. I'll go get a nurse to move her back to her room." Aunt Vi waddled out of the room.

Javier's face told me the odor had wafted in his direction. He moved farther away.

"You okay in there?" I called out.

The groans and exaggerated wails spoke volumes. "Do I sound okay? I'm retching my innards out in here."

"Help is on the way." My body broke out with cold sweats. "I can't believe this. Why would someone want to kill us?"

Javier placed the damp towel on my head. "We don't actually believe anyone made an attempt on Betsy's life. She wasn't supposed to be in the van with you." Javier turned to stare out the window.

"Oh." I rested my head on the pillow and processed his words. "But they did try to kill me. And said person would know I would be driving the Peach catering van." I blew out a deep breath and tried to calm myself. "Wait. Y'all searched the van. Wouldn't you have noticed a bomb?"

"The sheriff searched your van personally. Either he was in a hurry or it didn't occur to him to search the undercarriage."

Why would he? Eddie had no experience dealing with bombs. If it had gone off a few minutes earlier, Betsy and I wouldn't even be here.

What a minute! Another thought occurred to me. I'd only seen Mama for a split second before we crashed. She always appeared when my life was in danger, but usually she helped prevent what occurred, or tried to. Perhaps she saved us from the explosion, delayed it somehow. And perhaps I'd begun to rely on her instinct, especially when it came to the deceased. Maybe I depended on her a little too much.

"Y'all. I sort of made a mess." Betsy groaned from the bathroom as there was a knock on the door to my room.

The nurse. "Knock, knock." A graying stout woman with skin the color of rich caramel and kind honey brown eyes came into the room wearing pink scrubs. "I'm Natasha." She wrote her name on the whiteboard on the back of the door. "I'll be your nurse this evening."

"Nice to meet you, Natasha." I smiled, feeling the exhaustion overtake me. "Um, my friend who was in the accident with me is in the restroom there. She's really sick."

The woman rushed into the bathroom. "Oh, you poor thing," the nurse cooed. "Let's get you back to your room. You really shouldn't be out of bed." She wheeled a pitiful-looking Betsy out.

Javy and I remained in silence. The nurse came back a couple of minutes later and I assumed Betsy's nurse took over my friend's care. The woman checked my vitals. "How are we, Miss Brown? Your coloring isn't so good." She glanced from Javy and then to me. "Sir."

Javier turned around as he rubbed the back of his neck.

"I think Miss Brown should rest. She's been through quite an ordeal."

"He isn't bothering me."

"Hmmm. Well, I hear you and your friend are lucky young ladies. Don't you worry about a thing. We're going to take wonderful care of you. You'll be good as new in no time. You just relax and leave everything to me." She smiled in a mothering sort of way, and I instantly wanted to keep her forever.

How nice it would be to have her around when I wasn't feeling well. Mama wasn't the pampering motherly type. We were lucky if she didn't spray us down with Lysol at the first sign of a sniffle.

"On a scale of one to ten. How would you rate your pain?"

"A fifty. I'd love a bucket of ibuprofen."

She released the blood pressure cuff. "I can give you

Tylenol. We must avoid any medications that may poten-
tially worsen bleeding. I'll also bring you an icepack for
the goose egg on your head."

"That'd be amazing. Thank you."

She smiled broadly at me. "I'll be right back. And I'll
have someone come in and clean your restroom." She
cast a disapproving glance in Javy's direction. "Don't
upset her." She pointed her finger at him before leaving
the room.

"I hadn't planned on getting into the details with you
just now." Javy took a seat in the chair, looking guilty.
"Betsy blew in like a hurricane and forced my hand."

"Don't blame Bets." My eyelids were getting heavy,
despite the razor blades rattling around inside my head.

"I don't. She's just as much a victim as you."

"You gonna distract me again?" I smiled and held out
my hand, needing the feel of another person, and didn't
dwell on the fact that I didn't want it to be Paul.

"I try not to take advantage of hospitalized women."
I could hear the smile on his lips. "It worked though,
didn't it?"

I nodded, and when his fingers curled around mine, all
the terror caused by the fear of events of the day washed
away with a wave as safety fell over me.

CHAPTER 8

Several days later, on a Wednesday, I was released from the hospital and Eddie drove me home. I'd threatened to leave the day prior when I'd had enough of the interruptions from nursing staff during the night, robbing me of the possibility of solid rest and, while I appreciated their attentiveness, I longed for my own bed, the serenity of my cottage, and a full night of uninterrupted slumber.

My head still ached but had improved from skull crushing to a throb, and I was grateful to sink onto my mattress and under my sheets. I reminded myself to thank Yvonne for insisting I up the thread count when she returned from the trade show in New York.

Eddie put a glass of water on my bedside table. "You want me to close the curtains?"

"No. Crack the door a little so I can hear the waves. It soothes me." I'd missed my bedroom decorated in a mixture of soft blue, periwinkle, and hints of green. I pulled the soft blue-and-white paisley comforter up to my chin. According to my discharge papers, I wasn't to sleep for long spurts, but I could have a few hours at a time, and I planned on taking advantage of them. Doc Tatum would be by to check on me frequently to make sure I didn't develop any other symptoms.

"Are you sure that's wise?"

"The screen door locks. Mr. Wrigley enjoys sitting by it at night." When Eddie didn't move toward the door, I gave up with a sigh.

"I wasn't worried about your odd cat." Eddie ran his hand through his graying blond hair and stared at me as if I were in a coffin and he'd been responsible for my death. "Marygene, I . . ."

"Don't. This isn't your fault." I shook my head; the idea he kept blaming himself worried me. "You're not all-knowing, and you've never had to deal with bombs before. And hopefully you never will again. I'm okay and so is Betsy." *Thank God.*

"There's no excuse. I should have checked under the vans." The lines on Eddie's face appeared to have deepened, and I could tell he was taking this personally. I needed to talk to Mama in the worst way. Under the circumstances, it felt extremely odd she hadn't made an appearance. The way she told it, her job wasn't to simply help me when I needed it with the departed but also to try and keep me safe when my life was in danger.

"Listen, I've been thinking about it. This whole thing could have been orchestrated to create a diversion. Take out the sheriff's daughter and the killer could drive right out of Peach Cove and onto Cove Ferry, landing in Savannah before anyone was the wiser."

"I thought of that. And there's something else. There must have been some holy intervention because we found a bomb on the underneath side of Paul's van as well."

"What?" I pushed up in the bed. Paul hadn't said anything about it when he visited me in the hospital. I'd expressed my gratitude, and he immediately insisted he'd done what anyone would do in that situation. He seemed embarrassed by the attention, which was a different side to him I'd not seen before.

"It didn't detonate. Whoever installed it must have been in a hurry and screwed up the wiring. We're having a former colleague of mine that works for the bomb squad in Atlanta take a look at it. It'll be a few weeks before we know more."

With this new development, I wondered if Mama had intervened on Paul's behalf. It made sense. Paul survived and then he saved Betsy and me. But that also meant no one had checked under Paul's van either. This looked bad. Especially if Paul made noises about it, and the man was a stickler for details.

"How's Alex?" Surely, after all this, his mother no longer suspected Betsy or me.

"Dealing. The boy's been through it. He's lost his wife and unborn child on his wedding day."

"Still no sign of Lucy or um, her body?"

Eddie gave his head a shake. "We have a few leads. Nothing that has panned out so far."

The weight of the predicament nearly suffocated me. I hated that Alex was in pain. *Hated it.* And as much as I'd not been a Lucy fan, she certainly didn't deserve her fate. I thought of Jena Lynn's little bundle of joy and a sob nearly overtook me. Eddie handed me a Kleenex from the box on the vanity in my en suite. "Thank you. Do you think someone came after Lucy from her past? We hardly know anything about her."

"It's possible. We've been looking for an unidentified man who rode in on a Harley. From guests' accounts, he wore wraparound sunglasses and kept his distance and never joined the other guests." He patted my leg. "I'm going to let you get some rest. Lindy will be by in an hour or so. She'll stay the night."

"That's so nice of her. You picked a good one, Eddie."

He smiled a little before his face took on his sheriff look. "Now I don't think you're in any real danger. With both vans rigged, the diversion idea makes the most sense. Still, either I or Javier will periodically do sweeps of the house until I'm satisfied there isn't a shred of a threat."

"Alex now believes she passed away, right?"

"He still holds out hope. Even though, according to the Gaskin boy, she didn't have a pulse." Eddie raked his hand over his mouth. "It's a puzzler." He leaned down and gave me a light kiss on the head. "Get some rest. And stay put until Lindy gets here."

"Okay. Drive safe." My eyelids grew heavy and the space next to me vibrated. Mr. Wrigley and I had formed a bond since I'd taken him in from Tonya, Peach Cove Sheriff's Department's receptionist, the summer before last. She'd had a family emergency and the situation was supposed to be temporary. When I first saw the senior cat with his gray fur that stood up with static electricity and his one white eye, it hadn't been love at first sight on either of our parts. Now, the little guy and I had grown together through our trials. Both of us wore our battle scars from life proudly. We understood each other's trust issues and had found a kinship. When Tonya returned home, she didn't have the heart to separate us, and now, here we were. My hand moved across the blankets and I stroked his furry head. "Night, Mr. Wrigley."

The next morning, to my surprise, I felt worlds better. The nausea had subsided a great deal and my head was a dull ache. Nothing Tylenol wouldn't fix. The bruising and body aches were probably going to hang around for a while. Every time the soreness on my breastbone became apparent, I thanked my lucky stars I was alive to feel it. I'd called out to Mama for several minutes, really needing to discuss things. By the inconsistency of her responses, it wasn't clear if she ever heard me when I called, and I wished I had some surefire way of reaching her when I needed to. This whole island-spirit business needed to be revised. For the living person attached to the spirit, it was highly inconvenient on more than one level, and when the person wanted to reach the spirit, we had no pull. There should be comment cards or something. I'd fill that sucker out in a heartbeat.

Jena Lynn had come by with Olivia while Doc Tatum— well, Lindy—had been here and brought me some cheesy potato soup, my favorite. Sam called to see if I needed anything, which was nice. Yvonne had called after him. Her mama had informed her of my accident when they last spoke.

Despite the last couple of days, my friends and family gave me a warm sense of being blessed beyond measure. I wasn't on the schedule to work until tomorrow morning, and I decided to luxuriate over my morning brew. I had my coffee on the back deck, staring out at the waves crashing on the sandy beach, and called Betsy. She answered on the fifth ring with a grunt.

I kept my tone low. "Head still pounding?"

"It's not too bad. What time is it?" I heard the rustling of sheets.

"Eleven. I haven't slept this late in eons. You heard anything from Aunt Vi or Meemaw about Alex?" I set my mug down beside me.

"Yeah. Meemaw said he went from meltdown to madder than a hornet faster than she could turn around. He's frustrated with the lack of progress on the case."

"That's understandable." I stood and stretched my aching muscles.

"Yeah. It is. But what's got everyone in a tizzy is the hissy fit he threw last night. He seemed to be adjusting, having a hunk of Meemaw's prune cake and a beer, when your dad called. When he got off the phone, it all hit the fan and he swore a blue streak before he stormed out the front door."

"Was he angry with Eddie or the situation?"

"Both, I guess. Eddie's name was dropped a few times in not-so-glowing terms. And yours too."

"I bet it's because Eddie won't let him work this case. He's probably lashing out at the world. I should try and call him." The thought of Alex being alone with his pain tore me up.

"I wouldn't." The way she sounded told me Alex must've said some dreadful things about me. "Let him cool off. He'll turn up when he's ready. He didn't seem all that tore up about our accident either. He shouted at Meemaw, 'They're alive, aren't they. Lucy could be dead!'"

"Oh." I inspected my herb bed for weeds. Alex must be on edge if he shouted at Meemaw. Alex wasn't a disrespectful guy. It made me even more determined to reach out. Plus, he may know more than he thinks he does. Like who might have been hanging around Lucy before she died, and if she said anything that might clue us in on what the heck was going on. "I'll tread lightly."

"Of course you're not going to leave it alone." She sighed. "Don't say I didn't warn you. I'm going to hop in the shower 'cause I feel disgusting, and then I'm going to run to the diner for some food. I don't have anything in this house, and I'm off till tomorrow."

"Same. I'll meet you there."

The second she hung up, I phoned Alex. It went to his voice mail. "Hey, it's me. I . . . I know we haven't been on the best terms, but please know I care about you. I'm here if you need me."

An hour later, the tinkling of the bell above the familiar door and the married aromas of all the food being either fried, scattered, or smothered gave me comfort as I entered my home away from home. The Peach Diner was decorated in a fifties motif with its black-and-white checkered floor tile that offset the peach vinyl booths and chairs with a white stripe down the center. The long counter, where I'd spent many years of my life doing homework, ran the length of the room and was fitted with eighteen high chairs. It was completely full this afternoon.

Betsy waved to me from the back booth. I glanced at the walls adorned with old photographs of the town and townspeople, with the back wall dedicated to Peach Cove's high school football team. I passed the framed image of Alex and me in high school and sighed. My sister hurried out of the kitchen to replenish the displayed pastries. When she noticed me, she shot me a scolding grimace.

She'd given me strict instructions last night to stay in bed today. "What are you doing here?"

I snatched a napkin from the holder on the counter and waved it. "I'm here for nourishment. Don't shoot on sight."

"Fine. But you should be in bed. I'd have sent someone over with food."

"I know. You're the best. I just had to get out of the house. I've been in bed for days."

She relented with a grin. "I can understand that. Still, be careful and don't push yourself to recover too quickly. It takes as long as it takes."

"Promise." I held up two fingers in scout's honor as I passed by her. Not that I'd even been a scout.

"Hey, Bets." I slid into the booth and snatched a fry from her plate. "How's the head?"

She shrugged and chewed on her Sam's Surf and Turf burger. It couldn't be too bad the way she was devouring her food and slurping down a peach milkshake. "Sorry. I couldn't wait. You took forever."

"No worries." I snagged another fry.

Rebecca came over and gave me a hug, her sweet, young face full of sympathy. "We prayed for you and Betsy at my prayer group last night."

"Thank you." I smiled at her. "Keep it up. We can use all the prayers we can get."

Betsy nodded in agreement since her mouth was full.

"My nanny said she'd never seen anything like what happened at that wedding, in all her days."

I wouldn't suspect anyone had. We all three shook our heads mournfully.

"What can I get you?"

"I'll have a potato waffle, two eggs over easy, and a side of bacon. Coffee to drink."

She jotted down my order, placed it on the wheel for Sam, and went to see to her other tables.

Betsy took a second to breathe between bites. "I should've gotten a potato waffle instead of these fries." She finished off her milkshake, slurping loudly as Rebecca placed a fresh cup of coffee and a couple of creamers in front of me.

"I think I'll get a slice of key lime cheesecake and a cup of coffee. No hurry, though. I see your section is full."

Rebecca smiled. She and Betsy had become good friends.

"I'm on it." She pre-bussed the table and went about her business.

"I've decided I'm not going to worry about stupid things like dieting no more. Livin' through a near-death experience changed me. Think about it." Betsy wiped her greasy hands on a napkin. "We worry about the dumbest things. Stress about stuff that, in the grand scheme of life, makes absolutely no difference. This here's the new-and-improved Betsy. I'm taking life by the cahonies and juggling those suckers."

I nearly spat my coffee at her word picture as someone tapped me on the shoulder from the booth behind me. As I sputtered and turned, I saw Miss Sally dining with her twin sister, Miss Glenda. Both ladies were shaking their curly permed heads with the corners of their mouths turned downward.

"We heard about your car accident, dear. Sister and I were so happy to hear that you and sweet Betsy were okay. Gotta get those brakes checked real regular-like. The whole car really. You never know when you got a belt loose or a leak somewhere." Miss Sally patted my back, her wrinkled lips pursed. "You poor girls. Y'all gotta think about these things when you ain't got a man around."

"That's right, Sister," Miss Glenda chimed, putting down her coffee mug. "We know all about having to fend for ourselves. You gals need any advice, feel free to stop by the house. We'll have us a glass of iced tea and sit a spell on the front porch. We had a new ceiling fan installed last week. Puts off a nice breeze."

The old ladies scooted from their booth with their ticket and dropped a couple of singles and a few coins on the table. The sisters always tipped exactly twenty percent.

"Thank you, ma'am. We'll certainly keep your offer in mind." I smiled and Miss Sally pinched my cheek lovingly.

As they left, I turned back around to Betsy, her mouth agape. "I can't believe it. You know what that means, don't you?"

"Yeah, they think we're going to be old maids like them. The nerve!" Betsy folded her arms.

"No, you nutcase. It means the word spreading about our accident doesn't include the"—I lowered my tone and leaned in—"bomb."

Rebecca walked up with her tray laden with our food. Betsy and I sat back as she placed our plates on the table.

"Thanks so much. Looks like you're going to have a day of good tips." I picked up my fork.

"Yeah, we've been slammed."

The door chimed and another crowd was coming in just as the counter and booths were emptying.

"I'll check back."

"No need. If we need anything else, we'll get it ourselves. If things get too desperate, give me a shout. I could take a table or two for you."

"Jena Lynn would kill me. Besides, she's helping out on the floor when she's done in the back."

As if on cue, my sister came out of the kitchen and began filling mugs with coffee and scooping up ice in cups for drinks.

"Great. She finished in the kitchen early." Rebecca had a bounce in her step as she left us.

"You see what I'm saying?" I took a bite of the deliciously crispy waffle, topped with cheese, chives, and bacon. Comfort food at its finest. I couldn't help the groan that escaped.

Betsy grabbed her fork and dug into my plate. "I just want a bite. Yum." She chewed. "Now that you mention it, Alex didn't know about the bomb either. And that's beyond weird. I mean, I guess since he's all torn up about Lucy and they haven't kept him in the loop, he wouldn't know. Well, unless Aunt Vi told him."

"Did she?"

"She didn't say she did."

I pondered this for a minute and another interesting fact hit me. "Has anyone even mentioned Lucy? By name? The twins didn't say a word and Rebecca seemed concerned about our accident."

Betsy appeared thoughtful and then shook her head. "No one other than Aunt Regina and Alex, of course."

"The few people I ran into on the square before I came into the diner didn't say anything about Lucy specifically.

Most of the talk was about our accident. In fact, Bonnie said the ordeal was quite a show and you never know about outsiders." Bonnie Butler owned the boutique next door to the diner and the senior was always a source of breaking news and island gossip.

Bonnie'd been in such a hurry she hadn't elaborated as she normally would've. Her daughter had opened her boutique for her, and Bonnie expressed her annoyance at the change in the window display. I hadn't paid much attention to her meaning. Or my assumption of her meaning, anyway.

"Dude." Betsy swallowed a bite of cheesecake.

"Enough with the dudes." I sipped from my mug.

"You don't like it? Not even a little bit? It's like we're in high school again."

I raised my brows. "Not even the tiniest bit."

"Fine. I'll can the dudes. Back to Lucy. I guess folks just didn't like her none. I mean, why would they? She was horrible."

"I believe it's more than that. They don't think it's one of our own who committed the crime. I mean, look around."

We both surveyed the dining room. We received several waves and well wishes from those who took notice. Not a single person appeared to be rattled or upset by what happened. Betsy started humming *The Twilight Zone* theme song.

I finished my meal and dropped a ten on the table for Rebecca; the girl could use a mood lifter for her efforts. Then I went around the counter to have a word with Jena Lynn. She was busy. I couldn't help myself as I rushed into the kitchen, gave my hands a wash in the employee sink, and jumped in to help. After the customers at the counter were served and their mugs full, I asked my sister about customer chatter. She'd had the same experience I had.

"I thought it was odd no one mentioned Lucy, other than a few folks saying horrible things like Alex dodged a bullet and it was too bad they didn't get any cake."

My eyes went wide.

"I know. She didn't make the best impression in the year she lived here. I mean, surely there are those that must've liked her. Alex obviously saw something good in her. You know me, I don't like to talk bad about anyone, and I think it's dreadful what happened to the girl. On her wedding day, no less. But she could've done well to take a lesson in manners and etiquette. To be so pretty, some ugly things came out of her mouth. And you know what mama used to say."

"'Ugly words shouldn't come out of pretty mouths. No matter how much paint you put on the barn, the ugly taints the whole structure,'" we said in unison.

CHAPTER 9

Betsy and I took our time leaving. We chatted with a few customers and made pleasantries with our regulars before I grabbed a box of turtle brownies to go. We took a stroll around Cove Square. The brick square where most of the businesses in town were situated, including the Peach, was filled with pedestrians at all hours, from shoppers to diners and those enjoying the bluegrass bands that set up on the corners to play. Tourists were snapping pictures around the fountain recently added near the dog park area. Everything appeared to be business as usual. To the casual observer, today looked like any other.

Poppy Davis, my brother's girlfriend and the owner of the Beauty Spot, sidled up next to me. "Oh, Marygene." She squeezed me with all her might, my sore ribs protested, and I squeaked. "Sorry. I'm just so glad you're okay."

Poppy was a petite five-foot-nothing with ever-changing hair and gorgeous big brown eyes. Today she had mahogany brown hair pulled up in a messy bun.

"Thanks, Poppy. We were lucky, for sure."

She kept her voice barely above a whisper when she pulled me off to the side. We were on the sidewalk across the street from the giant glimmering peach sign above the diner. "Have you noticed how no one is too torn up about Lucy?"

I nodded. "It's surprising."

"It is."

Betsy joined us from where she'd been doing some snooping of her own around town.

Poppy gave her a quick hug and expressed her well wishes before continuing. "What's really odd, y'all, is the gossip at the salon. You know how I get a lot of seniors early in the mornings. The ones who are usually the most caring about town issues and drop off the get-well baskets from the church."

Betsy and I waited while Poppy paused to allow a group of tourists to pass by.

"Well," Poppy began conspiratorially, "they're getting baskets together for you and Betsy. A lot of 'poor things' were shared about y'all. They made up a bereavement basket for Alex too, but the consensus seemed to be no one was all that concerned about Lucy or her body's whereabouts."

I found this information on the seniors a tad shocking. "That is odd."

Poppy bobbed her head. "This is the real kicker and

the reason I came out to chat with y'all when I saw y'all out here. That strange man, the one who drove up on his Harley during the ceremony—"

Betsy and I nodded eagerly to show we weren't only following along but also anxious for her to get to the point.

Poppy's eyes were lit with intrigue. "Well, Trixie said she saw Lucy talking to him outside one morning before work a few weeks ago and asked about him. At first, Lucy acted like she didn't know him, and Trixie let it drop." Poppy stepped a little closer. "Then when she took Lucy home one evening after work 'cause her car broke down and Alex couldn't get off work, the biker was waiting for her in her driveway. Lucy got all jittery. And when Trixie was leaving, in the rearview mirror she saw him grab and kiss her."

Oh my God!

"How did she explain that?" Betsy asked, red faced.

"Well, Lucy had to come clean then. She said he was her ex and was upset when they broke it off. She said it was definitely over and swore Trixie to secrecy." Poppy was a wealth of information.

Betsy huffed. "I bet she didn't say a word to Alex, 'cause he would have lost it at the wedding when the guy rolled up the way he did."

She was probably right about that. Alex had jealously issues to the nth degree. I patted Betsy's shoulder to try and calm her down and faced Poppy. "Did Trixie see him again? Could she describe him?"

"She might've." Poppy's shoulders rose and fell. "I'm not sure she can describe him very well. She said he always kept his distance and wore those wraparound sunglasses, a biker jacket, and a skull bandanna. Like a sexy man of mystery. And Trixie said when she kept pestering Lucy about him, Lucy wigged out and shouted at her to drop it."

I'm sure Trixie conveyed her concerns to Eddie. Though he'd not mentioned it when he told me about the biker.

"He always wore a biker jacket in this heat?" Betsy turned her nose up. "Idiot would surely attract attention in that getup."

"Right?" Poppy held up a hand toward her assistant, who'd just walked out of the Beauty Spot and waved in our direction. Poppy signaled she'd be right there by holding up her index finger. "Trixie thinks he's the one responsible. You know, some shady love triangle."

Gotta love the gossip at the Beauty Spot. And Trixie might be on to something. I also wondered if the man of mystery knew how to make a bomb. "Hey, Poppy, how'd Trixie seem to be holding up?"

Poppy's light brown eyes lit up. She loved being the bearer of juicy gossip. "She seemed fine when she came in to have her nails done. She wanted something with color instead of the French manicure she got for the wedding. She enjoyed the attention since she'd been the maid of honor and all. She made the comment that she and Lucy weren't all that close. They'd had lunch a few times at work and she took her home a few times, but that's it. She was shocked when Lucy asked her to be in her wedding, and the maid of honor no less. She said she got a gorgeous dress out of it and Lucy paid for her highlights and manicure, so it'd been a good deal."

"Wow."

"I know, right. I have to go. See y'all." Poppy darted back across the street.

"We should probably find out what we can about the biker. I wonder if anyone else noticed him hanging around anywhere." Betsy spotted Meemaw and Aunt Vi walking toward Bonnie's Boutique. "I'm going to do some recon with Meemaw and Aunt Vi. I'll be all sneaky-like, but don't worry, I won't go mouthing off about the biker being Lucy's ex. With Alex losing it, I don't want to cause nobody to get out the straitjackets."

"Good thinking. I'm going to run by and have a chat with Teddy, then I'm going home to take a nap. You should too."

Betsy saluted me and went to catch up with her family. With Poppy's news, I was more eager to have a word with Teddy. I felt uneasy with the idea that some motorcycle madman could still be lurking on our island, and I wanted to see if he could shed some light on the situation.

After I conversed with a few more well-wishers, who happened to be diner regulars milling around the square, I proceeded toward my car in a hurry, a little concerned about the effects of the heat on the box of turtle brownies. My hand was on the car door when I heard my name being called. I turned to see Paul trotting over. We embraced the second he reached me.

"You are quite literally my hero." I grinned at him when he released me.

His face flushed under the praise. "I did what anyone would do. I'm just thankful I was there." He rubbed a hand over his thinning scalp.

"Betsy thanks you too."

His face creased in a large grin, making him look years younger. "Oh, I know. She caught me on the way over here and gave me a bear hug. I think she cracked a few ribs. She proceeded to tell me my scarecrow nickname was more of a term of endearment than anything else. It took her a few minutes to realize I hadn't the foggiest idea what she was referring to."

We both laughed and I searched his face. "How are you? I tried to call you when I got home from the hospital." I'd been really surprised he hadn't dropped by or stopped by my house. I left him a message while at the hospital. I did know how when you're involved in the accident, especially as the most important witness, you could be tied up for days with the police.

"My phone was left in the van and, as you know, it was impounded by the police. I came by the hospital after you were discharged and then by your house. Your dad was leaving and said you needed your rest. He told me he'd tell you I stopped by." Paul's scowled. It must have been clear by my expression that none of those things transpired. "He didn't though."

I shook my head. Eddie had a lot on his mind. He certainly deserved a pass.

"They're supposed to release my personal effects today. I was planning to go by the sheriff's office now, pick them up, and see if they've found any leads. I really need my phone back."

"It's certainly been a rough few days for all of us." I tucked my hair behind my ears and glanced around the square.

Betsy was right about one thing. We worried too much about insignificant things and failed to appreciate the beauty of our island.

"Marygene? You okay?" Paul tenderly stroked my arm with his fingertips and I smiled. "You zoned out there."

"Yeah, just grateful to be here. If you'd been a few minutes behind us, Betsy and I might not be here."

"Yeah, I get it. The sheriff is taking the position our incidences were to be used as a disruption of some kind. What kind of person does that?" Poor Paul. He had no prior experience with trauma, it seemed.

"There are some real sickos in the world." I opened my car door.

"Where are you off to? I was hoping you'd want to accompany me to the sheriff's department."

"Actually, I've got an errand to run." I leaned in, started the engine, and put the box of brownies onto the passenger's seat. The heat would ruin them if left out too long.

Paul's lips were pursed and his hands were resting on his narrow hips.

"Listen, I can appreciate how unnerving all of this is for you. Eddie will be in touch when and if he deems it necessary or if he believes you're in danger. You're going to be all right."

"Aren't I supposed to be comforting you with those words?" He glanced away.

I reached out and took his hand. "I'm running over to have a chat with Teddy. You want to join me?"

"Yeah, I think I do."

Ten minutes later, Paul and I were going up the steps of the two-story redbrick Gaskin Funeral Home. The funeral parlor had belonged to the Gaskin family since the first Georgia red-clay brick was laid. The front door was framed with large white columns to match the trim. Theodore Gaskin, "Teddy" to all those who grew up with him, had taken over the business after his father had been diagnosed with stage one lung cancer. Now his time was split between funeral director and coroner.

"He might be working on a body." Paul appeared uneasy as the sickly sweet smell of flowers and air freshener accosted us.

"Maybe, but he's usually in his office this time of day making calls. It's this way." We took a left and traveled down the narrow hallway on the threadbare burgundy runner. The dark cherrywood-paneled walls of the old funeral home gleamed. I knocked softly on the closed door.

The second I heard him grumble something, I popped my head inside. "Hi, Teddy. You got a minute?"

Teddy shut his laptop and motioned to the chairs in front of his desk. Paul and I went inside. "You know Paul, right?"

Teddy stood and extended his hand. "I'm not sure I've had the pleasure. Theodore Gaskin." Teddy had a wiry build and little brown eyes, with inky-black hair and mocha skin. He wore little round glasses that sat at the end of his pointy nose when he worked, which he had to constantly push up.

"Paul Fowler." The two thin men shook hands.

I placed the brownies on the large mahogany desk in front of him. "Turtle brownies, your favorite." I perched on the leather chair opposite the desk. Paul sank down in the chair next to mine.

"Thank you. You sure you should be exerting yourself after your accident?" Teddy pushed the box to the corner of his desk. His demeanor was vastly different from what I was accustomed to. His easygoing personality was replaced by a cautious, more solemn one. Attributing the change to Paul's presence, I realized my tactical error. Teddy probably felt ambushed.

"Thanks for the concern. I'm okay." A fact, though my head had begun to ache a bit and my muscles were more than a little sore.

"Teddy, when you went to help Lucy—"

Teddy cut me off. "We shouldn't be discussing this."

"I'm not delving into state secrets. You initially said you couldn't find a pulse. I heard you're backpedaling on that now. If Lucy isn't dead, then we have an abduction on our hands and a town in danger." Honestly, we might be in danger either way.

The cords in Teddy's thin neck were visible. "The woman didn't have a pulse. Alex kept pressuring me to be positive and, under duress, I might have given him hope. I deal with the deceased day in and day out. But a pulse check isn't a job requirement. I don't know how she vanished in the ten minutes I turned my back."

"Is that customary? For you to leave a body unattended?" Paul asked tersely.

Teddy held Paul's attention unwavering. "Nothing about what happened at the wedding was customary."

Recognizing my lapse in judgment at bringing Paul along, I rushed to intervene. I should have known better. "It's awful the ambulance was so late. Maybe they could have revived her with that machine."

Teddy shook his head. "Contrary to what you've seen in movies, it doesn't work that way. A defibrillator is useful when the heartbeat of the patient is erratic, or out of rhythm, if you will. Not to bring the deceased back from the dead."

I propped my elbow on the arm of the chair and massaged my forehead with my thumb and index finger. If Teddy was right, Lucy had died and there wasn't anything left to say. Some maniac killed her and displayed her body for all to see. Then the lunatic attempted to pull another theatrical stunt by killing Betsy, Paul, and me. What kind of crazy monster must we be dealing with? Then there was the issue that Mama hadn't believed her to be deceased. Could Teddy have been wrong? Perhaps? He was a fallible human, after all. Which led me to wonder what in the world would be keeping Mama away? Then we had the issue with our residents. No one seemed to be the least bit bothered by what happened to Lucy. Something mighty unusual was taking place on our island. Again. I was beginning to wonder if Peach Cove was cursed. The cursed island of Peach Cove. Wouldn't that bring the tourists? Ugh.

Paul spoke up. "I'm new to small island life and local hometown police procedures, and, with what happened to the bride, followed by Marygene's accident, which could've ended catastrophically, I wondered if I could ask you a couple of questions about procedure and protocol."

Teddy and I both sat stunned for a brief second.

Teddy managed to pull himself together before I did. "Mr. Fowler, if you have questions regarding law enforcement, you're speaking to the wrong man. Besides, I'm not sure what Marygene's brake malfunction has to do with Lucy Carmichael."

"You don't think the suspicious death of a newly wedded bride, who was then laid out openly by some sicko, and the tampering and attempted bombing with both my and Marygene's company vehicles, are linked?" Paul's tone wobbled slightly.

Teddy's eyes went wide as saucers as he sat forward. Clearly, he had no knowledge about the tampering. "Attempted bombing?"

"Indeed. I got Marygene and Betsy out of the van before it detonated. For some reason, the bomb under my van malfunctioned." Paul surprised me by tracing a cross, beginning with his forehead and then across his body with his right hand. I'd never seen him do that before. It wasn't something Baptists did. There was much I didn't know about Paul Fowler.

"I had no idea." Teddy deflated against the back of the high-back executive-style chair. He stared off in thought. "God, Marygene. Does your dad have any idea who's responsible?"

"That's what I want to know." Paul pushed the chair back when he became upright. "He won't discuss it with me. Doesn't have the time or the manpower, I suspect."

I slanted my eyes toward Paul with a glare I hoped he read as I didn't appreciate his comment or his mistrust in my father's ability.

I abruptly stood. "Thank you for taking time out of your busy schedule to speak with us."

Teddy nodded and rose, keeping his eyes narrowed as he appraised Paul with what appeared to be great scrutiny.

As we started to leave, Teddy gently grabbed my arm. "Hey, can you hang back a second?"

I met Teddy's dark gaze. "Sure."

"I'll wait for you outside." Paul closed the door behind him.

"What is it?"

Teddy sat on the edge of his desk. "During the chaos, I might not have paid close enough attention to the crime scene. I mean"—Teddy folded his arms—"I didn't know it was a crime scene and went in to try and help the woman. But I think I saw an injection mark on her upper thigh."

"Injection mark?"

Teddy nodded. "At first, I didn't think anything of it, but, after she disappeared and with this new information about the attempt on your life, I don't know. Without an autopsy I can never be positive. Still, it's possible the murder weapon could have been a drug."

"Who would do that? And why would they come after Paul and me?"

Teddy shook his head. "What does Alex say?"

I closed my eyes for a few seconds. "He isn't talking to me. I mean, I get he's hurting and all. He, um, sort of lashed out at Betsy and me."

"He's angry and distraught, as anyone in his situation would be." Teddy pushed his glasses up on his nose. "He's probably lashing out at everyone."

"Yeah, he probably is. I think he's also dealing with a little guilt as well. He came to me the night before the wedding visibly upset. I'm not so sure all was bliss in their union, and maybe they argued or something."

"Sounds like you're dealing with a little guilt yourself."

I leaned against the closed door and crossed one arm over to the other, thankful Teddy was a friend and would listen without judgment. I met his gaze. "Yeah, maybe a little. He wanted me to give Lucy another chance. For Betsy and me to befriend her."

"He shouldn't have put you in that position. And now he has to see how you've been through your own ordeal." Teddy reached out and squeezed my arm.

"Eddie thinks what happened to Paul and me was simply a diversion."

"Makes sense. It would give whoever time to get the body out of the area."

"Now I'm hearing about the biker that showed up at the wedding." I rubbed my forehead.

"What about him?"

"It's just rumors. He might've been involved with Lucy. Her ex or something."

"Does Alex know about that?"

I shrugged.

Teddy rose and put a hand on my shoulder. "Be careful. If Lucy got involved with the wrong person and you go doing what you always do, this could end badly."

He was right. And there was no reason for me to delve into this further. The deceased hadn't intercepted my path as they usually did when they needed my aid. And for that I was grateful and planned to enjoy my reprieve. I held up my hands. "Not this time. I plan to steer clear and let Eddie and Javy handle it."

CHAPTER 10

Paul and I parted ways after we left the funeral home. He acted miffed because I didn't share what Teddy told me, and I was irritated because he had an issue with my father. Paul had to get to work anyway, and I needed a nap. I pulled into the small space in front of my home. Beach Daze circa 1932 renovated raised cottage, with its slate-gray shutters and lovely gazing deck and tall palm trees, always felt like a retreat for me. "Come in and rest," the old place whispered over the salty breeze. My heart warmed as two large gift baskets sat on the front stoop, full of fruit and home-baked goods from our senior ladies.

The screen door closed behind me, the cool air a welcoming change from the ninety percent humidity outdoors. I punched in the code on the security keypad. I placed the baskets on the bar and flung my bag on the natural hand-shaped and handwoven rattan bar stool. Yvonne had insisted the natural beauty against the marble bar would relax the room. She'd been right. The cool colors in my home put out a soothing vibe, which I appreciated. My home felt safe. If the diversion theory was correct, and it made perfect sense to me, even if the biker was responsible, he wouldn't come after me again.

I opened the refrigerator and extracted a pitcher of tea. My replacement cell in my bag rang with Yvonne's ring tone. I'd been thankful I could sync it with my computer after losing my old iPhone in the explosion. I popped in my new AirPods and answered. "Speak of the devil."

"What?"

"I was just thinking about you and the wonderful job you did on the cottage. You on your way home?" I filled my glass with ice and poured the amber liquid over it. I took a few deep sips from the glass.

"Yes. I'm on the ferry." Her tone sounded off.

Something is wrong. I set the glass on the bar. "Tell me."

"Alex is here, and he isn't alone." I heard the car door shut. "Remember your favorite detective?"

"You've got to be joking. Detective Thornton is with him?"

"I'm not joking, and he certainly is."

That's who Alex lit out in a hurry to go and see. I slumped down on the bar stool and my chest constricted as if the wind had been knocked from me.

"And, Marygene, the man is not himself. Alex has always been prone to explosive, irrational reactions, especially in anger; though, I've got to say, this is edging on the need for medical attention. He told me I should have stayed away from the screwed-up island when I had the chance. He droned on about the crooked Peach Cove Sheriff's Department. How Eddie would sacrifice truth to protect islanders. That no one ever accepted Lucy, and their prejudices toward her caused her a great deal of pain."

"Oh, for the love of God! Lucy was no saint. I understand how people idolize the deceased once they're gone and all, but this is going too far. If Lucy didn't make friends while she was living, it was due to her sparkling personality. Forgive me for speaking ill of the dead or perceived dead."

"What's that? They're not sure she died on her wedding day?"

"No, well, I don't know. Teddy said yes, then he said he wasn't sure. Now he's back on the yes bandwagon. If she is alive, that would explain her disappearance. Yvonne, I kid you not, people aren't at all affected by her death. And it has nothing to do with prejudices. They've accepted plenty of transplants." I popped open a bottle of Tylenol and took two, washing it down with more tea. "Plus, she had a shady ex. Did Alex mention him?"

"Not to me."

"I bet Thornton is loving this." I went and opened the pocket doors and walked out onto the deck.

"I can't believe Alex would stoop so low. That detective was horrible to you."

I hoped the Tylenol kicked in soon. "Did Alex say anything else?"

"No. He seemed eager to end our conversation. Not that I wanted to stay engaged. He didn't seem like Alex, you know? Really unhinged."

"He's grieving. He'll come to his senses. Drive safe."

"I will. Should I call off the trip?"

I scanned my memory and came up blank before asking, "What trip?"

"Remember, I'm taking Mama on the Alaskan cruise she's always wanted to go on."

"Oh, right." There was a knock at the front door. "No, you should definitely go. Y'all have been looking forward to this. Go, have fun. This will all sort itself out."

"Okay, then. I probably won't see you before we leave. So be careful and don't let Alex drag you into anymore of his bull. You're seeing Paul now, and he's a nice step up from Alex."

"I won't. Have a great time." I checked the peephole. Javy stood on the stoop.

"We will. I'll catch up with you later."

I disconnected the call, shoved the buds into my front pocket, and swung open the door. "I thought you'd be down at the station house helping Eddie with all those interviews." I stood aside for him to enter and went to make him a glass of tea.

"That's why I'm here." He took the glass I held out for him and thanked me with reserved politeness, making this visit feel more formal.

"Right. You need to speak with me again. You'd think y'all would get all the questions you need to ask together before having someone give a statement. I bet y'all get a lot of complaints from folks tired of retelling an event that brought them trauma."

He sipped some tea, his brows raised over the rim of the glass.

"I know, I know, other questions come up during an investigation. Well, things are about to get even more dicey. You're never going to believe what Yvonne just told me."

"I'm listening." His expression conveyed nothing.

"She's on her way home and called from the ferry. She saw Alex and he isn't alone. He has a detective from Atlanta with him."

"What detective?" Javy put his glass on the counter and took a seat at the bar.

I took up purchase next to him and put the cool side of the glass against my forehead.

"Head still aching?"

After I swallowed a sip from my glass, I nodded and placed the glass on the bar.

"God, Javy. This is such a mess." I rested my elbows on the cool marble and covered my face with my hands. "Alex is teetering on the edge from grief, Paul is angry with me because I won't share everything, and now this horrible man is on his way back to the island. He's like the grim reaper, and I'm not being melodramatic, I swear."

"I take it you've had some run-ins with the detective in question?" Javy rubbed my back and I froze.

I lifted my head and met his gaze, feeling the reservation fall away.

"I apologize." He dropped his hand and seemed surprised he performed such a familiar gesture.

We'd shared one kiss. A kiss used as a distraction technique. His words before the kiss could've also been to divert my attention from Alex's wedding. I had to remember that.

"It's okay." I had a boyfriend, or sort of did. We were dating. Not that it was exactly relevant at present, and I focused on the current predicament. "A couple of years ago when Joseph Ledbetter died suspiciously, I met the Atlanta detective. There were rumors he wasn't on the straight and narrow. Alex worked with the man and is aware of this. He also knows bringing in outside law enforcement will send the island into a panic. And his mistrust of his own sheriff."

"Maybe that's what he's after. To shake up the island, I mean."

"How do you figure?" I leaned on one elbow, facing him.

"Well, the level of concern for his missing bride is strangely low among Peach Cove residents. After interviewing guests, the only reason a lot of them showed up for the wedding was to participate in the murder mystery."

Sam and I had surmised correctly.

"The drama hasn't hurt Sunshine at all. In fact, when I went by to speak with the new director, he claimed they were booked solid for the next three months."

"You're kidding?"

He shook his head. "And the theories the wedding guests have come up with in their statements. It's enough to give me a neck ache."

"Everyone's talking about the guy on the Harley? I heard about the love triangle theory from Poppy."

"That's one of them. Those mainly come from Trixie's friends. It's a ton of work. We have to look into anything that sounds remotely plausible. Odd thing is, the mystery man seems to have vanished. He checked into the inn your cousin runs, a few weeks ago. He used the name John Smith, paid cash and kept his distance from guests and staff, and then two days after the incident, he checked out. The sketch we got of the guy could've been anyone and everyone."

"Huh . . ." I drummed my nails on the counter. "What

about a driver's license? They would've made a copy of it at the inn for booking purposes, since he wasn't using a credit card as payment."

"We ran it, it was bogus." Javy pulled out his cell from the pocket of his brown uniform pants. He didn't have to explain who he was going to call. Eddie would require immediate notification of all developments. "Sheriff, I'm at Marygene's and have been informed of pertinent information."

I pondered the ramifications of Alex's decisions and worried about his mental state while I half listened to Javy relay to Eddie all I had told him. This would be the second time Detective Thornton got involved in Peach Cove business. And this time at the request of Eddie's own deputy. Alex and my father weren't simply colleagues who worked well together. They were more like, well, family. I found it devastating Alex would believe Eddie would cover up the truth, and seek outside help. A chill ran up my spine and the energy shifted. After days of no real contact, Mama stood behind Javy.

"Honey, I'm sorry. I can see you're upset. I'm not even sure what happened. I tried to appear before you, even got into the van. Something went wrong." She buried her face in her hands. Mama was grieved. Her hands dropped. "There's a strange energy around you. I can see something is wrong, but it isn't clearly defined."

She'd shocked me. Again. I stood without realizing it and took a step around Javy, opened my mouth, nearly forgetting myself.

Javy disconnected the call and turned in the chair to face me. I stood extremely close to him. He glanced over his shoulder and back at me. "Now I have more bad news."

Taking a step backward, I groaned and waved my hands for him to tell me.

"Alex's mom is at the department."

"Stirring up more trouble?"

He nodded. "She's formally alleging you and Betsy threatened Lucy."

That woman would not let anything go. A dog with a bone came to mind.

"She claims Betsy bragged about being able to hide a body and even laid hands on the woman."

"That woman is a menace!" Mama's face heated. "I never liked Regina. She loved to stir the pot."

I nodded in agreement. "She's out of her ever-loving mind! Betsy didn't kill Lucy. She despised her, sure, murdered her, no way. You know how riled Betsy gets. She's all talk, as Regina Myers knows. She's her niece, for heaven's sake. That woman is kicking a hornet's nest. Those Myers women don't take too kindly for turning on their own." I shook my head where thoughts fired at a rapid speed. "Plus, someone tried to kill us too! Betsy wouldn't try to kill herself."

"Someone tried to kill you. Remember Betsy joined you at the last minute. It wasn't planned for her to ride with you."

"And Paul."

"Speaking of Paul, you said you saw him today? We've been leaving messages for him to come in."

"A little while ago. Need to speak with him again too?"

"Just a couple of questions we need cleared up. And sometimes after a tragic incident it takes a couple of days to remember the specifics clearly."

True. In the moment of panic, a lot of little things could slip your mind. Paul could be privy to a lot of clues he wasn't aware of in his current mindset. And today, he seemed to have his wits about him. The way he went after Teddy proved that. I kept glancing in Mama's direction, hoping for enlightenment. She stood with her hands on her hips and her brows furrowed. Waves of frustration rolled off her.

"He went to work. He's either at his office or on a job. He said his cell was impounded with the van, so I'd recommend reaching out to his boss. He'll know how to reach him."

Mama's amber gaze was zoned in on Javy. I could read how conflicted she felt. Mama wore her emotions, always had, and now I could almost discern her every emotion. Even the way she stood conveyed the turmoil within.

"Something is definitely off here." Mama stepped closer to Javy, and I wondered if he could sense her in some way. When he didn't show any response, I figured not.

"The sheriff requests you to come down if you're up for it. Betsy is already there. He picked her up at the square."

My stomach did a flip-flop. "Picked her up as in . . ."

"In the literal sense of the word. No cuffs were involved. She's a mess, he says."

As inconspicuously as I could, I searched Mama's face for answers. "What can you tell me?"

"I've been forthright with you." Javy appeared confused.

My gaze shifted onto his face, but my words were directed at Mama. "Am I going to see you later?" I had to communicate with her.

"I'm going with you," Javier said while I picked up my bag.

"Yes. I think I fixed the issue. Be careful, my sweet girl, and always remember to trust your instincts." Mama began to fade. "I plan to get to the bottom of this."

CHAPTER 11

Peach Cove Sheriff's Department was a small precinct. It always reminded me of something out of an old seventies police show, with its drab wood-paneled walls and white-tiled flooring. Whenever Eddie needed more seating, he borrowed folding chairs from the Peach Cove Baptist Church.

The phone was ringing off the hook at the front desk. Tonya Wrigley, the office receptionist/secretary, had the phone to her ear. "Could you please hold." Tonya hit one of the buttons on the phone and adjusted her floral scarf. "Marygene, hon, I'm so sorry to hear about what happened to you." She glanced around. "I thought Officer Reyes would be with you."

"Oh, he is. He's outside handling a dispute between two senior men. They seem to be arguing over a parking space."

Javy had sworn a blue streak when we pulled into the lot and the two old coots were going at each other. Both their vehicles parked half in the same space.

Tonya rolled her eyes. "That's Mr. Smith and Mr. Johnson. They're neighbors and they're here every other week filing a complaint about something or another. Idiot stuff like Mr. Smith allowing his grass to grow too high or Mr. Johnson letting his dog poop in Mr. Smith's yard. You'd think they'd let up when real trouble strikes." She took another call and asked them to hold. "Did you get my flowers?"

"I did. Thanks so much. Things are pretty hectic around here, huh?" I edged closer to the desk.

Tonya shook her thin dishwater-brown hair. "A madhouse. I can't believe all the tips that are coming in. Folks around here have been watching way too much Netflix. How's Mr. Wrigley doing? He's real sensitive. Is he being all protective of you?"

I smiled. Tonya had given the cat her last name when she'd adopted him. Oddly, it fit. "He's my snuggle buddy. I don't know what I'd do without him."

The phone started ringing again. "I'm so glad. Listen, I've got to take this. The sheriff is waiting for you." She made a face I couldn't discern.

"Okay. Thanks." I made my way to the back of the room around the corner. Eddie met me by the lockers. His face was set to stone, showing no emotion, and that always spelled trouble. "There you are." He gave me a hug and searched my face. "You feeling okay? No double vision or nausea?"

"I'm okay." I smiled reassuringly.

He released me and nodded. His brows were drawn together and his face weary. There was a lot of that expression going around lately. "If you're sure. I'm going to need you to help Betsy. She's in my office and is a real mess. I've called her aunt Vi for her as she requested but got her voice mail."

"I'm confused here. I thought you wanted me to come down and make a statement."

He patted his sweaty brow and, now that I took him in fully, he didn't look well.

"We have more pressing matters at the moment. Regina kicked a hornet's nest, throwing around accusations within the Myers family, and Betsy publicly threatened her."

Oh, Betsy.

"Regardless of what Betsy says in anger, Regina knows Betsy would never hurt her family and accusations aren't proof. What about the biker guy? All signs point to him, in my opinion."

Eddie sighed. "Regina has other ideas."

"Ah, ideas that just so happen to not paint her daughter-in-law as a cheater and her son as a moron for being blind to her stepping out on him."

Eddie raised his wiry eyebrows. "She isn't a reasonable woman."

"I know. I'm sorry. Even if Regina Myers is completely delusional and points the finger at Betsy, there's no body. So?" I raised my hands.

"Cases have been tried without a body before." Eddie's phone chirped, and he took a second to check it. His mouth thinned to a grim line. "I'm not even sure this can be ruled as a homicide, per se. We never had a death pronouncement or saw any visible defensive wounds. It was a crowded area and far too many contaminants to make a clear deduction."

My mind thought back to what Teddy had said. The injection site on her thigh. Betsy certainly didn't inject her with anything. Alex would never believe otherwise. *Would he?* I was beginning to second-guess my second guesses.

Perhaps my father needed a reminder of said injection site. Maybe with all the commotion it'd slipped his mind. Not that he didn't have it recorded somewhere. "Eddie, you—"

His phone chirped for the second time. "Not now, Marygene. I know you're upset, but I've got to go and meet the detective and Alex." He softened his tone. "Thanks for your help with Betsy." He rubbed the sweat from his brow.

"No problem." As I turned to leave, I thought I heard him mumble, "We've got to find the poor girl's body."

The small twelve-by-fourteen-foot space contained a metal desk, a couple of chairs, one of which Betsy was slumped in, and an old-school filing cabinet off to the side.

She leaped to her feet when I entered, and threw her arms around my neck. "I can't go to prison. I'd never make it. I'll have to get one of those awful prison tattoos on my neck and join a gang. Who knows if they even sterilize the needles." She let out a half-hearted sob. "And you know orange isn't my color."

"You're not going to prison." I patted her back. "Don't be silly."

"Marygene, think! Once they find the body, I might." She released me and wiped the tears from her blotchy red cheeks. She clenched her fists by her sides. "This is all Aunt Regina's fault! She's like the devil whispering into Alex's ear. She's a lowlife good-for-nothin' rat! If we were back in the olden days, the family would turn her in-side out for this." She began to pace in the small confines of the office. "Just because her precious daughter-in-law was a floozie gives her no right to pin this on me!" It wasn't surprising Betsy had come to the same conclusion I had.

Regina seemed to be more interested in protecting her and her son's reputations than finding out who hurt Lucy.

I sat on the edge of Eddie's desk, near two old picture frames holding a picture of a much younger me and a fishing picture of Eddie with his arm around Sam's shoul-ders as he held up his catch, both men beaming. The new frame I'd added contained a picture of the three of us out on Sam's fishing boat last summer. Our golden hair shone in the sunlight, and our tanned faces were creased in sim-ilar smiles.

Betsy wiped the tears streaming down her face before she clenched her fist and teeth in a grimace. She rode one wild emotional roller coaster, and I hated to see her deal-ing with all this. What was even worse, I was forced to add to her load and, in this moment, I loathed Alex's mother.

"You're mad and scared, I get it. I can't believe your aunt would stoop so low to blame her niece for something she knows darn well you didn't do. It's monstrous." I fid-dled with the name plate on Eddie's desk. "I have to tell you something."

"Oh, sweet baby Moses, what now? They found the body! Why didn't you tell me first thing?"

I shook my head. "It's not that. Detective Thornton is on his way here."

Betsy's mouth dropped open and her eyes went as round as saucers.

"It gets worse." I chewed on my bottom lip. "Alex is

the one that asked him here." I explained how I came to this understanding. About Yvonne calling and Mama's reappearance.

Betsy plopped down hard in one of the chairs. She sat with her hands braced on the arms of the chair, as if waiting for the next bomb to drop and hoping and praying that, this time, she'd not receive any injuries when it went off.

"It's a lot, I know." I groped for more meaningful words, but they eluded me.

Betsy whined aloud and scrubbed her face with her hands. "Alex has lost his mind. He must've. Myerses don't turn on each other. It isn't our way." When she dropped her hands, her pale face showed her shell shock. Alex's perceived betrayal cut her to the quick.

I moved to the chair next to her and wrapped my arm around her shoulders and gave her a squeeze. "We'll figure this out. Alex will come to his senses. He lost his wife and child on his wedding day. As much as we grieve, we have to believe he'll see you also as a victim. Someone tried to kill us. And whether it was for a diversion or not, the result would have been the same for us."

"Dead as doornails." Betsy chewed on the nail of her index finger.

Aunt Vi barged into the office red faced, wearing a pair of coconut-print yoga pants and a yellow tank top. "My poor baby! Don't you worry your pretty little head about a thing. I got you a killer of a lawyer and we'll fight this!" Her yellow flip-flops flapped against her heels as she stomped across the small space and gathered Betsy in her arms and clutched her to her bosom.

I fought to free my arm.

"Honey, the world's gone insane." She rubbed Betsy's

head and rocked her. "Aunt Vi is here, and I'm not going to sit by and watch blood turn on blood. Regina is poison. Always has been. Always will be. She infected Alex, and now he's turned against you. She's never been one of us, not really." Aunt Vi turned toward me. "Before my brother died, he asked us to always keep an open door to her. To help her financially. And we did, for Alex's sake. And this is how she repays us. I could scratch that woman's eyes out. And over my dead body will she receive another dime from us."

I'd been privy to all of that, but I supposed she needed to explain the situation aloud to make herself feel better. I simply sat there, nodding in agreement and shaking my head in disbelief in tandem. There would be no question I was inexplicably on their side, though I hated the fact there were sides to begin with.

Betsy mumbled something to Aunt Vi. When we couldn't hear her, she pulled her head back. "I can't breathe in here."

Aunt Vi released her. "Sorry." She adjusted the girls that had spilled out over her tank top. "When God was handing them out, he gave us Myers women an ample portion."

I couldn't help the nervous giggle that escaped.

Betsy gasped and began fanning herself as she nodded in agreement.

Voices were overheard outside the door. Alex and Eddie's were easy to pick out. Alex sounded angry, and Eddie's tone edged on placating. It was the detective's baritone grumbles that set our nerves even more on edge.

The three of us shared a long, wary glance and I whispered, "Stay strong. The man is pure evil."

Betsy nodded and began chewing on her nails again. Aunt Vi jutted out her chin, raring for a fight.

The door began to open and then stopped. We could hear them conversing and it closed again. *What?* We were prepared. Were they toying with us?

The seconds ticked on. Aunt Vi surprised Betsy and me by huffing and stomping over to swing open the door. The three men halted their heated discussion and turned their attention to Aunt Vi. The detective's eyes widened at her appearance.

"Well"—Aunt Vi put both hands on her hips—"y'all comin' in or what?" She strutted with vigor back over to stand beside her niece.

The detective had lost most of his hair since we'd seen him last. Living a hard life took its toll. His beady eyes still held contempt, for our island politics, I surmised. The arrogance in his demeanor taunted me in ways that had my blood on the verge of boiling. After what appeared to be a brief word with Eddie, Alex begrudgingly left, which was for the best. Betsy wouldn't have done herself any favors if she launched an attack, verbal or otherwise, and she'd been glaring daggers at him before he retreated. Eddie stood to the side as if ready to run interference.

Aunt Vi placed herself protectively in front of Betsy. Her chin jutted out farther than I'd believed capable as she faced the detective. "Who are you and what business do you have on our island?"

"Viola, this is Detective Thornton. He's here in an official capacity at the request of your nephew. We're allowing him limited access, out of respect for Alex."

Aunt Vi's eyes flamed. "I see. And why would the boy request such a thing?"

"Because, Mrs. Myers—"

"Miss Myers." Aunt Vi cut Detective Thornton off.

He inclined his head as if that were no surprise.

Rude.

"Miss Myers, your nephew and his wife's parents are concerned about political interference and the sheriff's department's inexperience regarding this type of investigation. I've spoken to the attorney general, a personal friend of mine, and he agrees I should oversee the case."

This is a nightmare come to reality.

Betsy and I exchanged a withering look, and I made my expression harden. We had to stick together to withstand this disastrous storm.

I dragged my gaze from my best friend. "Lucy's parents are here?" I directed my question to Eddie, but the detective answered.

"They're on their way."

"Odd." I rose, readying myself to launch a defensive strike.

"Why?" Detective Thornton shifted his briefcase from one hand to the other.

"Well, they couldn't find the time to come to their daughter's wedding. And from the way she told it, they were estranged. Hardly ever spoke."

The detective gave nothing away when he stared down his pointy nose at me. "Most parents, estranged or not, care when something happens to their child. From my conversations with Mr. and Mrs. Carmichael, they were unaware of their daughter's current wedding plans."

Current? "Huh."

"Marygene, if you and Viola would kindly wait outside while I have a word with Betsy." Eddie stepped out of the doorway. "Betsy, you'll need to stay."

Betsy glared at the detective standing to Eddie's left.

"Don't worry about him. You and I will have a chat. He's only here to observe at this juncture. Nothing more."

"No." Aunt Vi took Betsy's hand. "She isn't saying anything until her lawyer is present. Not with this bozo trying to get involved. I've watched plenty of programs where folks are railroaded by some crooked cop." She threw her shoulders back and glared at the detective. "You're an outsider, and I don't know you from Adam. And it seems the world has gone mad in a biblical sense. We must be living in the last days scenario with brother turning against brother. For all we know, we're on the verge of an apocalypse. We're taking precautions."

Detective Thornton lowered his chin to make direct eye contact with Aunt Vi. "I assure you, Miss Myers, God nor the Bible isn't who you or your niece should fear. At the moment, it's the law."

"I smell sulfur. Like a demon rising from pit of Hades. Get behind me, Satan!" Aunt Vi rebuked and held up two fingers to resemble a cross at the detective. Betsy leapt to her feet and joined in and gave me an encouraging nod to follow suit.

Oh, here we go. They took my figurative evil comment literally. I shook my head and massaged my temples. When I glanced back up, Betsy'd dropped her hands and sat back down.

Detective Thornton glanced at Eddie with raised brows. It was obvious to the entire room what the loaded question in his eyes was, and under the circumstances, I couldn't say I blamed him. Not that I would utter the words. I'd be on Aunt Vi's side till the end.

"Viola, she needs to be questioned by me. Marygene, Deputy Reyes will take your statement now."

I understood Eddie's attempt to disarm the situation by reminding Aunt Vi of the fact that he still controlled the department.

"Lawyer, now." Aunt Vi wouldn't be moved. "Marygene's invoking her right to counsel too."

I would have said something like I didn't need representation at present, but then Aunt Vi wouldn't have listened to me anyway.

"Are you sure you want to open that can?" Detective Thornton appeared intrigued. He loved a good confrontation.

"We're not the ones who opened the Costco-sized can. Y'all did." Betsy seemed to gain a bit of her strength back. She stood shoulder to shoulder with her aunt.

"If you want to call an attorney, that's your right," Eddie said to Betsy. "Keep in mind, though, you aren't being charged with anything."

"I'm being slandered, though, Eddie. Folks are pointing the finger at me, and I won't stand by and be railroaded."

She and Aunt Vi nodded in unison. *Railroaded* seemed to be the word of the day.

"All right." Eddie looked at me expectantly.

Betsy put a vise grip on my arm. "Get you a killer lawyer too."

"It's going to be okay." I gave her a weak smile. "Will you be all right if I go now?"

"Of course she will," Aunt Vi answered for her. "You go on, little Marygene. We've got this."

CHAPTER 12

After I gave my statement to Javy, going over every single detail I could recall the night before the wedding and the day of, we sat together at his desk. He'd been asking questions about Alex's visit for the last five minutes. There wasn't much more I could tell him, and the questions became tedious in nature.

"Since his engagement to Lucy, was it common practice for Alex to come by your place?" His tone came out serious and completely professional, yet I could detect an undertone of familiarity.

He'd once interviewed me when he truly had suspicions regarding my guilt in a crime, and I'd despised the sight of him. Times had changed us both. Though, at present, I wasn't enjoying his company one bit. Not that any of this was his fault.

I took a sip from the Coke can and shook my head.

"No. In fact, I don't think we spoke about anything other than wedding arrangements until that night. It was better for us to keep some distance." I didn't add why.

Javy scribbled something on his pad. He took extensive notes on every case.

He raised his brows. "But the night before he was to marry the woman carrying his child, he made a point to come by your house and have a heart to heart. Did he say anything that gave you an inkling he wasn't happy?"

"Did he give you any inkling? You were his best man." It came out snippy, and I paused and glanced away. "For the third time, no. Oh, wait . . ."

"What did you remember?" he pressed, and I felt annoyed with myself for behaving in the manner I had.

"It probably doesn't mean anything . . . but he asked if I loved Paul . . ." My voice trailed off and Javy raised his brows. "We have history and they, he and Lucy, were experiencing the usual bickering sessions in regard to the wedding. It didn't mean anything."

"It's strange, you have to admit. First, he plants the seed that Lucy is terrified of Betsy and then asks about your relationship with Paul. Let's face it, he didn't seem all that happy."

It certainly wasn't my place to judge and, not liking the direction this conversation headed, I wouldn't comment.

"Then the woman suddenly dies, he's the first to notice she's nonresponsive, and the bombs were strategically placed under your van and the van of the man you're seeing. His mother starts shouting foul play. Now he goes and recruits a detective who holds a grudge against the sheriff, and you. Maybe Betsy is a decoy of sorts."

I shook my head. "No. No way."

His theory could be plausible if we were talking about someone other than Alex. I'd known him my entire life. Spent years attached at the hip. Loved him, despite not being able to make a relationship work, and probably always would. I leaned closer to Javy. Our arms were touching. "Look, I get what you're saying. Shining the light on Betsy first would throw people off the scent of him framing someone. But that's not Alex. He's upset and angry. And you should know that when he's angry, he lashes out at the world." I shifted in my seat. "And as much as I hate the way he's turning on the ones who love him the most, I can't point the finger at him. Deep down, he's honest and loyal."

"I'm glad to hear you still think well of me when my best man and partner doesn't."

I jumped at the sound of Alex's voice. He stood outside the cubicle opening.

Javy hadn't flinched, as if he'd been aware of Alex's presence. "Just running down every possibility. You know the drill."

Alex snorted. His wavy hair curled around his ears and was in desperate need of a good brushing. He reeked of alcohol, even from several feet away, his eyes were reminiscent of a racoon's, his face was full of stubble, and his clothes were rumpled. He didn't look good.

I rose to face him and kept my tone gentle. "I know you're hurting, and I wish I could fix it for you. I hate it. Just hate it. But you need to end this ridiculous vendetta against Betsy. It's killing her and Aunt Vi, and I can't imagine your meemaw is happy about it." I started to reach out and touch his arm and he took a step backward. I let my hand drop. "Alex, I'm serious. It's time to put an end to the madness. Life sucks sometimes. We deal. We haven't any other choice." I shook my head. "You know Betsy and I had nothing to do with this. And I'll help you find out who did, and, honey, we'll make them pay."

He scoffed but seemed to be listening.

"How can we work any of this out with that Atlanta detective here?" I sighed and lowered my tone. "For the life of me, I don't understand what you were thinking bringing Detective Thornton back into our business."

His gaze darkened, and I could clearly see I'd lost him. "What choice did I have? Lucy's been missing all this time, and we have no idea what happened to her or any real leads to go on. And the real pisser is, most folks around here don't give a rat's ass." A little spittle left his lips. This wasn't a side of Alex I'd seen before.

When he took a step forward, Javy put himself between Alex and me before I even registered he'd moved. "Watch yourself, Myers. You're receiving grace for your tone toward Marygene because of your pain. But I won't stand for a second offense. She's recovering from her injuries from her accident. She didn't cause this."

Alex's gaze flickered from Javier and then to me and back to Javier. He gave a bark of bitter laughter. "I see. Well, partner," he began with sarcasm heavy in his tone, "I'll give you the same advice you gave me. Watch yourself. She seems all innocent and sweet. She has a quality that draws men in and then brings out the worst in them. Just ask her ex-husband." He shook his head in a deliberate fashion and met my direct gaze.

Astonishment overtook me, and I registered the foul words he spoke and the venomous way he glared at me. Javy's body tensed and he opened his mouth to speak, but I brushed past them before the waterworks commenced, keeping my stinging eyes wide as I rushed by the front desk, hearing Tonya call after me. I shoved both metal doors open and rushed outside, scurried around the corner of the building, and placed my hands on my knees. *How can he be so cruel?* So vindictive. Alex knew my deepest, darkest secrets. Including my ex and all the pain I endured. Yet, he alluded to the abuse being my fault. *My fault!* Despite the falseness of the accusation, turbulent emotions threatened to overwhelm me and make me lose sight of the present. I could hear the echoes of the past within my head. My thoughts were in such a tumult, I scrambled to make sense of them. The dam broke. Tears poured as I took timed breaths and fought for control. The man I'd known my entire life, and loved for most of it, had wounded me in a way only he could. I understood he felt desperate. Still, this behavior was unforgivable.

"Marygene." And there *he* was again.

I moved down the wall in an attempt to put more space between us. "How could you?" It came out rough and ragged.

"God, I . . . I didn't mean that." He thrust both hands into his hair, fisted, and pulled. "I'm going nuts. I—"

"I'll never forgive you," I managed to get out over gasps. "Ever."

"Forget I said that. I'm not thinking straight and . . ." He glanced around wildly. "Marygene, nobody cares. Everyone is just going on with their lives like Lucy never existed." He slumped against the wall. "I don't know what's going on, but you didn't see her after the rehearsal. She was terrified. Betsy cornered her in the ladies' room and told her she would never be a Myers and if she walked down the aisle, she'd pay for it."

My thoughts became clearer as I continued to work to slow my breathing and turned his words over in my mind.

"That doesn't sound like Betsy, Alex. She's your cousin, for heaven's sake. She's all bark." My voice started to sound more like my own.

"Is she? Remember Darnell and the bonfire she made of his belongings."

"He cheated on her. And that's not murder." I wiped my face with the back of my hand, thankful I hadn't had a full-blown panic attack.

Alex took a couple of steps toward me. He seemed to be seeing me clearly now. His face was drawn in what I thought was panic or perhaps pain. "Baby, I—"

"Don't call me that," I bit out. "You can't call me a monster one second and try to sweet-talk me the next. You said nobody cares. I care." I pounded my chest with the palm of my hand. "I wanted to be there for you and tried to be, and how did you repay me? You chose the am-munition in your arsenal that would inflict the most dam-age and *used* it." I managed to get myself upright. "Someone tried to kill me too! If it weren't for Paul, Betsy and I would both be dead. Now your cousin is in there being grilled."

Alex's confused gaze matched my emotions. "What are you talking about? Who tried to kill you?"

"We don't know! That's the point. But they planted a bomb under the van, and it detonated minutes after Betsy and I were dragged from the wreckage. It was close. Too close."

He dropped his head but said nothing. *Nothing!*

"I don't know who you are anymore."

"You know me better than anyone."

"I'm not so sure. The Alex I know would be seeking the truth, no matter how painful it might turn out to be. He also wouldn't allow his mother to go on some tirade with false declarations regarding his cousin's guilt. And from what I'm hearing, Lucy had some disgruntled ex-boyfriend hanging around. Maybe you should be hunting him down, instead of blaming the people who actually love you."

He opened his mouth and closed it a few times before he finally mumbled, reiterating Javy's earlier point, "We have to go where the case takes us."

Strength began to fill me once more, and I closed the distance between us and tilted my head back to meet his gaze. "Right back atcha, buddy. But don't you forget, you started this."

I moved around him and started to storm off when he grabbed my arm. "No. Whoever harmed Lucy started this, and I'm damn well going to finish it."

I jerked my arm away. "Just remember, some burned bridges can't be rebuilt."

CHAPTER 13

After I assured Javy of my well-being, which took a little convincing, I went to check in with Aunt Vi. True to Eddie's word, Betsy wouldn't be charged. She'd been rattled but held it together. We all left exhausted, and I went home and baked. It's how I coped with stress. Something about shoving my hands in a good dough, baking off a fruit loaf with a delicate crumb, or producing a perfectly crunchy batch of chocolate cranberry biscotti simply brought me comfort. I opened the pocket doors and invited the fresh, salty air and the sound of crashing waves inside while I tested a new recipe for chocolate peanut butter muffins, made a loaf of Irish soda bread loaded with dried fruit, nuts, and orange zest, along with two dozen pecan sandies, and finished off with cranberry pistachio biscotti.

"The kitchen smells dreamy. I wish I could eat one of

everything." Mama inspected the baked goods on the large marble island.

I poured myself a cup of coffee and dunked a piece of biscotti before taking a bite. When I turned to face her, her painted red lips were pursed.

"There's still a darkness around you." She reached out and stroked my face. "I want to protect you from it." Her hand dropped and she smiled. "You're so strong, my beautiful girl. So very strong. You're growing in ways that astound me."

"Thanks." I attempted a smile. "I don't feel all that strong at the moment. This darkness, is its last name maybe Thornton or Myers?" I lost my appetite and placed my mug and biscotti on the counter.

"All I can say is trouble is coming and not only for you. Be careful. I know you've learned to be vigilant and are cautious with regards to who you trust. Your father is going to be tested through all of this. Be there for him."

Her words terrified me. "I will." I leaned against the counter and studied Mama, seeking clarity.

She always looked exactly the same. Every hair in place, her makeup applied to perfection, showing off her high cheekbones and elegant features, and her manicure shined. "Mama, can you see the future? Always see what's going to happen before it does, the good and the bad? Or are you only privy to what's going to happen around me?"

She sat on a bar stool. I knew she was attempting to be casual because she told me before how she no longer had the physical limitations of the living. And when she behaved as a living person, it put me at ease. Aware why she did it, the effect remained the same. Odd how that worked.

"Some days I'm allowed to just enjoy my girls' lives. Like when I get to see little Olivia." She smiled. "Being around for her is a blessing in itself."

"Olivia is wonderful."

That child had the entire family wrapped around her little finger from the second she graced us with her presence.

"Um, since she's able to see you, does that mean she's susceptible to island spirits? I mean, she isn't going to have one, is she?"

Mama shook her head. "I don't think so."

I let out the breath I'd been holding. "Thank God."

"Is having me around so terrible?" Mama folded her dainty hands together. She didn't seem bothered, simply curious.

"Other than the deceased wanting my help and being the only one who can see you and taking a risk of being locked away in a mental hospital if I'm ever caught conversing with you in public, not to mention the constant warnings, no. It's been a dream."

"Touché. To answer your question, I do sometimes see what's coming but not always. It would be torturous to foresee danger ahead of your family and not be able to intervene. Making amends isn't as easy to achieve with all the limitations on my abilities. I'm able to maneuver certain aspects of life to allow happiness to come to those in my life that I wronged." Mama had helped her friends when she could while stuck on the island. And putting her reality in perspective the way she just had, I could imagine how hard all of this must be for her.

I reached out and took her hand. Something I could only do when she willed it. It took effort, she'd once told me. "Thank you. For all you try and do for me."

Mama's watery gaze held mine for a long moment. "It is my sincere heart's desire to help you, honey. I'm so thankful we have this time together and yet so regretful it puts you in harm's way so often."

"I'm okay. And I'm glad we have this time too." I meant it.

An hour after Mama left, her words remained. *All I can say is trouble is coming and not only for you. Be careful.* Since the day I agreed to cater Alex's and Lucy's wedding, I'd had an odd feeling. Then I'd chalked it up to the uncomfortable situation. Now, I wondered. I picked up the phone and called the credit union where Lucy had worked with her maid of honor, Trixie. A lady took the message and a few minutes later, Trixie called me back. After a few minutes of chitchat, I got right to my questions after she gladly retold the story of catching the biker kissing Lucy.

"So you're saying Lucy seemed happy to get married? She wasn't torn between her ex and Alex?" I took a bite of a pecan sandie.

"She said it was over with him and he was having a hard time letting go. Well, she did complain about how old and dated Alex's little house was. She couldn't imagine herself living there. She said a woman like her deserved beach-front property. She called Alex a loser without an ounce of ambition a couple of times."

I nearly choked on the cookie and coughed. "You're kidding me?"

"Nope." Trixie laughed. "She could be a bitch. Excuse my French, but I liked her okay. We had a lot in common. You know, fashion and such." A lot of background noise sounded. "One more thing before I have to run."

I listened intently.

"You didn't hear this from me, but I overheard her on the phone talking to a David. I think he's another ex or maybe that's the biker's name. I don't know. But she was giggly and promised him treats if he did as he was told. Didn't sound so over if you ask me."

My mouth gaped open.

"She caught me listening and shut up. Still boggles my mind why she wanted to marry Alex anyway, no offense. I know you had it bad for him for years."

"No, none taken. I can't believe she behaved that way. Why would she go through with the wedding if she was so unhappy?"

"Well, Lucy could be super moody. I'm talking like crazy moody. She even took some meds to help level out her moods." More background noises. "Yeah, I'm coming! Sheesh, can't a gal take a coffee break? Two minutes. Sorry about that. You wouldn't believe the BS I have to put up with at this dead-end job."

"Sorry to keep you so long. One last question if I may?"

She popped her gum loudly. "Shoot."

"Did you happen to get a look at the prescription bottle?"

"It was in one of those little days-of-the-week pill containers. She said they were for her raging PMS."

"Okay. Thanks for talking to me." I was so glad I'd made this phone call.

"No prob. See ya."

Maybe we'd all had it wrong and Alex had it right to question his bride's demise. It hadn't made any sense to me before but now, recalling Paul's declaration that Lucy liked death spreads, perhaps she got cold feet. If she was as unhinged as Trixie made out, she could've used the elaborate wedding mystery to her advantage. No one would bat an eye at the bride in the parking lot, or maybe she had help. She must've.

My next call was to the Blue Bird Inn. Nate Palmer and his siblings were cousins from Mama's side of the family. They owned and operated the Blue Bird Inn on the island. When development began, they assumed they'd be out of business with all the beach-front property available to rent. To their surprise, folks liked renting inland just as much. It was a lovely little place with a nice pond and large gazebo. We'd catered small weddings there from time to time. They had a large party checking in, and I'd been forced to leave a message with the front desk. If he didn't call me back, I'd ride over there.

Mr. Wrigley curled up on the sofa next to me. I plunged my fingers into his soft, gray fur. "Could Lucy have been so devious to have had someone make pipe bombs and plant them? What do you think?"

Mr. Wrigley purred loudly.

"Hmm. Well, she surely hated me enough to want me dead."

My little friend cracked open an eye as if to say, "Say what?"

"I know. I never did anything to her." I shook my head as he settled. "It sounds nuts when I say it aloud. Plus, Teddy had been positive she hadn't a pulse when he checked her. And Lucy was pregnant with Alex's child."

Light bulb! "Ah, the pregnancy." I jumped and Mr. Wrigley let out a meow in protest. "Sorry. Jena Lynn had major mood swings when she was pregnant with Olivia. I'd bet money the pills Trixie saw were prenatal vitamins." Hmm. Another brick wall. I sighed and sat back on the sofa, petting my cat, and finished the pecan sandie while I racked my brain. So much for my promise to Teddy about not getting involved. Clearly, I hadn't a choice in the matter. We had to find Lucy, dead or alive.

The doorbell rang and, on my stoop, stood Paul. He presented me with a bouquet of flowers the second I opened the door. "Peace offering." He smiled sheepishly.

"Come in." I took the flowers and retrieved a vase from under the sink. "Hey, how often would you say you met with Lucy? To discuss plans for the mystery reception?"

He scratched his chin. "I'd say maybe half a dozen times. Like every bride, she wanted the mystery to be perfect."

Wow, did she get her wish.

"And you talked about death spreads?" I shivered as the word *death* fell from my lips.

He shifted and cocked his head to one side. "Yes."

"What about the guy on the Harley, the one who semi-crashed the wedding ceremony. You ever see him around? See him with Lucy, perhaps."

Lucy might've been careless around someone such as Paul. She wouldn't have paid him any attention if he weren't the coordinator for Sunshine.

He visibly stiffened. "No. I wouldn't have given it any notice if I had." He shook his head. "I don't know. Why are you asking me all this?"

I gaped at him. "Because she's missing and lives have been turned upside down, including mine. My best friend has been accused by her aunt of being involved, and Alex, well, he's struggling and is suspicious of everyone. Some mystery man has eluded everyone, and Lucy, well, that chick had a lot of secrets. And someone tried to kill us, Paul. Kill you. It's scary! And I need answers."

He glowered. "I know it's scary, and I want whoever made the attempt on our lives brought to justice too. I just don't have anything more to add. And isn't it the job of the Peach Cove Sheriff's Department? It certainly isn't yours."

Ugh. As I turned my back on him and filled the vase with water and began adding the plant food included in the bouquet, from behind, Paul wrapped his arms around my waist and, for a long few moments, we just stood there. I did my best to not tense. I liked Paul, I truly did. Yet, after Alex today, my emotions, like my thoughts, were all jumbled, and I was second-guessing everything.

"I'm sorry. I don't know why I reacted the way I did. None of this is your fault, and I had no business taking my bad mood out on you. When we first went out, I knew you were out of my league. You were so outgoing and beautiful."

I started to protest, but he cut me off as he released me. "Now, we both know it's true."

"That's sweet of you to say. I like you too." *I'm not sure I like you romantically any longer*, I didn't have the heart to say. And honestly, I wasn't sure I could trust my current emotions in regards to men.

He loosened his grip and helped me finish putting the trimmed flowers in the vase. "It isn't fair for me to ask this, but I'm going to anyway."

This conversation was beginning to make me a tad uncomfortable. "Paul, let's—"

"I have to get this out. Please."

I nodded, and he took my hands in his when I turned to face him. "Okay. I'm listening." *Please don't let him ask for any commitment. I don't want to hurt him.*

"What happened with the accident and all has made

me take stock of my life. Where I am now and where I want to be in the next ten years or so. At first, I thought about moving back home. I mean, with some crazy nut roaming the island and abducting, or, even worse, likely killing people."

"I can understand that. We've been through a scary ordeal. And with all the questioning and the body still missing, it makes you feel sort of unstable."

He nodded. "Then I thought about not being able to see you regularly, and I knew I couldn't leave. Crime is everywhere." He smiled. "And statistically, the crime rate in Peach Cove is massively lower than most cities. I want a family and a couple of kids. I think I can be happy here. We can be happy."

Moving too fast! "Paul." I glanced away and tried to pull my hands from his grasp.

He held on. "Don't panic. I'm not proposing or anything."

I swallowed hard and got up the courage to meet his gaze. "I'm sorry. This has to be the worst reaction ever."

His smile didn't waver. "No. I expected it. You need security and safety. And that comes with preparing for the future. I've blindsided you and, for the distress it causes you, I'm sorry. It isn't my intent. I have strong feelings for you, Marygene."

My mouth fell open, and I broke out in a cold sweat. Not an attractive response or romantic reaction. Surely he'd back off now.

Paul acted as if he didn't notice and kept plowing forward. "I know we've only known each other for a short time, but the feelings are real." He glanced at my hands. "I saw there was something between you and the deputy."

Which one?

"But the two of you have never dated."

Ah, Javy.

"That leads me to believe you don't believe he's right for you. I'm good with giving you your space now. The casual nature of our relationship gives you a sense of control. After all you've been through, I can afford you that willingly." He glanced back up and he searched my face. "Not now, but when all this is over, will you consider advancing our relationship to the next phase?"

"The next phase?" I mumbled dumbly.

"Yes, moving from casual to seriously considering marriage."

I hesitated before responding. I steadied my tone. "I can promise you I will think about it."

His smile broadened and he leaned in and kissed me on the cheek. "That's good enough for me." He released my hands and his shoulders relaxed. "No more heavy stuff tonight, I promise. How about we order pizza and, just for tonight, forget what's going on out there and watch some TV?"

Forgetting was an impossibility. I had so much on my mind and friends in trouble. Still, this sweet guy in front of me had saved my and Betsy's lives. He wanted to consider a life with me, and the next few weeks were probably going to be rough on him. And still, he was offering an evening of normalcy, or attempting to. I nodded.

"Great! I'll order the pizza while you find us something to binge watch on Netflix."

CHAPTER 14

A loud thud caused me to wake with a start, sitting upright in the bed, disturbing Mr. Wrigley. The cat
yawned and gave a meow. "Did you hear something?" I
ran my fingers through his fur.

He peered around the room, though hadn't reacted
with alarm. Mr. Wrigley wasn't as effective as a watch
dog, but he'd alerted me to danger on other occasions.
Now he seemed nonplussed and my heart raced.

In the darkness of my room, I reached for my cell
phone, where I kept it on the charger on the bedside table.
It was three thirty in the morning. I threw the covers back
and listened, placing my feet on the cool tile floor. The
alarm wasn't blaring. Had I forgotten to engage the security system? Had the person who rigged my van come
back to finish the job? Was this more of the trouble Mama
saw coming? My heart pounded so loudly in my ears I

feared I wouldn't be able to discern sounds of an intruder if there was one. I moved through the bedroom on tiptoes, quiet as a mouse, and paused by the open bedroom door, trying to listen. Nothing. Not a peep.

My breath came in pants. I searched around the bedroom for something I could use as a weapon. I grabbed a giant conch shell off my dresser. I wasn't sure what good it would do, but it was something. Vacillating momentarily, I scrounged up the courage and moved into the living room, flipping the switch and bathing the room in light. I meticulously and shakily scanned everywhere. Everything was in its place and exactly the way I left it when I'd gone to bed. I checked the security system, and it was engaged. Every room was clear, and all was well in my little cottage. I let out a sigh of relief. It must've been a nightmare that woke me. I couldn't recall a dream, but it wasn't uncommon for me to wake startled, thinking I heard a crash or someone yelling, with the feeling of impending doom. PTSD could strip you of all logical thinking at times.

Placing the shell on the island, I poured myself a cold glass of water. Mr. Wrigley moseyed into the kitchen and had a drink. Seemed like the thing to do, I guess.

"We're all right. We should get back to bed." I wiped the sweat from my forehead. Sliding between the cool sheets, I pondered my life. I would be extra cautious moving forward. I'd make better decisions and consider my words before I spoke. I'd be watchful for anything strange or unusual and do my best to stay safe. With all these thoughts, I had no idea how I would be able to get back to sleep. I'd needed the rest too. I had an early morning ahead of me.

The next thing I knew, the alarm on my phone was

going off at six thirty. I groaned and stretched before climbing out of the bed and turning it off. I went straight for the shower and stayed in there five minutes longer than I should have. I dried my hair and put on my standard diner uniform of shorts and a peach polo, applied my makeup in record time, slung my purse across my body, and was about to rush out the front door when Mr. Wrigley's howling halted me. He was pacing in front of the glass doors. Like me, he loved to sunbathe during the day and, to his obvious dismay, the blackout curtains remained drawn.

I glanced back at Mr. Wrigley pawing at the hem. I left the front door cracked open. "Sorry, I nearly forgot."

He kept meowing.

"I said I was sorry." I gave the cord a yank and light began to spill onto the tile. I froze mid-pull. Flutters took up residence in my midsection. *Oh . . . no no no no!*

Sequins on a once-white garment escaped a large black bag that lay in front of my back door. My head spun when I slid down the glass onto the floor as I stared at the half-open body bag. A glimpse inside caused me to shriek, and I scrambled backward. The horribly decomposed body was one I wouldn't forget.

Mr. Wrigley leaped on my lap.

"It's okay, fella. We're going to b-be okay." I stroked the cat's fur before my brain caught up and I put the cat on the floor and dug into my purse for my cell phone. I stared at the sleek device in my hand and panted. This was going to look so bad. Still, I had to get help. I called the first person I thought of, which happened to be the closest person. When he answered, I choked out without preamble, "Lucy's body is on my deck. It's bad, so terribly bad . . . Javy, I . . . I don't know what to do."

"I'm coming." His gravelly voice, thick with sleep, became alert, "Don't touch anything."

Minutes later, Javier came racing through the front door shirtless and in low-slung pajama pants, barefoot with his gun in his hand. Through my watering vision, I saw him carefully taking everything in. He walked past me on the floor and moved to the glass pocket doors.

"I . . . I was on my way out the door and Mr. Wrigley likes to sunbathe," I rambled. "If I hadn't come back to open the curtain, I wouldn't have seen it." I wiped my nose with the back of my hand.

"Did you see anyone around?" Javier opened the doors and a gust of wind brought the scent of decay and death. I gagged and scooted farther away as he squatted near the body.

"No. Oh, wait . . ." I thought back to last night. "At three this morning. I thought I heard something. I went through the house and everything seemed fine. But I didn't think to check outside."

He got up and looked around. He took a pen off the side table and used it to open the bag more. "Okay. What about your security lights? Were they on last night?"

"I . . . I don't know. I didn't check. I should have. I just didn't think to. Nightmares wake me up like that a lot. And with the blackout curtains, I wouldn't have noticed." I wrapped my arms around my knees and hugged them to my chest. "It's her, isn't it?"

"Hard to tell. I mean, she's in a wedding dress. The decomposition seems to be farther along than I'd expect, but I'm not an expert in forensics." He closed the doors and sat on the floor next to me. "The only reason someone would dump a body at your doorstep is to make an impact. Either to frighten you or—"

"Frame me."

We made direct eye contact. He'd tried to warn me. Like Mama mentioned earlier, this felt off. The whole ordeal. If the deceased had wanted my help as they had in the past, our paths would have intersected.

"They're doing a poor job of it, if they're trying to frame me."

Mama had said trouble would be coming for me, and boy, had that been an understatement.

"True, there are many other places to stash a body and plant evidence pointing to you that would be more believable. Perhaps they laid clues out, or what they believed to be clues, and we missed them." He rubbed the back of his neck. "They obviously wanted the body found and now. He's desperate and making mistakes."

My head whipped toward him. "Mistakes or not, this is damning evidence."

"They probably called the tip line to give a heads-up on where the body would be. That's how this type works. If the detective and the sheriff found it before you, a lot of theories could be presented on how you were about to get rid of the evidence and were caught before you succeeded." His gaze was intense, and I could see he was rapidly thinking through different scenarios.

Being the daughter of a sheriff and an ex-girlfriend of a deputy, I'd seen that look many times. Somehow, though, Javy's seemed different.

He'd seen more; his life experiences were quite vast. His theories would go many directions that Alex and Eddie probably wouldn't consider. "I don't know what's going on here, but something is rotten. I've been a cop a long time, and I can smell the deceit. That might not even be Lucy Carmichael out there."

"You think she . . . she's alive?" I wiped the remaining wetness from my cheeks, surprised by my strength and ability to have rational thoughts. "She'd have to be beyond ignorant of police procedure to try something like that and, honestly, Lucy struck me as an intelligent person when she wasn't playing the bimbo. Besides, what would her motive be?"

"I don't know. And she'd need an accomplice. Maybe Alex . . . But we're speculating. DNA will tell the story." He scratched his head.

"Oh God! You can't be serious? You think he hates me that much?"

He stood and held out his hand for my cell phone. "I don't want to believe it of him either. It has to be this way. Anyone and everyone is a suspect. I have to call this in."

I handed him my phone. "Even me, huh?"

He held my stare. "Except you. By my calculations, I'll be able to explain the time lapse of your call to me and when I called this in. Any more time passing and it'll seem suspicious that I waited, especially with the Atlanta detective overseeing everything." He hit a few buttons on my cell. "The sheriff won't be able to keep him out of this crime scene. You need to prepare yourself."

His words struck fear deep within. I fought to keep my knees from knocking together. I took a deep breath and got to my feet while I listened to Javy explain what he'd discovered at my house. He went dead silent and his face hardened and he disconnected the call.

"We have an even bigger problem." He stormed past me and went into my bedroom and then into my en suite. He searched underneath the sink and I felt a tad embarrassed at the disarray he found. He froze.

"What?"

He snatched my hand towel off the rack and picked up a tiny bottle and showed it to me.

"What is that?" I put my hand on his back and tried to get a look at the label on what he was holding.

"Fentanyl." He rose to his feet.

"What is fentanyl?"

"It's an opioid about a hundred times stronger than morphine. It's usually for hospice patients in patch form. I've had experience with it being adapted into a street drug. We must turn this over. The tip about the body and this drug were reported on the tip line. It's recorded and time stamped. Followed by anonymous calls to the sheriff and Detective Thornton."

My entire body tingled as I stared at the tiny half-used bottle. "What am I going to do?"

CHAPTER 15

My cottage swarmed with a forensic team, Teddy the coroner, the entire Peach Cove Sheriff's Department minus Alex, and the horrible detective. I sat at the bar and waited to be spoken to again. I'd already given my statement to the detective and now he was speaking with Javier, who'd run home and changed into his uniform. Teddy rolled the body out on a gurney through the front door of the cottage, a must since the sand would make it a struggle to wheel it up the side of the dunes. Strangely, and for some odd reason, I kept focusing on how in the world I was going to get the odor out of my house.

I must've said it aloud because Mama said from the stool beside me, "You'll open the windows and doors and steam your floors."

Slowly, I spun the chair around, facing the kitchen,

and put my face in my hands, my elbows on the bar, and kept my tone barely above a whisper. "I know you warned me, and I appreciated it. It would have been nice, though, if you could have given me some clue about the freaking dead body. My life is destroyed. I honestly don't know how I'm supposed to come back from this one. They have a body and evidence. Motive won't be hard to establish. She was marrying my ex. Any decent lawyer could run with that. Alex will hate me forever."

She rubbed my back. "Your life isn't ruined. I am going to help. I am helping."

Eddie put his hand on my shoulder. And just like that, my mama and daddy were both consoling me. I tried not to focus on how weird it was that Mama was dead and no one could see her but me.

"Pumpkin," Eddie began softly, "we're going to need to take this to the office and get your statement down officially. I've called Mr. O'Malley, the attorney in Savannah that I know, and he's agreed to represent you. Now, it's up to you if you want to give a statement today without his presence. I'll be there and will interject if I feel it's taking a bad turn."

My heart fluttered within my chest. "Am I going to be charged?" I couldn't stop the wobble in my voice as I glanced at my father.

He stroked my cheek with the back of his fingers and leaned in closer. His gaze held mine and his tone edged on fierce when he said, "Over my dead body." His declaration was swift and, from what I could tell, undetected by the others in the room. Eddie meant it, and understanding how hard he'd fight gave me the courage to calm myself and slide off the stool.

My tone sounded stronger when I spoke next, but his

face remained pale. "What about my house? You're not going to seal it off as a crime scene, are you? I can't be homeless again." The body was found outside my cottage. Surely that meant I'd be okay to stay here.

"No, I don't have any plans to do that." His phone rang and he pulled it from his pocket and checked it. "I've got to take this. Trust me." He squeezed my hand and I nodded before he stepped aside to answer the call. "Sheriff Carter here."

The energy in the space changed and Mama faded. Her face revealed she hadn't wanted to leave. A lot of times she disappeared before she felt ready to. She didn't always have a choice in the matter. I lifted my hand in goodbye and then scratched my face to hide the motion. My sister's face appeared on the screen as my cell vibrated on the kitchen island, where Javy had placed it after his call to Eddie earlier.

I hit the answer icon. "Hello."

"Hey, your text was beyond terse. What's going on?"

"Did you get Hannah to come in and cover my shift?" I slid off the stool and walked around the counter and stood by the refrigerator, keeping my back to everyone.

"Yes," she said tentatively.

"Good. I'm going to be a little longer than I initially expected. Someone dumped Lucy's remains, or what we believe to be Lucy, on my deck."

"Oh my God!"

"Say that again," Eddie said into his phone, breaking into my and Jena Lynn's inconspicuous conversation. His tone, more than his words, caught my attention. "I'll be right there." Eddie shoved his phone into his pocket. "Deputy Reyes."

"Listen, I've gotta go, but I'll speak to you as soon as I

can. And tell Betsy what's going on when you see her." I knew she'd be at work today. She called me before I went to bed, with a play-by-play of her interrogation and how they had nothing on her and were forced to let her go.

"She's here now. I'll tell her. And, Marygene, be careful." Jena Lynn sounded worried.

The detective stayed on the other side of the room while Javier and Eddie conversed. Eddie clapped his deputy on the shoulder before he started for the front door. He paused by the island, and I went to meet him. He pierced me with his blue-gray gaze and placed both hands on my shoulders. "Deputy Reyes will drive you. I have to go. I want you to make your statement. Stick to the facts. Don't elaborate, and then leave. Go to work or come back home, if you wish. Don't talk about this case with anyone. You understand?"

"Yes, sir." He would get no arguments from me.

He kissed me lightly on the forehead and left.

"Is there something I should know, Deputy?" Detective Thornton asked with his brow raised.

"The sheriff received a call from the president of Peach Cove Credit Union. There's been a robbery attempt. I'll drive Marygene in and take her formal statement."

"I can drive myself." I needed to exercise a little free will when I could. It gave me a sense of control.

"You're sure?"

I nodded.

"I'll be right behind you. And, Deputy, I'll be conducting the interview." Detective Thornton spoke to a member of the forensic team as I was gathering my things to leave. "Miss Brown." He paused beside me.

"Yes, Detective." I repositioned my bag across my body.

"I'll have the team lock up when they leave. Would you like to give them a key or just lock the bottom lock?"

I walked over to the table behind my sofa and opened the drawer. After extracting my spare set of keys, I handed it over to the detective without compunction. I had every intention of calling Harold's hardware store and having him send over a locksmith to change the locks ASAP.

He nodded and I forced my legs to carry me out the front door.

Ten minutes later I sat in the little interview room. Everything had to be official and above reproach. No one could accuse Eddie of special treatment. At least from my point of view. Javy, like Eddie, had cautioned me to tell the truth but not to elaborate. Keeping my answers to the point wouldn't be a problem. Obviously, I wouldn't mention my and Javy's conversation regarding a setup, or that we'd had to turn over the bottle of fentanyl. He was a protector by nature, and I wouldn't betray anyone who stuck their neck out for me in any capacity. Loyal friends weren't easy to come by. I'd given my statement for the second time and now we were in the questions portion of the interview. Sadly, this wasn't my first time being questioned. I knew the drill.

"Miss Brown, your account for your day leading up to the discovery of the body leaves a little to be desired. Could you expound upon what you told us?"

"I'll try. As I said, I've recently been released from the hospital and some of the time is foggy."

"Do your best." He didn't sound sympathetic in the slightest.

"Well, when I got home, there wasn't much food in the house. I met Betsy at the diner for a meal. We chatted with friends and neighbors." I fiddled with the paper cup on the table marred with scratches.

"This is when you and Mr. Fowler visited Gaskin Funeral Home and spoke with"—he glanced at his pad—"Theodore Gaskin, the island's funeral director and coroner?"

I nodded. "On the way to see him, I bumped into Paul. He decided to go along with me."

"What was the nature of your visit?"

The detective's meaty hands fiddled with the pen. His unexpressive eyes watched me with laser intensity. He gauged everything. I recalled the last statement he ever made to me before leaving the island. He'd been waiting for me outside the diner before he left, with an unpleasant gleam in his eyes. "Something is off about you. I can't quite put my finger on it." That day he'd watched me as if I was some caged exotic animal. I recalled the way my skin crawled.

I rested my back against the metal backrest of the folding chair and met his steely gaze. Why was this man so hell-bent on being involved with our island? Of all the cases he could be working right this second, career-making cases, why this one?

"I brought Teddy a baker's dozen of turtle brownies," I finally answered. "It's his favorite."

"Theodore gave us a statement, Miss Brown. He claims you didn't have a meeting scheduled. You and Mr. Fowler showed up with questions and accusations."

"Not accusations. I simply asked an old friend if, in a state of confusion and chaos, he could be certain the bride died. Nothing more than that." I lifted the paper cup to my lips and was proud when my hand didn't shake.

This man rattled me more than any other.

"Your father is dating Doctor Lindy Tatum."

I didn't react, kept my posture relaxed, and waited for the question while taking another slow sip.

"They've been together for about a year, and she is also your primary-care physician?"

Placing the cup back on the table, I left my hands where he could see them. Steady and calm. "That's right."

"She organizes the support group you are a part of for battered women."

"Doc Tatum has done a lot of good for the community, and she has taken over the role, but she didn't organize the group. Her associate did. When she retired, Doc Tatum stepped up. And it isn't just for battered women. It's for everyone in all walks of life that have suffered abuse or oppression. Not that I mind discussing our support group, but I fail to see what is has to do with the body on my deck."

He clicked the back of the pen slowly several times. "Was Lucy part of your group?"

I shook my head. "Should she have been?" I wondered what secrets Lucy kept that he was privy to. Had I misjudged her rudeness? Perhaps it'd been her survival tactic to keep people at arm's length. Had she had a tragic past that scarred her and made her mistrust everyone? Or was this man trying to trip me up by playing with my nurturing side?

"Miss Carmichael wasn't one of your favorite people, was she?"

"I don't know what you mean."

"I mean, she was marrying your high school sweetheart and having his baby." *Click. Click. Click.*

I worked hard not to focus on the pen. "Alex and I haven't been together for over a year. Lucy and I weren't besties, and we were never going to be. She had a different idea of how to treat folks."

"Meaning . . ." *Click.*

"Meaning, she was the self-centered type. Everything revolved around her. Like I said, we weren't going to be best friends. But I was kind to her. I catered her wedding, after all."

"A wedding she was murdered at." *Click. Click. Click.*

"Allegedly murdered at. And if she was murdered, I certainly didn't kill her." I slid my hands onto my lap and discreetly wiped them on my shorts.

"Can you explain the fentanyl in your cabinet?" He kept clicking that stupid pen.

My fear gave way to anger. I'd been more than cooperative, and I'd had enough.

"You've already asked me that twice, and I've answered each time, no, I can't." I finished off the last of the water. "Detective, you once told me you've worked cases in a lot of small towns."

He put his pen down on the pad and folded his hands on the table. "Yes. And most towns are the same. Some are better at keeping secrets than others. Instinct, whether wise or not, causes people to protect their own. Eventually, everyone cracks, though. I just have to find the right weakened spot and apply the appropriate amount of pressure. I'm good at my job, Miss Brown."

"Uh-huh." I folded my arms. "And all those years of experience taught you anyone is capable of anything. I can understand that. People never cease to amaze me either. Let's lay this case out, shall we." I unfolded my arms and opened my hand and held it out for his pen, "May I?"

An intrigued expression floated across his hard features. "By all means." He handed me the pen, flipped the page, then passed the pad over to me. Probably thinking I'd hang myself if given enough rope.

"A woman that most people disliked is allegedly murdered at her wedding." I jotted down a timeline like I would if I were putting this up on the whiteboard at home. It's something I did to work out a case when a deceased needed my help. "A wedding which she orchestrated so she could be the victim in her own murder-mystery-themed reception. Then she vanished into thin air. Later that day the caterer and her employee are nearly killed in an accident involving foul play. The person in charge of the murder mystery reception's van is also tampered with. Then—and here's where it gets really exciting—after the caterer is discharged from the hospital, the body suddenly appears at her house, along with an alleged murder weapon. Wow. If that isn't riveting entertainment, I don't know what is. The problem is, most murders like this one would be considered a crime of passion. Yes?"

He nodded.

"This is not such a case. This one has been meticulously planned." I passed the pad back over to him.

He studied it for a moment before glancing back at me. "Looks like you've had some practice."

"I grew up with a father in law enforcement." I scooted my chair back and stood. "I plan to hold you to your word that you're good at your job. Because you and I both are aware of how absurd this is." I pointed to the pad on the table, still open to the page I'd written on. "I didn't kill her, nor did I put her body on my back porch, if that is indeed her body. Someone is trying to frame me, and I expect you to find out who." I smoothed out my shirt that had wrinkled from sitting so long. "I'm through here. If you plan to charge me, go ahead and do it. If not, I'm leaving."

The detective stood and allowed me to register his size. He towered over me. I tilted my chin back and met him glare for glare. We stood there in silence for a few long heartbeats, and for a couple of those, I almost expected my hands to be put in cuffs. Instead, he reached around me and opened the door. "Before you go, can I ask one more question?"

I nodded and folded my arms in front of me.

"Do you have a lot of visitors? Men sleeping over, perhaps?"

I scratched the back of my right hand and glanced behind him at the old-fashioned two-way glass, where I knew Javy stood. His question made me uneasy. On one hand he could be attempting to defame my character, and on the other, perhaps the detective didn't think I was guilty or he wanted me to believe he didn't. I refocused on the detective. "I have visitors. My family and friends."

"Betsy Myers frequents your cottage?"

I locked my emotions down. "Betsy didn't do this. Alex is her cousin. She likes to spout off, but she loves deeply. She would never, ever hurt a family member and, as you know, this is ripping Alex apart. Besides, Betsy isn't proficient in bomb making." I half snorted. "And she certainly wouldn't be framing me."

"Do you know anyone who is proficient in bomb making?"

"No."

"Alex claims Lucy was frightened of the two of you, and, like you say, you grew up with a parent in law enforcement. This does appear to be an obvious setup, and you would know that."

I gave a bark of laughter; I couldn't help myself. My nerves were frazzled, and my resolve wavered. "You give me far too much credit. Not to mention there's no way I'd attempt to blow myself up. Over an ex-boyfriend, no less."

I took a step toward the open door.

"Your boyfriend, Paul Fowler, ever stay the night?"

I paused midstep and tried to read what he was thinking. The man gave nothing away.

"Paul and I have only been seeing each other a little while. He's never slept over. Though he was in my house the day . . ." I hadn't meant to allow my thoughts to trail off. This man had me suspecting the man I'd chosen because he was so different from all the others I'd dated. Paul rarely even raised his voice. Now I worried he might be involved.

"What do you know about Mr. Fowler?"

"I know he's kind, and if it wasn't for him, Betsy and I would probably be dead." Yes, that didn't make sense. Why would he save us if he'd intended to kill us? Unless he hadn't meant to kill us. I chewed on my bottom lip.

"Yes, Miss Brown, you see why we have to look at everyone. People always surprise us. We may need to speak to you again."

"I expect you will. Goodbye, Detective Thornton." I walked out of the room and into the little hallway and mumbled, "Everyone is a suspect."

CHAPTER 16

The diner was in the lull between the lunch and dinner rush when I arrived. There were a couple of people in the back booth, but other than them, the place was empty.

Betsy sat at the counter eating a California BLT and fries. "Marygene!" My friend rose from the counter and rushed to embrace me. She whispered, "Sweet Lord, I've been worried sick. Aunt Vi has been waiting to see if we need to get that attorney to represent you too."

I hugged her back. "Eddie has already called one for me. We can't talk here. Let's meet at my house after work. It's time to get out the whiteboard. Someone is trying to frame me."

Betsy released me and her eyes went as wide as saucers. "The nerve! First me and now you. They have no idea who they're messing with." It was good to see Betsy with all the color back in her cheeks. Our island bred survivors, for sure, and I had the urge to sing out the chorus of a Destiny's Child song.

"Is that you, Marygene?" Sam peeked through the service window. "You all right? Want something to eat?"

"I'm okay. I've got to get in the back and help Hannah out. She's probably overwhelmed with the added workload."

"Gotcha. Stop back here before you start work." Sam reminded me of Eddie. He wasn't a softy or anything, but he had become mighty protective of me lately. He was a good brother.

Betsy and I parted, and I paused next to the grill line, where my brother was cleaning up the work area in prep for the dinner rush, on my way to the bakery side of the kitchen. He turned to face me, securing his favorite American flag bandana in place on his head. "Why didn't you call me first? Or Dad?" His gray-blue glare told me of the anger brewing beneath the surface.

I blinked. "Hey, don't get all snippy with me. It all happened so fast. I called Javier because he lives the closest to me."

He leaned in closer and lowered his voice. "Marygene, do you need reminding how this family sticks together? If you'd called Dad or me, maybe we could have done something. Prevented this BS from hurting you."

Aww, my brother loves me.

I fought tears and put my hand on his shoulder. "Whoever dumped the body had already called in an anonymous tip. If we'd moved the evidence or tried to cover it up and missed anything, I'd be locked up right now. Not that I don't appreciate you'd get rid of a body for me."

Betsy hollered, "Ticket, Sam!"

Sam moved to the window and grabbed the ticket and

placed it on the clip above the grill line as he shook his head. He poured batter for three pancakes on the griddle and put the cast-iron steak press over three strips of extra-thick slices of applewood smoked bacon. He seemed to come to his senses. "It was really her then? Lucy, I mean?"

I nodded, then shrugged. "Looks like it. She's wearing the wedding dress. Although, it was hard for me to make a positive identification with the, um, condition of the body." I shivered, thinking back to the condition of the heavily decomposed remains.

He flipped the bubbling pancakes. "You think some-thing else is going on? Lucy's not really dead?" Sam edged a little closer to keep his voice down. "You know the credit union she worked for was just robbed."

My mouth dropped open. Eddie wouldn't want the news made public. "How'd you know that?"

"Trixie and her friend Cindy came in for lunch. They closed the bank early for the investigation. The way they tell it, a few of their larger customers called in with dis-turbing news that their accounts had suspicious activity on them. Massive amounts were requested for with-drawal and to be rerouted to another bank in the Cayman Islands."

"Wow. Whose accounts was it? Can they trace it? Did Trixie know?"

"Not that they told me. But the point to all this is maybe Lucy was the inside person on the job and who-ever was in on it with her took her out so they wouldn't have to share and could flee with millions. Or maybe she's still alive and planted an unrecognizable body in her place. One forensics can't ID." Sam looked both pleased and disturbed by his theory.

"I don't know. That would take a lot of planning, plus I'm not sure anybody would be able to pass it off as her. Besides, she'd have to be stupid to think they'd get away with that. And you'd think whoever she trusted would be someone close to her. She didn't have all that many friends other than Trixie." I drummed my fingers on the work top.

"That we know of. Peach Cove Credit Union hasn't ever been robbed. This outsider comes along and wreaks havoc on the lives of folks, lays in wait for the perfect patsy to use, i.e. Alex, and then puts her plan into action."

"I know you don't like Alex, and right now he isn't my favorite person on the planet. Still, I have a hard time seeing him being used like that. And you can't possibly believe he'd rob a bank."

Sam shrugged. "You never know. He's been moaning a lot about not making enough money to keep up with what Lucy envisioned as their lives together." Trixie's words came back to me. I guess Alex got an earful on how she deserved beach-front property. I wondered if she'd ever mentioned a David.

"He's been moaning to you?" Alex and Sam weren't exactly getting along these days.

"Yeah, he's been moaning to everyone. Ask around."

The Alex I knew felt content with his life. He was happy in his modest brick home his father left him. It was nearly paid for by now and he had money to burn on things he enjoyed. Like football and baseball games. No wonder he'd looked so downtrodden when he came by my place before the wedding.

I contemplated his words. "Even so, that's ludicrous. Alex—"

Sam cut me off. "Think about it objectively. I mean,

this is real *Ocean's Eleven* kind of stuff here. You know I've seen those movies a thousand times. If I really wanted to rob the bank, I could've done it."

"Uh-huh. And you think Alex is George Clooney good?"

"Not a chance. That's why he botched it." Sam snatched another ticket from the wheel and hung it.

I fought an eye roll. This theory verged on fairy-tale status. However, seeing my brother really get into this had lightened my mood considerably.

He threw a couple of burgers on the grill. "You know I've never been a fan of the guy. I mean, he certainly isn't the one I'd choose to join our family. But besides that, he hasn't been himself lately. And he would have knowledge of how a robbery would be investigated. Time frames and all that. Plus, he came in here a little while ago. He was asking customers a lot of questions and stirring junk up. He and Betsy almost got into it. Jena Lynn got upset, and I *politely* asked him to leave." Sam's emphasis on the word *politely* gave me a picture of what went down.

"I'm not saying I buy any of this. It's as far-fetched as a theory gets, but I'll play along. What kinds of questions?"

He plated up the pancakes and bacon and put the plate under the ticket in the service window. "He asked the staff who worked the wedding about their whereabouts, and what they witnessed when Lucy went into the tent to set up for the murder mystery. He had the nerve to even question me. I laughed in his face and told him he could take his questions and shove them where the sun don't shine."

"What you're saying is you think Alex, the guy we've known our entire lives and I dated, suddenly decides he's going to enact a giant screw-you to the island by robbing it, killing his pregnant new bride in front of a massive crowd, and then pin the murder on his ex-girlfriend and escape with millions?"

"If she's dead."

I pursed my lips.

"Okay. When you say it like that, it doesn't sound so plausible." Sam's brows furrowed. "I have a bad feeling things are going to get ugly."

Things are already ugly. I chewed on my bottom lip as three more tickets were hung and Hannah called me from the back. She sounded frazzled. We had a big pastry order to deliver in the morning. Sam and I shared a loaded glance, both of us feeling the weight of what was to come. We understood island politics and both knew this would be an issue for our business if it wasn't resolved soon. I couldn't wait to be fist-deep in dough, where I could get some stress relief and do my best thinking.

Hannah was covered in powdered sugar and standing over the commercial mixer with a bewildered look as she precariously balanced a large bag that had torn awkwardly down the side. I rushed to help her heft the large bag back to the stainless-steel work top. White powder went everywhere, but we managed to salvage most of the bag.

"Tyler!" I called our dishwasher and kitchen cleaner for help.

The skinny boy came running. "Yeah?" He took one look around the kitchen and nodded. "I'm on it."

"Thank you," Hannah and I said in unison.

"Where's Jena Lynn?" I poured the remaining sugar into a huge mixing bowl.

"Her sitter called and said Olivia is running a temperature and pulling on her ears. Poor baby is inconsolable."

Jena Lynn usually called or texted when she had to

leave. I washed my hands and checked my cell in my pocket. Sure enough, I had a text containing a huge apology and strict instructions to call her later with an update on what happened.

I texted her back with all-is-fine tidings and that I had things under control at the diner. The last thing she needed was to be worried about me when little Olivia was unwell.

Time to get to work. I still had a business to run. "What have you finished?"

Hannah showed me what on the order had been completed, and I rushed to begin the four baker's dozens of our good-morning muffins. They were a big hit with the health-crazed folks on the island. The muffins were packed with grated carrots, chopped apples, raisins soaked in vanilla, coconut, and pecans. The mixer was whisking the eggs, vanilla, and oil while I sifted the flour, Sugar In The Raw, baking soda, and salt into a large bowl. I worked on autopilot as I wondered what was going on at the bank. The robbery wasn't what I'd typically think of. A masked man hadn't burst through the doors with a sawed-off shotgun and demanded the tellers to empty their registers and open the safe.

Sam had been right about one thing: The robbery did sound like a theatrical-style crime, which meant someone had to be a genius. Still, that theory had crater-sized holes, like Lucy being killed. Honestly, if someone wanted to rob the bank, timing it after Lucy suspiciously died would be an ideal time. When law enforcement was all distracted. I needed to take a look at her former cottage rental.

* * *

My favorite Realtor, Tara Reynolds, looked stunning standing in front of the small cottage on the west side of the island where the tourists rented, wearing a flowing tan satin bell-bottom pantsuit and the highest heels I'd ever seen. Her attire made me feel a little self-conscious in my Peach Diner uniform of khaki shorts and a peach polo.

I smiled as I reached the porch. "Thanks so much for doing this for me."

"You're lucky you caught me. I was showing a place at the end of the beach." She unlocked the door and it swung open. "Luckily, the tragedy with Lucy and Alex hasn't hurt tourism or development. Weird how she just vanished."

I nodded as she moved aside, thankful she hadn't heard about the discovery of the body yet. "Do you handle rentals as well?"

"I do. Long-term rentals, anyway. Lucy was a good tenant. Paid on time and never a complaint about her from the neighbors."

The house, though a basic sea of beige with tropical accents and dated floral furniture, was spick and span. "She ever have anyone else on the lease with her?"

She gave her head a shake. "Why are you looking again? I would've thought you were all settled in Beach Daze. You seemed so happy when we found it, and I heard from Vi the renovations went beautifully."

"I am perfectly happy where I am. Betsy wanted me to have a look, since the sellers decided to put it on the market."

"Betsy, huh." Tara sounded skeptical. "I'm not sure she could afford the asking price."

As I moved through the space, I wondered if Lucy and the biker had rendezvoused here. The bedroom was empty and clean. Nothing in the dresser or bedside table. Same with the bathroom. *Well, this is pointless.* There wasn't a single piece of evidence that Lucy ever lived here. After I thanked Tara again, seeing how eager she was to get back to work, I didn't ask any more questions.

"Tell Betsy if she's serious about buying a new place, I have a couple of fixer-uppers coming on the market soon. We'll probably have to get creative with financing, but I'll do what I can." Tara opened the door to her sleek black Mercedes. Tourism had been good for her career, and I was glad.

"I'll do it. You know Betsy. One minute she's eager to leap and the next she's content to stay put." I waved and gave her a bright smile.

CHAPTER 17

Walking into my cottage took guts after what transpired today. I'd inserted my key three times, and each time I had a change of heart and went to wait in the car for Betsy to arrive. Someone had dumped the body and, unlike Sam, Alex wasn't the one I suspected. I let out a deep sigh when Mama appeared in the passenger seat. She reached over and took my hand. We both sat there for a long time in the air-conditioning, staring at my home, and I was thankful she'd shown up. How different would life have turned out if she and I had been like this when she lived? She might have crossed over when she passed, and perhaps I would never have left the island and never married Peter. Maybe if she'd told me about my father earlier, we could have all been a family.

"Lucy Carmichael has crossed over." Her tone sounded monotone, and I could tell she felt like she'd let me down.

Well, that was that then. Lucy died. "That's so crazy you couldn't tell." My stomach began to swim as I wondered why anyone would take her body.

"Yes."

"And the drugs in my cabinet?" I held my breath.

"Killed her."

I released Mama's hand when I thought I might throw up, turned the air to full blast, and leaned toward the vent while I tried to steady my heart rate and calm my churning midsection.

"There won't be any prints on the bottle, though, I saw to that. I have no idea how your prints even came to be there in the first place. I did leave the partial print from an unidentified person on it, though."

I glanced over at her. Her brown curly hair gently danced around her neckline, and I wondered what was truly real and what was a fabrication of my mind. I suddenly understood that like when she sat next to me or made a point to breathe, it put me at ease and allowed her to do her job and help me. Nor did it matter how or why she sat here. My life could have unraveled the same as it did now, but under different circumstances. Alex and I still might not have worked out, and he still might have married Lucy. Someone would still have murdered her, and I could have still been the one they set up to take the fall. All those what-ifs would tie you up in knots and keep you from growth. No more.

"Mama, what do I do?"

She reached out and took my hand again. "Things are going to get rough, but you keep moving. And I'll be here, no matter what. I'll never stop trying to help, and I'll never abandon you."

Gratitude overwhelmed me and the tears began to fall.

I squeezed her hand. "Thank you. Your growth and love haven't gone unnoticed."

She smiled one of her rare smiles that lit up her entire face. And even on this dark day, it brought light into my heart. "Darlin', I wouldn't be any other place. Javier you can trust. Let him help when you can, but, other than him, keep whatever you do to yourself."

"Eddie?"

"Your father will always be by your side and do everything in his power to solve this case. That Thornton is a puzzler. I can't get a good read on him. So be careful where he is concerned."

"No worries there." I swallowed hard and tried to calm myself. "Am I going to be arrested?"

Mama's head shook. "I honestly don't know."

Betsy's car came rumbling down the street. There was no mistaking her roaring candy-apple-red Camaro.

Mama squeezed my hand one last time. "I know you and Betsy share everything."

"She's my sister from another mister." I smiled as Betsy pulled in behind me.

"Give her a message for me. Tell her to always guard her heart." She began to fade before I could inquire further. Not that the advice was unsound. Obviously it was great advice for everyone; I still needed to know what impending situation made her bring this up.

Betsy jerked open my door seconds later as I sat alone in the car. "You ain't ever going to believe what happened!"

"What now?" I turned the car off and stepped out. The humidity slapped me in the face, and I instantly broke out in a sweat.

"The Carmichaels, Lucy's folks from South Carolina."

We walked up to the front door and I inserted the key for the fourth time today as I nodded for her to continue. "They're loaded. Like *vacation homes in France* loaded."

"Okay." I left the key in the door but didn't open it.

"Yeah, well, Aunt Regina offered them to stay with her, being hospitable and all. Initially they agreed, until Alex drove them up to her house. Then Mrs. Carmichael got all fidgety and made up tons of excuses why they just couldn't impose. This is all coming from Meemaw, 'cause I ain't speaking with Aunt Traitor at present, and neither is Aunt Vi."

"Right." I shifted my purse to my right shoulder.

"Anyway, they called a cab from Aunt Traitor's place and rented the old Ledbetter house, which, as you know, Rainey Lane is asking a pretty penny for."

Rainey Lane Ledbetter, our archenemy all through school, inherited the place from her father-in-law several years ago. She never came back home to visit anymore. She did, however, enjoy profits from all the rental properties she now held deeds to.

"I know it's the most expensive rental on the island. It's private, with a gorgeous view of the ocean. Plus, she put a lot of money into fixing up the place. If she ever decided to sell, it'd move quick."

"True." Betsy stared at me for a long moment. "Why are we still standing out here on the porch?"

"Because I'm scared to go inside."

Betsy humphed and dug through her shoulder bag, pulling out an old revolver. I raised my eyebrows at her as she pointed it at the front door and squinted one eye to aim.

"Don't shoot my door, you nut!"

"I'm not going to, and I refuse for us to live our lives

in fear. If some bozo wants to mess with us, they're going to get it right between the eyes. I'm a deadeye." Betsy couldn't hit the side of a barn. Still, it was better to do this together with a weapon than to go inside alone and un-armed.

Slowly, I unlocked the door, twisted the knob, and be-fore I could push it open, Betsy's sneakered foot flew past me and kicked. The knob slipped from my fingers as the door swung open, hit the wall, and slammed back shut in our faces and a shot went off. Betsy fell back into me, and we both went tumbling off the porch and into the mulched flower beds.

Something hard hit the side of my head. "Oh my God!" I rubbed the achy spot and crawled to my knees, flinching as the mulch imbedded into my skin. My right elbow stung, and blood rolled down my arm. Then some-thing shiny flickering in the sunlight caught my attention. I reached under the mature lilac bush planted by the pre-vious owners and felt the warm metal against my finger-tips. It took me a minute to figure out what it was as I held it up. It was a money clip engraved with *A.M.* on the front and *With all my love, Lucy* on the back. I froze.

"Betsy . . ."

"Yeah, you okay?" Betsy sat up and picked a couple thorns from her legs. She'd fallen right into my Knock Out roses. Petals were everywhere. Thankfully, I'd fallen just left of them and into the shrubs.

"Yeah." I inspected my skinned elbow full of nasty dirt. "Just scraped up a bit. Why would Alex's money clip be in my front flower bed?"

"Say what? Help me up, will ya."

"You really shouldn't be allowed to carry a gun." I dusted myself off and stood, holding a hand out to her.

She grabbed it. "Technically, I'm not actually allowed to carry concealed, but nobody checks those permits anyway."

My mouth gaped open. "Detective Thornton would. Not to sound cliché, but he'd lock you up so fast it'd make your head spin. Quite literally, Bets."

The alarm started going off. I guess Eddie must have come back and set it after they finished up here.

She grabbed my hand and scrambled to her feet, taking the clip from me for inspection. "I didn't think of that. Still, I'd rather be alive and deal with a charge than end up like Lucy." Betsy whistled. "It's his, all right. Lucy gave it to him at the rehearsal dinner. She made out like it was something important." She dusted off her backside, handed me the clip back, and looked around. "You see my gun?"

I glanced around the flower beds. "Yeah. It's over there in the shrubbery. It conked me on the head when you threw it." I sent a silent prayer above, thanking the good Lord for sparing my life. If some crazed maniac didn't kill me, Betsy might. My attention went back to the clip.

"I didn't throw it. You spooked me when you shrieked and knocked it from my hand. You're lucky another shot didn't go off. It's not the most reliable gun I have."

She stooped down and picked up the gun as I gaped at her. "Oh man! It's got a scratch on it."

My cell phone rang. I didn't have to guess who it was. "This is Marygene Brown." Not all that worried about a predator anymore, I marched up the steps and opened the door and hit the code on the keypad. "I apologize, I forgot to disarm the system when I came inside."

Betsy waltzed past me as she licked her finger and began rubbing at the mark on her gun.

The service, now satisfied I didn't have an intruder, warned me that if another false alarm occurred, I'd incur a charge.

After we searched the house for anything out of the ordinary, Betsy sat at the bar eating a slice of fruity Irish soda bread and a glass of iced tea.

"How's Aunt Vi holding up?"

"She's settled down. Our attorney put both our minds at ease. Unless they come up with some real evidence, all they have is stupid hearsay."

I nodded and put the money clip on the island and took a biscotti from my cookie jar while I fired up my Keurig. "If Alex received this as a gift the night before he got married, that would mean he had to lose it snooping around my house after it all went down or when he dumped her body here. It scares me to think that way."

"Yeah, me too."

My cell rang again, and I was surprised to see it was Teddy. I hit the speaker icon and placed the phone next to me on the counter. "Hey, Teddy."

"Hey. You holding up okay?"

I opened the cabinet and retrieved my favorite *Make It Happen* mug Betsy gave me for Christmas last year. "I'm okay. How about yourself?"

Betsy waved her hand toward the cookie jar.

"I've been better. I wanted to tell you I didn't say anything bad about you to that detective. I did, however, tell him how hostile your boyfriend was behaving."

"Don't worry about it. You have to tell the truth, and Paul isn't exactly my boyfriend, we're just sort of . . ." I didn't know where to go with it next as I handed Betsy her biscotti and cup of coffee. "Seeing where it goes, I guess."

"Oh, I see. Well, it isn't any of my business anyway." He went silent on the other end, and I could tell he was wrestling with whether he wanted to discuss something with me. He always went silent when he had one of his pros-and-cons mental debates.

"Teddy, is there something you think I should know?"

Silence.

"Teddy, are you there?"

"Maybe he hung up," Betsy whispered.

"I'm here. I didn't know this call was being broadcasted. I probably should just—"

"No, wait. It's just Betsy. Here, I'm taking you off speakerphone. Okay, we good?" I scowled at Betsy as I put the phone to my ear.

She got up and sliced herself another piece of bread.

"Yeah, okay. Listen, I'm not sure why I felt the need to tell you this so badly, but ever since I discovered some anomalies in the autopsy, I couldn't shake the desire to call you."

Thank you, Mama! "I appreciate you looking out for me."

"It's odd, Marygene. You and I have grown closer as friends over the years, but I'd never jeopardize my career for even my closest friends. Now I'm overcome with emotion to unburden what I found to you. On one hand I can rationalize it out as obligation for what you did for me when everything happened with Dad. And on the other, maybe I just want to see justice served. This is new, for sure. I'm not positive this new development between us is a good thing for either of us. No, I didn't mean that. I'm here for you. You know that, right?"

I suddenly felt extremely bad for Teddy, and I decided to have a talk with Mama about the effects of her influence on others. "Of course I know you're here for me. Honestly, though, if you feel like this is the wrong move, we'll hang up the phone right now and pretend you never called. Or maybe you called to ask about the specials at the diner tonight and want me to have someone deliver dinner, since you're so busy."

He got quiet again, and I held my breath and waited. Betsy was mouthing *what* and lifting her hands. I held up my index finger.

"No, we're here now. I'm just going to dive in." He groaned loudly, and I thought he was about to hang up. "The body's decomp is farther than what is typical. It isn't unusual if the body was exposed to the elements, as this one certainly was. I've sent tissue samples off to be analyzed to determine if drugs were the cause of death. There isn't any other evidence of trauma, other than a couple of healed bone fractures that were old. I'm guessing from childhood. Her parents will be able to clear that up. Another interesting discovery is the victim claimed to be pregnant, three months along, according to Alex, and there is absolutely no way that could be true."

My mouth gaped open and hope bloomed. *Could Mama be wrong?* "Are we sure it's her, then? Surely she showed Alex some evidence. A sonogram picture, a pregnancy test, or something."

"It's her, all right. The dental records her parents sent over are a match."

I held my hand over the receiver. "Lucy lied about being pregnant."

Betsy's face turned red with irritation. "She trapped him!"

I held my finger to my lips. "Wow. Anything else? Evidence that will lead us to find out who killed her maybe?"

"Nothing conclusive. She wore sweatpants and a sweatshirt under her wedding dress, which I found unusual. She wasn't on her wedding day; I saw the injection mark on her bare thigh. Again, I'd been right."

"I wasn't questioning your abilities, Teddy. And that is weird about the sweat outfit. Why would someone dress and redress the body?"

"I don't have an answer for that."

Yeah, I didn't figure he would. "Hey, I heard fentanyl can be adapted into a street drug. Is it possible she dosed herself and just got the amount wrong?"

"It's hard to tell. I'll know more when I get the toxicology report back."

"How long will that take?"

"Some tests take days, others weeks to months. We should have something definitive on cause of death in a few days, though. Even if she was a long-term drug user, someone wanted the authorities to believe you were responsible. It'll help define the case, of course. And for the record, I don't believe for one second you had anything to do with this girl's murder. And I'll voice that opinion to the detective. I imagine he and I'll be working closely during this investigation, since Eddie has agreed to work the robbery case."

We settled into silence for a few beats, and I supposed he was pondering what all this meant, as I'd been.

"Thanks for being my friend."

"You were there for me during my time of need. I won't ever forget it. I'll always have your back." Teddy's voice wobbled.

Overcome with emotion, I teared up as we disconnected the call. Teddy was one of the good ones.

Betsy stuffed the remaining corner of bread into her mouth. "Well, what gives?"

I laid out everything Teddy told me and my concerns about Mama affecting him negatively.

"I wouldn't worry about Teddy. He's tough. Besides, it isn't like your mama is making him *bawk* like a chicken or somethin'. She's doin' some real good. We need all the help we can get. With my stupid Aunt Traitor fingering me for the murder and someone trying to frame you, we've got some serious problems. I mean, I can't quit stress eating. I keep thinking if we have to do hard time in the slammer, we'll never get good food again. We'll have to eat moldy bread and tasteless bologna for God knows how long." Betsy hopped up and opened the door to my fridge. "You don't have nothin' real in here to eat. Let's order something. We've got an entire murder case to crack, and I can't do no cracking on an empty stomach."

CHAPTER 18

After we ordered dinner, we stood in my office, where I had a huge whiteboard hung above the white-washed desk. I tossed the teal throw pillow that had fallen off the chair back on it and rolled the white office chair aside. I put Lucy's name in blue at the top of the board. Sam's theory was shot, now that we knew Lucy was un-equivocally dead. I put Alex's name under hers in red, with *money clip* in parentheses, and beside his, *the biker* with a question mark. We still didn't have a positive iden-tification on him. To the left of their names, I added the body being dumped at my house and evidence planted. In parentheses, *fentanyl*.

Under the evidence, I put the names of everyone who had been inside my home after the murder. If it was a murder. I put a question mark after Alex's name.

"Alex had to have been outside your house after."

Betsy put the money clip on the desk. "I hate to say it, but we ought to call him over here and have it out with him. It'll be better if we go at him together."

I shook my head. "I don't know, Bets. You should have seen him at the sheriff's office. He practically foamed at the mouth. I mean, I've never seen him like this. And once he finds out Lucy wasn't ever pregnant, and the evidence against me, he's liable to blow a fuse. And when that happens, I don't want to be anywhere near him." I tapped the marker against the desk. "I would like to know if Alex has been snooping at my house, and why."

She made a face and folded her arms, just as the doorbell rang. "He's my own blood and I don't go accusing folks without cause, but how could his clip get here if he hasn't been? Maybe he's lost it, or worse, is on drugs."

"All right, fine. He was probably outside. I just hate to even think he might be behind setting us up." I followed Betsy out of the room and into the living area.

"Me too," she said sadly. "I'll grab the pizza. You get the plates."

"Okay." My cell rang as I was putting the plates on the bar. I hit the speaker icon when I saw it was Javier. "Hey." I grabbed two wineglasses from the cabinet.

"Hey yourself. I need to come by and have a word with you later." He sounded rushed.

I had the wine fridge open and decided on a bottle of merlot. "Is this officially or unofficially?"

"Like I was never there and way unofficially."

"Now I'm nervous." I searched for my corkscrew. I needed this wine now.

Betsy came trudging back in with a large box of pizza and a small box of breadsticks. She had to have her breadsticks. "Where are the salads?"

"I didn't order no salads. This here's a last meal sort of thing. Ain't no one ordering salads for their last meal." She plopped down the boxes and lifted the lids.

"Pardon me?" Javy asked.

"Sorry. Betsy's here and we ordered pizza."

"Ah." He answered as if that explained everything perfectly. "I'll see you tonight. It'll be late."

"How late?"

"Late."

Betsy started fanning herself. "Phew, that hunk of burnin' Latin love is a sweet-talker. I think I'm going to faint. Jump on that! This could be like your last conjugal before the big house. If he was here for me, I would. Desperate times calls for desperate measures." She kept fanning herself and took a bite of super supreme pizza. "Now that's a hot scene."

I pointed to the phone just as Javy said, "Goodbye, ladies." I heard the smile on Javy's face, and it added much-needed levity to the day.

Betsy nearly choked. "I thought he'd hung up. He's gonna think I want to jump his bones."

"Don't you?" I laughed and so did she as we loaded our plates with pizza. "Let's get back to the case." I sat down and a took a deep sip of wine.

Sam's ringtone blared and his smiling face came up on the screen. I was a popular girl today. I hit the answer icon. "Hey, what's up?"

"Turn on the news!"

"What? Why?"

"Just do it!"

"I'm on it, Sam." Betsy was already searching for the remote I always seemed to lose. She began digging between the couch cushions.

"Good, you're not alone. And for the record, everything I ever said about Alex Myers will be validated in the next minute. Call me back."

"Yeah, okay."

Betsy and I exchanged a wide-eyed glance as she came up with the little black remote and clicked, turning the flat-screen on.

On the steps of city hall stood Alex, who'd cleaned up since I'd seen him last. He wore a blue blazer and khaki slacks. Next to him stood an older couple, who I assumed were the Carmichaels. The woman with silver hair, wearing dark sunglasses and a pleated cream dress, held tightly to her husband's arm. Detective Thornton stood opposite them, and Eddie, along with the man I recognized as his attorney friend Mr. O'Malley, stood off to the side. My jaw dropped open as Alex stood in front of the microphones and his voice traveled through the speakers. "No, that's not what I'm saying." Alex smoothed his hair after a gust of wind caught it and he shifted on his feet.

"Really?" The female reporter held her ground. "Because I have a statement from a personal friend of yours who insisted that is exactly what you've said and why you left the island to seek outside help."

"I don't know who your source is, miss, or what they thought they heard, but I refute it one hundred percent. This has nothing to do with mistrust of the Peach Cove Sheriff's Department or our sheriff. After speaking with my in-laws"—Alex turned back and motioned to Lucy's parents—"we made a collaborative decision to reach out to the Atlanta PD and ask for help. Having Detective Thornton lead on my wife's case is advantageous for everyone involved."

A balding reporter I recognized as one of Betsy's high

school exes raised his hand. "Is it true your cousin Betsy Myers is a suspect in your wife's murder case? Your mother went on record last night that the victim and Betsy had an altercation and quoted threats your cousin made toward Lucy only days before her death."

Betsy sat on the floor in front of the TV. "I can't believe Larry would even ask such an awful thing."

I could. This was big news for Peach Cove and probably one of Larry's only chances to make any serious headlines.

Detective Thornton touched Alex's arm and Alex took the hint and stepped aside, not that he looked happy about it. "Everyone is being questioned at this point and, as of this moment, no arrests have been made."

"How can you drag your feet on a murder case?" Larry pressed.

"No one is dragging anything. The cause of death is still undetermined. While we appreciate the public's concern, we cannot and will not jeopardize our case to satisfy curiosity. As to any more specifics of the case, we cannot comment. Thank you."

A roar of voices went up with more questions. It was hard to make them out. Until we heard my name. "Isn't it true, Deputy Myers, that your ex-girlfriend Marygene Brown, owner of the Peach Diner, has been called in for questioning on your wife's murder as well? So, it isn't just your cousin in question but also your ex-girlfriend."

"I'll take this one, Deputy Myers." Mr. O'Malley moved in front of the microphone. "No, that is not accurate. My client, Marygene Brown, has not, nor has ever been, a person of interest. As Detective Thornton said, everyone who was present the day of the unfortunate incident is being questioned. Also, as the detective stated, the cause of death has yet to be determined. It is in the best interests of everyone involved that anyone with information regarding the case to please come forward and speak with the Peach Cove Sheriff's Department. A tip line has been created, and you'll find it at the bottom of your screen. Even the simplest detail could aid law enforcement in solving what happened to Lucy Carmichael."

"Myers, Lucy Myers." Alex sounded a little agitated as he shouted behind Mr. O'Malley.

The old man turned and stepped aside.

"Sheriff Carter." A chorus of voices rang out. "Can you tell us anything about how the body was discovered?"

I held my breath and perched on the edge of the sofa.

Eddie stepped forward and rested both hands on the podium, and I wondered if he needed it to steady himself. His face appeared paler, and he was sweating. "We are unable to comment on the specifics of the case at this time."

"Sheriff Carter? Is there a murderer on the loose here in Peach Cove?"

"Now, it's questions like that, Larry, that spread pandemonium." Eddie pierced Larry with a pointed glare, and the reporter slinked backward. Eddie faced the cameras and wiped his brow. "I urge the public, if you know anything, we do indeed have the tip line set up and ready to receive any and all information you have. Also, I'm told there is a number below the tip line at the bottom of your screen that we urge you to use to express your concerns. There is absolutely no evidence that anyone else is in danger at this time. Be vigilant, as always, but go about your lives and leave the case to the authorities."

A female reporter blurted, "Isn't it true the body was discovered by Deputy Reyes at your daughter's residence?"

Alex's head whipped around. He hadn't known where Lucy's body had been discovered.

I gasped and Betsy reached out and patted my knee.

"We cannot comment on the open investigation. However, I will say this, check your facts before starting rumors."

"Are you protecting your daughter, Sheriff?"

"I have nothing else to add."

"Sheriff, are you fit to serve under these circumstances?"

After another reiteration about the tip line and the safety of the islanders, the station took us back to the studio.

Betsy turned the TV off, and I slid onto the floor next to her.

CHAPTER 19

It took us about twenty minutes to get off the floor and try to articulate what we'd just seen. The shell shock we'd both experienced had us each in a state we'd never been in before. And Bets and I had been through a lot together. Betsy had recommended eating, and we'd both shut our phones off. The texts and calls were incessant. I'd spoken to my attorney, Eddie, my sister, and my brother, of course, and Betsy had spoken to Meemaw and Aunt Vi. After that, we'd made the decision to set our iPhones to do-not-disturb. My attorney had advised me not to speak to reporters, and I felt certain Betsy's would do the same once she spoke with him.

I pulled my plate from the microwave and grabbed a fork. I wasn't sure I could stomach the pizza now, but I'd felt light-headed and knew my blood sugar was rapidly dropping. "We need to find out everything we can about

Lucy. I want to know who she was before she moved here. Where she lived, where she went to school, who her friends were, and what happened to cause the rift between her and her parents. If I can get to know the woman whose body was laid out on my deck, then maybe I can determine why they wanted her dead." I chewed and swallowed the bite I'd taken and forced it down with a sip of wine.

"We better get on that fast."

"I intend to." I hurried to my office and came back with my laptop and got busy on Facebook, searching Lucy out. Her posts weren't public, so I couldn't see those, but I was able to peruse her friends list.

"Wow. That's sad." Betsy peeked at the screen. "She ain't got but a few friends. I've got loads, close to four thousand."

"You better be careful accepting any and all requests you receive."

She made a *pfft* sound and took another bite of pizza. "Those peeps are my followers. They love them some Betsy. I post all sorts of helpful tips on food and fashion." She glanced at the ceiling while she chewed. "I'm thinking her ex, the biker, has a story to tell. Is he on her list?"

"Hmm," I scrolled for a man with the first name David and filled Betsy in on my conversation with Trixie and my recon of Lucy's rental.

"Well, that's proof then. Stupid Lucy did have a piece on the side. She never stopped diddling her ex. You sure you searched that place good? Maybe you should've waited for me. I'm like a bloodhound when it comes to investigatin' and finding evidence."

"I'm sure. It was clean."

"Hmph. Either that biker fella is a killer on the run or

just her lover who doesn't want to be found. His name is David, huh?" Betsy poured herself another glass of wine.

"Trixie said Lucy chatted with a David. Until we find the mystery man, we'll have no way of knowing his identity. They may be the same person."

"We're this close from being arrested." She showed an inch between her thumb and index finger. "We have to find him. What's the stupid detective doing? Sitting on his hands? Having dumb press conferences."

It sure felt like it, and I exhaled loudly. "No luck." Could it be possible she really hadn't had many friends? She must've had a few back home.

"Figures. She probably didn't want nobody knowing her nasty beeswax. And I'm guessing her ex, the killer, didn't think nobody would believe you could pull this off on your own, so they roped in the cousin who obviously had misgivings about the marriage." She gulped from the glass. "Why couldn't I have been born with a filter? I mean, it's the Myers's hot-bloodedness that causes me to fire off like I do. It's out of my control. I probably need to get Doc Tatum to run one of them brain scans on me. It might be good to have in case we have to stand trial and I need an insanity plea."

"Don't be ridiculous." I half laughed unenthusiastically, hoping to show my friend her concerns were unfounded. Deep down though, my insides were doing flip-flops. What could Eddie really do if Betsy and I were skillfully framed? And if anyone could put the nail in our coffins, it would be Detective Thornton. All he needed was a reason to believe we were guilty, and he could put the whole case to bed. He'd been accused of framing jobs in the past, by people I trusted.

We'd settled into silence, the sounds of forced chewing and swallowing nearly deafening. A knock at the door startled both of us.

"Probably some reporter. I better not go anywhere near them." Betsy wiped her mouth with a napkin. "They'll get me mad and I'll convict myself."

"Just answer 'no comment' whenever they start pestering you. Don't let them bait you. Walk away, or you could say, 'Direct all questions to my attorney.'" We ignored the knocks until the doorbell began to ring incessantly. Whoever it was had no intention of giving up.

"Persistent jerks." Betsy grabbed another slice from the box. She didn't mind cold pizza.

Sliding off the chair, I went to the door and glanced through the peephole. I had to steady myself with my hands against the frame. Detective Thornton stood staring right into the opposite side.

"Who is it?" Betsy wanted to know and crammed her mouth full. "Reporters?"

Shaking my head, I leaned back and whispered, "Detective Thornton."

She dropped her pizza back on the plate and leaped from the stool. "This is it! I thought we'd have more time." She started running in place and flailing her arms as her voice rose. "Why didn't we spend our time buying fake passports on the black market and stockpiling money instead of sitting around here eating? Call someone! Do something!"

"Calm down!" I hissed.

"Miss Brown, you might as well let me in, I can hear everything out here," Detective Thornton said through the door.

"Be cool," I mouthed to Betsy, who gulped.

"I'm always cool. I'm as cool as a cucumber." She

bent over at the knees and started doing some deep breathing.

After a couple of deep breaths myself, I let the detective in.

The man waltzed right past me as if he owned the place. I supposed he familiarized himself with the layout earlier. He cast a glance over to Betsy. "Caught the news report, I see. Relax, Miss Myers."

"We better be on the same cell block is all I've got to say!" Betsy hollered, then slapped her hands over her mouth. She looked like she'd swallowed a stinkbug. She dropped her hands as my brows raised. "I mean, we're innocent! I want my lawyer. We want our lawyers!"

I'd never seen Betsy so panicked in my life. "Betsy, we haven't done anything wrong and I don't think the detective is here to arrest us."

The way the man walked in without reading me my rights or being in the company of another officer, he was probably here on a fishing expedition, which he was going to have no luck with, and I hoped he didn't make up a tall tale about the big one he caught.

The detective raised his hands defensively and smiled. The expression appeared awkward and forced. I'd never seen him smile before and for some reason, I got the distinct impression he didn't smile regularly.

"Miss Brown is correct. I'm only here to have a conversation with your friend. May I?" He motioned to the living room.

"Of course."

Mr. Wrigley appeared out of nowhere and leaped on the back of the sectional sofa with his hair and back raised, looking positively possessed as a god-awful noise came from his overweight body.

"Um, is that cat okay? It doesn't have rabies or something, does it?" Detective Thornton scooted to the corner of the sofa.

"No. He's just old and doesn't like strangers."

Betsy snatched her bag off the chair, grabbed the box of pizza, and said with the utmost speed, "Well, if y'all don't need me around here, I'll just mosey on my way."

"You're leaving?" I gaped.

She leaned toward me and whispered out of the corner of her mouth, "You know what they say about animals. They can sense evil. I advise you to come with me. Get out before whatever entity took over that man's body is unleashed." Before I could respond, Betsy hightailed it out of my cottage, leaving me alone with the detective.

I straightened and faced my unwelcome guest, who was still watching Mr. Wrigley with what was clearly trepidation. He'd even begun to sweat a little.

I walked over and stroked the cat's gray head. "It's okay, buddy. You run along." I hefted the cat, making a mental note to talk to the vet about some diet cat food. Being so overweight couldn't be good for my little fella. I kissed him on the head and placed him on the floor. "Can I get you something? A glass of wine or tea? I'd offer you some pizza, but Betsy took what was left with her."

"No, thank you. I'm fine."

"Very well then." I perched on the far edge of my tweed sectional. "What can I do for you, Detective?"

The man regained his composure the second Mr. Wrigley left the room. "I thought you and I should have a talk off the record."

I blinked several times before what he'd said actually registered. This had to be some trick to get me to entrap myself somehow. I got myself together. "Why would you want to do that?"

"Because, Miss Brown, something about this case is off. Way off."

"Ya think?" I closed my mouth the second the last word slipped out. I knew better than to poke the bear.

"I was hoping you and I could work together on this. You be forthcoming with me, and I'll do my best to solve this murder case and leave this island. You'll never see me again." He stared at me with a different air. Not that I trusted him. No, not by a long shot. The air shifted and Mama sat next to the detective. This was an omen. Danger.

"Be careful. There is a conflicted vibe coming off this one." Mama kept her gaze trained on the detective.

"I have been forthcoming with you. I told you what happened. It was the truth. I had nothing to do with Lucy's death. And I don't know who did." I sat back against the sofa to show I was calm and collected. I hoped it portrayed a calm demeanor anyway.

Having Mama here calmed my nerves a bit. She smiled at me.

"You haven't been when it comes to your relationships," Detective Thornton said.

"I beg your pardon?"

"I'm sorry, honey." Mama's tone was full of emotion, and I couldn't very well ask why.

I scratched my brow to glance inconspicuously from Mama to the detective. The pitying expression on her face spoke volumes. Nerves took up residence in my midsection and began to spread throughout my body. *Great, just great.* I couldn't stand being blindsided.

"Oh, you didn't know. Paul and Lucy had a relationship a few months back. Under the circumstances, I'm surprised he didn't tell you."

I crossed my legs and laced my fingers around my knee. "Are you sure your information is solid? Alex and Lucy have been together for . . ." A head tilt from the detective halted my speech. *First, I find out Lucy is fooling around on Alex with this biker fella, now he's adding Paul into the mix.* "Okay. Well, are you now inferring Paul might be responsible for Lucy's death and is framing me?" Mild-mannered Paul would be the last person I'd suspect, which gave me pause, and instantly I suspected him. Probably the intent of the man sitting across from me. Although, something about him made me almost trust him. Almost.

"I'm not inferring anything." He sat forward. "We're just having a friendly chat about how much you don't know about the people in your life. The ones you keep close company with and seem to trust with your life."

I gave his words some consideration. I wouldn't say I trusted Paul with my life. He felt different and, on some level, that gave me a sense of security. And from Mama's drawn lips and sad eyes, I gathered Paul and Lucy hadn't ended their contact months ago.

"I'm not comfortable with this conversation. I'd like you to leave."

"We'll have the lab results soon. Once they're in, an indictment will be forthcoming." He rose and strolled toward the front door.

"You mean *my* indictment?" I swallowed the lump in my throat and rose to my feet.

"Honestly, Miss Brown, I don't figure you for the one behind this one." The way he said *this one* didn't bode well for his opinion of me. "Someone wants me to, and when all the pieces of the puzzle are this elementary, I begin to become irritated. Either the perp believes I'm a fool, or he is." He left without another word.

A text came through while I still stared at the closed door. Javy had to cancel for tonight. Something came up in the investigation. It took everything I had not to reply and ask for details or to tell him what I found out from Trixie. I set my phone aside.

"He's not coming."

"No." I turned toward Mama. "It's fine. What's going on? Why is this different from all the previous times the deceased sought my help?"

She shook her head. "Are you feeling the pull to help Lucy like you have in the past with others?"

No stranger to death, not anymore, anyway, I thought about it for a few long seconds. And most of the time I had a strong pull to locate the person responsible for ending a person's life. The deceased were sort of like those in my support group. They'd been abused in the worst possible ways. This time with Lucy, it'd not happened like before. Perhaps because I hadn't liked her in this life. My determination to find answers was mainly to protect Betsy and me from ending up in jail. The day of the wedding I'd felt confusion but nothing more. Now, though, and since the discovery of her body, I did. With all the commotion, I'd not given it the necessary consideration. This was what my life had been reverted to. Pondering motives and attempting to right wrongs in the only way I knew how. My life hadn't exactly turned out the way I planned as a girl. A couple of years ago, I resented that fact. I let out a sigh. Today, though, I had the presence of mind not to fall into the depression trap. Because I wouldn't be who I was today without all the trials and turmoil I'd had to endure. Now I certainly was a person who took stock of life. Made the most of every blissful moment and took people as they came. I never expected anyone to be anything other than who they were, and knew life wouldn't always be a bed of roses. Yes, unlike the naïve Marygene, who ran away from home and expected to find greener pastures away from Mama and the island, I was a woman who could face death and live to tell about it and learn from it.

"Yes," I answered. "I need to find out who killed Lucy, not just for myself but for her as well. I'm not sure why, but I get the sense we never knew the real Lucy. And I plan to do everything in my power to find out who she really was. So far it hasn't been easy."

Paul and I met for dinner the next night. I studied him for a few minutes while he made small talk, and we enjoyed our favorite meal of fajitas for two. I thought about how much fun we'd had when we first started dating. There hadn't been any expectations and we were just like two new friends hanging out and getting to know each other. We'd spend hours binge-watching old movies and eating popcorn. I thought of the day we went to Six Flags over Georgia because he said he'd never ridden a roller coaster in his life. I could still see his flushed cheeks and his eyes wide with excitement, coupled with a little trepidation, as we rode up the nearly two-hundred-foot incline of the coaster Goliath, and then his shouts as we careened right back down. Paul looked like a flushed child, giddy for his next adventure, when we exited the ride. Such a fun day we'd had. I realized it was a side of him I'd never seen again.

Things seemed so different now. The more I considered it, the more I realized we were never going to cross from the initial flirty fun zone into a serious relationship.

After his second beer, I came out and asked about Lucy.

He choked on a forkful of rice and beans. I leaned back, wiping my mouth with my napkin. Then I sipped from my margarita while he got himself together.

He laughed, but his upper lip had beaded up with sweat. "I don't know where you heard that crazy rumor from." He hadn't said it wasn't true. "People on this island sure like to talk."

"They do. Funny thing is, I didn't hear it from an islander."

He glanced up, and I caught the tiniest flicker of panic.

"Detective Thornton told me." I scooped up a little guacamole on a chip and ate it casually.

"Oh." His face reddened. "Well, I can explain. It isn't what you think."

"From your reaction, I think it is. Not that I care. I just hate when I'm lied to or kept in the dark about things that directly affect me. You were aware of the problems I was having with the law, and yet you thought it best to keep silent about a relationship you had with the deceased. You allowed me to be blindsided and look like a fool, since we're supposed to be dating and all. And just the other day you asked if I'd take our relationship to the next level." I snorted in disgust.

He threw his napkin on his plate. "It isn't like you were jumping for joy at my offer, though, was it? You could barely hold back your repulsion to the idea. And for your information," Paul huffed, "Lucy came on to me. I resisted her advances because of you."

"I hope the fact she was engaged to Alex restrained you some!" I retorted with equal huff. "Still, even if what you say is true, you should have told me."

Paul looked exasperated and ready to blow a fuse. He and I had never had a blowout of this nature. "That goes both ways, baby. There's loads you don't tell me. You and that Javier are toying with a sexual escapade." His voice rose. "Don't deny it. Everyone can see it. You made me appear the court jester!"

Court jester? "You've completely lost it." We were attracting attention now.

"I've lost it? Look at your disaster of a life."

The waiter slinked by and dropped the check and hurried away.

"Keep your voice down. My life is none of your business, just like what you do is of no consequence to me. We were both fools to think this would work."

"You said it." He stood so abruptly the chair clattered backward. "You're as nuts as they say you are!" He stormed from the room, leaving everyone to gape at me. My face burned and I wanted the ground to open and swallow me whole. The jerk even left me with the check.

Boy, Marygene, you sure can pick 'em.

CHAPTER 20

I slammed the door to my car and stomped up onto the stoop, shoved my key into the door, and swung it open. It was one disaster after the next. In the mood I was in, I dared an intruder to come at me. I'd rip him to shreds with my bare hands. Stupid Paul. Stupid need to date. Stupid murder investigation. I jerked open the refrigerator and grabbed a half-empty bottle of wine. When I closed it, Mama was there, then she vanished, then she was back again.

"Mama, what's going on?"

She opened her mouth, and nothing came out, and once again, she faded away. I placed the bottle on the counter and called out to her a few times.

When she finally appeared again, I could hear her speaking when her mouth moved. "I'm fighting the pull.

I need to . . ." Her face contorted in pain. She doubled over at the waist, "Edward. No." And she was gone.

Everything else in my complicated life vanished, and Eddie consumed every thought. Without a moment's hesitation, I called his cell. I called more than a dozen times, and each time it went to his voice mail. *No, God, please! Please don't take Eddie.*

As I fumbled with my keys and dropped my purse, everything scattered on the ceramic tile flooring. With shaky hands, I gathered up all my essentials and left everything else where it was and rushed out the front door. As I pulled out of the driveway, I had no idea where I was going. All I knew was I had to find my father. When the phone rang through the speakers, I jumped, and a squeak left my lips. I hit the answer button on the steering column. "H . . . hello."

Doc Tatum's voice came over the speakers. "Marygene, honey, where are you?"

"I'm in the car driving toward town."

"Pull over, dear."

A sob nearly overtook me. "Why? You're scaring me."

"Stay calm and just pull over for a second. I need to tell you something."

I focused on the sounds of shells crunching under my tires as I pulled over into the sandy parking lot by the beach access entryway. "O . . . Okay."

My trembling hands were in my lap.

"Your father had a heart attack."

The dam broke and an audible sob left my lips.

"He's in surgery now. Your brother and I are at the hospital. I can come and get you if you don't feel as if you're able to drive."

Hot tears traveled down my cheeks. "Is he going to be okay? They're going to fix him, right?"

"Honey, they're doing everything they can."

"They *need* to fix him!" I sobbed.

Mama had crumbled in front of me. I'd never seen her do that before. I couldn't lose Eddie.

"Sweetheart, let me come and get you," Doc Tatum said.

I heard Sam ask how I was in the background and got myself together.

"No. You should stay there. I'm fine to drive." I forced myself to stop and focus on my brother and Doc Tatum. I felt positive I wasn't the only one paralyzed with fear. Sam must be gutted.

"You're sure?" Sweet Doc Lindy Tatum sounded so together, but I knew deep down she had to be feeling what Sam and I were. She loved Eddie. The two of them were even discussing marriage.

I wiped the tears from my cheeks. "I am."

"Okay then. Do you want me to call Jena Lynn for you?"

"Yes, please." If I heard my sister's voice, I'd break down again, and she had enough on her plate with a sick baby. "Betsy too, if you don't mind."

"Of course not. We're in the waiting room on the third floor. You'll have to get a guest tag at the front desk. I'll let them know you'll be coming."

"Thank you." I put the car into drive and pulled back on the road and punched Bay Memorial into the GPS. With my brain clouded, it would behoove me to have directions ringing in my ears.

"I'll see you soon. I love you, honey."

"Love you too. Tell Sam I'll be there as fast as I can." I disconnected the call.

Eddie hadn't looked good to me during the interview. And I prayed the Lord would see him through this. A lot of people made it. Eddie was strong and a fighter.

"Mama!" I called into the empty space. "Mama, please. If there's anything you can do, anything at all. Please help him."

It was a long shot, I knew that. She'd been able to intervene and help me in situations in the past when my life was in danger, but she'd told me she didn't have the power to do more than that. Still, I had to ask.

I prayed the entire way to the hospital, with only the monotone digital voice guiding in the background. When I pulled into a parking space, I forgot to put the car in park and the curb reminded me of that fact. Once I had, I snatched my purse off the seat and rushed into the hospital. My entire body felt numb as I clipped the tag onto my shirt and rode the elevator up to the third floor. There were two elderly women crying next to me, and I had to force myself to not break down. My heart hurt for all three of us. I'd *hated* hospitals before little Olivia was born. The sterile smells, the whirling machines, and the stench of illness was all I could focus on before the glorious night she emerged into the world with a red face and balled-up fists. When my sister first asked me to be in the room with her during the delivery, I hadn't wanted to. I knew nothing about babies or the pain the mother endured to give them life, before experiencing it with my sister. Now I was so glad I'd been there to witness the miracle. The joy and the love that knew no bounds I'd instantly had for the little stranger astounded me. The memory almost made me smile. Almost.

When the doors opened, I had to face the other reasons people were admitted. The smell of Lysol and bleach greeted me as I moved down the hallway toward the waiting room. Standing in the open doorway, I took it all in. In the corner in the back sat Sam, slumped over with his elbows resting on his knees and his hands in his hair. Next to him sat Doc Tatum on the phone. She rubbed his back in a motherly sort of way.

Sam lifted his head and looked directly at me. Almost as if he sensed my presence. The lost-puppy-dog look in his blue eyes broke my heart. He rose and we crossed the room and embraced. "I was worried about you. You took forever getting here."

We went to sit in the chairs.

"I'm sorry. It took me a minute to pull myself together." I dabbed at my eyes.

Sam nodded. To my utter surprise, Sam wrapped his arms around me and buried his face in my neck and sobbed.

We cried together while I murmured soothingly into his ear and rubbed his back. "He's strong. He'll make it. I have no doubts."

"That's what Lindy said too," Sam said.

"Lindy is right." I smiled in her direction. Her face, stricken with worry, creased in a small smile.

He lifted his head and wiped his face with his large palms. His face reddened with embarrassment. Stupid macho guy stuff.

"Of course she is. Besides, the old man is too stubborn to die," Sam said.

We laughed.

He rose. "I'm going to go get us all some coffee." He

didn't look back as he left the waiting room. He needed a minute alone. I understood that.

Doc Tatum—no, Lindy—moved to his abandoned seat and wrapped an arm across my shoulders and gave me a squeeze. "Your father is in capable hands. I have the utmost confidence in Dr. Zeke's abilities. It could be a long operation, though. He's undergoing a triple bypass. He's lucky. I know the warning signs, and he showed nothing except for his fatigue levels."

"Where did it happen?"

"He collapsed beside his truck outside the sheriff's department. Tonya was just coming back from lunch and saw him fall. She dialed nine-one-one and then me. I made it a minute before the ambulance and rode with him here. I was terrified I'd lose him right there on the pavement." Her voice wobbled, and I squeezed her hand. It was evident how much she loved him.

"I'm so glad you were with him. I would hate to think he dealt with such a terrifying ordeal alone."

We settled into silence. I stared at the striped pattern on the commercial carpeted flooring. Several other people strolled into the waiting room, taking seats around the perimeter of the room. One family in particular kept glancing our way. I didn't recognize them. The young man, with what I assumed were his parents, showed them something on his phone. They weren't far from us. It was easy to pick up Larry's voice asking Eddie if he was protecting his daughter.

I wanted the ground to open and swallow me whole.

Lindy took my hand. "This girl's father is on the operating table. Doesn't she have enough turmoil to deal with? I'd appreciate it if you'd show some respect."

The older woman had the decency to appear embarrassed. "We apologize to you both."

Her husband stood and came over to where we sat, while the woman instructed her son to put his device away. He didn't appear the slightest abashed, shrugging and shoving the phone into the cargo pocket of his pants.

The man, wearing jeans and a gray T-shirt, held out his weathered hand to me. "I know Sheriff Carter. We fish in the Peach Cove tournament together every spring."

I took his calloused hand as recognition struck. "Oh, that's right."

"Our grandson didn't mean anything. He's young and anything exciting is fair game as far as entertainment goes. His mother is fighting for her life too."

I shook my head. "No, of course not. Emotions are running high. I'll be praying her surgery is a success."

He dropped my hand; his eyes were kind and warm. "Thank you. And we'll be praying for Eddie." He took Lindy's hand next, and she stood and hugged the man. Then she followed the man back to his seat and hugged his wife. She would've hugged their grandson, but he slinked back into his seat. I could hear her offering kind words and apologizing for her outburst.

I sat there fiddling with my hands in my lap until she returned. She'd spoken up for me, and I wouldn't forget it. Lindy and I would be closer from now on. She was family.

A few minutes later, Lindy said, "I better go check on Sam. You want anything from the cafeteria?"

I shook my head and she walked away. It appeared Sam and Lindy were a lot closer too.

My phone chirped several times in succession. I dug

through my bag, hoping I had enough battery life to get me through the night. It would be tight with only forty percent remaining. Betsy had texted with her prayers and asked if I needed anything. I texted back with my thanks and that I was good. I had a few texts from my sister, but before I could reply, my phone rang with her ring tone. Heads whipped in my direction.

"Sorry." I fumbled with the buttons on the side of the phone before answering. "Hey," I whispered and moved to the chair in the corner.

"Hey, hon, how are you?" Jena Lynn's voice held that motherly concern. It didn't matter how old we were, she'd always act like my big sister.

"I'm okay. Eddie's still in surgery. I don't know anything yet." I placed my elbow on the back of the chair and glanced out the window to see the sun falling behind the tree line below the parking lot.

"We're praying for him. He'll pull through." I heard mumbling in the background.

"Thanks, Sis. Someone there with you?"

"Zach's mom. She's been a lifesaver. When Olivia is inconsolable, she has the patience of Job. She walks her up and down the driveway for hours. I don't know how I'd get along without her help."

Jena Lynn won the mother-in-law jackpot. Zach's mom had the capacity to love like no other. She treated Jena Lynn just like one of her own.

"I'm so glad. How is Olivia?"

"She's okay. The pediatrician said she has a little cold and that, compounded with teething, has her fever up and her ears bothering her. It's nothing serious."

"That's good."

"It is. But we don't have to talk about this."

"No, I want to. Distraction is good. Vent away." I tapped on the window lightly with my fingernail.

"Don't be silly. You don't want to hear about my debate to wean Olivia to formula so I can have my body back, or how I'm worried I'm spoiling her by picking her up the second she begins crying."

I attempted to laugh but failed. "Sure, I do."

"Listen, you don't have to be tough with me. It's okay to be afraid. It's okay to worry, and it's more than okay to express those emotions. I don't want you to have to go through this on your own. You've done your fair share of suffering in silence. The limit, I'd say. I'll be free in an hour if you want me to come and sit with you and Sam." She meant it, and I appreciated it. But she sounded exhausted and she'd need to pump or feed the baby every few hours. She had enough on her plate. Despite all of that, she'd sit with me all night if I allowed her to.

"Thank you, but you should be with Olivia. I'll call the second I know anything."

"You're sure?" Her voice betrayed her hurt feelings.

"Oh, Jena Lynn, you know I love you and always want you with me. I just thought you could use the rest, and Lindy is here too. She said it could be hours before we receive an update. Please don't be upset."

"I'm not. Of course, I'm not. Forgive me. It's my hormones. Don't mind me. I love you, Sam, and Eddie is all. If you change your mind, call me day or night. Promise?"

"Yes. I promise. Love you."

"Love you too."

I heard Olivia crying in the background before she disconnected the call.

I sat staring at the phone for a few minutes. I could go

on social media and catch up on the happenings with all my Facebook friends. That would pass a little time. I slid my phone back into my bag and decided against it. I couldn't handle negative energy in my current headspace, and social media could be blowing up with the interview and conspiracy theories regarding the murder or politics.

My phone chirped again, and I hurried to dig it out of my bag quietly. When the Blue Bird Inn came up on my caller ID, I hit the answer icon. "Hello."

"Marygene, I just heard about Eddie," my cousin Nate said. "I'm so sorry to hear it."

"Thanks. He's in surgery now. He'll pull through." I wiped my nose.

"Of course he will. Um, you left a message for me to give you a call the other day. I'm sorry it has taken me so long to get back to you. If this is a bad time—"

"No, it's okay. With everything that's happened, I completely forgot. I wondered if you had a guest registered there with the first name David. He might be the biker type."

"Um—" I heard the clicking of computer keys. "Surprisingly, we do have a David Commons registered."

I sat up straight in my chair.

"He and his wife checked in two days ago. They'll be here until tomorrow. But I don't think he's the biker type. They're here for bird-watching. They came with a small group. I think he's about seventy."

"Oh, okay. I know the sheriff's department spoke to you about the man who stayed and paid cash."

"Yeah, haven't seen him in a while. We currently just have the McCall Bird Watchers as guests. Hey, I'll be praying for Eddie. We all will."

"Thanks. Bye." I put my phone away and rubbed my

aching head, so overwhelmed I could bawl my eyes out. When I glanced up, I spied Javy filling the doorway. His presence always seemed to take over a room. I waved. Javy took the chair next to me.

"Hey." I smiled at Javier.

"Hey." He smiled back. "No news yet?"

"No. How about with the investigation. Any new developments?" I stared into his face expectantly.

"Afraid not."

I took in a deep, shuddering breath and shook my head. Javy reached out and took my hand. I allowed him to wrap his large fingers around mine.

CHAPTER 21

I woke with a start and my head on the seat of the chair next to me. "Marygene, the doctor is here," Sam whispered, and shook my shoulder.

"Oh." I wiped my mouth. The waiting room had cleared out with only Sam, Lindy, and me left in it.

Lindy was standing in front of the man in a white coat. I slid my feet off the chair. Sam took my hand, and we joined Lindy. We stared like two lost children waiting for the nice man with salt-and-pepper hair and a creased forehead to tell us our daddy was okay.

"He came through the surgery well." Dr. Zeke looked from Lindy to me and Sam. "We had a small incident where his vitals dipped and we almost lost him."

I sucked in a breath, and Sam swayed on his feet. I gripped his forearm with my free hand. He squeezed my hand so tightly it almost hurt.

Dr. Zeke rushed to add, "He's stable now."

"Can you explain exactly what was done?" Sam cleared his throat. "I've heard of folks getting bypasses done, but I'm not sure I understand the procedure. I mean, how long till he's able to be back on his feet and all that?"

"Of course. We performed what is known as a coronary artery bypass graft surgery. It treats blocked heart arteries by creating new passages for blood to flow to your father's heart muscle."

Sam nodded and so did I as I attempted to absorb what the doctor was saying. Numbness spread throughout my limbs. It was almost an out-of-body experience. Listening to some stranger tell about how he'd held your father's life in his two hands and saved him.

Dr. Zeke's coffee-colored eyes softened. "Let's see if I can break this down a little. Basically, we take the arteries or veins from other parts of your dad's body and use them to reroute the blood around his clogged arteries." The doctor's lips flattened into a thin line. "Now I must inform you that during the procedure his heart experienced failure and we nearly lost him, but we managed to stabilize him and right now, he's okay. We'll be monitoring him closely."

"Thank you, Doctor." Lindy shook his hand.

He covered hers with his. "You're welcome. It's a lot to process when it's someone you love, I know."

"When can we see him?" I asked.

"As soon as it's possible, I'll send the nurse out to inform you when he's able to have visitors. It'll be a little bit. Take this time to grab some coffee or a snack."

"Thank you," Sam and I said in unison.

"Take care."

The doctor left and then the three of us embraced, and tears of gratefulness flowed all around before Lindy excused herself to go to the ladies' room. My stomach audibly growled. I hadn't eaten in hours.

"It's going to be a while before we can see Dad. I could eat something too," Sam said. "The cafeteria isn't open yet, but we could pop down and get something from the vending machines. We'll feel more awake when we see Dad if we get some sugar in our systems."

I glanced at my watch. It was five in the morning. "Yeah, okay."

We sat in the dark cafeteria with our tabletop full of crackers, granola bars, and a variety of chocolate bars. Sam braved the ham-and-cheese prepackaged sandwich while he talked to Poppy on the phone. The coffee tasted burned, but I drank it down with vigor while I texted Jena Lynn. She usually put her phone on do-not-disturb at night so it wouldn't wake the baby if she received a call. She'd see that Eddie came through the surgery when she woke. I did the same for Bets.

"Javier stayed until he absolutely had to leave," Sam threw out there after he hung up with Poppy. "He made me swear to call him if you needed anything."

"He's a good friend." I got up and put some change into the machine and pressed the buttons for another cup of disgusting caffeine.

"Friend?"

"Don't make mountains out of mole hills. We're just friends." I sat back down at the table.

"Well, he's protective in a way that appears he's more than just a friend, Marygene. He watched over you while you slept and made sure you weren't disturbed. He stroked your hair like you were some prize."

My fingers froze on the package of crackers I'd been about to open. "Really?"

Sam nodded. "Yeah. It's not like you're in a relationship or anything."

I opened my mouth to refute his assumptions on my love life, but he cut me off.

"Don't even say you're seeing Paul. I can tell the guy's just a placeholder."

"That's not true." I tore open the package.

"Hey, it's me you're talking to. You started dating him on the rebound. He's the complete opposite to every other guy you've ever shown interest in. That made him seem safe in your book." He raised his hands. "I get it."

"Maybe there's a little truth to what you're saying." I shrugged. "I thought he was a great guy, or at least a different kind of guy."

"Really? If that's true, where is he? A great guy wouldn't stay away without even checking in. Have you even thought about calling him?" Sam finished off his sandwich in two bites and, from his facial expression, it must not have been so tasty.

I froze mid-sip as I pondered Sam's words. He had a point. Paul hadn't entered my mind when I found out about Eddie. I'd never even thought about contacting him, especially after our dinner. Nor had I been devastated when I found out he might have had a relationship with Lucy, or by his reaction to my questioning. Was embarrassed by it, yes, but not hurt. I'd been more concerned about Lucy's death than his deception. I felt awful that I could've been using Paul.

"The reasons don't matter now anyway. We had a fight. It's over." I sipped from my cup. "It's not a big deal. I forgot all about him when I got the news about Eddie."

"See! I was right."

"Yeah, okay." I smirked. It felt good to be sitting here chatting with my brother, knowing our father would be okay. "Still, that doesn't mean I don't care about him. I'd like to be friends." Even as the words fell from my lips, I wondered if being friends with Paul, after everything, would be possible.

Sam grinned. "I don't see it happening, Sis. One thing I've learned through this nightmare with Dad is when catastrophe strikes, who you think about first is who you really care about. I called Poppy first thing. She'd have been here with me too, but she has a cold and Lindy said it wouldn't be wise."

"I don't see the correlation."

"Well, this also shows Paul's true colors. A man with good character would've reached out, even if it's over. Y'all had a thing. He should call and at least check in on you and your dad. Surely word has gotten around by now."

Sam had a point. I checked my phone and confirmed I hadn't received a call from him. I shrugged and slid my phone on the table. "We parted badly. I'll tell you about it sometime, just not now. It isn't like I loved him or anything. All that matters is Eddie's alive and in the care of great physicians. He's what's important." I concentrated on the black liquid in my paper cup.

My phone rang, and Sam and I both glanced down to see Alex's face. The guy who loved Eddie too. His sheriff took him under his wing and taught him everything he knew about law enforcement. He'd been more like a father to him, really. That was why it'd hurt so much to hear Alex turn on him the way he had.

"Don't answer it. That pain in the ass is probably what triggered Dad's heart attack." Sam's face was beet red.

I wouldn't do anything to go against my brother right now, and a little part of me agreed with him about Alex being the straw that broke the camel's back. I declined the call and slid the phone back into my cross-body bag. Sam settled when he saw we were on the same page.

"Let's not talk about anything that will stress Eddie out when we see him. We'll only talk about positive things and put on a happy face at all times." I placed my cup back on the table.

"Agreed. He's always tried to shelter us from the ugliness in the world. Now it's our turn to do the same for him. He won't like it at first, though." Sam held his stomach, which rumbled audibly, and Sam gave out a little groan.

"Did you check the date on the sandwich? I told you prepackaged meat and cheese could be risky."

Sam shook his head. "It tasted okay. A little wangy, but I was starving." Beads of sweat appeared on his upper lip and his hair looked limp. "I gotta find a bathroom and now." The chair slid back loudly, and Sam bolted from the room, leaving a lingering odor in his wake.

I held my nose. "Oh yikes, Sam."

Maybe next time he'd listen to his little sister.

CHAPTER 22

Three hours later, Sam and I were allowed to visit for a short while with Eddie. We took turns because hospital policy required they limit visitors. Lindy assured us that once they got him into his permanent room, they'd afford us more freedom on that front. Sam went in first with Lindy. She'd offered to let me go in with Sam. I'd declined, needing to get myself together first, and I could tell she was eager to get to his side. She came out fifteen minutes later, and I hung back for a few to give my brother some alone time with his father. While I waited, Lindy and I discussed how we'd care for Eddie once discharged. She would take a short leave from her practice and care for him full-time. Now that she had a partner in her family practice, it would be doable. I would make his meals, per his new cardiac diet plan, and deliver them. We planned to freeze as many meals as possible so he would have options. He wouldn't like it at first. In time he'd adjust. I even toyed with the idea of adding more heart-healthy options at the diner. I made a mental note to discuss the idea with Jena Lynn later.

When it was my turn, I nearly gasped at the sight of my father, so pale and weak. Tubes and wires were attached to him and he was hooked up to several bags of IV fluids. Machines beeped and whirled, and I suddenly felt ill. Eddie had always looked so strong and unbreakable.

"It's not as bad as it looks," he rasped when he saw me.

I went to his bedside, bent and kissed his cheek, berating myself for allowing such a reaction. I would remain positive even if it killed me. Eddie deserved nothing less.

I swallowed the lump in my throat and pulled the chair closer to his bed, smiling as I took his hand. "You look wonderful."

"Overselling it a bit." He managed a grin. "I'll be all right."

I nodded and blinked to hold the tears at bay. "Of course you will. You're alive and awake and, to me, you've never looked better." I sniffed. "And I don't want you to worry about a thing. We're going to all pitch in and make your life a bit easier while you recover."

"I don't want a fuss." Eddie's head rolled back and forth on the pillow. The best he could do at shaking his head, I guessed.

"Don't be silly. We love you and want to make your road to recovery a bit easier." I kissed his hand.

He smiled. "I appreciate it, pumpkin. I guess this stubborn old goat is going to have to let go of the reins for a bit on some things. Not all, mind you. I still want to be in the loop with things. It'd drive me crazy to be shut out." He blinked his eyes a few times and when he focused on me again, they were more serious. "What's going on with the case?"

I smiled as if everything was perfectly fine. "There's nothing for you to worry about. Javier is on it. Don't even think about it. Your job is to rest up and get well."

Some beeping went off at the machines and Eddie's face relaxed. The drugs they had him on were good.

His head rolled to the side, facing me, and he got a far-away, transfixed look. "You know," he slurred, "I almost died, pumpkin. I saw myself leaving this body and everything. It was extraordinary. You know who came to me?"

I shook my head, hating this conversation, yet so grateful he lived. "You must've been dreaming while under."

"No, it was real. Your mama came to me." He smiled dreamily and tears began to flow. "She's changed, somehow. I mean, she was still as beautiful as I remembered her to be, healthy before the cancer. Tonight, her countenance had a sweetness about it, kinder, I guess. She told me she loved me and apologized for her failings between us while living. She thanked me for being a great father to you and made me swear to continue to look after you since she isn't able to do it properly. I told her I didn't know how to be any other way. My kids are my life."

I smiled at him through blurry vision.

"Then she told me I wouldn't die if I agreed to her terms. She wanted me to take better care of myself, eat right and exercise. She made me agree." He chuckled a little. "Stubborn, amazing woman. When I did, she physically pushed my spirit back into my body." He sounded groggy as he smiled and squeezed my hand. "It was the most unusual feeling." A little sigh left his lips. "Then she kissed me and promised, with her blessing, I'd heal faster and my recovery would be speedy. I didn't want her to go . . ."

Mama appeared beside him and ran her fingers through his hair. "He won't remember this when he wakes."

"My Clara. I will remember." His eyelids fluttered, and he fought to open them and focus on her face. "My Clara, we did good with our little Marygene."

I sobbed openly. "Mama, thank you. I couldn't bear to lose him too."

"I know, my sweet girl. Edward and I are connected still." She stroked his face lovingly, and his lids closed and he drifted into slumber. "I suppose you're never free of your true love. I'm not sorry. Although, I will reap the repercussions of intervening where I wasn't supposed to, yet again." She sighed. "You'd think they'd see reason. My job is to do good and help those I love. How am I to do that with all these confounded rules to follow."

For the first time since Mama returned, I could see what a struggle all of this was for her. And I saw what Eddie mentioned. She did have a sweeter countenance, a goodness. A knock at the door broke into our moment, and Mama began to fade. "Trust yourself and rest assured, your father is going to make a full recovery."

The door creaked open. "Miss Brown, there's a deputy here to speak with you. He says it's urgent," the young nurse in pink said.

Javier stood just outside the doorway, looking grim.

"Okay. I'll be right out."

The nurse nodded, her eyes shifting around as she glanced from Javier to me. She'd probably seen the news broadcast, like everyone else.

"I'm sorry to intrude. I need a word."

I stood and kissed Eddie's forehead.

"How's he doing?" Javier whispered.

I smiled. "Better. He's going to pull through. Thanks for being here for me."

Closing the door softly behind me, I met his hazel gaze. Sam had certainly given me a different picture of how Javier thought of me. I wasn't ready to explore the idea yet. Maybe I would be one day soon.

"I'm glad to hear he's doing well." His eyes shifted around, and I could clearly read regret on his face. "I'm sorry to add to your burden, but we have a problem. A big one."

I deflated. "What now?" I closed my eyes and massaged my temples with both hands. "Honestly, Javy, I can't take any more bad news. If someone is slandering me or calling the tip line with bogus theories, just deal with it. I'm so over this. I know it's not a rational reaction under the circumstances, but there it is."

"Paul has been abducted."

I dropped my hands and stared at him. "Is this a joke?"

The hard set of his jaw spoke clearly.

"What do you mean, abducted? Like literally abducted?" I sounded like a broken record in my current state of brain fog.

"Literally abducted. And it gets worse."

How can it get any worse?

Javier pulled his phone from his pocket and hit play on a video.

My eyes widened at the image on the screen. *What in God's name is going on here?* I pulled the phone closer.

Paul, bruised and bloody, sat tied to a chair in a dark room with what appeared to be a bomb strapped to his chest. I watched as he held up a paper with today's date on it. A gloved person took the paper and replaced it with a whiteboard that read, RELEASE THE BANK FUNDS OR HE, LIKE LUCY DIES. DON'T MESS WITH US, YOU'VE SEEN WHAT WE CAN DO. WE MAKE BODIES DISAPPEAR.

"My God," I gasped.

Javy slid the phone back into his pocket. "It was posted to YouTube late last night, and about an hour ago, the media got wind of it and it made the early morning news."

"So . . . the robbery and the murder are now officially linked." I rubbed my neck. There was a multitude of knots.

"It would appear so. And since the airing, we've had a couple of calls about the fight you had with Paul at La Cocina Mexican restaurant."

"Oh . . . yeah. I can see how bad that looks. Especially with that message."

"Want to tell me about the fight?"

I met his gaze. I told him about the detective's visit and confronting Paul. I even confessed to not really caring about his relationship with Lucy.

"He was angry with me and left in a huff." I shrugged. "I care about him as much as I would anyone, but not enough to do something stupid like that. I mean, really?" I pushed through my muddled fears and shock-clouded brain to focus on the message. "Whoever is behind this is making people believe Betsy and I are to blame. It doesn't take a decipherer to see they used Betsy's words." The statement about making bodies disappear was all Bets. Ugh. "Combine that with the fight I had with Paul, the body being found on my back deck, and you've got your case." I leaned against the sterile wall and glanced at deputy Javier Reyes. I smiled as an overwhelming melancholy overtook me. "You aren't here to just share this with me. You're here to arrest me."

He stared at his tactical boots for a few long seconds. "Not arrest, just to bring you in."

I gave a bark of bitter laughter. "Right. As a person of interest that will be held upon arrival."

Once the toxicology report came back with an overdose of fentanyl, and it would, of that I felt completely certain, case closed. Someone really wanted me gone. And this person or these persons understood police procedures, the media, and small-town politics. Taint the populous views and ruin my and Betsy's reputations.

"Can I say goodbye to my family first?" I glanced back at the door where my father lay recovering.

Sam and Lindy would care for him, and it would give me comfort while I was away. I wasn't giving up, never would I give up, but it gave me peace of mind to know he had others.

"I just thought . . ." I rubbed my index finger between my brows as I fought emotion. Consumed with the weight of a thousand tons of impending doom, I began to break down. "I really believed everything would work out. I feel so alone."

Javy gripped my shoulders firmly and placed his forehead to mine. His face was fierce as his eyes flashed with a combination of anger and determination. His voice sounded thick. "I'm on your side. Always on your side. I'm not like your ex-husband, Alex, or that pathetic Paul. I'm not weak, nor do I shy away from a fight. I don't give up on people I care about. You need to trust me. I'll do whatever is necessary. Do you understand me?"

Unshed tears stung my eyes as I flung my arms around his neck. And as if he shared his strength with me, all the tears that threatened to pour in waves dried up. There are moments in life that alter you. Moments you know will change you forever. This moment, this critical moment in time, I knew this man before me would hold a permanent place in my life. And I swore to never give up on him either. I would get through this. One foot in front of the other.

I said goodbye to Eddie with a smile and stayed strong, assuring him all was well. He didn't need any other concerns that would hinder his healing. When I hugged Sam and Lindy goodbye, they didn't ask questions after I told them I had to go in and give a statement. Their minds were filled with concerns for Eddie. It was as it should be.

CHAPTER 23

Betsy and I sat shoulder to shoulder in the little holding cell in Peach Cove Sheriff's Department. It wasn't the first time I'd sat here. No, I'd been here before, under different circumstances. And oddly, life had prepared me for this. It struck me as funny how when you got battered around for a while, you toughened up enough to handle what life brought. Acceptance, though, now that was another matter altogether. The amiable person I'd once been had vanished, leaving a woman who didn't face adversity trembling. Well, not trembling as much. After my statement, I had to wait a while, alone. When they brought Betsy in, I'd been relieved and upset. Javier had prepared me the best he could. Still, nothing could truly prepare you for such an ordeal. Seeing my best friend's bottom lip quiver as the detective escorted her inside the cell caused my heart to break.

"Don't fall to pieces, Bets. We're going to get out of here. This isn't the end."

"Fall to pieces, me?" Betsy huffed. "I'm not going to give that jerk the satisfaction of seeing me cry. And the person responsible for framing us will pay."

I gave her a nod. "When we get out of here, we're going to tear this island apart. The killer is still here. And I think Sam might have had a decent theory after all. Lucy must have been an integral part of the plan to rob the bank. She might have gotten in over her head and someone offed her. And now they have Paul. The video was awful."

Betsy shivered. "I'm not sayin' I don't feel bad for Paul, I do. We owe him our life. But man, I'm glad it isn't one of us in his place."

"What kind of psycho could do that to another person?"

"I think you answered your own question with the psycho bit," Betsy said.

"Yeah, you're right. I hope they have some solid leads. I don't want Paul to end up like Lucy."

"Me either."

"It's weird how no one saw the biker other than those at the wedding. Maybe we're completely off about him. He could have seen whatever he wanted to and drove right onto Cove Ferry. And this David might be a different man altogether. He might not even be on the island. He could've been clear across the country when he and Lucy spoke." I ran my fingers through my messy hair. "Perhaps we and the police have been wrong about everything and that's why we're not getting anywhere."

"Well, it sure ain't us!" Betsy humphed. "And I'm still

having a hard time feeling sorry for Lucy. If she had gotten in over her head and she'd been the least bit decent to us, we'd have helped her." Betsy smoothed her wild hair behind her ears.

"Decent or not, I have every intention of helping her now."

"Why? She's the reason we're sitting here."

I scrunched up my face.

"Oh, the crazy mama juju thing. That's so annoyin'. I get helping folks out that deserve it. The dead being dead and all. Still, Lucy doesn't deserve our help."

"I'm beginning to believe we didn't know Lucy as well as we thought. The detective alluded to her past troubles."

"What sort of troubles?" Betsy curled her lip.

"I don't know, and it doesn't really matter. I just have to help her rest in peace."

"Fine. Only after we help ourselves, of course. And poor pitiful Paul, if we can, then Lucy."

Betsy and I locked gazes. "Yes. After that."

"Where is she? Where is my niece? I won't ask you again!" Aunt Vi's voice rang through the building.

Betsy smiled, despite her worry. Good ole Aunt Vi always brought some much-needed levity.

"Myers. Your lawyer and aunt are here." Detective Thornton came around the corner and unlocked the door.

"It's about time!" Betsy rose. "Come on, Marygene." She pulled at my shirt sleeve when I didn't rise.

"Only you, Miss Myers." The detective fumbled with the keys in the lock.

It stuck sometimes. Eddie kept a can of WD-40 in his desk drawer. I debated telling him about it and decided against it.

"It's fine." I squeezed my friend's hand. "You go on. I'm sure I'll be right behind you."

"When is her lawyer gettin' here?" Betsy fired at the detective. "My aunt ain't going to shut her trap if you don't let Marygene out too. Hell, I won't shut mine either."

"Miss Brown isn't who you should be concerned with. And I'm sure your aunt doesn't ever shut her trap, so that isn't much of a threat." Couldn't argue with his logic. "Would you like to speak with your attorney or not?"

Betsy hesitated.

I released my grip on her. "She does want to speak with him."

"I should wait on you." Betsy chewed on her fingernail. "We're a package deal. I'm your ride-or-die BFF."

"I haven't got all day, Miss Myers." The detective's impatience grew.

"Go!" I urged.

"Okay." Betsy threw her arms around my neck. "I'll see you on the outside."

She sniffed, wiped her eyes, and shuffled out of the cell. She lifted her hand right before she went around the corner.

The door remained open after she'd gone. The detective inclined his head, and we traded inquisitive stares. Was this a mind game? If so, I wasn't about to break down.

"Well," he said.

"Well what?" I crossed my legs and laced my fingers over my knee.

"Would you prefer to stay inside the cell or join me in the sheriff's office?" The heavy set of keys jingled as he shifted them to his other hand.

"Are you serious?"

"I'm never not serious. Life hasn't afforded me a sense of humor."

He could say that again. Slowly, I rose. The hour and a half had felt more like an eternity inside the cell. And if I reacted true to my emotions, I'd run from the room. Instead, I held my armor in place and followed the detective out the door. My armor slipped a little when the door clanged shut behind me, and I jumped. I squared my shoulders and marched after him anyway.

Aunt Vi charged me the second she spied me coming around the corner. She wrapped her arms around me and squeezed until I thought my ribs would crack. "It worked! He finally relented. I told that Latin fella and the surly detective I was going to be a boil on the backside of this department if they didn't let both of my girls free." She rocked me back and forth. "I'm so glad your daddy is okay. I prayed for him. We all did."

"Thank you." I hugged her back.

"I can't believe the nerve of some folks. Harassing a poor girl who nearly lost her father."

I didn't have to see to Aunt Vi's face to know the intense threatening glare she aimed at law enforcement.

"Don't you worry, sweet girl. We're going to get this sorted out. That detective has more brains than he lets on. He knows you and my Betsy are innocent."

I patted her back. "You're right. It's going to be okay. I'm going to go and speak with the detective now." I stared into her sweet round face and smiled. "Thank you for praying for Eddie."

Aunt Vi bobbed her head and then placed herself protectively in front of me. The glare I imagined was there and in full force. "Remember this, Detective Big Shot, you're not the only one who can call a press conference. You mistreat my girls and I'll shout it from the rooftops. I'll use every dollar I have to investigate your background and ruin what life you have left." With that, she spun on her sandaled heels and left. I had to hand it to her. It was a hell of a way to leave an impression. I felt grateful to have her on my side and to know she cared about me.

"You ready?" Detective Thornton opened the door to Eddie's office, and I walked inside.

The second the door softly shut behind me, I fought tears. I smelled Eddie's cologne lingering. Even though I knew he had a bottle stashed in his desk, I wanted to believe it came from him. I scanned the images on his desk. I caressed his smiling face with my index finger before I sat in the chair opposite.

"I hear your father pulled through." The detective handed me a Coke from the machine and propped himself against the desk.

I took the can and cracked it open, more parched than I realized. I assumed it was from the machine in the break room because it felt semi-cool. The other machine never kept the drinks cold.

"He did." I swallowed and steered away from personal family stuff. "What are y'all doing to find Paul?"

"Everything we can." He stared straight through me. "We have quite a predicament on our hands, don't we?" The detective folded his arms.

I didn't respond, unsure as I tread these unfamiliar waters. My attorney wasn't here, and I certainly had no intention of accidentally incriminating myself.

"Let's discuss the facts."

"What are the facts as you see them, Detective?"

He turned, leaned back, and took a file from the top of

the desk. "We have three crimes. A murder, an attempted robbery, and now a kidnapping. On the murder, we have the drugs found in your cottage. A match per the toxicology report. The body was found on your property and your boyfriend has been kidnapped after a public argument you two engaged in. We have witness testimony stating Betsy threatened the first victim after the victim started an argument with you." He dropped the file back on the desk. "We have a video where your boyfriend is holding a sign with similar threats Betsy made."

Nerves did somersaults in my stomach. Yeah, I sounded guilty, all right. Anything I said could and would be held against me in a court of law. "When is my lawyer arriving? I would feel better if he were here before I answered any questions."

"Wise of you. But the thing is, Miss Brown. I don't think you're guilty."

The inner warning alarms were blaring loudly. *Trap! Trap! Trap!* I straightened in the seat and took another sip from the can.

"Skeptical. Sure. I understand. I don't know what's going on here. Something is wrong. I've been a cop for over twenty years. I have a sixth sense."

Javy had said something similar the other day. What was with law officers and their analogies? The phone on the desk rang and the detective leaned over and answered it. He grumbled a few clipped sentences into the receiver that, in my current state of mind, sounded like gibberish. I only caught *Mr. O'Malley* and *agreement*. My mind still spun with the declaration he'd just made, and I had to get it together. He set the phone down and went to open the door.

In walked my attorney, briefcase in hand. The older

freckled man had a strong posture. His face showed no fear or concern. I wished I had his confidence.

"Has the detective been treating you well?" he asked as he reached me.

"Yes. He's also just been telling me an interesting story."

His eyes slanted toward the detective, and I read a warning within his gaze. "Yes, I can imagine he did."

"She was never at risk. We were just having a friendly chat." The detective appeared to remain stoic. He leaned forward and placed both palms on the desk as he faced us. "Weren't we, Miss Brown?"

I glanced from the detective to my attorney. "What's going on here? What am I missing?"

Mr. O'Malley turned to me. "We can have a private discussion first, or if you're ready to get out of this place, you can trust I'm doing everything in your best interest. With your long night, I assumed you'd want the latter."

His blue eyes were clear and reassuring. Eddie trusted him implicitly. I would too.

"Whatever you think is best. I'm okay to move forward."

He smiled approvingly before wiping his expression clean and digging into his briefcase. For some reason, I felt proud I'd given him the correct response. He pulled out a printed document and put his cell phone on the desk. My eyes went wide as he opened the voice recorder app. He spoke clearly and concisely, announcing the date, time, and names of everyone in the room. Then he turned to the detective.

"Everything Detective Thornton requested has been added to the agreement. I'd like the record to state that anything spoken here or hereafter regarding said agreement will have no impact on my client in a negative way. Even in the event the department should later decide to pursue a separate set of criminal charges against her. Which I would advise against. I would also state that any information spoken here may be used in my client's case if the department dares to pursue such a case."

"Agreed and duly noted," the detective said.

The ruddy-faced man pulled a chair close to me. "Some new evidence has come to light, my dear. This evidence has led Detective Thornton to the conclusion that it would have been impossible for you to have committed these crimes. Time-stamped evidence of your presence at the hospital after the wedding, a traffic camera recording, plus the hospital footage when you were there with your father. There's no way you could be at two places at once, and Paul held this morning's paper."

My heart hammered so loudly in my ears, and my head felt clogged. It took me a minute to process the information. I glanced from Mr. O'Malley to the detective.

"Not only that. We also managed to get a partial fingerprint taken from the drug in your cottage. Plus, upon further analysis of the video, the reflection of a person with dark curly hair was captured. A forensics team has swept through Paul's apartment and found the place cleaned out. Not a single personal effect was able to be located. And someone did a proficient job of wiping it clean."

My mouth dropped open, and I instantly closed it. Could I really be hearing this? A professional clean-out job, here on the island?

Mr. O'Malley took a seat next to me and placed his hand over both of mine. They went still, where I'd been twisting them subconsciously in my lap. It was a sweet, fatherly gesture, and I had to fight back tears.

"I had this drawn up this morning. It's to protect you from any prosecutorial endeavors the department may decide to pursue if the case they are attempting to make falls through. All it needs is the detective's signature. He has his own copy. This one is for you." He passed the document over to the big man looming over us. He signed in a perfunctory manner. This detective truly didn't believe me to be guilty.

As if reading my mind, the detective met my gaze. "You were correct in your analysis. This isn't a crime of passion. These are carefully planned and executed crimes. Someone would have to understand police procedure. And I don't mean a daughter of a local sheriff." The detective picked up a photo and presented it to me. My heart nearly stopped. They'd blown up the image of the reflection in the video, showing the back of someone's head. A head that reminded me of Alex's. Curlier perhaps, like when he didn't dry it after swimming or showering.

No, it can't be.

My hands trembled as I handed the picture back. "Okay. If you don't believe I'm guilty, why did you have Deputy Reyes haul me out of the hospital while I sat by my father's bed?"

"I regret having to order that. Like I said before, someone is trying to frame you and your friend Betsy. If we allow said person to believe we're considering filing charges, we'll have a better chance at catching them. Deputy Reyes has been working tirelessly to prove your innocence to me. He had an old colleague analyze the video in record time."

My bottom lip quivered. *Thank you, Javy.*

"Betsy is being questioned by Deputy Reyes in the other room about her cousin."

I could have fallen from my chair. Sweet Lord, they caught the resemblance too. "You actually believe Alex Myers is capable of killing his wife, framing his cousin and ex-girlfriend, along with orchestrating a bank robbery while playing the grieving widower?" It all sounded like something out of a movie. A horrible B-level movie.

"It's something to consider. He has motive, he had opportunity, and he has the means."

I scrubbed my face with my hands. "Detective, in the last forty-eight hours, I've been accused of murder and kidnapping, along with attempted armed robbery. My father almost died, and I've spent two hours in a stinky cell. My best friend is beyond stressed out because of all of this mess, and a guy I was seeing has been abducted. Now you tell me a man I've known my entire life is behind it all. It's too much."

"I believe this concludes our meeting for today." Mr. O'Malley shut off the recording. He helped me to my feet. "My client is exhausted. We'll discuss this at a more opportune date."

"It's your decision, Miss Brown. But like you said, a guy you were seeing has been abducted. Don't you want to help?"

"Of course I do. It's just, right now, I'm fried and wouldn't be of use to anyone. I'm having trouble thinking straight. My brother is at the hospital by our father's side. I need to shower and take a nap and then I'm going back to be with my family. I'm taking Betsy with me. She needs a break."

I shook Mr. O'Malley's hand. "Thank you, sir."

I started for the door, pausing with my hand on the knob. I turned and pierced the detective with my own stern glare. "After that, you have my word. I'll help you. Under one condition. I will work with Deputy Reyes and only Deputy Reyes. Not that I'm saying I believe Alex is guilty, but whoever it is needs to be stopped, and poor Lucy deserves to rest in peace."

The detective's face held marginal surprise at my mentioning Lucy. "You are a good woman. We'll find your boyfriend. Rest well, Miss Brown." The detective rose to his full height. "I apologize for what you've endured by my hand. Your request to work with Deputy Reyes is granted."

I still didn't like this man, and if framing me would suit his purposes, I believed he'd do it in a heartbeat. I thought about replying with a mocking retort. Something like how generous he was for granting me such a kindness while I helped him build his case. Or perhaps he could take his grants and shove them where the sun didn't shine and make his freakin' case on his own. It would've been childish, and I hoped he'd keep his word and find Paul.

Instead, I nodded, turned, and left the room.

CHAPTER 24

A shower never felt so good. I shampooed my hair twice for good measure as my mind spun with a plethora of worries. Where was Paul? Was he okay? Were they hurting him? Who would hate me enough to want to frame me for theft and murder? *Please don't let it be Alex.* I tried to be a good person, love my fellow man, and give back where I could. I jumped, poking myself in the eyes, as my phone blared from the other room, where it charged. Rubbing my left eye, I turned off the water, wrapped up in my terry cloth robe just as it went to voice mail. I held my hand on the tie and considered hopping back in the shower. Mr. Wrigley rubbed against my bare legs and meowed loudly.

"Is your feeder empty?"

As if he could understand me, he lifted his tail and marched toward the kitchen.

"It has to have just run out. I checked it earlier this week." He was right, only a few small pieces remained. Like I thought, just ran out. "I'm sorry, little fella. It's been a chaotic couple of days."

He gave me a look that said he didn't care one bit.

"Gee, thanks for the support."

He meowed as if to say, "Who me?"

I hefted the bag of cat food and went about the task of refilling His Majesty's meal dispenser. I leaned down and we engaged in one of our staring contests. Mr. Wrigley gave me a bemused expression as he glanced in my direction with his head cocked to one side, looking positively adorable.

"Yeah, yeah, you always pull that you're-so-innocent routine, and I'm the one with a couple of screws loose. I've got your number, fella. You and I are way too much alike."

My cell rang again and, with a good scratch behind the ears, I left Mr. Wrigley to enjoy his meal. My mood had lifted marginally; Mr. Wrigley had that effect on me. I missed the call again and I checked the number. Unknown number. Huh, probably a telemarketer. I placed the phone back onto the bedside table as I stretched out on top of the cool comforter. My last thought was I should probably dry my hair and I hoped I wasn't getting sick.

Betsy, Aunt Vi, and I sat out on the back deck drinking coffee and gazing at the sunset. They made me promise to allow myself a few minutes to breathe and not be consumed with guilt about Paul. I was trying, but how could I enjoy a lovely evening while he remained captive? I needed to rest or I'd be no use to him or anyone. I had real limitations and needed to address them when they reared their ugly heads. It was okay to take time for self-care.

"Eddie's doing well then? He'd have to be for them to have him up and walking to the bathroom." Aunt Vi took a cookie from the platter I'd placed on the table.

"He is. I spoke to Sam after my nap." I sneezed into my elbow and took a tissue from the box.

Betsy held out her hand for the box of Puffs I had next to me, snatched it from my outstretched hand, and loudly blew her nose. She and I both seemed to have come down with some sort of cold or bug at the same time. Which was the reason I was sitting here instead of at the hospital with my family. Eddie's immune system couldn't be compromised.

"I bet you girls caught something from that nasty cell they had y'all in. Someone should do something about the uninhabitable conditions of the correctional institution on this island." Aunt Vi shook her head.

"They really should!" Betsy took a sip from her mug. "I think I saw black mold growing in the corner. We probably got a disease or somethin'."

"Relax. We didn't get a disease in a couple of hours in a holding cell. And it's not technically a correctional institution, Aunt Vi." I succumbed to yet another sneezing fit.

Betsy handed over a box of cold medication.

"Ugh." I popped two pills and knocked them back with the last of my coffee.

Aunt Vi had steadily headed for the steps. "Listen, y'all know Aunt Vi is all about her girls. And if I thought my presence here would be of aid, I'd stay. However, now that we know where the detective's head is on this case, there's no need for me to put this ole bod through a bout of whatever y'all have."

"You're right. Save yourself while you still can." Betsy moaned melodramatically.

I waved to a descending Aunt Vi, not blaming her one bit as she waddled down the beach toward her cottage.

"You know what I think?" Betsy said as the breeze blew and we both shivered. Not a good sign. "I think we should head over and have a conversation with my cousin. If the detective thinks he's behind this, we should show our cards. I mean, I don't believe in a million years that Alex, even as stupid as he's being, would ever set us up for murder. If we call him out, we might actually get somewhere."

"On one hand, I don't think that's such a bad idea. Why wouldn't he see reason and look at the situation objectively? If he did, he would see how absurd his notion that we're involved is. But now that I've had a moment to consider things, something else is at play here."

"I'm listening." Betsy ate a lemon shortbread cookie.

"The detective is a smart guy. He'd have to be. He's a decorated lawman. He had a vendetta against towns that hide crime, which is good, though he also has been accused of being dirty when it suits him. I know he signed the agreements ensuring they can't come after me again. I'm still having a difficult time trusting him. I mean, what if he wants to sink our little island." I raised my hands. "Metaphorically speaking. I'm going way out in left field here, using the whole what-ifs to suit us. All our other theories proved fruitless."

"Sure, we never get anywhere without the what-ifs." Betsy ate another cookie.

"I made a call to our friend Calhoun earlier, and he agreed it could be plausible. You know, he's always had a special interest in our infamous detective." Roy Calhoun was a reporter who I'd become close friends with a few years back. He and I shared a moment in time that bonded folks together like no other: death. Calhoun was now a family man with a couple of stepkids and a pretty wife. He was still in the field and still pursuing the theory that Thornton framed his brother for murder. He'd gladly share intel.

Betsy's eyes went wide as she nodded. "I like it. Thornton is digging up our past, why shouldn't we dig up his?"

"What if the detective had a personal interest in the fraudulent wire transfer? From what Calhoun's gathered, our eager lawman has a mountain of debt and will be facing retirement soon."

"You think he might be behind all of this?"

I shook my head. "Not all of it, but perhaps the bank heist. It's way out there, I know. Just a what-if."

"Hmm. That's a lot of what-ifs." Betsy wiped her running nose.

"Yeah, I know. I just keep worrying about Paul. I got the impression the detective didn't believe the abductors would kill him and lose their leverage. I'm just not sure if me helping will do all that much good. Especially if they're using me to trap Alex." I drummed my nails on the table. "Come on." I hopped up and decided to put all these what-ifs on the whiteboard.

Five minutes later I had it all written out. Betsy sat on the chair sipping from her mug. In the middle of the board I drew a large circle. Inside the circle I wrote a few dollar signs. I placed all of those affected around the circle: Lucy, Alex, Paul, Betsy, and Me. "Okay. Maybe we've been going about this the wrong way. What if the robbery was the main focus the entire time. Lucy worked at the bank and had access to all the pertinent information regarding bank transfers, routing numbers, and bank procedures." I drew a line from the circle to Lucy. "Lucy's murder, followed by the attempt on our lives, showed skill in diversion tactics." I used a red dry-erase marker to write *murder* beside Lucy and *car bombs* next to Betsy and me. I added a question mark between Lucy and Paul. Now that he had become the killer's latest target, the alleged relationship between them was plausible and relevant to this case.

"Don't forget that someone placed a bomb under Paul's company vehicle as well."

I added it, as well as the abduction, next to Paul's name, along with the unidentified dark-headed person from the video, and then wrote the detective's name at the top of the board before stepping back and examining my work. I'd spent a minimal amount of time in Paul's apartment. It'd been basic, with masculine furniture and nothing hanging on the walls. He had a mother somewhere who suffered from dementia. Other than her, he had no other family to speak of. He sent money to the care home monthly. I recalled him discussing with the proprietor regarding her health and care. Now I wished I had paid more attention to his life. Unfortunately, I couldn't go back to his home. All evidence of his existence there had been erased. Who would be able to accomplish such a task? Alex? Hard to believe. The detective certainly would. Another stretch. What about the biker? How had he vanished like he had without another soul seeing? Had they checked the ferry registry?

"What's that buzzing sound?"

I glanced around, listening for the buzzing Betsy refer-enced. "I don't hear anything. Your ears must be clogged." I sneezed a few times and sat next to Betsy. "We need to go over to Alex's. Preferably when he isn't there." I wanted to go through Lucy's things without upsetting him. And I knew from Aunt Vi that Lucy had practically moved in with him before the wedding.

Betsy sat up straighter. "I can have Aunt Vi case the joint before we go over. I'm sure she could get Meemaw to create a diversion." She tapped her chin and jumped. "Oh, I've got it! Meemaw has this pinhole leak under the sink in her kitchen. She's been after him to come over and repair it for over a month now. You know how she is about paying for repairs she believes are an easy fix."

"It's been leaking for months?" I picked up my mug of now lukewarm coffee.

Betsy nodded. "She put a bucket underneath it." She whipped out her cell phone and called Aunt Vi. While those two chatted, or more accurately schemed, I thought about Lucy and the Carmichaels. I couldn't get their dis-traught faces out of my mind, and I wondered how they were coping. There were so many victims. So many hurt people, I wished I could help. I had to be careful too. The person behind all of this could be out to use me to hurt others. And I was beginning to feel royally pissed by the audacity of the selfish evil person who wreaked havoc on all involved.

"Okay, it's all set. Aunt Vi is on it!" Betsy stood. "There it is again. The buzzing."

Betsy and I went to investigate.

We followed the sound into my bedroom and to the source, my cell.

"I must have accidentally switched it to vibrate."

"See! I knew I wasn't hearing things. I've got amazin' hearing. Superpower hearing." She flopped down face-first on my bed. "Your mattress is so comfy, and this comforter is so soft. Maybe we should take a nap." Betsy sniffed loudly.

I quickly handed her another tissue in attempts to avoid having to have my comforter dry-cleaned, and then checked my phone.

Whoever they were left a voice mail. Oddly though, the unknown voice mail had been recorded while I'd been in custody, according to the time stamp. I'd not noticed it. I hit the voice mail icon.

"Marygene, babe, I need your help," Paul rasped.

A vise gripped my heart. Betsy flopped around and sat up straight on the bed, her eyes wide.

"You're going to receive some instructions soon. Please do everything you're asked to or they'll kill me. Please. I love you."

Some scuffles were audible. A combination of guilt, fear, and anger consumed me.

A robotic voice said, "He'll die, slowly and painfully if you notify your lover-boy deputy or the authorities that we contacted you or share our instructions. Get it? No police! Go about your life as normal and don't alert anyone or you'll start receiving pieces of your boyfriend."

Horrific, agonizing screams came next.

Chills ran through my body and the phone slipped from my fingers to clatter to the floor.

"Sweet Lord," Betsy gasped and leapt to her feet.

We stared at the pink case that encompassed my iPhone, and we clutched on to each other. The little device gave me such terror, as if at any second it could reach out and strangle the life from me. Blood thrummed in my ears. My knees gave out, and I slumped down on the bed, taking Betsy with me. She pulled me closer. We just sat there. Staring.

"What should we do? We must do something. I have to call the sheriff's department or at least Javy."

Betsy shook her head. "They said not to contact your lover boy."

"You think they were referring to Javier?" I gaped.

"They certainly don't mean Alex. You know any other deputies with the Peach Cove Sheriff's Department?"

The phone vibrated against the floor. I squeaked.

"Answer it!" Betsy shouted, and released her hold on my arm. "No, don't!" She grabbed my arm again and jerked.

"Stop it. I have to answer it." I went to my knees. My trembling fingers groped to gain purchase on the rubber case. The unknown number caused tendrils of panic to swirl within my midsection as I hit the speaker icon. "He . . . hello. Paul!"

"Marygene!" Paul's shaky voice rasped.

"Paul! My God. Are you okay? Where are you?"

"Follow the instructions . . . Please . . . A-and don't tell a soul. I can't t-take much more of this . . ." The line went silent.

"Wait! What instructions? Paul!"

He was gone.

I paced the floor in front of the whiteboard after I'd added the incident to the board. Bets and I had gone back and forth on the right thing to do.

"I really think I should call Javier. What if they kill Paul?"

"They're probably planning to kill him anyway." Betsy chewed on the nail on her index finger. "I mean, they have no reason to keep him alive. They're already in this for murder and attempted robbery, what's another count?"

I hated to agree with her as I rubbed my aching head. "Why would they contact me instead of the sheriff's department? They have the authority to back everyone off. I sure don't."

Betsy shrugged. "Poor Paul. He's boring as dry toast, but he did save our lives. No one deserves to die for being born a bore. Besides, you're the closest person to him on the island and he said he loves you."

"Yeah, I heard that." My shoulders slumped forward. "What if they took him because of me, Bets?"

Betsy waved her hand in the air, "Maybe he was just an easy target. You think they said no cops because the detective has him?"

"I don't know. Calhoun swears the detective's dirty." I began pacing again. A light bulb in my brain fired to life. "We have to think of this logically. What could they possibly be after? Easy. Money. I don't work for the bank. I haven't any way of releasing funds." To borrow an expression from Sam, my brain wasn't firing on all cylinders. I whipped around toward Betsy. "Okay, at the risk of sounding redundant, let's go through it again."

Betsy nodded.

"The killers wanted to frame us in the first place. Every decision they made was perfectly calculated to enact a crime that pointed to us. Lucy died in the reception tent. The poison was placed under my sink. They dumped her body on my back deck and your words were used on the abduction video. That, along with your aunt pointing the finger at you, makes you a perfect accomplice."

"Oh, right!" Betsy clapped her hands loudly. "If they have us following some lame-ass instructions, it'll probably be a trap. Another piece of the puzzle to frame us."

I paused to blow my nose. "On the other hand, they must have someone watching us. Whoever they are must've known we were in custody and later released. And they certainly wouldn't want me to involve the authorities."

"Who would have that knowledge? And know about the sexual tension between you and that hunk of burnin' Latin love. The detective, of course and . . ." Betsy pulled a tissue from the box and froze.

"Alex," we both said in unison.

CHAPTER 25

Betsy and I fell asleep around one a.m. The drowsiness side effect of the cold medication had been a huge help, since otherwise we weren't going to get any sleep after the phone calls. Both of us had shifts at the diner, and we did our best to work without spreading germs and acting as if everything was normal. We shared worried glances in passing. Nothing more.

My hands were dry from so many washings and my sister fussed over me like a mother hen. "I'm fine. I swear." I dutifully sipped the hot tea with honey that she'd thrust into my hands a moment ago.

"You don't look fine. Your eyes are peaked, just like Olivia's." Jena Lynn put the back of her hand to my forehead, her face drawn with concern. "Not feverish. That's good. Still, you need to take care of yourself."

My sister cared deeply and put me at such ease, I almost unburdened about Paul before shoving the absurd idea away. None of this touched her, and I wouldn't do anything that would draw her in. I put on a smile. "I will, and until I'm fully recovered, I plan to keep my distance from Eddie."

"That's a good idea. Your immune system is probably low because of all the stress that stupid detective put you through. I have a good mind to go over to the department and bless him out. How dare he come onto our island and throw his you-know-what around as if we're all so impressed." Jena Lynn's face flushed red. "Somebody should do something about his incompetence. And now that poor Eddie is down and out, he'll probably try to take over Peach Cove."

I shook my head and coughed in my elbow. "I don't think so. I have a feeling he wants to be off this island at his first opportunity." Especially if he had anything to do with the attempted robbery and abduction. Even in my thoughts it sounded crazy. Too crazy to fit.

"I sure hope you're right."

In hustled Jena Lynn's sister-in-law, her face bright red and glossy. "Sorry I'm a tad late. My stupid car wouldn't start." She rushed toward the sink and wet a kitchen cloth. "I had my neighbor give me a jump." She turned and leaned her tall, lean frame against the sink as she dabbed her face with the cloth. "And to make matters worse, the compressor went out on my air conditioner again." Her small almond-shaped eyes darted from Jena Lynn to me. "I interrupted something, didn't I?"

My sister and I both smiled. Hannah brought a great energy to our staff.

"Not at all. I was just telling my mucus-filled sister to take it easy." Jena Lynn squeezed my hand. "Now Hannah's here, you go have some food and cut out early. Some rest will do you good."

"Oh, yikes. I hope you feel better, Marygene. There's a nasty bug going around." Hannah took a step away, and I laughed.

"I get it. Y'all don't want my germs, and I don't blame you. I'm going." I left the kitchen after thanking them both. Some distance from me would be good for them in more ways than one.

Sam had also given me a wide berth today, which was wise. One of Eddie's kids needed to be available in case Lindy required assistance. Not that she would. She had a full staff she could call on if she so chose. Eddie would be the best cared for patient on Peach Cove. I thought back to his confession that he saw Mama. I couldn't thank her enough for sacrificing her atonement for our benefit. She really had made some changes during her time here. And I certainly could use her input in my current predicament.

Betsy and I ate together at the counter. I ordered cheesy potato soup and a salmon BLT with spicy garlic mayo. It was difficult to eat with a sore throat and swimming nerves. Knowing I needed my strength, I forced it down anyway. The more I considered things, the more I wondered about Detective Thornton and battled in disbelief with his theory Alex had something to do with all of this. Sure, Alex hadn't been himself lately. And he'd showed his worst side toward me and everyone else since he lost Lucy. Deep down, I still didn't believe it. I couldn't believe it. I loved him. Always would. No, we'd never be as we were; still, I hoped for our friendship to continue. I tested the temperature of my soup before spooning some into my mouth.

"It's all set," Betsy whispered out of the right side of

her mouth. "Alex is going over to Meemaw's at four. Aunt Vi will pick us up here at the diner in a few and drive us over to his house. She'll stand lookout in case he or Aunt Traitor comes over." Betsy huddled over her double-stack burger and took a huge bite. The cheese oozed out from in between the patties.

Betsy had insisted last night that her aunt Regina might be Alex's accomplice. She'd been known in the Myers family as a gold digger. I forced myself not to argue the point that the Myers hadn't wealth to begin with, so that didn't make any sense at all. I got the point that Alex's mom wasn't and never would be popular within the family. From the day of Lucy's death, the woman hadn't wavered on her stance. We'd just been lucky we hadn't seen her around lately.

"Marygene, girl." Miss Glenda came by the counter and broke into my reverie. "I just can't believe all this mess. We heard about your and Betsy's unfortunate incarceration. Terrible, just terrible."

I decided not to correct the old woman by reminding her we hadn't been charged, much less incarcerated. It wouldn't have done a bit of good.

"Thank you, ma'am. It was rough," Betsy said, and I glared at her. She snickered a little in response.

"That's why Sister and I always said we didn't want no outsiders butting their noses into our island's business. With all these new folks around, there's no wonder we have those darn thieves too. Incompetent ones at that. Please, if they wanted to rob the island blind, they should've nabbed someone we cared about, not that skinny boy who was always skulking around with the dead girl. Folks round here don't need an investigation to know you and Betsy aren't guilty of anything. It's ludicrous." She grabbed a couple of sugars from the caddy in front of me and went to sit back down in her booth. I supposed the detective's plan to allow rumors about Betsy and me being persons of interest had worked. It was a no-brainer on this island.

"That's right," the couple from the booth behind us agreed. "Y'all aren't the ones responsible. My bet is on the delinquent on the motorcycle. Riding that loud machine to show off. Idiot."

I turned around on my chair to ask if they'd seen the man again when Miss Glenda's words sunk in. *Wait a minute!* "Miss Glenda. You're saying you saw Paul and Lucy together on multiple occasions?"

She nodded. "Oh, yes. I told the detective I saw them arguing by the tulip bulbs at Harold's Hardware a spell back. When they saw me, they hushed up real quick. It was shameful behavior, but I didn't think anything about it because that Lucy girl always seemed to be arguing or fooling around with some man." Her eyes narrowed, and she shook her head in a disapproving fashion before leaning in close and whispering conspiratorially, "I'm not one to speak ill of the dead, you know—however, I also saw her carrying on with the wild boy, you know, the biker fella."

Betsy gasped and my eyes widened.

Betsy asked, "You positive, Miss Glenda?"

The older woman gave a solid head nod. "One hundred percent positive. I saw them behind Mason's Market a few weeks before she died. Mr. Mason always lets me go around back and use the spoiled produce for fertilizer for my garden." The woman smiled. "It really works wonders with my tomatoes."

"I do the same thing, Glenda." Miss Susie, the senior woman having lunch with her husband, Forest, in the booth across from us, agreed. "And I use my used coffee grounds too."

Miss Glenda nodded approvingly. "I heard of that on the lawn-and-garden program. I might start using my coffee grounds too."

"Excuse me, ladies." I kept my tone as calm as I could manage. "I don't mean to be rude, but you were telling me about Lucy and the biker, Miss Glenda . . ."

She bobbed her head. "Yes, of course. I went back there to meet Mr. Mason at the shipment door and the two of them were really going at it, arguing about him showing his face on the island. She said something like, 'I'm done. Forget it.' The girl was waving her finger in his face, hollering about she wasn't dying for him."

"And the tall fella grabbed her arm and said, 'I guess we'll see about that' and jerked her to him and kissed her right on the mouth."

"Say what? We have another eyewitness account?" Betsy began coughing.

"That's right, and she seemed none too eager to get out of that lip lock. Her hands were all over him until Mr. Mason opened the doors and they saw they had an audience." She shook her head again. "Trashy behavior when she was engaged to the Myers boy."

The fact he threatened her with death before they went at it made a lot of sense, with her loving those disgusting death spreads. I bet she didn't believe she'd actually die.

"Here's your order, Miss Glenda. I put in the end pieces for Miss Sally. I know how much she likes them." Rebecca handed her the bag and smiled.

Miss Glenda held out a five-dollar bill. A nice tip from a senior on a fixed income. "Thank you, honey. Sister sure will be grateful." Miss Glenda finished her coffee and turned to Betsy while my mind whirled with this new development. "You get yourself a good peach brandy from the liquor store. Pour yourself a jigger full and mix it with some raw honey from Mason's Market. He has the local honey with all the wonderful antibiotic properties still in it." She made a face. "Not that cheap industrial stuff. It'll cure that cough in no time. Help you sleep too." She winked at Betsy.

"Glenda's right. We use cinnamon whiskey and honey. Works like a charm every time." Miss Susie smiled. Her face lit up in that warm, loving, grandmotherly way.

"I better get this food home to Sister while it's still hot. Y'all take care." Miss Glenda gave my arm a squeeze. "Send your daddy our love and tell him we're praying for his speedy recovery."

"I sure will. Thank you, ma'am."

Miss Glenda patted Betsy and waved bye to her contemporaries.

Betsy and I returned to our food and attempted to process the elderly woman's revelations regarding the biker and Paul. What was he doing arguing with her? And was Lucy cheating on Alex with two guys? I couldn't imagine that. I had a hard time keeping up with one. Betsy nudged me and hitched a thumb over her shoulder to the rumblings behind us. Conversations regarding the investigation, Eddie, and new gossip about Paul and Lucy commenced around us, though softly. I spun on the stool, intending to digest the chatter in case another little nugget of relevance presented itself.

"Yakety-yakking, that's all you women do," said Mr. Forest, and the natives went from unified to downright hostile.

Every female in earshot turned to glare at the old man, who seemed unperturbed and swallowed another bite of pie. "It's all the sheriff's department seems to do too. Ain't no one been arrested yet. If the sheriff hadn't fallen ill, he'd have done something. That makes me wonder if he was targeted. Perhaps someone wanted him to have a heart attack." He tapped his forehead with the back of his fork as if proud of his deductions.

"Ya think it's possible?" Betsy asked with big eyes.

The old man gave a solid nod. "I do. Those confounded outsiders." He made an obscene gesture that made Betsy snicker.

"Hush, Forest. Quit showing these girls your worst side." Miss Susie gave her husband a warning glare.

"It's the only side I got, woman." He turned back toward Betsy and me. "I'm on y'all's side. I told the idiot detective that dog just won't hunt. You gals have lived here all your lives. Marygene's mama was well-known and respected. Her daddy's the sheriff, for God's sake. All y'all banked with Peach Cove Credit Union, like the rest of us. Only a moron would believe that one day, out of the blue, you'd decide to rob folks and leave behind everything your families built." He shook his head in obvious disgust. "You know. Now that I think about it. I have the perfect solution!" He tossed his napkin, which had been tucked under his chin, onto his plate.

The old man was riled up now.

"Do nothin'," he sneered. "Let that crook, who I recollect is the biker fella, blow the boy up like they threatened on that YouTube thingy my daughter showed me."

Betsy and I exchanged a glance. Guess they hadn't taken the video down soon enough or shut the media down in time. Making the case yet again, secrets on this island were difficult to keep, and I worried about repercussions if I kept the one Betsy and I were sitting on.

"Something was off about him anyhow. You heard Glenda. Catting around with that woman engaged to the Myers boy. He's been through it because of them. Although, that does beg the question why they don't have a manhunt going on. Betsy, if I was Alex, I'd root the bastard out myself instead of laying back and coming across as weak."

Miss Susie shook her gray head, and I was speechless as the man ranted. I got the impression he enjoyed conspiracies and low discussion, where he held everyone's attention. Betsy ate her fries and leaned forward, listening intently, and I could tell she worried now more than ever about Alex's involvement. There wasn't a Myers breathing that could stand weakness.

"Hell, maybe they'll blow each other up and rid the island of the riffraff altogether and stop bothering you girls and give the Myers boy closure. I don't know about y'all, but I'm tired of it. Aren't you tired of it, Betsy?"

Betsy nodded with vigor. "I am! You're right! Guilty or not, the nerve of them defamin' our characters." Betsy wiped her nose and leaned forward. "Mr. Forest, you think that blast would take out more than the killer and Paul?"

The man shook his head, and I shot Betsy a warning glare. I didn't want her encouraging the man or publicly incriminating herself.

People are listening, for heaven's sake.

The old man leaned back and picked something from between his front two teeth. "Well, I reckon if it's a pipe bomb, probably not."

Betsy clapped her hands together. "We just need the blast to be big enough to—"

"While we appreciate the sentiment and belief in Betsy's and my innocence, we certainly wouldn't want anyone harmed. My goodness. The department needs to root out this lunatic and save the innocent. Paul is a victim here too. Wouldn't it be better to wish for peace and harmony on the island?" I quickly interjected.

The old man huffed and folded his arms. Miss Susie shot him a glare that said, *You're going to get an earful when we leave*. She'd do a way better job than I could, too.

"Peace certainly would be ideal, dears. You'll have to forgive ole Forest here. He doesn't know when to hush up. I keep telling him to keep his disturbing opinions to himself." The older woman scooted out of the booth and tossed her large carryall over her shoulder. "I'll be praying for your daddy and the rest of this mess. The Lord will sort it all out, you'll see." Miss Susie cast a scowl at her husband. "Come on, Forest, we need to get to the house before Dana brings the kids over."

The bald heavyset man scooped up the last of his pie, humphed, tossed a couple of bills on the table, and leaned toward Betsy. "You've got a good head on your shoulders, gal, and a heart of a warrior, like me." He thumped his chest with his fist before he followed his wife toward the door.

Heart of a warrior. I rolled my eyes and turned back around in the chair toward my meal, though my appetite had waned. Betsy was still smiling to herself. Lord help us.

Moments later the door jingled open and in waltzed Aunt Vi in a pair of tie-dyed yoga capris and a florescent yellow tank top. Her spiked red hair had bright platinum tips today. She huffed and waved her hand at her face as she charged toward us. "Hot flashes are the bane of my existence." She reached over and grabbed a laminated menu and started fanning herself. "You'd think, with all the advances in medicine, they'd find a way to rid us women from this affliction."

"The doctor said she'd give you a prescription." Betsy sipped from her glass.

Aunt Vi slapped the counter with her menu. "She wanted to give me hormones. Whose hormones are they? Not mine! I bet they stole them on the black market."

"They do not steal hormones. That's out there, even for you."

"Betsy! Don't sass me, child. I read it right there on the internet."

"If it's on the internet, well, it must be true." Betsy gave an eye roll and stuffed the last of her fries into her mouth, and Aunt Vi gave her a light smack on the leg.

Betsy snickered. "Hey, I didn't mean nothin' by it. I'm trying to help, Aunt Vi."

Rebecca came over.

Aunt Vi's greeting smile appeared more as a grimace. "Hon, if you'll just bring me a large peach tea with extra ice and a couple of those peaches-and-cream bars to-go, that'll do me."

"You went to the Beauty Spot this morning, I see." I changed subjects as Betsy finished off her food.

"Yeah, all this stress was making me feel down. I needed a pick-me-up and little Poppy had one of her girls fix me up. Do y'all like it?"

Betsy and I exchanged a glance that said *tread carefully* before we both smiled and nodded with a mm-hmm.

That was all Aunt Vi needed, anyway. She didn't struggle with self-confidence. If anything, when God handed the confidence out, he delved an extra helping her way. Besides, what most folks couldn't pull off, Aunt Vi could.

We finished our food and said our goodbyes and went on our insane mission of breaking and entering.

CHAPTER 26

"Why, pray tell, do we need to lay down in the back seat?" My question came out muffled from underneath the blanket Aunt Vi had tossed over Betsy and me.

We were slumped down nearly perpendicular in the back seat of the big brown late-'90s model Cadillac. She'd insisted none of the models made after the '90s was suitable for her. The body styles went to pot, I believe she'd said. Followed by she needed a car with size, class, and panache. I guess the large pink dice hanging from the rearview mirror added to said panache. I held out my hand to Betsy and she passed over the box of tissues.

"Yeah, it's stuffy under here, and I'm already having trouble breathing out of my nose." Betsy succumbed to a coughing fit, and I shielded my face with my arm.

"Because, girls, if someone checks the traffic cameras, y'all won't be seen on them." Aunt Vi sounded pleased to have thought of this. "Whoever is trying to frame you girls will use anything and everything against y'all. I mean, I don't know what the world is comin' to. None of this ever happened in my younger years. We took the law into our own hands. Someone spoke against us, we took 'em to the woodshed. And if it comes down to it, I'll root out the culprit and handle it myself."

I held my aching head and pictured Aunt Vi, the vigilante, running amok.

"Hold on. We're turning onto Alex's street."

Betsy and I held on to whatever we could grab. Aunt Vi navigated the behemoth into the sharp turn, and I swore we must have gone on two wheels at one point.

"Once we can knock some sense into that ignorant nephew of mine, he'll help us."

Betsy cleared her throat. "Unless he's involved."

Aunt Vi slammed on the brakes, and Betsy and I were flung into the back of the front seats. The blanket had somehow managed to come completely off me and wrapped Betsy like a burrito.

I righted myself just in time to see Aunt Vi peering over the tall seats with an angry scowl. "That boy is *not* involved! He's gone a little cuckoo, but who in this family hasn't at one point or another? Ain't no cause for slander."

Betsy had lain perfectly still while Aunt Vi ranted, opened the door, stomped out, and slammed the door shut.

"Come on. Let's get this over with before your aunt has an aneurism." I reached around the front seat to open the passenger's side door. A car this big should be a four-door.

Aunt Vi marched toward Alex's side door, keys in hand, and I climbed out onto the small carport and sighed. It'd been over a year since I'd visited Alex at his house. It'd belonged to his daddy's side of the family and was willed to him. The all-brick ranch home sat on a large, private corner lot with a privacy fence and a gigantic double carport with a large storage building in the back. Alex had painted the beige shutters recently, and the clay shingled roof was new. The large palm tree in the front yard, which Alex and I had taken one of my favorite pictures of us in front of, had been recently trimmed.

My attention was pulled back toward the car as a thumping commenced. Betsy had yet to emerge from the back seat.

"Well, come on. We don't want any nosy neighbors driving by seeing you or Betsy," Aunt Vi said just before we noticed the car had begun rocking.

I hurried around the car and opened the driver's-side door. Betsy was yelling and thumping around on the floorboard.

Aunt Vi stomped over, her flip-flops flapping loudly. "Sweet Lord, Betsy. We ain't got time for games. Get on out of there."

A not-so-nice response came from beneath the blanket.

"I'm going to wash your mouth out with soap and then take a hickory to ya." Aunt Vi put her hands on her hips. "Out. Here. Now."

"I think she's stuck." I reached down and tugged at the blanket to no avail. How she managed to roll herself so tightly, I'd never know. One last tug, and I stumbled backward as the blanket came flying off her. Betsy crawled out of the vehicle. Her frizzy hair stood up all over her head. When she managed to look up from her hunched-over position, her eyes were bloodshot, and snot had run all down the left side of her face.

"Sweet fancy Moses, you look possessed!" Aunt Vi jumped back.

Betsy wheezed and coughed with her hand over her chest. "I nearly suffocated in there. I saw my entire life flash before my eyes. The light was coming for me."

"The light, huh." I held out a hand to Bets.

Aunt Vi leaned down. "Did you see Daddy in the light?"

Betsy was about to launch into one of her tirades when someone called out, "Yoo-hoo!" from around the side of the yard. It sounded like Mrs. Davies, Alex's sweet elderly neighbor.

"Quick, hurry," Aunt Vi hissed.

Betsy and I scampered, hunched over, through the carport and through the side door that led directly into the galley kitchen. Aunt Vi closed the door behind us. We made sure to steer clear of the window over the kitchen sink. Betsy hovered low to wash her face over the white ceramic beauty. I did a double take. The deep sink with hook sprayer was the exact one I'd picked out for Alex when he'd considered a remodel three years ago. In the end, he'd decided he was happy with things as they were and would rather spend the money on a new fishing boat.

I spun slowly around the kitchen. The new granite countertops were the ones I'd chosen as well. The new stainless-steel appliances gleamed against the creamy cabinetry. And my heart nearly stopped when I spied a set of double ovens.

"What is it? You look like you've seen a ghost, and not a friendly one." Betsy patted her face dry.

I swallowed hard. "This is *my* kitchen."

"Huh?"

I shook my head and attempted to discern what I saw. "Not my kitchen. The kitchen I chose for Alex when we were together. The one I told him I could prepare Thanksgiving and Christmas meals in. When did this happen?"

"Oh, I thought this was all about Lucy. He remodeled six months or so ago. Not that Lucy cooked or anything." Betsy scratched her head. "Now that I think about it. It was during their separation period, right before they got engaged . . ." Betsy's green eyes widened, and she sat at his farmhouse dining room table. "That's why she told him she was expecting. He'd cut her loose and was planning on winning you back. Then when nothing else worked, she came up with the pregnancy scheme."

"Don't go down that rabbit hole. I'm not the reason he remodeled. She wanted a nicer house and Alex, not having imagination for it, went with what I chose in the magazine Yvonne gave me. Knowing Alex, he didn't even remember I was the one who chose it." Part of me wondered if Betsy could be on to something, the other decided I'd take my own advice and not go down that rabbit hole.

I moved through the house on the brand-new hardwood flooring past the living room with a large leather sectional and sixty-inch flat screen that I hadn't picked, and down the narrow hallway toward their bedroom. I paused in the doorway of the tastefully decorated room and blew out a breath.

"Here." Betsy handed me a pair of purple latex gloves.

Once snapped into place, I began snooping in my ex's and his wife's bedroom. *Lord help us.*

When the bedroom provided nothing in the way of insight, either to Lucy's character or if Alex had any involvement, I moved to the bathroom adjacent to the master bedroom. It was spick-and-span. Alex's mom must've cleaned everything. There wasn't any evidence that a woman used this bathroom. I sat on the closed toilet and sighed. That was when I noticed a dark black spot on the back of the tile beneath the sink. I went down on all fours, thinking it might be blood. I opened the cabinet beneath the sink and found a Q-tip. If it was blood, it would flake. Nope. Not blood. I added a bit of water to the tip and rubbed it over the stain. Hair dye. Brown or black hair dye. I carefully scanned the contents of the cabinet for a brush. What I found belonged to Alex. Not even Lucy's comb or toothbrush was there.

"Hey, Bets," I whispered down the hallway.

"Yeah? Find somethin'?" Betsy popped her head around the corner, chewing.

I narrowed my eyes. "What are you eating?"

She paused and mumbled around a mouth of red goo. "Hot Tamales."

"You're eating Alex's candy?" I hissed. "He'll know we've been here."

Her face reddened. "But I love Hot Tamales."

"So does Alex." He kept boxes of those things everywhere. I shook my head and focused on the task at hand. "Go into the kitchen and get that snake Alex keeps under the kitchen sink."

She nodded, looking a bit sheepish about her blunder. In these older houses, clogged drains were always an issue. Especially in the bathroom sinks.

Betsy returned and began the task. She didn't even argue about how gross it was or that she was too pretty for such a job, like she normally would. When she pulled the contents from the drain, we both made a face and put a hand to our noses. I leaned forward and felt deflated. A couple of strands of hair looked to be the length of Alex's, but maybe a strand or two could be longer. I bagged it anyway.

Betsy and I had gone through everything, and the three of us sat at the kitchen table. Not much belonging to Lucy remained. Other than several articles of clothing, a couple of designer bags, and a bag of makeup. Sadness crept over me. They'd planned to begin their lives together here, only for someone to cut short their chances of happiness. Sure, their union hadn't had a perfect beginning, especially with Lucy's deception. Nor had she made many friends on the island. Still, I couldn't help but mourn her. I let out a cleansing breath. What did this recon give us? Nothing. Well, a few strands of black hair. My first thought when I found it was the person's reflection caught on the video. The one they believed was Alex. Perhaps the person in question frequented Alex's home. Colored their hair in his bathroom? Mrs. Myers colored her hair. Could it be? Had her whole reaction to Lucy and all her finger pointing at Betsy been a ruse? No, surely not. A hard reach, for sure. Desperate even. Ergo, nothing.

"I don't know what to think, y'all," I said after I relayed my thoughts to Aunt Vi and Betsy. I left out the what-if about Betsy's aunt Regina. I wouldn't add fuel to that fire. Plus, as flawed as the woman was, she loved her son. "Maybe we should move this discussion to my house. We're pressing our luck here." I checked my watch. In a little under half an hour, we'd done all we could do here.

"True that," Betsy said as we all rose from the table.

I snapped the gloves off and shoved them into my cross-body bag.

"Well, you gals satisfied now?" Aunt Vi shook her head.

Betsy sneezed. "Not really. We didn't find a thing."

"That's the point. If Alex was involved, you'd have found some evidence. Y'all even looked through his shed."

Nothing inside there had changed. It held nothing but the same old lawn furniture and broken-down riding mower Alex had insisted he'd repair. And I didn't argue the point that technically, since he was in law enforcement, he'd know not to hide anything in his house. This was a fishing expedition to clue us in more on Lucy.

Keys rattling at the side door startled us. Betsy and I ran in place before turning and bumping into each other. Aunt Vi waved for us to go and hide. Before we could even get out of the kitchen, the door swung open and Alex stood there gaping at the three of us.

"Now, honey, before you go bursting a blood vessel, let your aunt Vi explain." Alex's gaze narrowed and zeroed in on me, and I froze where I stood. "We just wanted to come by and clean up the place." Aunt Vi went over to her nephew and wrapped an arm around his waist. "You've been hurtin', and we just wanted to do our part. Show our kindness without getting you all riled. We all love you."

"I don't mean to be rude, Aunt Vi. You know I love you, but I want y'all out of here before I say something I might regret."

"Alex," Betsy whined.

"Out." The single solitary word, gritted out between clenched teeth, was all we needed to excuse ourselves.

Alex barely moved aside to let Betsy and Aunt Vi pass. I didn't make eye contact as I started to scoot by.

His hand closed softly around my arm. "Not you." His face was close to mine, and his breath hot against my neck.

Bets and Aunt Vi stood, appearing unsure of how to respond.

Aunt Vi was the first to act. She rushed forward. "Son, Marygene rode with us. She doesn't have any way of gettin' home."

"I'll drive her." His burning gaze sizzled my skin.

Aunt Vi placed a hand on her nephew's back. "Honey, let the girl come with us. You're not thinking clearly."

Alex released my arm and turned around to face his aunt. "You think I'd actually hurt her?" The pain in his tone caused a knot to develop in the pit of my stomach. Of course he wouldn't hurt me. All this craziness had addled my thinking.

Aunt Vi put her hand on his cheek. "Of course not, honey. But maybe it's best if she comes with us."

"Yeah, and Marygene don't want to stay. Do you?" Betsy waved for me to slide through the small opening between Alex and the doorway.

I started to leave, but then he swung his head around and faced me, his nose mere inches from mine, and I couldn't do it. The pain written all over his expression was too much.

"It's okay. I'll let Alex drive me home." My tone was only marginally shaky.

"Have you lost your mind? He might be the one——" Betsy shut up the second Alex's gaze swung to her.

"Not you too! I'm your damn cousin. The one who beat up that boy for picking on you in the third grade. The one who always comes when you call with a flat tire or need your oil changed in your car. And now"——he flung an arm toward them——"my own family makes sure I'm away so my house can be snooped through! And believes me capable of the most horrendous acts . . ." His voice caught in his throat.

Betsy smiled sheepishly and her face flushed red. "You've been acting crazy since Lucy, and your mom has completely lost it. We just want to find out who's doing all this and get life back to normal. I didn't mean to turn on you."

Alex ran a hand through his untamable hair. "Yeah. I get it. I've been a little on the unhinged side. I think I deserve a little slack. I've kind of had a lot to deal with here. And you know Mom, always looking for the conspiracy. I think she likes all this." He glanced toward me, and I turned away, still hurt. It seemed we'd all suffered in one way or another.

"Okay." Betsy blew out a breath. "I'm sorry. Of course you had nothing to do with this. But someone sure wants me to believe you're involved. I've had a lot to deal with too, you know. First, we were bombed and in the hospital. Then they put Marygene and me in the slammer."

Aunt Vi rubbed Betsy's back.

"Not that we're not tough chicks who can handle it, but still. Plus, I don't feel good." She leaned her head onto Aunt Vi's shoulder. "I'm going home to take a hot shower and get some sleep." Betsy started for the car, yawning loudly.

"Finally seeing reason. I'm glad to hear it." Aunt Vi looked pleased that her niece and nephew had made up.

"All right then. Y'all be sweet." Aunt Vi wagged her finger in our direction and she followed Betsy toward the car.

I stepped out the doorway and watched them slowly back down the driveway. It took Aunt Vi three tries to fully back out onto the street. Betsy waved and Aunt Vi blew the horn as they drove off.

I turned and followed Alex back into the house. Butterflies took up residence in my midsection when he shut the door.

CHAPTER 27

Alex stood at one side of the kitchen, leaning against the counters, and I stood on the other. The silence that stretched between us deafened me. It also made me keenly aware of even the most trivial things. The clock on the oven blinked. The whirling of the ceiling fan in the living room. The slow drips from the faucet in the sink caused by Betsy leaving the valve partially open. It was so quiet I could almost hear Alex breathing. The silence overloaded my senses.

"The house looks great." Small talk. Alex hated it, still it'd slipped out.

To my surprise, he smiled. "Thanks. God. How did we get here?" He turned and opened the refrigerator and pulled out two beers. He opened mine and handed it to me and then sat down at the table.

A second later, I did the same.

"Sorry I don't have any lime."

"This is fine." I swigged from the bottle. Strangely, even under these circumstances, it felt nice sitting here with someone who knew me so well. I'd need to bring this up in therapy. The emotion couldn't be healthy. I sighed and set the bottle on the table. "Alex, we have a serious problem."

He finished his bottle in a few long, loud gulps. "Don't I know it. The woman I married lied to me about being pregnant with my child. Lied to me about loving me. Lied to me about everything. God, I don't even know if I was in love with her. She was like a hurricane, you know. One minute we're dating and having fun with glorious peaceful skies and the next she swarms over me, engulfing and destroying everything. She dropped the baby news on me after we had a huge fight. Even showed me one of those test thingies. I don't even want to know how she got a positive one of those. Then she said we had to get married, for my child's sake, knowing I'd do the right thing." He got up and got himself another beer. "Now, she's dead and I can't even be pissed off with her. And the kicker is, I was about to end it before the baby, and she knew it." He sat back down hard on the chair. "I don't know if I'm coming or going anymore. And the fool who took her life decides to infect all the areas of my life by dumping her body on my ex's porch."

The lump that developed within my throat felt like a stone. I wasn't sure what he was looking for from me, and I didn't have the luxury of time to figure it out. "Alex. This situation goes way beyond you being tricked into marriage. I mean, I'm brokenhearted about you losing your wife. I wouldn't wish any harm to come to you or yours. Ever. But something really odd is going on here." I debated divulging what I knew. Sharing it with Alex could blow up in my face.

He was in a real raw place, and I needed to heed the warning within my gut. Plus, I saw the flicker of Mama behind him. She kept shaking her head, and that settled it for me. Not the time.

I reached across the table and took his hand. "Alex, someone terrible is wreaking havoc on our island. They've taken your wife, flawed as she was. That was heinous, and I'll be darned if I'll stand by and allow her to go un-avenged." The strength in my tone no longer surprised me. When it came to the wronged deceased, I was em-powered by the level of vengeance that overtook me.

Alex, however, appeared surprised. "I thought you hated Lucy."

"Hon, she wasn't kind to me, and I wasn't her biggest fan. None of that matters. She didn't deserve her end. And I won't stand by knowing she isn't resting peace-fully. Her voice has been silenced. Mine has not. And I will speak for her. Stand for her. And do whatever is nec-essary to bring her killer to justice."

Alex held tightly to my hand. "My Lord. You look like an avenging angel. You mean that, don't you?"

I squeezed his hand. "I do. And as God as my witness, neither Betsy nor I had anything to do with her death or the robbery. And we certainly don't have Paul stashed somewhere with a bomb around his neck."

He stared into my eyes for a long few moments. "I know I should care that Paul was abducted. If not for him, for you. You love him."

"Paul and I were finished before someone decided to use him as leverage. And I never said I loved him." I waved my hands in the air in an erasing motion. "Not that it matters. We need to rescue him. Save him, no matter what it takes.

Alex's eyes hardened. "The Carmichaels think I had something to do with it."

So does Detective Thornton.

"They're probably just hurting and looking at the most obvious." It came out wrong, and I wished I could take it back. I'd opened my mouth to utter an apology when he snorted and let go of my hand. "That's not what I meant. They don't know you."

"If I were investigating this case, I would take a hard look at me too. I don't know who or why someone is trying to lay this at your doorstep." He picked at the label from the bottle. He knew something, and he was having one of his inner debates on whether to tell me. "I've been in a bad place. Making sense of all of this hasn't come easy, and I'm still doing my best to figure it out. I'm not allowed back on the job until the case is solved and—" His eyes went wide. "Oh hell, I didn't even ask about the sheriff." He went to his knees in front of me and wrapped his arms around me. I stiffened as he held on tight. "I'm sorry. So sorry. You know I love Eddie. He's been like a father to me, and I've been lost in the minutiae of this nightmare. Is he doing all right? Since you're here, I take it he's going to make it."

Alex held on as if I were his lifeline. Mama's head dropped as if she believed I was going to be sucked in again. I wasn't, and I shook my head to attempt to signal such as I wrapped my arms around one of my oldest friends. "He's doing well. I won't lie, I was terrified, but he pulled through, and he's on the road to recovery. I came down with a cold and thought it wise to keep my distance." I patted his back softly, the way I did to sooth Olivia.

"Alex, did someone dye their hair in your bathroom? Your mom perhaps?"

He let go and leaned back to face me. "What an odd question to ask."

I shrugged. "When I went to use your restroom, I noticed hair dye on the floor. I was just curious."

"I can't believe y'all searched my place." He retook his seat. "Like I could do any of this." He shook his head, as if his brain was misfiring. "I don't know about the hair dye. Maybe Lucy did."

"Did she ever color her hair dark? Because I've never seen her as anything but blonde." I treaded carefully.

"No." He folded his arms and glanced away. "This is like a nightmare I can't wake up from. If they'd let me work this case, I'd find out who was behind this, and I'd kill the bastard."

"Then the wisdom behind you staying out of the investigation should be crystal clear."

Detective Thornton would be watching Alex. And how ironic that was. Since he'd enlisted the man's help in the first place. I slumped down in my chair and realized he was probably watching me too. He'd know I was here if he had surveillance on this house. Probably betting on me coming here. Darn. Stupid, stupid mistake.

"Hey, did Lucy talk about ex-boyfriends, childhood friends, her life before moving to Peach Cove?" I kept my tone placating, bordering on soothing.

He shrugged. "Not really. She didn't like to think about her past."

"Not even her parents? From what I saw on the news, they were wrecked by her death."

He nodded. "Yeah, that part doesn't make much sense. They're both devastated beyond belief about losing her. It doesn't fit the image Lucy portrayed. Her parents loved her. And her mom is the most docile woman I've ever met. And I'm a good judge of character."

I refrained from pointing out he might not be the best judge around. It seemed he and I both struggled in that area.

"This whole case is riddled with holes. Who would want to murder Lucy? What's their motive? And I know they're linking the crime with the robbery, that someone used it to throw the authorities off their scent. I don't buy that."

"What about the bombs at the wedding? Someone knew enough about them to use them in both crimes."

He thumped his elbows on the table and massaged his temples. "People are saying the man on a Harley that showed up at the wedding was a disgruntled ex of Lucy's."

This was all too much for him. I shouldn't have said anything. I kept silent. He picked a girl who got around.

"If we took a hard look at the biker, with the working theory that he killed Lucy because she chose to marry me, he had to be onsite to take her body after we found her. And we all saw him drive away. But say we missed it and he came back. Why leave her to be found, only to take her minutes later? And how would he know the tent would be cleared? And there's no way he could haul a body away on a Harley." He shook his head. "Doesn't make sense. This sort of crime takes planning. That profile fits more of a crime of passion. A man gets angry and lashes out and someone dies. That I get." He held out his index finger. "Add to the case the attempt on your life and the attempted robbery at Lucy's place of employment. A lousy botched attempt." He scratched his head and his eyes widened. "Don't forget, someone would have to inform the guy that Lucy was marrying me in the first place. That didn't happen. Lucy was a private person. She didn't even tell her parents about me."

I chewed on my bottom lip but said nothing.

He narrowed his eyes. "Oh, I see what y'all are thinking. And no way! If Lucy wanted me bad enough to trick me, why would she take up with an ex?"

I sighed and decided he needed to know. I decided to use Miss Glenda's account over Trixie's. It would carry more weight with Alex. "Miss Glenda said she saw the biker and Lucy kissing." Alex bristled as his dark eyes flashed hot. Jealousy proved he had deep-rooted feelings for his late wife, whether he believed it or not.

"When was this?"

"Not long before the wedding."

"Then he has to have something to do with all of this! God! I'm such a fool. What else am I missing?" Alex hit his forehead with the heel of his palm.

"That's not all. Detective Thornton said she had something going on with Paul too. While he and I were together. Paul confirmed they had toyed with the idea." I rubbed my brow.

He gaped as if it were ludicrous for anyone to believe a woman could prefer Paul to him. Then his eyes bugged. "Then maybe Paul killed her. You know, jealous because she chose me, and enacted revenge. He was there. Had time and motive."

I gave him a level look. Sure, blame the victim who was strapped to a chair with a bomb around his neck. "Paul is the most unassuming man I've ever met. He doesn't fit the profile of a murderer. Not to mention, he's been abducted. If the crimes are linked, Alex, how does that make any sense?"

Alex leaned forward. "I hate to burst your bubble about that guy, but he probably isn't what he seems. What do you really know about him? Nothing, right?"

I matched his posture. "I know enough to say he isn't a killer! And someone is using him as leverage, and I won't let him end up dead. And right back atcha, buddy. What did you know about Lucy? Obviously, not nearly enough and *you* married her." It was a low blow, and I instantly regretted it. "Alex"—I reached out and tried to take his hand, but he snatched it away and got up—"I didn't mean it. I'm sorry. I'm all discombobulated." I pulled a tissue from my pocket and wiped my nose.

Alex paced the kitchen. I'd said too much. Alex wasn't ready to hear any of this, and I'd been selfish to throw his issues right in his face. I had to get myself together and put my feelings aside for the greater good.

Alex braced his hands against the counter and lowered his head. I couldn't handle seeing him so distraught.

"Alex, please, what can I do? I hate that we're at odds. Hate that you've seen me as your enemy. I would never intentionally hurt you. Ever."

He shook his head and then, a moment later, he turned around. "I know that. And I'm sorry for the horrible way I behaved at the department. I was way out of line. My life is a mess of my own making. Not what happened to Lucy, but with us and the family. Forgive me?"

"Yes. Certainly. Always."

Our gazes locked in shared pain and desire for normalcy. For closure.

"I have a favor to ask. It's a big one."

I waited.

"Would you be willing to have a conversation with the Carmichaels?"

I leaned back farther against the chair. "I don't think that's such a great idea."

He closed the distance between us, pulling a chair close to me as he sat. "I can't stand the idea they believe I'd do something like this. She was my wife. And despite the deception surrounding our marriage, I would have done right by her."

"Of course you would have."

"See, you know that. Because you know me. If they hear it from you, the kind of man I am, they'll focus on pushing the detective to focus his effort on actually solving the case, instead of wasting time looking at me." Alex's eyes were wide, pleading.

On one hand, this could be disastrous. On the other, I might gain some insight into who Lucy was before she reinvented herself in Peach Cove. It might aid me in seeing what was hidden. Plus, Alex's predicament disturbed me. The detective did have his sights trained on him, or at least he wanted me to believe he had. And if the Carmichaels made their suspicions known, it was highly probable Detective Thornton had been on the up-and-up with me.

"Well?" Alex wrapped his hands around my tissue-stuffed ones. "Will you do this for me?"

His demeanor and tremulous tone reminded me of myself and the other people at my support group when they first arrived. It was desperation mixed with an out-of-control feeling. Life had become an overgrown monster who had us by the throat and refused to release us. No one should have to experience such turmoil or fear. "I will."

CHAPTER 28

I spoke with Eddie the next morning on my way into work. He sounded stronger and more himself. I'd missed the steadiness he brought to the family and our community. But I was happy to be able to offer it to him now. Lindy was by his side, and for that I could never repay her. He'd even grumbled playfully about the flavorless diet they had him on and how Lindy was being a drill sergeant, making him follow the rules to the letter. God love her. Our family gained an angel when she joined. I promised him when I recovered, I'd be working on some recipes to improve his meal plan. I heard the smile across the phone. My cold had given him no reason to question my absence. And Sam and Lindy had kept the case from him. Wise. All Eddie needed to concern himself with was getting well.

I hadn't been contacted by the abductors again and

jumped every time my phone rang, and had butterflies when I refreshed my email or checked my snail mail. Going on every day, like all was fine, when I knew Paul was being held against his will was brutal. The rest of the island didn't seem to share my feelings, and that made me sad. We should care about all our residents, whether they were newcomers or not. Tourism had brought wealth back to our island.

I finished icing forty cinnamon rolls and thanked Hannah for all her help as I rounded the corner with a tray of replacements for the front display case.

"Just in time." Jena Lynn took the tray from me.

The diner sounds were soothing to me. Forks on plates, low rumble of conversation, and occasional bursts of laughter. I busied myself with refilling mugs with piping-hot coffee.

"This place is hopping." Mr. Mason smiled and held up his mug. The man reminded me of an overstuffed teddy bear with his round face and fluff of chest hair always peeking up from the opening in his button-down shirt.

"It certainly is."

"Can't complain about that."

"No sir, no complaints here." I moved down the counter refilling mugs and trading smiles.

"Where's Betsy?" I overheard Mrs. Foster ask Rebecca when she approached to take her order. It happened all the time. I'd reassured the girl on numerous occasions that she was as good at her job as Betsy, and soon she'd have regulars of her own. In time, customers wouldn't constantly be asking for Betsy. It had nothing to do with her service but everything to do with familiarity.

"She's off today," I answered to save Rebecca the trouble. "Can I get you a cup of coffee? It's fresh."

"Yeah, I'll take a cup. Make sure the mug is clean. I want one just out of the dishwasher. Last time there was lipstick on the side." Mrs. Foster shook her head.

"You got it."

Rebecca followed me to the back to retrieve a mug.

I wrapped my arm around her shoulders. "Mrs. Foster is cantankerous. Just give her an extra slice of bacon, extra crispy, and act like you didn't notice the mix-up, and she'll be happy as a clam. That's what Betsy does."

Rebecca nodded. Her long brown ponytail swung with the motion. "I just don't understand it. I've been working here for a year now, and I'm still referred to as the new girl."

"And you will be until someone else comes onboard." I placed a steamy mug onto her tray.

"Look at it this way." Sam passed us, tying on his apron. "You'll always be the pretty young new girl. Not an old'un, like Marygene here." He winked at her and she fell into a fit of giggles. Sam had that effect on women, a chip off the old block, as they say.

"You look like you're feeling better." Sam pulled a tray of chuck patties from the walk-in.

"I am. Thanks." I smiled.

"You should see Dad. He's charming all the nurses when Lindy isn't around, trying to get them to sneak in a burger and fries."

I laughed and shook my head, not at all surprised. "We'll come up with a good alternative. Our suppliers sent a brochure about a new plant-based meat product. It's pricey, but I've been wanting to expand our menu to include more vegetarian options anyway. I have a recipe for meatless meatballs I'm dying to try."

A lot of our new tourists had asked about such options. It could be profitable. We could start out with a limited menu and then expand if it did well.

"It's a good idea. Though, I won't be having any fake meat." Sam thumped his chest. "Me carnivore."

That gained him a few chuckles. And we started toward the front.

"Any news on Paul?"

I kept my smile fixed in place, trying hard not to show my nerves. No news in this situation wasn't exactly good news. "Nothing yet."

My brother's face suddenly became serious, and he reminded me so much of Eddie. "Marygene, be careful. Dad can't take much more in his current state."

My heart sank within my chest. I had no desire to cause my father distress. But I never did, yet somehow it just happened.

"Don't get involved, as much as you want to help. I know your heart is in the right place, and it's admirable, but for once, think of yourself and your family first." He leaned in and kissed me on the forehead.

"I'm always thinking of my family," I managed to croak out.

He gave me a head nod, and I patted his shoulder as he slid behind the grill line and I numbly walked back to the front. My sister sidled up next to me as I was putting the pot back in its place.

"Alex is here with Lucy's parents."

I closed my eyes; I'd completely forgotten about my promise to Alex, and my brother had just asked me to steer clear. If only there was a way to help my brother understand my predicament. The best I could do, under the circumstances, would be to tread lightly and take care. I'd only help in safe ways, from this day forward.

"You want me to ask him to leave? I will. It's really bad form for him to show up here like this."

Rebecca be-bopped over with a bounce in her step. "Marygene, the table in the back is asking for you."

"The nerve!" Jena Lynn was incensed. "I'm going to take Alex outside and give him a piece of my mind. I told him to wait and let me speak with you and look at him! Pressing. He's used up all my sympathies. I've tried to overlook the fact he treated you poorly and then pointed the authorities in your direction as if he believed you to be capable of such a horrific thing. You've been mis-treated, and someone tried to kill you, for heaven's sake. And all of this is in relation to his life." Jena Lynn began taking off her apron. "Well, I'm not taking this lying down another second. If he thinks he can continue this abhorrent behavior, he's going to have to go through me."

"Dang!" Rebecca exclaimed.

I knew firsthand how surprising it could be to see my sister go off like this. Her personality didn't lend itself to this sort of behavior.

I put my hand on my sister's arm, halting her advance around the counter. "It's okay. Don't get all stressed out. Let me deal with him."

"Are you sure?" My sister's amber orbs were watering with emotion.

I wrapped my arms around her neck and held on to her. My sister always smelled wonderful, much like Mama used to.

"I'm so grateful for you. You're a wonderful sister and

the best business partner in the world." I released her, and she stared at me, shell-shocked.

"Well, I love you too." Her angelic smile was now fixed back into its proper place.

I returned her smile and quickly moved around the counter, snatching three laminated menus on my way. "Good afternoon, and welcome to the Peach Diner." I handed out the menus. "Can I start y'all off with coffee or some drinks?"

"I think we'll just have coffee, young lady," Mr. Carmichael said, and I relayed their order to Rebecca and met the sad hazel gaze of the man who'd lost his daughter in one of the most horrendous ways. The lines around his eyes were deep, and the dark circles and bags were evidence of his heartache.

His wife, with her neat plaid skirt and white blouse, nearly broke me when I made eye contact. The steel-blue gaze was distant and hollow. I tore myself from her and asked Rebecca for three coffees and some pastries for the table.

Alex rose. "They've agreed to speak with you. I'll leave you to it." He escaped like a thief in the night, and I wanted to join him.

Instead, I slid into the booth. Emotion welled up and a soft sob broke from my lips. I couldn't control it. I placed my hand over my mouth and glanced away. The overwhelming sense of loss and grief consumed me.

I took a wobbly breath and faced the couple. "I'm terribly sorry for your loss, Mr. and Mrs. Carmichael. No one should ever have to endure such grief."

"No. No one should," Mrs. Carmichael said, her tone low.

Rebecca placed three mugs on the table and filled them

all to the brim with hot coffee. She dropped the creams. "Are we ordering?"

Mr. Carmichael shook his head and waved a hand, dismissing her. "Alex said you wanted to speak with us. Why, I haven't the faintest idea. But we're here."

Alex shouldn't have put me on the spot like this. He was supposed to be the liaison, not run and hide like a coward. I regretted ever agreeing to this.

"Honestly, Alex asked me to speak with the both of you." I took a sip from the mug.

"Is that so. Well, I suppose that makes more sense. I knew it seemed an odd request, especially since the police considered you a suspect and we'd obviously harbor some prejudices against you because of that fact." The man placed both hands on the table.

"Mr. Carmichael, I had absolutely nothing to do with your daughter's death. She and I weren't best friends or anything, and our relationship was complicated for sure, but I didn't wish her dead. Nor would I even have the ability to harm her if I did. I come from a background of abuse, and I would never, ever inflict that sort of fear or agony on another person." I glanced from Mr. Carmichael to his wife, who still sat with a vacant stare.

"So you say." The man glared down his nose at me. "From what I heard, you despised her."

How to respond to that without causing more pain and offending this grieving couple stumped me for a second. I cleared my throat. "I honestly never spent enough time with your daughter to really get to know her. The person she was deep down."

"Deep down." He sighed. "She'd been an angel once." The older gentleman took a sip of black coffee and cast a sad glance toward his wife. "The girl who left our home wasn't our little girl, not the one we raised to be a kind, caring individual. You see, Miss Brown, our daughter left home with some ragtag, claiming to be in love. We told her we would in no way support a marriage to a man without a solid career or means to support her. She broke our hearts."

Mrs. Carmichael began digging into her purse, placing her wallet, keys, and nail polish amongst other personal items on the table.

"I'm sorry to hear that. I had no idea she told you about Alex, and I assure you he isn't a, as you refer to it, ragtag."

Mr. Carmichael's phone rang. He pulled the phone from his front pocket and groaned. "It's Garrison. Will you be okay if I go take this?" He shook his head as Mrs. Carmichael continued to place her items on the table, ignoring his question. The man was obviously concerned about his wife's mental stability. Not that I blamed the woman. Losing a child must be the worst trauma on the planet.

With a quick evaluation, the man looked me over appraisingly and must have decided I would do no harm because he left his wife alone with me to answer the call.

"No." Mrs. Carmichael spoke for the first time since arriving.

"I beg your pardon."

"No," she said again. "The boy wasn't Alex." She held a picture out to me with a shaky hand.

I took it and examined the image up close. A tall, thin girl stood laughing poolside. Her hair was wrapped up in a scarf; wisps of blond hair spilled out.

"That's my Lucille. That's the real Lucy. This girl, the one whose body lies on a cold slab in the morgue, isn't her." A sob broke through, and she covered her mouth with a napkin.

I couldn't stop the tears as they spilled over my cheeks.

"She got lost along the way, and I always thought we'd get her back. Now . . . now it's . . ." The woman sobbed.

"I'm so sorry. I know it doesn't help." I wiped the tears from my cheeks. "But it's all I know to say. I want the responsible person caught. I hate, and I mean hate, what happened to your daughter."

Our gazes locked, and something was shared between us.

I wasn't exactly sure what it was, but I believed the woman understood me in that moment, as I did her. "I will do anything and everything in my power to help the authorities find her killer. I'll answer any questions you have if it will put your mind at ease."

"You didn't do this, child." She reached across the table and gave my hand a quick squeeze before putting it back in her lap. "I see the goodness in you. My husband won't. He's too hurt to be able to see anything other than his grief."

That was understandable, and I told her so.

"My girl was beautiful, loving, and wanted to become a nurse. She almost had her degree when that boy came into her life." The tears flowed freely down her cheeks now. "He wasn't a good boy. I mean, he acted like one. Said all the right words and offered all the appropriate assurances. But he pushed for marriage because of her trust fund, and her father and I knew it. They barely knew each other before he popped the question without a ring. He put the notion of backpacking through Europe in her head and said they'd live off the land, which Lucy found romantic."

To be swept away by a man you were enamored with and who offered you a life of fun and adventure would be appealing to any young woman. Years ago, I had a similar experience with my ex and made the same mistake of buying his lies. Thankfully, I'd broken away before it was too late for me. It seemed Lucy and I had more in common than I'd realized.

"He turned her against us. Got her addicted to drugs. She changed, my little girl, it felt like overnight. One day she sat in our kitchen chatting away about her plans, her friends, and her adventures, and the next . . ." She pulled a few more napkins from the dispenser on the table. "She . . . she was replaced by a stranger begging for money and threatening to leave and never return if we wouldn't release her trust fund and agree to allow her to marry without a prenup. The last words I ever uttered to her were, 'Don't call me when your life is ruined, expecting me to pick up the pieces.'"

That sounded like Lucy, and I wondered about her drug problem. Trixie said she took pills, and they certainly weren't prenatal vitamins as I once believed. Perhaps she injected herself before the wedding and misjudged the dosage. Teddy hadn't mentioned any other needle marks and perhaps she only used pills or the patches Javier mentioned to satisfy her cravings in the past.

"I know it isn't any consolation, but I am truly sorry." I felt like slapping myself for overusing that platitude condolence. "My heart truly breaks for you."

"Thank you. I just want my baby to find peace. To be

at rest." She lowered her head mournfully, and the dam broke as she crumpled into sobs.

Mr. Carmichael rushed back to the table, sliding into the booth. He pulled her to his chest and held her, rocking gently. My hand went to my mouth and now, more than ever, I wanted to help Lucy and her mother and father. She mumbled to him that she'd confided in me about their child.

"As you can see, my wife is distraught. She shouldn't have told you those things. But they're all true. When Lucy met that boy, the one before Alex, she changed. Stopped calling and emailing. We haven't spoken with her in over a year, and then one day we get the call that she's . . . she's . . ."

This time I held my tongue, even though condolences kept rising. Words would do nothing here, unless they helped put Lucy to rest.

Mr. Carmichael shook his head. "Not that Alex is much better than a motorcycle-riding deadbeat." He scooted out of the booth and helped his wife out.

"Excuse me. The man before Alex, did he ride a Harley? Was his name David?"

He shook his head. "I don't know. The bike was loud. We have to go."

The dead silence in the diner showed the reverence everyone felt for the grieving parents. I still had the picture in my hand and rose quickly to give it back to Mrs. Carmichael, who moved through the diner clutching her husband.

Jena Lynn raised her hands in question.

Lifting my shoulders, I mouthed, "I have no idea what just happened."

My sister placed her arms on her womb, and I could only imagine how she couldn't help but relate to the grieving couple. The loss would be so bone-crushing deep, and Jena Lynn hated the thought. Olivia was her and Zach's whole life.

The couple had already made it through the doorway as I made my way to the front of the diner and outside, under the overcast sky in the late afternoon, needing some air. Alex intercepted, blocking my path. "What did you say to them?"

"Nothing. They just shared their hearts." I gazed around him to where the Carmichaels were getting into a Lincoln Town Car.

"You were supposed to help, not cause the woman to collapse." Alex groaned in agitation. "Whatever. Thanks for nothing." He left me standing on the sidewalk, clutching the picture Mrs. Carmichael had given me to my chest. I guess we were back in cloud cuckoo land, where Alex was concerned.

Mrs. Carmichael glanced up as they pulled from the curb and lifted a hand. I did the same.

CHAPTER 29

Detective Thornton crossed the sidewalk in three long strides. "Miss Brown, do you have a minute?"

I paused, glancing over my shoulder. "I do, and I'd like to have a word with you too."

He appraised me in an entirely different way and, gauging from his expression, he'd seen the display with the Carmichaels and Alex. In this moment, I didn't care. My heart was laden with burden for the family and Lucy. My inconvenience during this ordeal paled in comparison to what her mother and father were going through. I wrestled with the portrayal her mother laid out, the contrast between the Lucy before her addiction and the Lucy I knew.

I motioned for the detective to join me in my car. I started the engine and blasted the air-conditioning to combat the thick humidity we were experiencing. The detective had difficulty folding his large frame into my compact car. He moved the seat back as far as it would go and closed the door. It was the first time I'd been in such close quarters with this man.

I got right to it when he closed the door. "When you ran the toxicology report, did you check for long-term drug use?"

He angled his body toward me. "For someone who wants to be left alone and kept out of the fray, you sure have thrown yourself headlong into the muck."

"I said I'd help, and I will. I am." Squaring my shoulders, I decided he deserved an explanation. Sure, he'd believed me capable of despicable things before. And in his line of work, with all the horrors he'd seen, why shouldn't he? He didn't know me, and his job was to close cases the best way he knew how. Was he crooked? God only knew. In this instance, I would trust my gut and say *not at present*. He could've built a case and thrown the book at me. Left the island and left the case for the prosecution to sort out. Through all of this, I'd had many epiphanies that shed light on myself and others in my life.

"Life isn't always black and white, Detective. Years ago, I believed that gray was invented by those who didn't want to abide by rules and created their own realities as they saw fit. But it isn't that simple, is it?"

He shook his head.

"Our mutual acquaintance, Roy Calhoun, would put money on you being dirty."

The detective adjusted the vents in front of him, pointing them at his face. When he turned to face me, his gaze was serious. "Like you said, there's a lot of gray in life. But I haven't been, nor will I ever be, a dirty cop. Some would say different. There's always controversy surrounding men in power. Take your father, for instance. He's a good man and a good sheriff. He has heart, and that's a quality that makes him perfect for this island. Though, in the opinion of some, that quality can cloud judgment and be a weakness."

"You call it weakness. I call it strength. Once one loses the love for their fellow man, they lose their ability to govern them. Each person has their own story, has lived their own journey. They've loved and lost and hurt. What makes one worth more than another? I care what happened to Lucy. Care deeply. And until the person responsible pays for the crime, no matter who they are, she'll never be able to rest. Nor will her parents ever find closure."

"We're not that different then. You have your reasons for wanting the culprit behind bars, and I have mine. Either way, we're on the same side here and now." He waited and I gave him a solid head-nod, and he returned it. Oddly, in this car, he and I found common ground. Still, the issue of trust hadn't been established, but we were close. Perhaps I could share the call from Paul and handle it delicately, without alerting the killer to his involvement. I needed to be sure, since I'd be risking another person's life. A person I cared for.

"You spoke with Alex last night. Did he seem agitated or unhinged?" He adjusted his position again.

And now we were venturing into deep, dark, shark-infested waters, and instantly I recoiled.

"You said you want the person responsible charged. This is the way we go about it. I will find the one responsible. And I'm convinced the robbery and murder are connected. This crime is way too sophisticated to have been pulled off by a local. I don't believe Alex is the mastermind behind any of this, but I still have my reasons to suspect his involvement. Beauty wields a lot of power. If Alex is innocent, we'll rule him out."

Put up or shut up, Marygene. "I've known Alex my entire life. He's a lot of things, but a crook he isn't. He'd never steal from anyone, much less his neighbors." I rubbed the space between my eyebrows with my index finger. "But . . . he isn't himself. Like you, he believes himself to be good at his job. Can you imagine what it would be like to think you knew someone, only to find out later you'd been manipulated into marrying them, they had a drug problem, and then they were murdered right under your nose?"

"Like I said, beauty wields power."

I nodded. "He's frustrated by the Carmichaels. According to him, they believe he's involved. And Mrs. Carmichael, Lord bless her, is in shambles. That's why I asked about the hair samples to see if her drug use might've been embellished. She believed it was the reason her daughter wasn't herself. And why she fell for some lowlife who aided in her addiction and attempted to use her to gain access to her trust fund."

Several people stopped in front of my car, glancing through the windshield oddly at the company I was keeping. I smiled and waved as if everything was perfectly normal. Just me and my good buddy, Detective Thornton.

In his usual fashion, he ignored them. "From the hair samples we were able to determine Lucy frequently used drugs."

I nodded. "Then it's completely possible she injected herself and overdosed. Perhaps her ex used her to gain access to account numbers and gave her the filled syringe, knowing she couldn't resist. She'd be out of the way and he could keep all the money for himself. It fits the profile drawn by her parents. He obviously never left the island. He could've easily changed his look and hid among the tourists. We wouldn't be the wiser."

"I need to speak to the Carmichaels again." His hand went to the door, and I reached out and wrapped my fingers around his forearm. He glanced at my hand.

I pulled out my phone. This sounded far more complicated when I spoke it aloud. I blew out a breath. Here and now, my best chance to save Paul was sitting next to me. No longer suspecting he had anything to do with the robbery, I hit play on the voice mail from Paul's kidnapper. Every visible muscle in his body went tense. He checked the time and date on the message and listened to it again.

"They called again. I answered it the second time. Paul sounded petrified, and they threatened to kill him, slowly and painfully, if I didn't cooperate or if I called the authorities. Obviously, now, with us sitting here out in the open for the world to see, I'm not equipped to handle any of this. And I'm tired. So very tired. I just want everyone to be safe. For people to refrain from killing one another and let me get back to baking and helping out at my support group." I shook my head and met his scrutinizing gaze. "I'm just a diner owner who loves a great dough and making people happy with good food. My father nearly died of a heart attack, my ex is struggling to find his way, and my best friend and I were nearly killed. The guy I was seeing has been abducted, and the lunatics are calling me! I'm at my wits' end here, and I'm hoping, no, I'm trusting you'll be able to handle this delicately and another person doesn't die." I slumped down in the seat and rubbed my face.

To my surprise, he put his hand awkwardly on my

shoulder. The act made me feel more lonely than comforted.

"I've brought in more of my team to aid on the investigation. This will end and your life will resume some sense of normalcy. Would you be willing to wear a wire and have your phone tapped and your cell records released?"

We were back into uncomfortable but necessary territory, and I agreed.

Javier stood on my back deck when I got home. No doubt the detective sent him right over. I'd still insisted I wanted to work with him. I noticed Javy when I crossed the threshold and stumbled over a flat envelope shoved through my antique front door mail slot. I'd kept it purely for aesthetics, and it wasn't usually used by my postal worker. I smiled through the glass door at him. My comfort level with him made the ordeal easier. Thankfully, I'd begun to feel a bit better physically. Emotionally, not so much. I'd take what I could get.

"Hey." I slid open the back door.

"Hey, yourself." Javy's steely gaze searched mine. "You want to explain?"

I moved aside for him to enter. "Do you really need me to? I'm sure Detective Thornton gave you every single detail."

"I'd like to hear it from you. I mean, you and I are a lot closer, or so I thought. Hearing all of this from my superior disturbed me." Javier made himself at home and sat in the living room while I used my tissue to pick up the flat unmarked mailer and deposited it on the counter. Deep breaths did nothing to slow my heart rate. Having doubts about my actions would be pointless. It sucked that your heart didn't always comply. The mailer surely held the instructions, and I had no idea if the abductors were privy to my actions.

I went to the fridge and pulled out a pitcher of peach tea. "Want a glass?"

"No, thanks."

Taking my time, I filled a glass with ice and tea. "I'm in over my head here. The detective was there, and as I struggled to the surface for a breath of air, I let it all out." I told Javier everything I had told the detective. "He's having the voice mail analyzed now by his tech-savvy guys. Did you know, by a simple signature from me, they can access my phone records and gain access to all my voice mails? It's all in the cloud." After a few long sips, I placed both pitcher and glass on the bar.

"It's a virtual kind of world."

I nodded. "I guess. I sure hope I did the right thing and Paul doesn't pay the price." I pulled the band from my hair and rubbed the sore spot on my head. "Hey, could you find out the identity of a person by a hair sample?"

"No, why?"

I sat on the sofa and attempted a smile. "That would have been too convenient for my life. I found black hairs in Alex's drain. It might be his, but I found some hair dye on the tile underneath the sink." Admittedly, this was all getting to me, and I probably sounded desperate and reaching. I didn't care.

He moved next to me and wrapped an arm around my shoulders. "Hair cannot be positively matched to a specific person."

"Are you sure?" I leaned in to him.

"Fairly positive. To tell us much of anything in an examination, it must contain the root pulp. During a struggle, hair that's been ripped out by the roots will contain nuclear DNA. This hair was probably hair that shed during the coloring process. It won't contain the correct DNA."

Here I'd hoped I'd found something of consequence. Nothing that I expected could be used in a court of law, mind you, but maybe a clue that would point us in the right direction. On the other hand, Betsy would be thrilled to know her shedding problem wouldn't be credible evidence to frame her. I'd been right to ask for help.

Javier sat straight and strong. Confidence oozed from his pores, making me wonder if he ever struggled with anything, and feeling guilty that I wanted to borrow some of his strength. Or at least bask in it for a while. I opened my mouth and told him everything. All that happened at Alex's. My conversation with the Carmichaels in more detail. I even let him in on my fears.

After a few long minutes inhaling his scent and feeling safer than I had in a long time, I got up and went to retrieve my purse and the mailer. I used a paper towel to pick up the mailer this time. Javier maintained his silence. There was something about him that reminded me of Eddie. It was his demeanor. Like Eddie, he brought a palpable calm to the room. I sat back down, keeping some distance between us. I played the voice mail. He needed to hear it firsthand.

Javier sat forward as Paul's voice came over the speaker. His body tensed as if he were prepared to leap into action at any second. He played it three times, listening closely. "Did you speak to Alex about this?"

I shook my head and handed over the mailer. "I'm guessing these are the instructions. I have latex gloves in my purse if you want them."

He didn't comment. He simply held out his hand for my gloves. I handed them over. Betsy had insisted I keep some with me, and she carried some as well. Clearly, we had a problem.

Javier struggled to get them over his hands, but they were on enough to keep his prints from transferring. I moved closer as he ripped open the tab and dumped the contents out. A key clattered onto the table, tagged with a safety deposit box number. A printout with instructions, along with a time and date I was to retrieve the contents of the box and where I should deliver it.

I sucked in a breath. A sticky note attached to a picture of the inside of the diner read, *You've been naughty. One more misstep and boom!* All the hairs on my neck stood at attention.

I leapt to my feet. "I have to call Jena Lynn. We need to evacuate the diner!"

Javier took the phone from my hand and threw it on the sofa.

"What are you doing?" I wailed. "That maniac is going to blow up my diner with my family inside!"

Javier took me by the shoulders and peered into my face as he spoke calmly and assuredly. "We need to call Detective Thornton and have him issue a quiet evacuation of the diner. If we create a pandemonium, they might set the bomb off."

I held on to Javier's forearms. My eyes stung. "Oh God, what if—"

He gave his head a firm shake. "No. We aren't playing the what-if game. This was a threat to ensure you follow their instructions, when Paul wasn't enough. They had to threaten what you hold most dear. Your family and your business. They won't do something stupid and ruin their most valuable leverage." Javier navigated me to the sofa, where I perched while he made the appropriate phone calls.

Yes, I believed his actions were correct. Reacting could prove disastrous in a situation such as this. And I wasn't planning on risking anyone's life by betting on the crazy people behind all of this. Still, I prayed nothing went horribly wrong. Mr. Forest's words ran through my mind and, for the briefest of moments, I did wish they'd blow up. All the horrible, evil people who had the audacity to threaten me and mine. Acting with a cool, level head would always prevail. I tried deep breathing while Javier moved through my space. The way he was looking under tables and in lamp shades, I suspected he was concerned my place had been bugged.

Mama appeared beside me and took my hand. She sat there, and her presence calmed me slightly. I didn't say anything when she started speaking. I listened to every word she said. Every bit of advice I took to heart. My mama had drawn a line in the sand. She would do whatever it took to help me, even if it meant tying herself to this island for the rest of her existence. Putting herself aside for me now, after all these years, proved people could change if they chose to. The last thing she whispered to me hung in the air long after she'd faded. "Trust this one, my sweet girl. He's seen enough and lived enough life to understand the nature of people. He's on this island for a reason."

I'd come to trust Javier, and it was rooted deeply. That Mama agreed gave me more confidence in my discernment. Still, she puzzled me with the statement that he was here for a reason. My phone rang, and my sister's face showed up on the screen. I glanced at Javier, who gave me permission to answer it with a nod.

"Jena Lynn, are you okay?"

"Marygene, oh my God! We've received a bomb threat! The diner is swarming with plainclothes officers." Her voice shook. "They've evacuated our entire side of the square. It's bedlam."

"I'm sure. Are you home yet?" I couldn't help the tears. Hearing my sister so shaken up rent my heart into pieces. This was all happening because of me, because I hadn't followed the instructions. I *needed* her safe.

"I'm driving there now. Honey, are you okay?"

I sniffed. "I'm fine. Don't worry about me. Just go home and snuggle with Olivia and Zach."

"You come over too. We need to be together at a time like this."

Boy did I want to. "I'll try. The detective will want to speak with me first."

"Right. Okay. I just pulled in and Zach's here."

I let out a silent thank-you. "Good. That's good."

"Love you, stay safe, and get over here at your first opportunity. I don't care what time it is." Jena Lynn recovered enough to use her mama voice on me.

"I will. Love you too." The second I hung up, I nearly collapsed.

Javier scooped me up in his arms. "It's okay. We're going to get this guy. I swear it." Determination and anger shone through in his tone. I held on to him and sobbed until nothing was left inside.

My cottage was swept for recording devices. And if anyone was watching the house, they wouldn't know the detective, his crew, and Javier were inside. They came to my cottage on the beach side as discreetly as they could manage, anyway. We'd been over the plan about a dozen times, but still, it was hard to fathom I was in this position and would be the one entrapping the evil person behind these heinous crimes. Eddie would have never allowed me to do anything like this, and once he got word, he'd be mad as the devil. Still, it was our best chance.

I stared at my reflection in my bathroom mirror. I'd taken a hot shower and just finished drying my hair. My eyes were a tad red from crying, but the release had been warranted. I felt a little lighter.

A light rapping at the door caused me to pause with the comb in my hair. "Are you dressed?" Javier's soft accented voice broke the silence. "Everyone's gone."

I put the comb down and slid open the pocket door, putting me face-to-face with the handsome man who had been by my side since this whole ordeal began. The one who sat with me while I waited to see if my father would make it through surgery, who tried to help me even at the risk of his own career. I recalled his earlier words. *One day you'll stop wasting your time with the wrong men and see the right one standing in front of you.*

"You okay?" He brushed a strand of hair from my forehead lightly with his fingertips.

"Yes, and I think I'll stop wasting my time with the wrong men." I slid my arms around his neck and slanted my mouth over his.

He crushed me to him and, for a long few moments, we were totally lost in each other. Until he abruptly jerked away and put half a room between us.

"Damn. Your timing is god-awful." He ran a hand over his mouth, and I could tell he was struggling to keep his distance. His eyes kept glancing from me to the bed. He pointed a finger at me. "We'll revisit this at a better time. When you're not vulnerable and are thinking clearer."

I shrugged. "Suit yourself." I turned and walked into the kitchen, desperately in need of a glass of wine. Anything to numb the anxiety niggling within me.

"Do you want to talk about tomorrow? Have any questions you want to ask that you didn't feel comfortable asking the detective?" Javier asked as I pulled the bottle from the fridge.

"No, Deputy Reyes." My tone was thick and a little husky. "I'm going to indulge in a glass of wine and try to settle my thoughts. I would have chosen to indulge in you over the wine, but you said no." I poured a glass and offered him one.

"I didn't say no. I'm being respectful of your situation."

"How chivalrous of you." I walked past him and out onto my back deck. The sounds of the ocean and the salty air swirled around me as I sipped chardonnay. Tomorrow would be here before I knew it, and I needed to settle my nerves.

"I didn't say no, Marygene." Javier joined me on the deck.

When I thought of Paul, I should have felt guilty, but I didn't. Even though he'd been all over Lucy while we dated, until he was safe I should be more respectful. And would. It also wasn't fair to Javier. "I know you're right. I'm not in the best headspace at present, and I was just making light of jumping you."

Javier took my face in his hands and kissed me lightly on the lips. His breath danced on my lips. "Jump me any other time, *mi corazón,* and I swear things will turn out differently."

CHAPTER 30

The next morning, I dressed in jeans and big baggy T-shirt to hide the wire taped to my midsection, which ran up to the top of the sweatshirt. Javier had slept on the couch while I tossed and turned in my bed until I gave up and made some coffee.

"There. Is that comfortable?" Javier placed a tiny object in my ear. He would be there, in my ear, if I were to freeze up or forget something.

I glanced up. "It's fine. Guess you're my handler, huh?" I made a sad attempt at humor to add a little levity to the heaviness in the room.

"You don't have to do this. We can find another way." His words were sweet, and I smiled.

He and I both knew I had to go through with it. He'd done his best to persuade the detective to go with another plan. One that wouldn't put my life at risk. It felt nice to know he had my back.

With his big hands on my shoulders, he gave me a look I feared I'd never see from a man again. One that said, *If you say the word, I'll damn the world to save you.* "Promise me this. If you ever feel threatened in any way, use the code word and I'll get you out."

My code word was *coffee*. My idea. I was to yawn and say, *Wow, I could really use a cup of coffee.*

"I promise," I choked out as my phone rang with Eddie's ringtone.

With our gazes still locked, I fixed a smile into place and lifted the phone to my ear. "Hey, Eddie. How are you feeling today?"

"Hon, it's me, Lindy. Your dad is doing very well. So well he's become a pain in the butt to deal with. We're having a hard time keeping him from watching the news or reading headlines. He wants to talk to you. Please try and keep the stress off him."

"I wouldn't dream of adding to his troubles. The department has it all in hand and he'll be glad to know they can manage while he heals." I turned away.

"You know how he is. Unless he's in the middle of whatever case that's being worked, he's out of sorts. Thanks for understanding. Are you okay, hon? Sam was so enraged by what happened at the diner that he didn't come by last night." Lindy sounded like a concerned mother, and that made me smile. She'd taken a bit of ownership over Sam and me.

"I'm perfectly fine. The shock was earth-shattering, for sure, but I'm trying to hold it together, and I'm just grateful no one was hurt." I walked outside onto the deck and lifted my face toward the sun. The wonderful rays always made me feel whole.

"I'm so glad, honey. The last thing you need in your life is more trauma. You're a strong woman and can handle whatever is thrown your way. I just want a bit of peace for you."

I smiled. "A bit of peace sounds heavenly."

"Your dad's yelling for the phone again." Her voice went up a couple of octaves. "It was wonderful talking to you too. Here's the grumpy old man." She chuckled.

Boy, were we all going to pay when he found out.

A couple seconds later Eddie came on the line. "I'm not grumpy. Y'all are treating me like an invalid." I heard a little more grumbling in the background followed by, "Pumpkin, where've you been?"

"I've had a cold. Your immune system doesn't need anything else to fight. I'm positive Lindy and Sam told you. How are you feeling?" I kept my tone upbeat and my smile fixed into place.

"I'm right as rain." Typical Eddie. Downplaying anything to do with his health. "I need to see my baby girl. You don't sound all that sick. I think you should come see your old man. I'm home now and nearly losing my mind watching Lindy's home improvement shows."

I laughed and Javier poked his head out the doorway. I held up my finger. "I promise I'll be over the second I'm completely well. Lindy would skin me alive if I brought illness into the house. And—"

"Hang on a second, pumpkin. Lindy, could I have a cup of decaf? Thank you, darlin'."

Lindy mumbled something and there were kissing noises. Guess they'd made up.

"All right, we're alone now. Tell me what in the hell is going on?"

"N-nothing. I'm just getting ready to go in to work."

"Don't lie to me, young lady. Lindy won't let me have the remote or my cell phone, she keeps taking calls out of the room, and Sam's face nearly cracked in half, trying to keep his smile in place. He looked like the joker or an escaped mental patient. His constant *yes sirs* tells me something is going on. I want to know everything this minute."

"Eddie!" Lindy came in and saved me. "Let the girl go. You're getting yourself all worked up."

"She's my daughter and I want to know what's going on, and she's going to tell me."

I had no idea what I was supposed to do. I must have had a helpless look on my face because Javier held out his hand. I took the out he was offering me. "Look who's here! Javier wants to speak with his sheriff."

"What's he doing at your house? Has he overstepped his bounds?"

I shoved the phone into Javier's hand, mouthed a silent thank-you. And rushed inside to hide.

CHAPTER 31

The square was eerily silent as I took the roundabout and drove toward the credit union. They'd reopened most of the businesses after the buildings were swept for active devices. The Peach sat empty this morning, even though it had been cleared. I parked in a space close to the financial establishment where all this would be going down and took a second to exercise a little deep breathing.

"It's going to be okay," Javier said, and I picked it up crystal clear in my earpiece. "You're going to walk across the street and into the credit union like you would any other time. I'm here watching your every move, and there are several plainclothes officers inside the building." He reminded me of everything we'd previously discussed.

My hands were shaking in my lap. Being consumed with the fear that I'd somehow screw this up and Paul would suffer or someone else might die made it impossible to reduce the tremors.

I adjusted my rearview mirror, giving me a view of the Peach's catering van, where I knew the crew had set up shop. Javier and his team were inside and could be at the scene in under a minute. That gave me some comfort. Still, it was me going into the red zone. They were counting on me. *Me.*

When Mama appeared in the passenger's seat, I nearly leaped with joy.

"I don't like this." Mama shook her head, and the joy faded. "I don't like this one bit. Why in the world do they need you to do their jobs for them? My thinking on Deputy Reyes has changed with this asinine plan. He and that detective have everything they need to apprehend those two morons. It's right under their noses."

My eyes went wide. Mama knew who was behind this! How could I communicate with her without sounding completely insane? She vanished and I sucked in a breath.

I bolted from the car, glancing around frantically. *Oh, come on!* The energy around me lasted for a few long seconds before I spotted her several feet ahead of me. As I caught up to her, I gave her a look she'd understand. The one kids gave their parents when they felt like shouting *what the hell* but refrained because it was disrespectful.

"Slow down," Javier said, calmly.

"Marygene, my word, wipe that ugly look off your face. Your eyes are bugging out like a Pekinese. It's mighty unbecoming." Mama strolled across the parking lot with her shoulders back and her head high, carrying herself like the lovely Southern woman she was.

I followed behind her, feeling like a scolded misbehaving child.

Mama paused in front of the large white columns framing the Peach Cove Credit Union. "Come on now, let's get this over with."

I let out a derisive snort.

"Marygene. Everything okay?" Javier broke into my reality, reminding me that to others, I appeared like a mental patient, therefore adding validity to old rumors.

"All good." I kept my tone low and my cheeks burned as I caught up with my mother. "Just wish I had someone on the inside who could shed some light on who was really behind this. That would make *my* life easier." I glared at her.

"I'm here. We're going to get the guy." Javy's words did nothing to calm me. And when I overheard a deep voice saying, "She's losing it. I knew she couldn't pull this off," I nearly turned and ran back to my car.

Then Mama ignored me completely, and I wanted to scream. Really? Wasn't this the reason she was here? To help? I gave myself a mental shake. She was helping. I knew that. She'd been there with Eddie in his time of need. And for that, I could never repay her. Anxiety stirred deep within my gut and began to spread like tentacles throughout my entire body. My chest and face were on fire. Not now. I had to pull myself together.

"Now look at her, she's frozen." The voice came over loud and clear. Followed by Javier sending a harsh and not polite warning for the jerk to shut his mouth and hold his position.

I glanced around, with no luck, for a visual of where the jerk was positioned. "Everyone's a freakin' critic. I said I was good." I yanked the door open and stepped into the coolness of the bank and stopped, surveying the area. I forced my feet to move toward to the small area where people filled out bank slips and deposited their checks old-school. I couldn't spot the officers among the handful of people in the building. Mama stood next to me, cautiously glancing around. I couldn't speak verbally to her, but there were other means of communication. I took a pen connected to the table and scribbled on the slip. Nothing happened. I picked up another and again, out of ink. Seriously! For heaven's sake!

"I'll be back." I actually reached out for Mama before she disappeared and forced my hand to drop by my side. That was when I spotted Trixie. She was filing her nails at her station. I moved through the little roped-off line, even though there wasn't anyone in line. When I reached her desk, she appeared annoyed.

"Hey, Trixie."

"Hey. What can I do for you?" She put her file down and smacked her gum.

"I need to get a safety deposit box, please." I smiled.

"Alrighty," she said unenthusiastically. "Did you fill out a form? I don't see one."

"Oh, yes." I dug through my bag and pulled out the prefilled form I'd been given by the detective and presented it to her.

Trixie slid it over to herself with her super-long acrylic nails painted a mirrored blue color. "You didn't sign it."

"Well, the pens back there are out of ink, and I don't have one with me. Can I use yours?" I held out my hand for the pen next to her.

"They're so cheap." She handed me her pen with a pink pom-pom on the tip. "We shouldn't even be open today. Y'all closed, right? I mean that bomb could've taken all of us out."

"Change the topic of discussion," Javy said.

I quickly scribbled my name on the bottom of the slip and slid it back and nodded. "We're closed. We were asked to as a precaution."

"Well, we should've taken the same precaution. Our lives matter just as much, right, Jodie?" Trixie rocked back in her chair to speak to her older coworker. "We should walk out."

"Shut that down," Javy barked, and I jumped.

"How?" I squeaked.

Trixie made a face at me. "We just walk out. God, Marygene. If we all did it, they'd have to listen to us, like a union."

The older woman grunted and grabbed her mug. She took her time rising. She placed a closed sign in front of her window. "I'm taking my break."

"That Jodie, she's such an old hag. Her life is already over anyway. Mine's not! I'd just walk out myself if I didn't need this stupid job." She shook her head. "I miss Lucy."

I nodded sympathetically. "She was a good coworker, I bet."

"Not really. She was a real witch, but she hated this place as much as me. We went out for drinks and talked trash about this place. Security here is a joke. I mean, if we wanted to, we could walk out of here with every dime."

I kept shaking my head.

"Seriously. Our dumb bank manager is hardly ever here. And he cheaps out on everything. Not just the pens. The bill for security software went unpaid for nearly three months, leaving the customers vulnerable. He finally got that straightened out a few weeks ago. It was only by luck he managed to halt the robbery. And with the amount I heard they attempted to steal, this place would have gone belly-up." She leaned closer, placing both arms on the counter and whispered, "I don't even bank here. What's that tell ya?"

A throat cleared in the line behind me. She looked in their direction. Two men dressed in casual Hawaiian wear sold at the new souvenir shop that opened last spring—it was unmistakable. Now I knew who the officers were. Though the criminals probably wouldn't.

Trixie made a face in his direction as a couple of others joined the line. "Rude tourists." She slid the chair back and stood. "Can I just hand you the keys? There's nothing to it. You just go around the corner there, use this key to unlock the gate, and then this one will be for your box. The number on the key will match the box."

I nodded and took the keys. "Are you sure this is okay?" I'd been prepped on the box procedure, and Trixie was going off-book. If I went on my own, that would seem way more suspicious, I thought.

"Go with it. This works out to our advantage," Javy said. "The officers will add more pressure."

Trixie glanced back at the line and hesitated.

Another throat clearing. "Excuse me. I've been waiting here."

"Yeah, it's fine. I'll go and handle that jerk and be right back. Just don't tell anyone or I'll lose my job."

"I won't."

"Keep your shirt on," Trixie yelled to one of the undercover officers at the front of the line. She rolled her eyes and shooed me in the right direction. "I'll be right back."

My head bobbed up and down before I disappeared around the corner. Trixie wouldn't need to walk out; I had a feeling she'd be escorted out soon enough. The gate securing the room that held all the safety deposit boxes had a unique style lock on it. My heart pounded within my chest being so close to phase two of the plan. Get in and retrieve the contents of the box and somehow get out of the bank without seeming suspicious. The key didn't work. I tried again with the others on the ring. I even forced a few keys in that hardly fit, shaking the little gated door. "None of these stupid keys work. Now what?"

"Are you sure you tried them all?"

"Yes! I tried them all. I guess I'll have to—" A hand covered my mouth. I squeaked in protest as my back hit against a hard chest.

"You okay?" Javier's voice still sounded calm, and I wanted to say, yes, everything was perfectly fine and mean it. But as I glanced up at the ski-mask-covered man, it wasn't. Everything from there happened like a blur. The earpiece was dislodged from my ear and stomped under a large weighted black boot. He reached under my shirt, unhooking the wire and ripping the tape.

"Move." He hustled me toward the back of the building and out the back door into the alley. The alarm sounded. I fought like an alley cat when I saw the sliding door of a van open. The man grunted when I landed a shot between his legs, but he kept hold of me and flung us both into the van, pulling the door shut behind him.

The van swerved as it took curves on two wheels, and I was flung into the masked man. We both went down, hard. My head bashed into floor, but I didn't care. When his hand landed on my upper arm, I kicked out with all my might, landing a solid strike to his ribs.

"Dammit! Stop that!"

I didn't. I'd seen plenty of movies and knew darn good

and well what would happen if he managed to take me out to some secluded spot. I wouldn't submit to that sort of treatment. I'd rather die right here in this van, fighting. I launched myself atop him, ready to gouge his eyes out through the mask.

The man grabbed both my hands and held firm. "It's me! Stop it! I'm going to let go. Don't go all cat woman on me."

Wait. I recognized that voice. Slowly, he pulled the mask off his face.

All the breath left my body in a whoosh. "Alex?" I choked out and slid off him.

"I think you neutered me back there." He rolled to his knees, taking deep panting breaths.

"Hey, check me out! I'm driving like a bat out of hell! Ain't nobody gonna catch me."

I slid up to the cage separating the van. The driver was a wearing a black leotard with a cat tail, black tights, gloves, and a Michael Myers Halloween mask I knew belonged to Alex. He'd been Michael Myers for Halloween every year in high school.

"Betsy!"

"Hey, girl! Hang on!" She squealed tires and my fingers burned as they held on through the metal holes. "You were dead-on. Alex did drop his money clip while snooping on ya. He's so careless. I told him he gave himself away. He's lucky we found it and not the evil detective."

My vision went blurry, and suddenly everything went dark.

"Alex, Marygene, move!" Betsy shouted and the next thing I knew the sliding door opened and Betsy removed her mask, her face sweaty and her hair stuck to her forehead. She grabbed my arm and pulled me out of the van.

We were in a dark, damp, parking garage. "Come on! We've got to hightail it out of here. We're on a tight schedule."

Numbly, I followed her deeper into the garage. A still-puffing Alex stumbled behind us.

Betsy hurried around to the driver's side of an old yellow Pontiac. I stood there staring, as if shot with a tranquilizer, unable to move. She fired up the engine and smoke billowed from the tailpipe. I coughed and she leaned out the door. "Come on!"

Alex put his hand on my lower back now that he was able to stand upright. "I'll explain. But you need to get in. Okay?"

I blinked several times, looking from Alex to Betsy. I couldn't make sense of this. As much as I tried, I just couldn't. My best friend and ex-boyfriend, two people I would trust with my life, abducted me while I was working with the Peach Cove Sheriff's Department. Neither one of them had known about the arrangement, yet they were right on time.

"Marygene. We don't have time for this." Alex nudged me forward, and I slid into the back seat. "Scooch." I moved farther down the vinyl bench seat, and he got in beside me. Betsy smoothed out her hair, slammed the heavy metal door, and backed out of the space.

CHAPTER 32

The car bumped along the dirt back-roads Betsy took. The police scanner Alex had alerted us to where they were casting their wide net. Javier's voice came over the speaker as he barked orders. Gone was the calm, soothing tone. It was replaced by one that promised steep repercussions.

"Oh man." Betsy started fanning herself. "He's got it bad for you. I bet he'll tear apart anyone that gets in his way of finding you too. It's too bad he and I weren't soul mates."

She glanced in the rearview mirror and her smile faded. "What's wrong? You look like you could burst into tears at any moment."

"She thinks we're the killers." Alex held up his finger. "No wait, killers and robbers." Alex scoffed and picked up a box from the floorboard that resembled an English dictionary.

"She does not." Betsy started laughing. "She's just had a lot on her plate lately, and she's in shock."

I didn't, did I? Yeah, I had there for a few minutes, followed by disbelief about what had transpired.

"I know that look. I've been there a few times in my life too. I mean, I'm rock solid and all, but everyone's got a breaking point." Betsy's face contorted with worry. "You didn't break, did ya?"

"Betsy! Watch the road!" Alex yelled as the car swerved and skidded off the road, flinging me into Alex.

She jerked the wheel, saving us from landing in the ditch.

"Good God, Betsy! You have one job. One! Driving!"

"I've done a great job! And the only reason you gave the job to me is because you couldn't chance being seen. Face it, without me, your plan would have been dead in the water. Besides, I was just worried about Marygene."

I used the back of her seat as leverage to sit back up. "I'm okay. I have no idea what's going on anymore, but I haven't flown over the cuckoo's nest yet."

Alex handed me the box and inside was what looked to be several thousand dollars, three passports, and several fentanyl patches. In the first two passports, Lucy was pictured under different identities. On one passport she had red hair and in the other, black. When I opened the third, I met Alex's dark gaze.

"After you left, I tore the place apart. I found the hair dye you were talking about and then, in the back of the closet in the guest bedroom, I found a loose board." He nodded to the box. "That was inside. The space beneath the floor was big enough to hold a lot more. This was wedged way back against a stud. If I hadn't looked in there with a flashlight, I would've missed it." He pointed to the third passport containing his picture. "This is the smoking gun. How they were going to frame me. They could say to avoid needle marks, I used the drug patches to get enough drugs in her system. The final dose having been in a syringe from the planted vial in your house. The passport and cash prove I had an escape plan and tried to pin it on you and Bets."

"He called me and told me everything," Betsy explained. "That's when I told him about that scary voice mail from Paul and the killer. We were worried the killer would come after you to get to Alex. We drove to your house to warn you. That's when we saw Deputy Latin Love was there and it was too late."

Alex shook his head. "They never should have used you like that. And if Javier cares about you, he wouldn't have allowed it. I sure as hell wouldn't't've. The plan was so obvious too. You followed the instructions they laid out while they watched from close by. When you made the drop, they'd swoop in and apprehend the suspect. They tapped your cell line, right?"

I nodded.

He exchanged a look with Betsy, and she said, "Yeah, you were right." She whipped her gaze back to me. "You disappoint me. Have I not taught you anything? Never ever give the po-po more ammunition against you."

"It wasn't against me! I was terrified for Paul, my family, and my diner. Which includes you. If that bomb had gone off, you could've been inside."

Betsy visibly gulped. "Your hands were tied. I get it."

Alex said, "That there was even a bomb threat proves

how dangerous these people are. Eddie would have never agreed to any of this. And God help them when he's back on his feet." He had me there. "They had fake passports made up for Lucy and me. God only knows how long they've been planted in my house. And I've been so distracted I never even noticed my personal space had been invaded."

"And we found some keys to two different storage facilities." Betsy pulled deep into the tree line. Where Alex's pickup truck sat. "We're going to check them out."

A hissing came over the scanner, followed by broken speech we found hard to make out. When they said *Alex Myers*, it came through loud and clear, though. Betsy's hand went over her mouth. Alex didn't seem surprised.

"I don't want y'all anywhere near me when they pick me up. Pop the trunk."

I followed Alex as he retrieved a black duffel bag from the trunk. He loaded all the evidence in it with his bottles of water and what appeared to be a stash of granola bars and the unmistakable arsenal of firearms.

"Are you going on the run? Seriously, Alex, that's nuts." Sweat rolled down between my shoulder blades. Mosquitoes feasted on my limbs. Betsy's too, by the way she was swatting all over her body.

"No. I'm going to go and wait for the bastard in the storage facility." He tossed the bag over his shoulder. "You tell Javier the truth. That I got you out of there and dropped you off out here where you'll be safe. By the time they catch up with me, hopefully I'll have enough evidence for a case." He took my face in his hands.

Both of us were panting from the blistering heat as he rested his sweaty forehead against mine.

"I'm sorry they came after you to get to me. None of

this is your fault, and I've been a giant fool and treated you inexcusably. I'll avenge my wife and then make them pay for what they've put you and my cousin through." With a swift kiss on the cheek, he stalked around the car and held out his hand to Betsy for the car keys.

"We're going with you! The three of us are a team! The three musketeers. All for one and one for all."

"You want to be a team?" Alex asked.

She nodded.

"Even if being on my team means you'll spend the rest of your life behind bars?"

She slapped him on the arm. "That's not going to happen."

"It's a risk. The department knows I was at the bank. They know Marygene was snatched. The detective and my in-laws believe I was involved. In my possession is the drug that killed Lucy, along with fake passports and enough cash to get me off the island and into hiding for a few months. Now I'm on the run, conducting an unsanctioned investigation on a case I've been warned to stay away from. Shall I go on?"

Betsy threw herself into his arms and squeezed. His bag flew off his shoulder and hit the ground hard. Some of the contents spilled out.

"I'm sorry." Betsy went to her knees as a sob broke. She began shoving things back into the bag. "I just love you. You're my favorite cousin."

Alex helped her up and took the bag.

"I'm going to keep this water. It's hot out here and Marygene and I might get dehydrated."

"Ah, Bets. Don't fall to pieces on me now. I need you to be my rock." He wrapped an arm across her shoulders.

She wiped her face. "You're right. I've got this. Mary-gene is in good hands."

He nodded and handed me my own bottle of water.

"Thanks." I smiled sadly at him as helplessness overcame me, and I battled to regain my courage.

He glanced back a couple of times before he slid into the front seat of the Pontiac, fired it up, and started down the dirt road. Dust caused us to cough, and we both turned away.

Betsy smiled at me with a twinkle in her eyes, and I found my voice. "What did you do?"

"What needed to be done." She held out the keys to Alex's truck and one of the two sets of keys to a storage facility.

"You're a rock star!" I beamed, despite my raging emotions.

"Right? He thought I was crying. Ha! Betsy Myers is da bomb!" She started dancing around me and hooting. The next thing I knew, her eyes bugged out, and her hands went to her throat. She gasped for breath.

"What is it?" Terror griped me. I grabbed her arms, searching for what I'd missed.

"I think I swallowed a mosquito! Oh my God! What do I do?" She jerked away and began running in place in front of me. "What's going to happen to me?"

And just like that, the doomsday mood I'd been in was replaced with laughter. Even in this scary moment, while I was sweaty and stinky, with swollen bites covering my face and body and so many things at risk, I was laughing.

"Come on, crazy. Let's get out of here." I wrapped my arm around Betsy, and we trudged over toward the truck while she guzzled from her bottle of water.

* * *

We waited until we could drive to the storage facility under the cover of night. According to Betsy, the one Alex planned to go to first was clear across the island. It would also give him time to let the heat settle before chancing being seen by the authorities and hopefully find evidence to clear himself. Plus, by the time he realized Betsy had stolen them, he'd be an hour away and forced to stay put. At least I hoped he would.

Sandstone Storage had a gate with keycard activation and under that a keypad.

"Now what?" I glanced over at her.

"I don't know. There wasn't a keycard in that box that I saw."

I sighed and leaned out the window, searching around. That was when I spied cameras placed strategically around the facility.

Betsy caught me staring. "Don't worry 'bout them. Alex made a few phone calls and found out they don't work. Haven't in years."

"Hey, what's the number on the key?"

Betsy turned on the light in the cab and read off the four-digit number to me. I punched it in but still, nothing happened. We came all this way to help Alex and now we couldn't even get inside.

"Try one two three four."

"That's not the code."

"Try it, Marygene! A lot of people use that. When I synced my cell phone to my car, that's the code I used."

To pacify Betsy, I leaned out and pressed the buttons. When the gate opened, I nodded to Betsy. "Good job."

She fist pumped. "Team Betsy bringing some major value."

I guessed I was a member of Team Betsy.

The units were clearly marked and in a row, but too close together for us to pull right up to them. Betsy used the light on her cell phone as we made our way down to the one marked 6074.

"This is it," I whispered. Even though we were the only ones here, it felt dark and creepy. The fluorescent lights that lit the paths were barely functioning, and the wind rattling the aluminum siding added to the creepy vibe.

Betsy leaned down with her phone light engaged and put the key into the padlock. It popped open and she lifted the sliding door. Hot, stuffy air was like a punch in the face. The light came on, and I stepped inside and gaped.

"It's set up like a studio apartment in here." We walked around the sofa and onto the area rug in the middle of the unit. Off in the corner sat a portable air conditioner. It would be needed if someone spent any time in here and, from the pool of condensation on the floor beside it, they had.

Betsy opened the small mini fridge in the corner and pulled out a can of Coke. "Want one?" She cracked it open and began gulping it down. At first it seemed like a well-organized unit. There was a bag of golf clubs in the front at the corner, and a few bookshelves. Then realization struck and I gaped.

"What?"

"This is Paul's furniture. All of it." I turned around in a circle, taking it all in.

"So, this is where it all went." Betsy put her can down and picked up a box. "Hey, look at this." She pulled out a makeup bag, a couple of wigs, and a video camera. I spied a suitcase over in the corner. I had it open before I thought twice, finding lots of clothing I recognized had belonged to Lucy, and several shirts I'd seen Paul wear. There was also a large Ziploc bag filled with meds prescribed to a Winona Howell. Was the killer a woman? She'd have to be a strong woman to have carried Lucy out in that body bag. A feat I certainly couldn't pull off. And why would she want all of Paul's furniture? I froze when I spied a biker jacket and several bandanas.

Betsy began snapping pictures with her cell, mumbling something about texting them to Alex. She kept saying, "Burn! I got evidence first."

"Bets, keep your voice down."

"Alex just makes me so mad. He thinks because we're girls, he's superior to us. Well pooh on him. We were the ones to find the crooks' hideout, and he thought I'd be baggage." She had a point there.

I opened a briefcase I found on the floor next to the sofa and sucked in a breath. There were driver's licenses for different states, with Lucy's picture on them and duplicates of the same states with Paul's picture. The gut punch, a single Georgia license with Lucy Carmichael's name on it. The girl with an angelic face a little older than the picture her mother had given me. I palmed the picture and began tearing through the unit. I spied a tarp in the very back, behind several boxes. I climbed over them.

"What is it?" Betsy was behind me.

I was a woman on a mission. I jerked the tarp off and there it sat. The piece of the puzzle that'd I needed. The Harley. It all clicked.

"Whoa!"

Betsy helped me back over to the couch.

Poor Lucy Carmichael. I rubbed the face of the young

woman staring back at me. I wished I'd been able to do something before she ended up needing my help.

"I'm sorry," I whispered to the image. I looked at Betsy, fighting the emotion welling up within me. "We were wrong. I was wrong. They're in this together, Paul and . . ."

The shadow of a man appeared, and he began clapping. Paul.

CHAPTER 33

"Well, well, well. Nancy Drew and her sidekick have cracked the case."

"Nancy who?" Betsy edged closer to me. "And what made you shave your head? It's a good look. We're glad you're okay. Marygene here was worried about you. Thought you were going to be blown to smithereens." Betsy had her phone behind her back and was typing away.

"Nice try." Paul held out his hand. "Phone. Now."

"Why should I? There's two of us and only one of you."

Paul smirked and reached behind his back, pulling a gun from where he'd had it hidden in the waistline of his jeans. He pointed it at her. "Still want to argue?"

Betsy put the phone in his hand. "So, uh, you got sick of Lucy's mouth and whacked her, huh?"

He laughed; the low, dark chuckling sound caused a shiver to climb up my spine. How could I have been so blind.

"Lucy, the real Lucy, the daughter of the Carmichaels, died months ago," I told my friend, not taking my eyes off the madman in front of me. "The woman who stole Lucy's identity is the one we knew. I'm assuming, when they weren't able to gain access to the poor girl's trust fund, they killed her."

"Wrong. I mean right but wrong. I'm not the monster you think I am. I'm the easygoing one of the dynamic duo."

A witch's cackle echoed throughout the space. Betsy and I jumped in unison, colliding into each other.

"He's right. The brains and brawn of this operation is me." In walked the woman who had wrecked our lives. She had short black hair and wore more makeup than any normal woman would find fitting, but it was her. "Poor, pitiful, drug-addicted Lucy. All she had to do is marry Paul here, make her parents turn over the money, and we'd have taken our spoils and left her to her devices." She tsked. "Sadly, she had to be difficult. Do you want to know how I killed her?"

"Winona . . ." Paul seemed to be cautioning, as his attention slid in her direction.

Winona laughed. "Who cares. I'm free." She ran her hands through her hair and cackled loudly. This woman was certifiable.

Paul looked uneasy. He wasn't smiling anymore.

"Okay, mum's the word." One of her eyes began to twitch.

Betsy grimaced and she shook off a shiver. "How did you manage to be somewhat normal all this time? I mean, you were always a whacko, but this"—Betsy waved her hands in the woman's general vicinity—"is a whole new level of cray-cray."

"She took her meds," I answered, making a face at my friend, hoping she'd read my nonverbal cues to not agitate the insane.

"Bingo." She pointed at me. "Those nasty things dampen who I really am. Dim my aura and detract from my raw beauty."

What?

"I can see from your friend's confused expression she's unable to see my otherworldliness."

"Say what?" Betsy face scrunched up in disbelief. "I think you need those little pills."

She rolled her eyes. "I took them, off and on, until I managed to play your boy toy for a fool. Got him addicted to all this." She ran her hands down her bright red skintight dress. "I mean, really, you have nothing on me. It was easy as pie. The closer I got to him, the more I learned about this little island's law enforcement. Alex likes to talk about his work. Things were going smoothly. Then his stupid family, including Miss Fatso over there, had to be a pain and I had to get creative." *The baby.*

I put my hand on Betsy's arm before she lunged and got herself killed.

"Oops. I hit a nerve." She smirked another creepy smile. "Anyway, I had to get my man here on the island to help me enact the plan of all plans. And desperate little you, so hurt by the rejection of the love of your life, ate up his false affections. I mean, really, you people on this island are such backwoods hillbilly morons, I had a hard time imagining anyone here would have the brains to make any real money. But lo and behold, people can surprise you. Now you've gone and ruined everything. You have to die." She made a pouty face.

Oh sweet Lord.

"Winona, enough. Let's lock them inside and get the hell out of here."

Betsy and I exchanged a quick, hopeful glance. It'd be stuffy, but we could find our way out after they left. At least they'd leave us alive.

She shook her head. "My man still has a weak stomach when it comes to the wet work." She teetered up to Paul, or whatever his name was, on her impossibly high heels and planted a huge openmouthed kiss. There were a lot of sucking noises.

Betsy squeezed my hand and gave me her game face. The one she got when we watched our high school football team play. Lord help me, I was in on this plan. We hadn't another choice. I nodded, hunkered down, and, right before they disengaged, we charged like two Georgia Bulldogs running backs with our eyes on the prize. My shoulder radiated with pain and my teeth rattled upon impact.

They went down with a thud; a shot went wild. Winona grabbed my purse and jerked. My foot shot out on reflex and connected with her face. She screamed like a banshee, swearing a blue streak about how she was going to disembowel me or impale me or something only lunatics dreamt up.

I scrambled to my feet and followed Betsy out the door, running as fast as I could. When we made it to the end of the row, we hid, panting. "Oh my God. Your boyfriend is a maniac!" Betsy gasped. "You and Alex sure know how to pick 'em. I never liked either of those nutjobs."

"Marygene! Where are you? You naughty girl. Come out, come out, wherever you are." Paul sounded as if he was a good distance from us but getting closer by the second.

"We have to get to the truck," I whisper-shouted to Betsy. Then I realized I no longer had possession of the keys. "That psycho lunatic has my bag!" I panted.

Betsy pulled at her hair with both hands. "What are we going to do? We don't have the keys, they took my phone, and I don't have my gun!" She mouthed all of this, but I could clearly hear the shout behind the words.

I grabbed her hand and we moved low together to the next bay. If I could find an empty unit, perhaps one that wasn't locked, we could hide in there. The chances of that were slim. Still, I had to hope. This wasn't run as a tight ship or anything. The security cameras didn't work, and no one seemed to notice that two insane people were living on the premises. My thoughts jumbled together as I desperately tried to come up with a plan. And slowly, I became aware of the fact this might be the end. When Mama appeared, a sob left my lips.

"Mama."

"I know, I want my mama too." Betsy sniffed and wrapped her arms around herself.

"No." I pointed to where Mama stood. "Mama is here."

Betsy's eyes brightened, and she wiped her nose. "Good, 'cause you were really gettin' scared and all worked up."

"Come with me," Mama instructed as I kept hold of Betsy's hand since she wouldn't be able to hear the instruction.

"Marygene, I'm trying to help you here," Paul called out. "I cared about you. I truly did. My hope was we'd be gone before you were any the wiser. Only your pride would've been hurt then. You broke Winona's nose. She's doctoring herself up now. Get out of here before she comes back, or your fate will be way worse than death."

Lord help me, I believed him about my fate if it were up to Winona.

Mama led us to the next bay with her fingers on her lips. I nodded and mirrored it to Betsy, who made a signal of locking her lips and throwing away the key.

"Follow my voice and I'll lead you out of here." Crazily enough, Mama was leading us toward him. My heart raced and blood pounded in my ears so loudly I could barely make out Mama's words.

I started to pull Betsy toward the next storage bay, but she dug her heels in. She'd picked up the direction we were going. Back to *their* unit. She kept shaking her head violently and turning to run the other way. I gripped her shirt tight, fearing, in this moment of panic, she might bolt.

"It's this way," Mama insisted, her face stern. "If she goes that way, she'll run into Winona. You're going to have to be fierce."

"Betsy"—I put my mouth directly at her ear—"they've got us boxed in. We have to go this way. Back to the unit. We have to fight for our lives here. Do you understand me? It's us or them, and, by God, I won't let it be us! Let's make them pay. Are you with me?"

Her head bobbed up and down. Her emerald eyes showed the fear within. Fear I understood, felt, and validated. We were in this together.

We wasted no time. We bolted forward with new resolve, slipping back into the storage unit. I hunted around for a weapon, anything I could use to protect Betsy and me. Betsy spied the golf bag at the exact moment I did. Each of us chose a club.

Mama said, "Get down on either side of the doorway. You here and Betsy there and wait for my signal." I pointed to where Mama instructed Betsy to go and her eyes bulged. Yes, she and I would both be exposed if we settled on either side of the opening. Still, I had to make a choice here. To trust my mama or not. I went with trust.

"It's going to be okay. I swear it," I whispered. Taking my place, I watched my friend take hers, and I prayed to all that was holy to have been right.

Tears stung in my eyes at the sight of my best friend shaking in the corner. We could hear them approaching. Winona taunted, calling our names. Promising pain like we'd never experienced before. Her tone sounded cold, callous—and worse, honest. She would enjoy making Betsy and me suffer. Something scurried and a shot fired so close to us it made my ears ring. Betsy screamed at the top of her lungs. Footfalls got louder and then the lights went out all over the facility, and we were plunged into pitch-black darkness.

"What the hell?" Paul shouted, and we heard loud thuds as they ran into aluminum siding.

"Do something!" Winona commanded.

"Like what? I can't control everything. We should have left after we discovered they were here. You really need to dampen your sadistic desires to hurt people." They were close. So very close.

"You're such a p—"

"Now!" Mama shouted.

"Now!" I shouted and stood swinging with all my

might as the lights came on and my club made contact. Betsy and I stood over Paul and Winona's bodies. Both were knocked unconscious. Sirens were blaring loudly.

"I guess Alex called them. When I sent him all those texts, he said *Get out now. I'm calling for backup.*" Betsy shrugged. "Sorry, in all the commotion I forgot to tell you."

CHAPTER 34

Next week's order was placed. The chair rolled back as I stood in our tiny office and closed the laptop before untying my apron and tossing it over my shoulder while stretching. Working a double shift always did a number on my muscles. Everyone had gone home, except for me; the diner was silent. I walked around the counter. In a few hours, the janitorial team would come in and polish the black-and-white checkered tile floors, wipe down the peach vinyl booths, and scour the kitchens and grill line. And Monday, we'd start a whole new week. New beginnings. I smiled.

I locked up and took my time strolling to my car. Everything had calmed down and settled back into life as normal on Peach Cove island. For weeks, following the fiasco with Paul, who turned out to be David Parsons, and his lover, Winona Howell, it had been a circus. Winona

was wanted for suspected embezzlement in three different states. They were still trying to figure out how she got
past her employment background checks. News and mag-
azines were running stories entitled "The Woman, The
Monster, The Genius." Winona was pictured behind bars
in full makeup, smiling. Just thinking of the haunting
image creeped me out.

David, who turned out to be the more normal of the
two, confessed and copped a plea. He'd laid most of it at
Winona's feet, and she'd seemed quite pleased—no,
happy—about it. At least from the interviews I'd seen.
She touted how it took guts to allow someone to inject
you with the drug tetrodotoxin, which slowed her heart
rate, reduced her metabolism, pulse, and breathing. As
long as she wasn't examined closely, she'd pass for dead.
And she had. David had the smallest of windows to move
her body, and they timed it to perfection. He'd even
changed shirts after relocating her body and no one even
noticed. The explosion was supposed to take me out and
create a diversion. David had spared us by not engaging
the bomb until he managed to get Betsy and me to safety.
She'd paused and made a pitiful face at her lover's weakness. Our names weren't mentioned, thank God. Still,
people around here knew. Later, he'd admitted he wasn't
sure why he'd spared us exactly, just, in that moment,
he'd been compelled to do so.

Thank you, Mama. Again.

Winona went on to explain why she'd chosen Lucy.
She believed Lucy had been gifted to her by a cosmic
force due to their doppelgänger status, with similar facial
structures and the same eye color. Losing a few pounds
and coloring her hair took the most effort and were nothing compared to the payoff of a hefty trust fund. If she

didn't allow close shots, she was golden. She all but ap-
plauded her own efforts before switching topics and
laughing maniacally and boasting of all her fan mail and
plethora of marriage proposals. The woman was de-
ranged, and we were all glad to rid the island of her presence. I took solace in the fact she'd remain behind bars
until she took her last breath.

The Carmichaels were grateful to finally have answers
and be able to take their daughter home and bury her. Detective Thornton seemed happy to close the case and
leave too. For good this time, he'd said. I'd heard rumors
he would be facing his own legal troubles when he got
home, although the detective showed no signs of concern.
Even if he skated from whatever charge they thought they
could make stick, my friend Calhoun would never rest
until he proved the detective's complicity in his brother's
death.

Eddie, like Alex said, had been furious with everyone:
law enforcement, Alex, Javier, Betsy, and me. Bless his
heart, he was cooling down now but swore he would
never leave his department in the hands of nitwits.

Alex was sitting on my stoop when I got home. He
held up a six-pack. This had become a semi-regular thing
since the case had closed. We went out onto the deck, and
he cracked open two not-so-cold ones. We sat shoulder to
shoulder, staring out at the ocean. We didn't talk this
time. Just sat there drinking and listening to the waves.
Alex was navigating the waters of trauma, a first for him.
In his life, he'd never been played the fool. Never been
used by anyone. It was a new experience for him, and I
promised myself I wouldn't let him flounder out there on
his own. He was already getting enough razzing from his
buddies when they'd had a few too many.

My job would be to support him as a nonjudgmental person who would allow him to lick his wounds without taunt. He needed this. What we all needed at one time or another in our lives. From the moment we came screaming into this world until the moment we left it, our lives were a series of blips. Blips of happiness, sadness, hard times, joyous times, and everything in between. When the good times came, hold on to them, and when the difficult times emerged, have faith another positive moment was on the horizon.

"Is this a private party?" an accented voice I'd grown mighty fond of called loudly, and it drifted over the sound of the wind and the waves, causing my heart rate to speed up. He was coming back from one of his runs.

"Nope. And I was just leaving." Alex was on his feet before I could say anything, lifting a hand in his partner's direction. I'm not even sure Javier heard him from the distance he was from the porch.

"You don't have to go," I told Alex, and he gave me one of his rare lopsided smiles.

"I do, though." He kissed me on the head. "Love ya," he whispered.

Mama materialized and we watched Javy stroll toward the deck in the bright moonlight.

I covered her hand with mine as she placed it on the banister. "You said he was on the island for a reason."

"Yes."

"And that reason would be?"

She smiled. "Let your hair down, my love. You have such beautiful blond locks. Jena Lynn's father used to call you Goldilocks. Do you remember?"

"No." I shook my hair out as I pulled the band out. I'd

been so young when he passed away. I wondered if my sister recalled the nickname.

Mama ran her fingers through my shoulder-length hair. "You're going to be so happy." Her smile was watery before she faded away and Javy made it to the top of the steps and grinned.

"You okay?"

I nodded, not able to speak yet as I searched Javy's face. For what, I wasn't sure. The joy welling up within my chest regarding Mama's revelation that I'd be happy threw me. In this moment, I suddenly realized that deep down, since the trauma from my ex, I never expected to be truly happy again. Just from the confirmation that happiness was possible, hope bloomed. Mama hadn't confirmed if the man who stood before me would have anything to do with my happiness. For now, I decided, it didn't matter, and I'd hold on to this moment in time for as long as it lasted. And either way, I'd be okay.

"I'm good." I couldn't help the smile that began to spread as I met his warm hazel gaze.

A smile began to play on Javy's lips in time with mine, and his eyes lit up with what I read as mischief. "If you're sure." Javy held out his hand to me. "Want to go for a night swim?"

Much to my father's chagrin, I had a reputation for enjoying the freedom and pleasure of swimming in the buff on my nearly private beach. I'd since curtailed the activity and, to be honest, I'd missed it. I didn't think, didn't worry, didn't weigh the pros and cons. And come what might, I decided to live and love fiercely. "You bet."

RECIPES

Healthy Pumpkin Muffins

1½ cups Medjool dates, pitted
4 tablespoons water
1 cup canned pumpkin puree
1 teaspoon salt
1 teaspoon pumpkin pie spice
1 teaspoon vanilla
2 eggs
2 cups oats
1 teaspoon baking soda
1½ cups dark chocolate chips

Preheat oven to 350° F and line muffin tin with paper liners.

Add all ingredients except chocolate chips into a food processor fitted with the S blade. Process until smooth. Pour mixture into a bowl and fold in chocolate chips. With a standard 2¼-inch ice cream scoop or a large spoon, scoop batter into prepared cups, filling them almost full.

Bake for 20–25 minutes or until they spring back when lightly touched. Serve warm or at room temp.

Note: Refrigerated leftovers will keep a week.

Note: Microwave a leftover cold muffin for 10 seconds and they taste freshly baked.

Prosecco Strawberry Cupcakes

For the cupcakes
1 box white cake mix
$\frac{1}{3}$ cup vegetable oil
3 egg whites
$1\frac{1}{4}$ cups prosecco
$\frac{1}{4}$ cup strawberry preserves

For the frosting
3 cups powdered sugar
$\frac{1}{3}$ cup butter, softened
$1\frac{1}{2}$ teaspoons pure vanilla extract
3 tablespoons prosecco

For the strawberry topping
4 sliced strawberries
1 teaspoon sugar

Preheat oven to 350° F and line a cupcake tin with cupcake liners.

Beat cake mix, oil, egg whites, and prosecco until thoroughly combined (it will be bubbly). Fold in strawberry preserves, then fill each cup of the muffin tin about two-thirds of the way full with cake mix. Bake according to the box instructions for cupcakes—typically for 18 to 20 minutes—or until a toothpick inserted in the center comes out with just a few crumbs (no gooey batter). Set aside to cool.

For the frosting: In a medium-sized mixing bowl, beat sugar and butter on low until combined. Gradually stir in vanilla and prosecco, starting with just 1 tablespoon and gradually adding more until the consistency is smooth and easy to spread. (If it gets too thin, add a spoonful of powdered sugar.) Frost each cupcake.

For the strawberry topping: Slice strawberries and add sugar. Let them sit for 18 to 20 minutes to release juices, then top each cupcake with a slice.

Irish Soda Breakfast Bread

4 cups all-purpose flour, plus extra for dried fruit
5 tablespoons sugar
1 teaspoon baking soda
1½ teaspoons kosher salt
4 tablespoons (half stick) cold unsalted butter, cut into
    half-inch dice
1¾ cups cold buttermilk, shaken
1 large egg, lightly beaten
2 teaspoons grated orange zest
1½ cups mixed dried fruit
½ cup chopped walnuts

Preheat oven to 375° F. Line a sheet pan with parchment paper.

Combine the flour, sugar, baking soda, and salt in the bowl of an electric mixer fitted with the paddle attachment. Add the butter and mix on low speed until the butter is mixed into the flour.

With a fork, lightly beat the buttermilk, egg, and orange zest together in a measuring cup. With the mixer on low speed, slowly add the buttermilk mixture to the flour mixture. Combine the dried fruit and walnuts with 1 tablespoon of flour and mix into the dough. It will be very wet.

Dump the dough onto a well-floured board and knead it a few times into a round loaf. Place the loaf on the prepared sheet pan and lightly cut an X into the top of the bread with a serrated knife. Bake for 45 to 55 minutes, or until a cake tester comes out clean. When you tap the loaf, it will have a hollow sound.

Cool on baking rack. Serve warm or at room temp.

The Peach Diner's Cheesy Potato Soup

½ pound smoked bacon, chopped
2 tablespoons olive oil
½ cup butter
1 large onion, chopped
3 garlic cloves, chopped
1 peeled carrot, chopped
3 pounds gold potatoes, peeled and cut into half-inch
    cubes
¼ cup flour
6 cups chicken stock
1 pound shredded sharp cheddar cheese
1 cup of heavy cream
Salt and pepper to taste
A pinch of thyme
Scallions for garnish

Cook the bacon over a medium heat until crispy in olive oil. Remove with a slotted spoon and set aside. Add butter onions, garlic, carrots, and potatoes cook for five minutes, stirring occasionally.

Stir in the flour, making sure to coat the vegetables. Add the stock and bring to a boil. Cook, partially covered, for fifteen minutes or until potatoes are tender.

Place the shredded cheese in a large mixing bowl and add a quarter cup of the hot soup, mixing until smooth. Return it to the pan. Gradually add in the cream, salt and pepper and thyme. Heat until almost boiling.

Serve garnished with bacon, chopped scallions, and extra cheese.

Some good crusty bread for dunking is also delicious.

Cranberry, White Chocolate, and Pistachio Biscotti

2¼ cups all-purpose flour
1½ teaspoons baking powder
¾ teaspoon salt
6 tablespoons (¾ stick) unsalted butter, room temperature
¾ cup sugar
2 large eggs
1 tablespoon grated orange zest
1½ teaspoons vanilla extract
1 teaspoon whole aniseed
1 cup dried sweetened cranberries
¾ cup shelled natural unsalted pistachios
6 ounces white chocolate chips

Preheat oven to 325° F. Line 3 large baking sheets with parchment paper. Sift first 3 ingredients into medium bowl. Using electric mixer, beat butter and sugar in large bowl to blend well. Beat in eggs one at a time. Mix in orange zest, vanilla, and aniseed. Beat in flour mixture just until blended. Stir in cranberries, white chocolate, and pistachios (dough will be sticky). Turn dough out onto lightly floured surface. Gather dough together; divide in half. Roll each half into 15-inch-long log (about 1¼ inches wide). Carefully transfer logs to one prepared baking sheet, spacing 3 inches apart.

Bake logs until almost firm to the touch but still pale, about 28 minutes. Cool logs on baking sheet for 10 minutes. Maintain oven temperature.

Carefully transfer logs, still on parchment, to a cutting board. Using a serrated knife and gentle sawing motion, cut logs crosswise into generous half-inch-thick slices. Place slices, one cut-side down, on remaining two prepared sheets. Bake until firm and pale golden, about 9 minutes then flip and another 7-9 minutes on the other side. Transfer cookies to racks and cool.

Pecan Sandies

1 cup pecan halves
2 cups all-purpose flour, divided
¾ teaspoon kosher salt
½ teaspoon baking powder
½ pound (2 sticks) unsalted butter, at room temperature
½ cup brown sugar
2 teaspoons pure vanilla extract

Preheat the oven to 350° F.

Place the 1 cup of pecan halves in a nonstick skillet and toast over low heat for about five minutes, shake the pan often to toast evenly. Set aside to cool. Place the cooled pecans plus ¼ cup of the flour in a food processor fitted with the steel blade and process until the nuts are finely ground.

Place the mixture in a medium bowl and add the remaining 1¾ cups of flour, the salt, and the baking powder. Stir to combine.

In the bowl of an electric mixer fitted with the paddle attachment, cream the butter and sugar on medium speed for 2 minutes, until light and fluffy. With the mixer on low, add the vanilla and the flour mixture, mixing just until the dough comes together.

Using a small ice cream scoop or your hands, form the batter into balls. Place the balls 1 inch apart on sheet pans lined with parchment paper. Bake for 20 to 25 minutes, until the cookies turn golden brown around the edges. Cool for 5 minutes. Place on a wire rack and cool completely.

Healthy Fudgy Brownies

1 medium-sized sweet potato (baked, cooled, and peeled)
¼ cup raw honey (if you like sweeter chocolate use ⅓ cup)
½ cup almond butter
1 teaspoon pure vanilla extract
¼ cup cocoa powder (the higher quality the better)
¼ teaspoon sea salt
1 teaspoon baking powder
⅔ cup oat flour
½ cup chopped pecans
⅓ cup chocolate chips (optional)

Preheat the oven to 350° F.

Line an 8 x 8-inch baking pan with parchment paper. Set aside.

In a food processor, add sweet potato, honey, almond butter, and vanilla extract. Pulse till smooth and pour into mixing bowl.

Add cocoa powder, sea salt, and baking powder and stir to combine. Then add oat flour and stir until a thick batter is achieved. Transfer batter to your parchment-lined baking dish and spread into an even layer using a spoon or rubber spatula. Then top with pecans and chocolate chips (optional).

Bake on the center rack for 28 to 32 minutes. The brownie edges should appear slightly dry and a toothpick inserted into the center should come out mostly clean with a few crumbs. Remove from oven and let cool in the pan for 30 minutes to1 hour.

Lift out of pan and slice. If you like a denser brownie, refrigerate for an hour or so before cutting. Store leftovers covered at room temperature up to 3 days, in the refrigerator up to 7 days, or in the freezer up to 1 month.

Connect with U(s)

Visit us online at
KensingtonBooks.com
to read more from your favorite authors, see books
by series, view reading group guides, and more.

Join us on social media

for sneak peeks, chances to win books and prize packs,
and to share your thoughts with other readers.

facebook.com/kensingtonpublishing
twitter.com/kensingtonbooks

Tell us what you think!

To share your thoughts, submit a review,
or sign up for our eNewsletters, please visit:
KensingtonBooks.com/TellUs.